Braelynn Galbraith wants peace for her beloved Scotland, marriage to her childhood sweetheart, and a house full of children. In that order. But evil incarnate, in the form of Gard Marschand, turns her life inside out and destroys all hope of a decent marriage.

Known in the Highlands as the legendary devil, Gard Marschand raids his way across Scotland and England amassing power and property in his malevolent wake. He will stop at nothing in his pursuit to regain what is lost—even conceal his true identity and associate with his enemies. His determination is all-consuming until he and his men lay siege to Ross-shire and one feisty Scottish lass obliterates his single-minded purpose.

Can Gard abandon his deep-seated need for revenge for a love that just might save his rotten soul? Or will he succumb to the demons that hound him and surrender to the devil within?

This book has been previously published.

The Devil Take You
Copyright © 2019 H.K. Carlton
ISBN: 978-1-4874-2423-7
Cover art by Martine Jardin

Published by eXtasy Books Inc or
Devine Destinies, an imprint of eXtasy Books Inc

Look for us online at:
www.eXtasybooks.com or www.devinedestinies.com

THE DEVIL TAKE YOU

BY

H.K. CARLTON

DEDICATION

To Susan, who wrangled this enormous undertaking the first time around, and to Nicki who helped me tame this devil a second. Thank you, for your never-ending patience, your expertise, and most of all for loving Gard and Brae as much as I do.

PREFACE

Ross-Shire, Scotland, April 1307

Braelynn Galbraith ran as if the hounds of hell were nipping at her heels. This time they might well be. "Please God, if ya get me outta this one last scrape, I promise I will never pass another message to the rebels again."

Since Brae had taken up the cause she had been chased many times, yet she had always managed to avoid capture. By now she should have learned her lesson. This would be her final escapade one way or the other. The territory was becoming much too dangerous for such folly.

The steady beat of hooves pounded in her ears as the unknown pursuers bore down on her. Brae ran for the cliffs. The strategy had worked in the past.

Brae rounded the dune with her plaid bunched into her fists to keep her legs free. With an additional burst of speed born of pure fear, she veered for the bluff. By the time she reached the crags, more horsemen had appeared on the rock face. She skidded to a halt, caught between the two. She had to make a decision, and fast.

Following her first instinct, she scurried over the rocks and ducked under the overhang, then slid through an arch that water and wind had eroded over time.

Brae launched herself into the shadowy mouth of the first tunnel she came to.

Molding herself against the cavern wall, she listened intently for the horsemen above while gulping much-needed air into her burning lungs. Though her chest heaved, she tried not to make a sound.

Trembling in the darkness and unable to keep the memories at bay, Brae found her thoughts returning, as they often did, to the one other time she had nearly been detained. On that occasion, she had hidden in a narrow crevice. Not by design and quite by accident, she had fallen into it while fleeing from her would-be captors.

Fortunately, the crag had been deep enough to swallow her whole. At the time, she had been certain she'd broken every bone in her body. Before she could take inventory of any injury, she'd heard the clip clop of a horse's hooves dancing very close to the gap. Luckily, she had not been wedged so far down that she couldn't see the surface.

Holding her breath, she had hazarded a glance upward, only to meet the most ferocious set of black eyes she had ever encountered in her eighteen years. His predatory stare had chilled her.

The stranger had been dressed severely, all in black. Everything about him was dark—his eyes, his hair and clothing, even the billowing overlong cloak that snapped like thunder in the wind. The fine whiskers covering his cheeks only added to his sinister air. For a split second, she had believed she was enduring her last moments. But to her utter shock, he had gestured to his men and reported the all-clear. As she'd stared up at him in shock and gratitude, he had directed his mount slowly away from her hiding place.

Much later, to her horror, she had discovered he was none other than the man they called the devil. His misdeeds were legendary in the highlands. If the stories were true, he was a thief, a murderer, and a rapist. His innumerable offenses appeared to have no rhyme nor reason. One scheme seemed to benefit the English, the next gave advantage to the Scots. No one knew for certain where his loyalties lay.

Since then, Brae had been plagued by his actions. Many a morning when between wakefulness and dreaming she roused to find his black eyes swimming before her. The devil stalked her dreams, taunting her. Why had he allowed her to escape and not dispatched her forthwith, as she knew he was capable? Whose side was he on? She spent hours thinking of possibilities. Was he—like so many of her countrymen, forced to make choices—pretending to conform to English rule while remaining true to Scotland in their hearts? Or had he merely considered her inconsequential. *His mistake.*

Brae knew the messages she passed between the rebels not only diverted senseless slaughter and aided the efforts to establish Scottish independence, but also thwarted the English in their pursuit of domination. However, she was equally aware the missives she had traded had also caused harm and even death. And that was something she had to live with. She longed for the day when peace could be taken for granted.

Snapping from her reverie, Brae realized there were no sounds from above save the wind and the waves crashing.

Fairly confident she had lost her pursuers, Brae lifted the hem of her plaid and picked her way through the empty passageways.

"Ahhh," she sighed in relief and even allowed a smile. She lowered her guard for just a moment and in the next instance found herself pinned against the slimy rocks. An unknown assailant slapped his filthy hand over her mouth.

Brae squirmed, while screaming into his smelly palm.

The man spoke in rapid French.

"I dinna understand ya," she mumbled against his hand. She knew a bit of the language but could not speak fluently.

"I will not hurt you, Mademoiselle," he repeated in broken English. "That is, if you can get me out of this hellish maze."

3

Brae continued to struggle until he pressed his knee between her legs, then leaned his big body against her. Afraid of what else he intended, she stilled. Her heart pounded even more now than during the chase.

"I may even reward you," he added, slowly removing his hand from her mouth, yet he kept her in his hold.

"Let me go," Brae demanded, thrashing about.

"Help me return to my men. I was separated from them and became lost in these passages."

"Why should I?" Brae's voice shook.

"Could you not use the reward and save yourself some bodily harm?" he threatened, shifting his leg still lodged in her skirts.

"I dinna trust ya. Release me and I will get us both outta here."

"And I do not trust you, Mademoiselle. 'Tis obvious you know these tunnels well. You could outmaneuver me and leave me here to die." He eased his knee away. Still crowding her, he kept a firm hold of her forearm with one hand while he rooted in his pocket. He pulled out a sizable oval stone then held it aloft. "Yours." Easing his grip, he stepped back. He lifted her hand and placed the cold mineral into her palm. "Help me safely rejoin my men and you may keep this bauble. Create a diversion so we can make a clean getaway, and *that* will bring you much more. 'Tis very valuable."

Brae hesitated to accept anything from him, leery of what the *more* might entail once she led him to safety. Ross-shire had been under siege many times in the last few years. Living under an enemy's rule had given Brae an extreme understanding of what men were about, especially in numbers.

"Mademoiselle!" Her latest captor snapped her from her musings, reminding her of the tight spot she found herself in.

She had no choice. "A'righ'. Follow me." She pushed off

4

from the rock wall.

"We will hold onto each other," he said, grasping her arm. "Until we reach our destination."

"Where are your men? Be they the ones above" — she pointed to the surface — "or the ones beyond?"

"Above." His eyebrows rose.

"They were headed for the waterside o' the cliffs," Brae explained. "We are best to go this way."

Carefully she led him through the darkness, using the filtering light to guide the way.

"What if your men are entangled in combat with the ones who are trackin' me?"

"They are not chasing you, Mademoiselle. 'Tis I they pursue."

"So, I'm leadin' ya to your death, then?"

"You would not be so lucky. When they realize I'm not with my men, they will continue their search. I am the target, not my men."

"And what will happen when they find *me* with ya?" Her stomach cramped.

"I will do my utmost to protect you."

She did not believe that boast, since he was the coward hiding in the caves.

"Shhh," Brae warned. "I hear voices up ahead."

Her kidnapper's hand tightened on her forearm.

"Stay here while I see who be aboot," Brae whispered as she approached a shaft of daylight beaming through a cleft in the rock above.

"Merci, Mademoiselle," he said, relief evident in his voice.

Cautiously, Brae boosted herself up, trying not to give their whereabouts away.

"Are your men dressed in opulent English splendor?" Brae asked acerbically.

"Oui." He chuckled. "Be there a white horse with a black

star on his left haunch?"

"Aye," she replied.

"And the others? Giving chase?"

"No sign." She eased herself down.

Immediately, the man took her place in the void. He took a moment, as if weighing his options.

"Merci, Mademoiselle," he said, athletically hiking himself to the surface.

Brae blinked. In the darkness of the cave, she had been unable to see him clearly. His sweat-soaked shirt clung to his muscular upper body.

He offered her his hand, which she declined. "Perhaps a wise choice, Mademoiselle," he said, with an indulgent grin. "What is your name?"

Uncertain she should tell him, she raked her lower lip.

"I only ask so you might collect your reward in the future. One day you may be in need of my influence."

"Who are you?" she blurted.

"Gaveston," he said with a flourish, then he narrowed his gaze.

Should I know the name? It did not ring any bells.

"Galbraith," she responded, in kind.

With a chortle, he bowed. "Mademoiselle Galbraith. I am indebted to you."

Fleetingly, she thought he was quite handsome.

"Do not forget, the gem will prove your identity. Return it to its true owner and you will be granted any boon you may ask, in payment for saving my life this day." He shrugged. "Or perhaps if you find yourself in need of coin, the bauble will bring a tidy profit. You cannot lose here."

With a disreputable grin, he ran for the white horse, then vaulted onto its back with stealth and ease.

Brae poked her head out from the rock face. "How will I ken the rightful owner?"

"You will" — he said with certainty — "if, and when, the time comes."

How cryptic. "How am I to find ya? You're fleein'?"

"I will not be gone long. Perhaps even less time than some might wish. Bonne chance, Mademoiselle." He kicked the horse into motion. "Keep up your end of the bargain now and create a diversion."

"And you, good luck." Brae slid the cold stone into her bodice for safe keeping, which left her hands free. She heaved herself onto the flat rock above, then ran in the opposite direction Gaveston had ridden. It was not long before the other Englishmen caught sight of her and gave chase. Once again, her familiarity of the terrain served her well. Within minutes Brae was safely ensconced in the maze of passageways while the soldiers above shouted and searched.

Having nothing but time while she waited for them to depart, she held the stone up to the light. The clear blue gem was hard and cold. "Beautiful," she murmured. "Whatever it is."

The precious stone was oval in shape, except for one damaged edge. She ran her finger over the flaw, convinced it had been sanded smooth.

"And what of the true owner?" she whispered. Gaveston had insinuated the person might be of some import. *Yet how am I to know?* She shrugged, dismissing it. Gaveston was most likely full of bunk, only concerned with saving his own skin. The bauble was almost certainly fake as well. She didn't care. It was very pretty. She fitted it into her bodice.

As dusk descended, Brae climbed stealthily from the depression. With no riders in sight, she scurried over the escarpment and headed toward Ross-shire. First, she would alert the vicar she had survived another mission.

Huffing and puffing, Brae burst into the chapel.

"Braelynn!" the vicar shouted. He scrutinized her disheveled appearance, from her knotted hair to her snarled dress.

To her shock he pulled her into an embrace.

"Thank ya," he said skyward. "Did ya deliver the missive, Brae?"

"Aye," she mumbled into his chest, before he cleared his throat and took a step back.

"I-I-I was b-b-beginnin' t-t-to worry," he stuttered — an affliction he was often stricken with.

"'Tis the last of it, Vicar Dufferin. As of this day, I'm retirin'. I made a promise to God if he got me outta this one, I wouldna do it again."

"Aye. I-I-I knew this d-d-day would come. 'Tis too dangerous for you to c-c-continue. Soon ya will be m-m-married, and Callum willna tolerate it."

"No one can ever learn what I've done," she said, frowning.

He tapped her shoulder. "We will keep each other's confidence, Brae."

For a moment she paused. Strange, he had not stammered. "Aye. We will. I must be off and pray I reach home afore my parents."

"They are busy at R-r-ross. I may have created some extra w-w-work for them this day." His blue eyes danced with devilment.

"Thank ya, Vicar Dufferin."

"I'm s-s-sorry to lose ya, Brae. You've been a great source of p-pride for me in this endeavor. Though I must admit, th-there were times I'd wished not to s-s-send ya. But I k-kenned ya would go regardless." He searched her gaze.

"Aye, I would 'ave," she admitted. "'Tis too important."

The cleric nodded. "But you are safe now. 'Tis all that matters. Shall I a-a-accompany ya home?"

"Nay, thank ya. I'll be fine."

"Take care, Braelynn."

"And you, Vicar." Brae closed the door, then sprinted home.

Once there, she washed her face and hands, then changed her clothing—stuffing her tattered dress behind the bed until she had time to mend it before her mother noticed its condition. She tamed her knotted hair and left it loose.

Brae barely managed to begin supper before her folks arrived home.

The following morn as she repaired her dress, she unearthed the gem Gaveston had given her, and after admiring its beauty yet again, she sewed it into the lining of her carpetbag for safe keeping. The case held her most precious belongings, including the irreplaceable tomes gifted to her from the saintly Vicar Dufferin.

CHAPTER ONE

Ross-Shire, Scotland, July 1307

At breakneck speed, Braelynn ran over the moors. Hardly ladylike, but she was late, yet again. Her father would have her head.

Often while she walked the moors, Brae's thoughts wandered to the future. And now that she had given up running messages, she found little to occupy her mind beyond her chores.

As she rounded the burm she spied Callum, her betrothed. He paced the perimeter like a caged animal until he caught sight of her, then he stilled and crossed his arms over his broad chest.

"Hurry, my sweet, your sire was raisin' the roof. He's oot searchin' for ya now."

Brae sighed and slowed her pace, delaying the first of the two lectures she was about to endure. As she strolled, she replaited her unbound hair.

When she finally reached her husband-to-be, Brae stared into his clear blue eyes. The wind ruffled his wavy blond locks over his forehead. "I'm sorry, Callum I seem ta have lost—"

"Track o' time. I ken. Ya do naught but. And I'll tell ya again, mistress, I willna tolerate your defiance the way your sire does, nor ya runnin' free." Roughly, he gripped her shoulder, but his eyes twinkled and his mouth curved belying his ire. "When ya disobey me, I *will* punish ya. Severely."

He leaned in, then took her lips in a scorching kiss. By the time he released her they were both breathless. "I canna wait," he said, his eyes heavy-lidded.

"Ya canna wait to punish me?" she teased.

"Nay, I canna wait for ya to become my wife that I may kiss ya and I dinna have to stop. Come."

Hand-in-hand, they walked slowly toward Ross.

Brae inhaled deeply. A relative peace reigned for now, a calm they had not witnessed for years. There had been naught but upheaval during Scotland's bid for independence and the uncertainty following the execution of William Wallace. But now it seemed they were transitioning into a precarious understanding with the English. Yet, it was rumored King Edward was in the midst of installing Englishmen and collaborating Scots to govern the country—Scots loyal to him, swearing their fealty. There were even talks of King-appointed Marches as border wardens to control the boundaries between England and Scotland.

Brae and Callum did not take for granted this sparse freedom, for who knew how long it might last. They had endured many months inside the demesne walls of Ross, protected from the violence that played outside, destroying their country and countrymen. Although their overlord was not a man given to violence, he was a fierce protector. At least, he *had* been. Of late, Lord Ross had become lax in the reinforcements of the county, growing accustomed to tenuous peace which the people knew would never last.

"Ya shouldna be walkin' alone, Brae. Ya never ken who might be aboot. There are English soldiers not far from here. Ya dinna wish to meet up with the like. I would hate for ya to be hurt. They would find ya too bonny to pass up. Scot or no, they wouldna care. Or worse, ya dinna want to meet up with the devil. I've heard his black self has been spotted along the border as weel. He is more brutal and savage than any Englishman. Ya ken this. Do ya understand?"

Unbidden, the devil's dark eyes swam before her. "Aye, Cal. I dinna mean to wander, but this freedom to walk beyond the walls beckons me after bein' confined so long."

"I ken your wayfarin' nature, my love. I only worry for your safety. Ya dinna wish to be accused of passin' messages ta the rebels, either."

She smiled softly as they reached her family's croft. Little did he know only a few weeks past the accusation would have been quite accurate.

He turned to snuggle the side of her neck. "I love ya, Braelynn, and I would hate for somethin' ta happen to ya tha' might change it." His blue eyes darkened.

"I love ya, too, Callum." She blinked, confused by the comment.

He kissed her again, until her mother's angry voice interrupted them.

"Braelynn Galbraith, hie yourself off to your corner at once."

"Thank ya for escortin' me home, Cal. I will see ya on the morrow."

"A fortnight, Brae," he said, hinting of their wedding night. "I have waited so verra long for ya."

"I canna wait, Cal," she replied over her shoulder.

Inside the gloomy hut, she greeted her mother.

"If ya think for one second Callum will tolerate your ways any better than your da, ya are sadly mistaken," Brae's mother ranted, wagging a finger in her direction.

"I'm sorry, Ma. I lost track—"

"—O' time. You've been usin' tha' excuse since ya were knee high. Go and await your da."

Brae repeated another apology.

"Aye, you're always sorry. But not half as sorry as me."

Brae hung her head and trudged to the back of the dwelling. She and her mother had never been particularly close. The woman was not compassionate or loving, not even toward her da.

Dispirited, Brae slumped onto the stool used for milking.

Raised voices signaled her father's return. It would not be long now. He would only take the time to wash up before giving her a good scolding.

As much as she detested the lectures, she realized he only did so because he cared. She felt sorry for him. He had so little joy in his life and marriage. Brae was determined her relationship with Callum would be different.

Brae took a deep breath when her sire approached. With a ferocious scowl, he took a seat, then placed his palms over his knees. A patch of graying hair near his temple drew her attention. She was most likely to blame for every ashen strand.

"I'm sorry, Da." She searched for other words besides *lost track of time*. "I didna realize 'twas so late."

"For the last time, Braelynn, ya are forbidden to go oot unattended!" His voice rattled her eardrum. "You've no idea what could happen to a young girl alone. You're temptin' fate. Ya are betrothed, ya canna be actin' this way. I dinna envy young Callum at'all. But I'll be glad when ya become his burden and no longer mine. Ya've no idea how I worry."

"And you'll not fret over me once I'm Callum's wife? Will ya quit carin' about me the minute I take his name?" Had she truly been such a dreadful daughter that he could not wait to be rid of her?

"I willna have ta worry. Ya may not mind me, but he willna stand for ya shamin' him."

"*Shamin'*?" She recoiled. "I dinna dishonor ya, Da. I'm not doin' anythin' wrong by walkin'."

"Ya dinna think everyone sees ya oot there. And then the next thing you're returnin' hand-in-hand with Callum. Folks are already bargainin' as to how soon after ya are wed that your first bairn will arrive."

Her cheeks bloomed with heat. "Ouuu! They are no'! Callum doesna accompany me onto the moors, and ya ken it. And 'tis you who sends him ta fetch me."

"I canna believe I'd say it, but I think I would feel better kennin' he was with ya. If you're gonna end up in tha' condition anyhow, I'd prefer it be your betrothed, than some brigand."

"Da!"

Never had she considered the possibility he felt that way, or that others might think her behavior disgraceful.

"Ya listen and ya listen fine. Come a fortnight, ya are no longer my problem. You've never minded me afore, but ya will heed me now." He stood, towering over her. "Ya are forbidden ta step foot outside o' this house without your ma until ya are wed."

Brae crossed her arms, not in defiance, but to stave off the misery his words evoked.

"Ya make me seem weak, Braelynn." He frowned. "Callum thinks I canna control ya."

"No, he doesna."

"Aye, he does, and he's not the only one."

She knew he meant her mother. She had overheard them shouting about the very subject often enough to know her mother thought her da was soft, especially when it came to discipline.

"Och, Da, I dinna believe that. 'Tis simply walkin'."

Anger mottled his complexion. She was used to her mother's fury, but not his. It stung. "Ya ken 'twould serve ya right if ya'd run afoul out there for the hundreds of times we've tried to warn ya of the dangers and the evil that awaits pretty foolish young girls who dinna mind their sires and think they ken better."

"Da!" she blurted in shock.

"Ya will obey me this one time, Braelynn," he command-ed, as he turned to exit. "Until the weddin' ya will remain here or ya will have accompaniment."

Three whole days she lasted before she couldn't stand be-ing cooped up in her mother's company any longer.

CHAPTER TWO

Gard Marschand rode alongside his second and friend, Hudson Grainger — accompanied by three other men, Aidean Ferguson, Robbie Cowan and Hugh Chamberlain — en route to meet up with another contingent at Ross-shire holding. The plan? To oust Lord Ross himself from the shire. Gard assumed the lead for this siege.

This was the third takeover in as many months. Gard grew weary of the constant warring. He was more than ready to take and accept his rightful place and reclaim his name and property.

As instructed, they were removing Scottish overlords who were not easily malleable and replacing them with select leaders. Not necessarily English overlords, but men who were more pliable. Gard was not particularly agreeable to these appointments but would do what was required in order to reclaim what was his. From the moment Wallace had been executed, everything had changed for Gard. He no longer wanted to fight what seemed to be a losing battle. His only desire was to seize what was rightfully his, hold on to it, protect it, and endeavor not to let *them* change their ways.

"Gard!" Grainger called his name, and by the exasperated expression on his face it wasn't the first time. "Have your wits about you, man," he murmured.

Gard resumed listening to the raucous conversation between the younger men.

"I canna wait to sample the new lot o' lasses." Robbie Cowan practically salivated.

"You will leave the lasses be, Cowan," Hugh Chamberlain, the British Captain, commanded in his most regimented voice. "You are here for one purpose only. Abusing the young lasses is not one of our goals. I am sick to death of compensating the irate papas after every siege. The next time, it comes directly from your recompense."

"Ya canna do tha'," Cowan fumed.

"Yes, I can."

"Ya forget who I am," Robbie snarled.

"You are no more or less than any of the rest of us, Cowan. You are here as our guide and a Scot. You will direct us and help us with the language if need be. That's it. Harming the women is not part of your post. Moreover, I'm sure your clan would be interested to know how you comport yourself in their name. I will be sure to include it in my report." Captain Chamberlain spurred his horse into a canter.

Robbie Cowan glared at Hugh's back while the rest followed Chamberlain's lead.

They traveled in silence and eventually met up with a larger contingent of men.

Gard issued their orders. "Fraser, take half the men and cross the river. Stuart, take the others and head northeast."

"Ya want us ta merely ride right up ta the front door?" Stuart asked, insolently.

"You've seen how lax Ross has become. We've scouted enough." Gard reassured them. "Ross' stronghold and reinforcements are laughable at best. It *will* be that easy."

"Chamberlain, take the rest and go over the moors, around that big burm. Grainger and I will take up the west side."

En masse they rode toward Ross, closing down on it from three sides.

Cowan kept up his incessant prattle. When he wasn't rutting, his other favorite pastime was belittling those around him. He had a way of identifying a man's weakness and then announcing it, to one and all. It was different from Grainger's good-natured teasing. Cowan set out to mock and humiliate. For the most part, the troop tended to ignore him where possible because of his notorious relation. But sooner or later, even that would not save him. He had singled out every man in the group so far before making his way to Gard.

"Marschand isna human." Cowan tried to draw Gard into confrontation. "I have yet ta see him partake in the bounty of lassies placed before us. Even Grainger, a married man, no less, has given in to his baser needs."

Gard sent Grainger a sidelong glance in time to see his comrade cringe at the reminder of his indiscretion.

"But not Marschand," Cowan continued. "It makes me curious."

"He exhausts the camp whores, Cowan," Grainger interjected. "Have you not noticed?"

"He has? I havena noticed. I keep them quite busy meself." He preened.

"Aye, 'tis the reason half of them have hied themselves off to greener pastures," Aidean Ferguson added. "Ya are a savage, Robbie."

"How do ya ken 'tis me brutalizin' 'em? Ya jus' said Marsch tires out the campies. He's a beast, in every way. Ye've all seen the violence in 'im. Ya canna tell me that he is not when he's ruttin' as weel."

Cowan was quiet for a moment, no doubt mounting a new attack.

"Or mayhap Marschand canna maintain his manhood because he is inta young boys." Robbie laughed hysterically at his own lewdness. "Tha's why he abuses the whores, as if 'tis *their* fault he canna keep it up."

While Gard struggled to rein in his anger, he turned to

Grainger. "I *will* kill him," he pledged matter-of-factly. But to Cowan he said, in a most sinister tone, "You had better ride faster, Robbie Cowan, afore my beastly tastes turn to red-headed cocksure Scotsmen."

Robbie did not heed the warning and provoked Gard further. "I wondered. But you Frenchmen have strange appetites. Beastly, ya say. Are ya inta animals, too then, Marsch?"

Inwardly, Gard seethed. Cowan was the animal. On former missions, he had prevented him from attacking several defenseless young women. Unfortunately, there were more he had been unable to save. And the last one—her face still haunted him. Gard thought he had warned her sufficiently, but she had gone out unprotected, and the rutting bastard had stalked her, cornered her then violated her. The poor lass had taken her own life by the time Gard had returned to the castle. Hudson had saved Robbie Cowan's worthless existence that day. And in essence, Gard's as well, considering Robbie Cowan somehow shared kin with the late John Comyn.

"How about tha' one, Marsch?" Robbie goaded. "Ya canna tell me tha' doesna stir ya."

A girl of no more than eighteen, if a day, wandered the moor. Alone.

Where are her men? They should be hanged for lending her to the fate that was about to become hers.

She wore a green on blue tartan. The azure hue was one of Gard's familial colors and captured his attention immediately, along with the wave of long dark hair that swirled about her slim waist. Totally oblivious to the danger lurking around her, she bent and picked a sprig of heather, then tucked it into her hair. Plucking another, she added it to the bouquet in her hands.

She *was* breathtaking. And it had been a long time since Gard had been with a woman. His body reacted. Yet he was not the only one affected by her comeliness.

19

The horses picked up speed. The soldiers bore down on the girl — a pack of hungry wolves on the unsuspecting lamb.

Run, lass. Run! As if she heard him, her feet took flight.

The stench of burning rotted wood permeated the air, signaling the first troops had breached the village. The initial wave of the siege had begun.

As usual, Hudson anticipated Gard's every thought and positioned himself to impede Robbie's progress at the precise time. Gard maneuvered his horse to the flanks of the other beasts, then hazarded a glance in Cowan's direction. The boy's eyes were alight with eagerness. He foamed at the mouth with the excitement of the chase. Gard was not about to let this happen again.

Each man had single-minded purpose.

"I dare ya, Marsch," Robbie taunted, grinning. "Take her. Afore I do!" With a vicious kick he urged his horse to sprint.

A plume of black smoke rose over the burm, swirling into the sky.

"Dear God, not again." Brae dropped the bouquet she had been fashioning and ran, perhaps stupidly, toward the village. Even with the wind whistling through her ears, the commotion and terror-filled shrieks of the town folk still reached her.

With her attention focused on locating her family, Brae didn't hear the horses behind her until the last second.

All of a sudden, her feet lost contact with the damp earth. She choked on a scream as some unknown assailant grabbed her by the hair and plucked her from the ground. The destrier never slowed its pace as she dangled precariously in midair.

In agony, Brae clamped her hands on either side of her head — her scalp threatened to peel away from her skull.

The kidnapper hauled her up in front of him and body slammed her stomach-first onto the horse's back. Brae's breath rushed from her lungs at the force. She bunched her hand into the rider's enormous black cloak and hung on for dear life.

While she struggled to breathe, the brigand wrapped his rather large leather-clad hand around her backside.

"This one be mine!" The sound of his deep voice chilled her. By his accent, he was English! Braelynn closed her eyes and recalled the warnings from Callum and her da. Had her own father's words cursed her? Was she to learn the lesson the hard way?

She was afraid to open her eyes, but she knew by the smell stinging her nose that they were close to the source of the acrid smoke.

The horses came to an abrupt halt. Brae barely had time to register the fact when someone from behind grabbed her by the ankles and attempted to rip her from her captor's lap.

"She be mine," her captor growled.

To her horror her skirt rode high.

"I want her!" the second brigand responded while caressing her bare leg. Brae's skin crawled.

In terror, she stared up at the raider holding her while the other slid his rough hands ever higher up her plaid.

Leather creaked when her captor leaned in the saddle. He placed one large booted foot in the center of his rival's chest and shoved. At once, Brae's lower body dropped as he fell backward from the blow. Her arms pulled taut, stretching painfully, supporting her weight.

Without warning, the man holding her suddenly released his grip. Brae slid down the horse's side and fell to the ground with a thud in a tangle of voluminous skirts. She did not wait to disentangle herself but seized the opportunity to flee. She leapt to her feet intending to run, but her captor was faster. He grabbed her by the hair yet again. Circling it around his hand, he reeled her in.

"Not so fast, *Caileag*." He sneered the last as if it were a nasty word. "You and I have some business to attend."

Brae fought him, kicking, punching, and scratching, but to no avail. With his enormous reach, he held her at bay until another one of the black-garbed knights gathered her from behind and pushed her into the lean-to attached to the smithy. She landed heavily on one hip on the sub-floor, with the stranger's hand still wrapped around her hair. He let it uncoil. Long strands hung from his gloves. Her scalp ached.

Petrified, she stared up at the small crowd now gathered. There were four of them, but more outside.

"Come, Marschand. You never take the women. Ya are just tryin' to prove yourself to Cowan. Give her to me. She's too bonnie fer the likes a you," one man jeered.

All the men were dressed the same, entirely in black. But her original captor, the one they referred to as Marschand, was truly pitch-dark from head to toe, including his hair and beard. Even his eyes were two bottomless orbs of bleakness.

Brae gasped. *'Tis him! The devil himself!* Absolute terror tried to climb its way up her throat.

"You had the last one, Ferg," Cowan complained. "Give her to me, Marsch. Ya dinna need to prove anathin'. You're a monster. We all ken it." The red-head's hands opened and closed eagerly.

Confused by the accents, Brae darted her focus between them. What were her own kind doing with the likes of the devil?

Marschand remained silent. His eyes glittered. The enormous black cloak he wore swirled around him as he stalked Brae.

"Marsch!" The tall one, yet to be named, barked. "We've no time for this."

"No, I like the look of this one," Marschand murmured. The announcement chilled her to the bone. "Leave us," he commanded with a wave of his hand.

"Naw way! I want her when yer done," Cowan said.

"Och, why would ya want anathin' that had him in her?" Another man grimaced.

"Come watch!" Yet someone else shouted.

The men crowded into the small space.

Helplessly, Brae gulped the bile stinging her throat. They were going to watch. *Dear God, this is truly happening.*

"Grainger," Marschand snapped, though he never took his focus from her.

"Just get on with it. Or give her over."

Brae cowered. The devil was almost to her. Skittering backward, she tried to create space, but his speed was astonishing. He fell on her.

"Nay," she screamed, kicking and flailing, but he subdued her easily. "Nooo," she cried as he yanked her skirts up.

Cold air hit her bare legs.

The men behind jeered, urging him on.

"Please dinna, do this!" she choked.

Sobbing, she bucked and clawed at him. But he was too strong. The mere weight of his big body smothered the breath from her.

A deafening rush of sound roared in her ears.

"Cease yer whinging, Lassie," another yelled from beyond. "Marschand doesna join often, but when he does, he is a brute. Make it easier on yerself and dinna anger him further."

The crowd's laughter blended with the drone in her head.

Marschand spoke, but she could not hear him, her mind too busy trying to save her from her fate. Her body had already accepted what was to come. She refused to allow his foul words to penetrate her consciousness, as she well knew his body was about to obliterate her innocence.

With ease he wrested her undergarments from her body, which whipped the crowd into a frenzy. She struggled anew as he loosened his trousers.

All of a sudden, he gagged her with his other hand, dulling the shrillness of her screams. But she continued to howl. In hysterics, she could not seem to stop it.

His hot breath scalded the side of her neck. He mashed his mouth against her ear. Brae cringed, certain he was going bite her. *He is a beast!* The legendary tales of his wickedness were true.

But to her surprise, instead of the sting of his teeth, his words broke through her outcries.

"I willna hurt ya. Keep up the struggle. Continue to scream and fight me. I will not rape you. But you must do exactly as I tell you. We have to keep up the show. This has to seem believable."

When he stopped whispering in her ear, he growled loudly. Braelynn tensed and shrieked in response.

"Fight me," he demanded harshly, while the men continued to heckle.

Marschand was still incredibly rough with her, but she did as he demanded. Hope gave her strength. Marsch pulled his voluminous cloak around them, as if he was trying to conceal her nakedness from the onlookers.

"There needs be blood," he said, as he pulled a dirk from his boot.

Lord, what is happening?

"Shout and fight me," he demanded, and he roared again as if angered or aroused. But in the struggle as he aimed the blade of his dirk, Brae's knee caught his hand, driving the sharp tip of the knife straight into the meaty part of her thigh.

Brae shrieked at the piercing pain. How could she have

been so stupid as to trust him? He was not only going to rape her, he was going to mutilate her as well!

While he endeavored to return the dirk to his boot, Brae attempted to shimmy away from him. But he grasped her shoulder with one hand and clamped her buttocks with the other. He thrust his rock-hard pelvis into intimate contact with her bared flesh. He pummeled her with his hips while groaning his gratification. Each jolt made her cry out involuntarily as he literally knocked the hysterical breath from her.

"I'm sorry," he panted, his harsh exhalations fanned her hair. "I did not mean to cut you."

He growled again for the audience, she assumed, but he continued to pound. Yet not into her. As he'd promised, he had not penetrated her.

Stunned and confused by his actions, she wondered why he had spared her, though she continued to sob pathetically.

He picked up the frantic pace and made sounds that not only repulsed her, but strangely made her skin tingle. His warm breath rushed past her ear. His deep throaty noises reverberated through her chest. Was this what she had to look forward to with Callum?

Callum! Oh dear God, Callum.

"Please," she cried.

"She's beggin' fer more, Marsch. Give it to her," one of the rabble yelled.

"Please. No more!" She sobbed and turned her head to the side. For a split second he met her gaze, and she could have sworn she saw regret. "Please," she begged, her voice now hoarse.

Forcefully, he plunged three, perhaps four more times, before he shuddered, then collapsed heavily atop her. Except for his harsh panting, he fell silent.

When Marschand shifted his weight, Brae scooted out

from under him, then skittered toward the rear wall of the smithy. Her mind and body were numb.

The devil stood, barely sparing her a glance while he adjusted his clothing.

With her plaid wrap still rucked up, Brae stared at her lower body. Her limbs were unrecognizable, her legs looking as though they belonged to someone else. Bright red blood oozed from the deep wound, staining her skin. A mournful keening sound escaped her throat.

"Gor, Marsch, you've ripped her apart," one man said, turning away at the sight of her.

"Ye've gone an' killed her, Marsch," said another. "She willna survive tha'."

With trembling fingers, Brae tried to toss her plaid down to shield her nudity, but found the fabric heavy from all the vital fluids she'd lost.

Was that why the devil and his men wore black, so the material would mask the brutality of their heinous crimes? Brae shuddered at the morbid thought and lifted her gaze just in time to connect with her assailant's. For a split second, Brae saw regret in his expression, before he quickly extinguished it, making her question whether she'd seen it at all.

In a swirl of his overlong cloak, he turned his back and abandoned Brae in the smithy—embarrassed, degraded, and humiliated.

Left alone with the remaining brigands, Brae was horrified by the excitement still lingering on their faces. They reminded her of men on the hunt, eager for the kill, stimulated by the scent and the sight of blood.

Brae jumped when the red-headed, Cowan, slithered toward her, as if in a trance. *He* scared her more than all the others.

A feral growl curled his thin lips and he bared his teeth.

His eyes glittered with madness. He gripped the hem of her skirts, then tugged, dragging her closer to him. She tried to scream, but her voice was all but gone.

Cowan jerked the material so hard it ripped. And as soon as he caught sight of the crimson spatter on her thighs, he dropped to his knees. To her utter disgust, he licked a path up her shin.

With a pitiful screech, Brae kicked at him. Cowan's fingers bit into her tender flesh. He reared, hand raised, preparing to slap her.

Cringing, Brae braced for the strike.

Out of nowhere, Grainger attacked, knocking Cowan aside. More blood, not her own, splattered, as Grainger struck him with his fists.

The other men were quick to break it up. They dragged Grainger off Cowan before carrying the inert red-head away.

Grainger swatted the dust from his clothes. "Get up, wench," he barked. "I suggest you run along afore it happens to you again."

When she attempted to gain her feet and gather what was left of her dignity, the unimaginable happened.

"Braelynn? Brae!"

Though Brae couldn't see him, Callum's wretched voice reached her through the din of awkwardness.

Suddenly, he broke through the crowd, then abruptly skidded to a stop. His eyes widened as he digested the scene before him.

Brae stared up at her betrothed. His fair hair and clothing stood out within the sea of men dressed in black, surrounding him. Like he didn't belong there.

'Tis all a bad dream.

Hopelessly, Brae whipped her plaid to her ankles.

Callum's shoulder's drooped. He mouthed the word *no* but did not make a sound.

Brae reached for him. "Callum," she cried, her voice weak and raw from screaming.

He stood frozen on the spot.

"Please, help me, Cal," she rasped.

Callum swallowed convulsively.

Brae waited for Callum's assistance, but it never came. Instead he ignored her outstretched hand as if he could not bring himself to touch it. Then to her utter shock he began to retreat, the crowd parting to let him through.

"Callum?" Tears coursed down her cheeks as he ran away, leaving her there in the midst of the brigands.

Brae stood on weak wobbly legs, fighting off nausea. She used the wall of the smithy to steady herself before she stumbled between the men. One tried to help her, but she swatted his hands away. Where was his aid when she had needed it?

As she put one foot in front of the other, the cut on her inner thigh pulsed. Every time her legs rubbed together, a fresh stream of warm blood trickled down her leg and pooled in her shoe.

She staggered toward her home, uncertain if it was even safe to return there. Yet she didn't have a choice. It was imperative that she stanch the blood flow.

Blindly, Brae staggered past the burned-out armory.

When Brae finally reached the croft, she found it empty. Where were her parents? Had they sought the shelter of the holding, or had her father joined the men to fight the fire? Surely her mother would have volunteered to help the injured.

"But I am injured," she wailed, feeling sorry for herself. "I need ya!"

Brae hefted the washbasin from its place by the door and tried not to spill the water—she had no time or energy left to heat it up. She limped to the rear of the hut where the family slept.

There she stripped out of her ruined clothing and discarded it.

The stains on her legs had begun to dry, but fresh blood still leaked from the open gash.

Wetting a rough cloth, she washed off the worst of the filth. When she had finally managed to clean enough to inspect the cut, the bowl of water ran crimson.

Gingerly, she fingered the jagged laceration. The flap of skin resembled a crescent moon, she thought fancifully. It had to be stitched closed, or it would never stop bleeding. What she needed was a doctor. But Ross-shires's physician would have escaped to the holding, not only for protection but to help with the casualties.

Leaning against a wooden chest for support, Brae pulled a fresh chemise over her head. The motion made her stomach lurch.

Her peripheral vision blurred as she groped along the wall in search of her mother's sewing kit and her father's whisky.

After securing the supplies, she perched on the edge of the straw mattress and tried again and again to thread the needle. Between trembling and crying she kept missing the eye.

As Brae worked, her mind strayed to Marschand. The demon had spared her for a reason. For the life of her she could not understand why he had gone to such lengths. But for some inexplicable reason she felt obligated to keep the affliction a secret, to protect him as he had done for her.

"Ah-ha!" she cheered as the thread finally caught. A small victory in a defeat-filled day. But as she sat poised to plunge the needle into her skin, she couldn't do it. There was no way she was going to be able to stitch her own flesh together.

Brae took a long drink of the amber liquor. It seared her raw throat, causing her to sputter and cough. As she waited for the blessed numbness to settle into her limbs, she poured some of the alcohol over the needle and thread as she'd seen her mother do countless times when sewing her father's wounds. But by the time she began to suffer the effects of the whisky, her fingertips and eyesight were impaired.

With her thumb and index finger she pinched the puckered lip of skin closed and took a deep breath. After taking aim, she closed her eyes and pierced the tip of the needle at the edge of the C-shaped lesion, yelping at the pain. "One stitch. Please jus' one stitch," she prayed, then opened her eyes.

Brae pulled the thread through her flesh. It burned like fire, worse than the stinging nettles she had gotten into as a child.

Breathing shallowly, she forced the needle into her flesh on the opposite side of the semi-circle. Brae managed one round suture. She pulled the loop taut, successfully gathering the two sides of skin together. Quickly she knotted it, cut it, then promptly passed out.

CHAPTER THREE

"So, 'tis true!"

Brae jerked awake at the sound of her mother's gravely tone.

Bleary-eyed, Brae tried to focus on her father. Relief flooded her. They were safe, but the respite was short-lived. Her mother gestured to the mess strewn about—the soiled rags, the blood-stained water floating in the basin, the ruined clothing.

"Where were ya, Braelynn? Where were ya when they took ya?" her father bellowed.

Groggy and confused, she took too long to answer.

Her mother shook her violently. "Where were ya, ya bloody fool?"

"Were ya on the moors?" her father demanded.

What difference does it make? They had been like a pack of wild dogs. Confident she was not the only girl attacked this day, she was luckier than most, because other than the cut, she was still intact.

Abruptly, her mother dropped her hold and Brae fell to the straw mattress.

"Ya have no idea what ya've done, ya selfish little chit." Her mother yanked open the chest of drawers and began removing Brae's clothing.

"Ma, what are ya doin'?" Brae swallowed, trying to wet her parched throat. "Are we goin' ta the holding?"

Her mother upended the carpetbag where Brae kept her precious tomes from Vicar Dufferin and unceremoniously dumped them out onto the dirt floor. She then tossed a day dress in Brae's direction. "Allotta good learnin' ta read did ya and us as well. Get dressed!"

Her sire turned his back, awarding her some privacy.

"Answer me, Brae. Where were ya?"

"I was on the moor, Da," she admitted.

The moment she stood, her thigh throbbed painfully. Her vision tunneled, and she was forced to grab the wardrobe to remain upright.

"Ya disobeyed me one too many times, and ya've cost us evrathin'," he roared.

"I dinna understand." Brae shook her head, threading her arms into the sleeves.

Her mother continued shoving her belongings into the bag.

"Ya ken we'd settled on a bride price with Callum," Da explained.

"Aye."

"Evrathin' we had left depended on your marriage to Callum." The big man threw his hands up in the air.

"Evrathin' we had left?" she repeated, frowning.

"We've no place ta go, ya stupid girl!" her mother screeched.

"No place ta go?" Brae echoed.

"I had nothin' ta offer for ya. Ya kenned Callum was goin' ta be me apprentice. And Callum bein' me helper was the only reason Ross the overlord accepted me latest bid ta build the new retainin' wall. It all hinged on Callum. He's even been payin' the rent 'ere. And now that he's begged off, we've nuthin'. We have ta get oot."

Brae's stomach cramped. "Callum's cried off?"

"O' course, he has," her mother said cruelly. "Ya are used. Why on earth would he accept ya now? You are worthless. Ta all o' us."

Brae ran her hand over her face. This could not be happening. Of course Callum thought the worst of what he had seen in the smithy. He thought she was no longer innocent. How would she ever be able to make anyone believe her? Marschand had made it look so convincing. And there were too many witnesses to count.

"Where is Callum?" Brae asked meekly as she dragged the dress over her head.

"It doesna matter. He doesna want ta see ya," her mother snapped.

"But I need ta explain."

"Close your mouth. There's nothin' ya can say. Ya got what ya deserved!" her father railed.

"I didna ask fer this, Da!" Brae cried.

"Take that." Her mother thrust the bag into her chest then pushed her toward the exit.

"Will I help ya pack, Ma?"

"Och, ya've done quite enough." Her mother forced her outside of the croft, then to Brae's utter shock, closed the door in her face.

"Ma! What are ya doin'? Please!" Brae croaked.

"Go away!" her mother yelled through the door.

"But, where will I go?"

"I dinna care!"

"Da?" she pleaded. "Da! Please!" Brae pummeled the door with her fists.

"Go, Braelynn," he said, sounding close to the door. "Just go."

His words cut her heart. Would he not stand up to her mother one last time in her defense? Especially now?

Defeated, Brae collapsed. She leaned against the hut and listened while her folks argued.

"I told ya she'd be nuthin' but a big disappointment. Just like me sister."

Brae's lip quivered.

"That's what ya get for strayin' with me sister, ya randy auld goat. And this is what *I* get for agreein' ta raise your begotten as me own."

Brae's mouth dropped open at that bit of truth. Her mother was not her mother? *Can this day get any worse?* She was dreaming, she had to be. The whole day had been a nightmare.

And where was she to go? With no money. No protection.

Callum. She would go to him and explain everything. Once he understood, all would return to the way it was before.

Dragging the satchel, Brae limped to Callum's, but found the croft empty. Exhausted and at a loss of what to do next, she slumped heavily on Cal's front stoop. Sitting there she felt like the only person in the world, it was so eerily quiet. The village was deserted. It was truly frightening.

She needed to find somewhere to go before darkness fell. Retracing her steps to her own front door, she pounded on the wood until her knuckles bled, pleading for her father to allow her return. She fell to her knees in complete despair.

"What have we here?" a male voice, drawled.

"Looks to be Marschand's leftovers," another replied.

How can I be so stupid? Twice in one day!

In no time, Brae found herself atop a horse at the mercy of the devil's men. Though this time she didn't even fight, allowing her body to hang limp, bobbing up and down with the trot of the steed. Her only regret was that she had lost her carpetbag with the gem sewn inside. But as her luck was going, she might not live long enough to reap the rewards of Gaveston's precious stone.

"I want her this time," one of the rider's laid claim.

"What!" another said in disgust. "I wouldna touch her after she's been with Marschand."

"I'm surprised she yet lives. Marsch really went at her. She bled like a stuck pig."

The man holding her brushed the hair from her face. It was the one called Grainger.

He dragged her to a sitting position. His gaze was chilly. Yet she felt somewhat optimistic finding herself in his custody. He had saved her from Cowan, who without a doubt had been about to cause her true harm. She shuddered recalling the red-head's tongue on her flesh.

"Did you not learn your lesson, young one?" Grainger whispered.

"I have learned many this day," she said in a raspy voice.

"I'm afraid you may not yet be done," he said, releasing her.

She sagged against his chest.

Not long after, they rode through the bailey of Lord Ross' holding. "Why are we here?" she asked, confused by the way he had ridden in with no resistance.

"Your Lord Ross is dead. Meet your new overlords." Fear ran down her spine. Grainger pulled her from the horse.

"And who are you?" she asked.

"We are mercenaries for hire." He grinned, and if possible, his eyes grew colder.

"Who be your hire?" she whispered, afraid of his answer.

"'Tis no matter. As long as we are paid and paid handsomely, the who or the why is of no concern. Follow me." Grainger dragged her along until they reached great hall. The town folk of Ross sat grouped together. Not a soul met her gaze.

Just then, two soldiers marched between the rows.

A tall man with sandy colored hair took the dais and began to address the crowd. "Fine townspeople of Rossshire . . ." He paused as if he had forgotten what shire they had been paid to overtake. The man at his side, leaned in and whispered. "Ah, yes, and Cromartyshire."

It was the other male who drew Brae's attention.

Marschand!

His hair was even blacker than she had originally thought. And his beard, though well groomed, gave his face a harshness, lending his features even more of a malevolent air. His mouth was hard and unforgiving. If the devil possessed human form, he would choose to look like this man. There was no softness in him at all. His dark eyes glittered as he stared down at her people huddled near his feet. Looking at him now, she could imagine him being as violent as his visage suggested. But that was not what she had experienced from him. For some reason, he had spared her.

"You are under siege." The new leader was English, like Grainger. Yet Marschand, though his accent was English, had a surname suggesting a French background.

Brae listened in.

"We are your new overlords. You will obey us, and we will in turn assure your safety. You will be assigned your duties according to your occupation or talents. You will do as requested, or no one eats this night." The speaker turned slowly in a circle and pinned each person in his vicinity with a self-assured stare. "We can work together without major bloodshed. Labor jointly toward a common goal. With the exception of your poor departed leader, Ross, there have been no casualties. His death was unfortunate. His poor heart could not take our usurpation."

"No casualties?" Someone had the courage to shout. "My smithy lies in ash."

"As does my croft," another added.

"And the armory!"

"As I said," the leader continued, " . . . common goals. We will rebuild together. Better than it was afore. See to your duties, comport yourselves kindly, and all will be well good people." He made a sweeping gesture. "Men?"

His troops fell in and began to assign tasks.

The superior stalked off. Marschand was about to follow when Grainger thrust Brae into his path. She collided with his broad chest.

"I believe *this* is yours," Grainger drawled.

Marschand spanned his hands about Brae's waist, steadying her. Disoriented, Brae stared up at him. For the briefest instant he looked horrified, before his gaze turned inhospitable. Grainger applied the same technique. She wondered if it was part of their training.

Assuming an air of boredom, the devil turned his attention to Grainger.

"You are mistaken, Hudson. *This* most definitely is not mine." He used the same offensive sneer as when he had referred to her as *Caileag*, during the catastrophe at the smithy.

Wait! Caileag is a Gaelic word.

Before she could puzzle it out Grainger said, "Then give her to Stuart. He has expressed interest in her. Or better yet, let Cowan have at her. He's splitting his breeches to finish her off." With that grotesque announcement Grainger stalked away, while the devil bristled at her side.

Marschand pushed her into the crowd with the rest of her people. "Sit," he growled.

Brae grimaced at the throbbing in her thigh as she bent to take a seat.

Without another glance, the devil marched away. Clearly, she was not his problem.

Brae wrapped her arms around herself. She was so cold and beyond tired she could not stop trembling. All she wanted to do was curl up and sleep. Since that wasn't about to happen, she scanned the crowd, trying to locate her father or Callum and his kin. But she saw no one familiar, not even her best friend, Katie.

The men garbed in black picked people at random and enlisted their duties.

"You." One pointed to Brae. "What do you do?"

Good question. Up until a few hours ago, she was going to be a wife. She had not planned on anything else.

"Speak up!"

She flinched. "I . . . I can sew and . . . cook."

"Of course, you can." He rolled his eyes. "To the kitchens."

Brae gingerly gained her feet—her leg already threatening to stiffen up—then headed for the scullery.

"Ya could be spared from kitchen duties, if ya like."

She didn't have to turn to know who offered such a disgusting proposal. The back of her neck tingled. *Cowan.*

"We could use your services in other ways."

"I prefer ta work the kitchens," she said, quickening her pace. Brae darted in and out of the other girls appointed to the galley. For the moment Cowan let her be, but she knew it couldn't be that easy to get rid of the likes of him.

In the kitchens, Brae peeled and chopped vegetables, washed dishes, and cooked. In general, she did whatever needed to be done. Like most of the others, she kept her head down and did as she was told. The odd person who voiced a complaint earned a quick reprimand before the entire assembly. The unspoken threat of violence kept the rest of the citizens in line.

For the most part, as a community, they had collectively given up. This was just another siege. Conform or die. No one tried to stand up to the marauders. No one fought. No groups broke off and plotted to overthrow. No weapons were passed or hidden. There was nothing left to fight with. They were tired. Weary of fighting. Warn out by war. Not just with the English, but battling each other.

This siege seemed different from the more recent takeovers. These men were reasonably organized and well armed, and other than what had happened to her earlier in the smithy, they did not seem out for blood. Or to eliminate as many Scots as possible.

Who had paid them, what was their goal, and why were there so many Scots among them? And the biggest question of all, what part did the devil play in all this?

By the time the evening meal was ready to serve, Brae's thigh pounded so painfully it was all she could think about. The site of the injury felt hot at times and she was convinced the wound had reopened and was seeping down her leg. Yet she dared not ask to have some privacy to check on it.

Brae was handed a large tray and herded out with the rest of the kitchen help. Long trestle tables lined the great hall.

As she served, she tried to locate a familiar face.

The only eye she caught was Robbie Cowan's, though it was swollen and bruised from Grainger's beating.

CHAPTER FOUR

Gard Marschand stood on the slightly raised dais overseeing the dinner service. He did not eat, for fear of poisoning. He had done this too many times to trust people under duress. He watched for any rapid movement or anything that might indicate revolt.

The people of Ross were different than the last two holdings they had taken. Chamberlain had led the first. The townspeople had been angry and difficult to overtake. Perhaps therein had been their first mistake with Robbie Cowan and some of the younger men. They had gotten a taste of power and how violence and fear could bring people to heel.

Hudson Grainger had led the second, which turned out marginally better as they had learned from the errors of the first.

This last one was Gard's. So far, it had been effortless. These people had no apparent fight left in them.

Hudson approached and took up his place next to him on the dais.

"I am tired of this," Gard confided.

"That is not obvious at all, Gard," he mocked. "That stunt you pulled this morn is proof."

"Served two purposes. The men will get off my back. And I saved at least one of them from Cowan."

"Suddenly developed a conscience since leaving England?" Hudson raised an eyebrow.

"One of us needs one," Gard retorted.

Hudson snorted. "What for? It's not likely they'll hold the

40

pearly gates open for us."

"Speak for yourself. I will own the pearly gates afore I get there," Gard boasted.

"I believe there are no gates in fiery pits. Oh. I forgot. You merely *act* like a rapist." Hudson frowned. "And how is it you're going to keep your *supposed victim* from lamenting that tiny fact to the fine townspeople, not to mention her grieving betrothed?"

Gard could not hold Hudson's gaze. "'Twill be her word against mine."

"And if a physician should check her?"

"Go to hell, Hudson."

"Meet you there, my friend, but you have more immediate problems."

Gard followed Hudson's glare, only to find Robbie Cowan once again harassing the *supposed victim* in question.

"Bloody hell!" Gard swore, stepping down from the platform.

Braelynn sidestepped the ever-persistent red-head. "Please, leave me be. I've no quarrel with ya," she croaked, wishing her damaged-voice was stronger.

Cowan ignored her and reached for her anyway. Brae cringed, but before Cowan could put his hands on her, she was seized about the waist. Brae landed against the solid chest of . . . she guessed whom, without turning.

"What don't you understand, Cowan? This one is mine."

Marschand's warning was issued with such conviction it made Brae tremble.

Without a word or backward glance, Cowan retreated.

Brae twisted in the devil's arms—he followed her rotation with his palms, still spanning her waist. He regarded her frostily.

"Thank you," Brae uttered. "Again."

His frown deepened. With that incredible speed he possessed, he lifted one hand and stroked her throat. The gentleness of his touch conflicted with his severe expression. "Your voice?"

"From screamin'," she explained.

Instantly his gaze darkened, and his mouth hardened as if he didn't care for her response.

"Continue serving." He inclined his head and strode away.

Confounded by his odd behavior, she stared at his broad back as he strode through the masses.

Once the meal and the trestles had been cleared away, the troops brought in pallets for sleeping.

As in musical chairs or Ye Olde Trip to Jerusalem, folks rushed to claim a mat before they were all taken. She was passed over several times, but after a nod from Marschand, one of the men handed her one.

Brae also kept watch on Robbie Cowan, who was lurking nearby. Darkness would present a whole new set of problems. She dreaded resting in the crowd. During every other siege, she had slept in a protective cocoon between her parents. But, she still had not located them. And even if she had, she knew they would not be receptive right now. Stupidly, she had taken her safety for granted. And that was the rub. Callum and her da had warned her time and again, and now she was alone.

The Dark Ones — she had nicknamed the devil's men for lack of something better to call them — stood sentry, scattered around the perimeter of the room.

Auld Myrtle waddled over near Brae. From as far in the past as Brae could remember Myrtle had looked the same — hunched shoulders, sun-wrinkled skin, and her thick white hair plaited in the fishbone style.

Brae's chest hurt as she watched the elderly lady struggle to get down on the ground. With work worn hands she swept the filthy rushes into a pile and was about to lie down. It was bad enough they were being forced to sleep on pallets when they had perfectly good homes to bed down in, but poor Myrtle only had the dirt floor.

Brae handed her the pallet.

"I thank ya, Braelynn. Ya always were a gud lass. Stick near me. I'll protect ya." She winked and showed Brae the dirk she had hidden under her wrap. "They willna mess with ya while I'm here."

Brae returned her grin. Myrtle certainly did not take her safety for granted. She took matters into her own hands. If she got out of this, Brae might think about arming herself, especially if she ended up living alone.

Placing her back against the wall Brae slowly slid down it, her thigh throbbing. At least with her shoulders to the wall, she would have one less place to guard.

Brae wished for invisibility. She tried to curl up in a little ball and take up the least amount of space as possible, but the pain in her leg made that position impossible. Instead, she leaned against the wall and tried to rest sitting up.

She should locate Callum and explain what had happened to her, but she was too tired to move. And what on earth could she say that would convince him she still retained her innocence? There was only one way for her to prove that to him, and until they were wed — *if* they wed — it was not likely he would believe her.

Tears rolled down her cheeks. This had been the worst and longest day of her life.

Myrtle patted her shoulder as she wept.

Gard and Hudson stood on the raised platform overseeing the multitude. The torches flickered in the sconces, making it difficult to see in the dimness.

"She's being watched. On many fronts, Gard," Hudson said.

"'Tis none of my affair," Gard replied, flicking a bit of imaginary lint from his sleeve.

"Then quit grinding your teeth," Hudson snapped.

"Where is Cowan?" Gard asked, scanning the room, after losing sight of the scoundrel for a moment.

Grainger did the same. "He is on the other side of the old woman who sleeps on the pallet at the young girl's feet."

"I'll kill him, Hud. I do not have a care to whom he is related. He will not ruin another innocent."

"Ahh, Gard, your divine afterlife is truly in jeopardy," Hudson said sarcastically, grinning. "Cowan knows we're watching."

"Good. Then perhaps all the women will be safe this night."

It was only a matter of time before the boy could not restrain himself.

For over an hour they watched, and when Cowan finally made his move, both Gard and Hudson stepped from the podium simultaneously. Like twin shadows, they maneuvered silently through the rows of bodies. But before they could reach their destination, Cowan squealed in agony.

When they reached him, Gard looked down to find Robbie's hand pinned to the dirt floor with the old woman's dirk. Gard could not help but respect her quick action and foresight.

"I ken ya were na good," she said to Robbie. Then she turned her wrath on Marschand and Grainger. "Is this how ya plan ta protect us. By lettin' your men ruin our youngin's? I've heard tell poor Braelynn 'ere has already been attacked this day." She sent Marschand an accusatory glare. The girl whimpered, then stared at her feet, as the wrinkled old woman broadcast her misfortune to one and all.

"Do you never learn, Cowan?" Grainger said and yanked the dirk from Robbie's hand. He coiled up in pain and grasped his bloody hand to his chest.

"Sleep wit' care, auld woman," Robbie warned.

"Are ya threatenin' me?" Myrtle's eyes glittered.

Hudson gripped Robbie by the scruff, then all but tossed him toward the exit.

"He is not, Madame," Hudson soothed. "I'm certain he will be truly apologetic and remorseful on the morrow."

"Weel, I should hope so."

"Thank ya, Myrtle," Brae whispered.

"Ya need to take her out of here, Dark One. She be too temptin' a jewel," Myrtle said.

"Sleep, woman," Gard ordered, but he grasped the young lass under the elbow and yanked her roughly to her feet

"Ow," she protested, but her voice faded.

Gard moved so fast, he was certain the girl's tiptoes barely touched the floor as he raced toward the raised dais. Once there, he pushed her down onto his pallet. He most likely wouldn't get chance to rest anyway.

"Sleep," he commanded. Turning his back on her, he resumed surveilling the room.

The unmistakable sounds of lovemaking filled the air. It set Gard on edge and made him completely and painfully aware of the woman behind him. That kind of behavior was known to produce more of the same, like a wave of sensation that moved people to act, driven by baser human instinct. Especially ones who thought their lives might be in peril.

Gard rubbed his aching temples and tried to shut out the

grunts and groans from the amorous couple. The whole day had been one he would like to forget, right along with the girl at his back.

She tossed and turned, obviously unable to get comfortable.

Minutes later, her teeth began to chatter.

Gard's patience was about at its limit. Angrily, he stripped off his cloak and covered her with it. After croaking a meek *thank you*, she pulled the material up to her chin.

Once more, he waited for her to quiet, and when he couldn't stand it anymore, he lay down beside her.

Her eyes widened as he draped the wrap over the two of them.

Without a word he glared in return, waiting for her to acquiesce.

"I willna hurt ya," he pledged—though he honestly couldn't guarantee the vow—but the lie seemed to work and she calmed somewhat.

Yet her constant trembling got on his last nerve. He wanted to draw her nearer and provide the warmth of his body she so plainly sought. She snuggled further under the cloak, bombarding his senses with her scent.

Finally, he yanked her against him, chest to chest. She stiffened, unyielding.

"Sleep!" he growled.

Gard gritted his teeth as she nestled against him, remembering what it had felt like to be buried between her thighs. How she felt underneath him. She had no idea how close she was to violence.

Brae knew not what woke her. Yet she was loathe to move—content to remain in this warm secure embrace. The foreign but appealing new smell pleased her senses. She breathed deeply, filling her lungs.

Awareness came slowly, This was not a dream, nor a nightmare, but her reality for the moment. She opened her eyes and stared into the blackness of Marschand's chest.

"Braelynn." A harsh whisper reached her.

Her gaze darted to the man holding her, and she waited to see if he had heard it, too. He did not budge — his even breathing signified sleep. Tentatively, Brae turned onto her other side. Her leg ached. She peeked out from under the devil's cape.

"Brae." Hovering just above the lip of the dais was Callum's best friend.

"Duncan!" she cried quietly. He was to stand for them at their wedding.

He opened his eyes wide — she saw the fear and determination therein. "Take me hand, Brae," he encouraged.

Brae knew even if she attempted to flee her captor, it would be bad for her but even worse for Duncan. She knew not what these men were capable of and she would not test it out on her friend. This brave man had put himself in jeopardy to help her — it was more than Callum had done. Though she longed to go with him, she could not risk Duncan's safety.

She shook her head. Sorrow flooded her being as her eyes filled. Although it killed her to do so, she turned her back on her would-be savior and returned to the arms and the warmth of her abductor.

As she listened to the faint sounds of Duncan retreating, she sobbed silently into the devil's chest. Had that one decision just sealed her fate?

Just when she thought she had managed the small deception without waking her captor, his deep voice broke the silence. "Good choice," he sneered and tightened his arms about her.

Chapter Five

When Brae awoke next, Marschand was gone. She was surprised he had been able to sneak away without waking her. Thankfully he had left his cloak. For one so cold and calculating, he was very considerate.

Ignoring her aching muscles, Brae sat up, then tried to finger comb the knots in her hair.

From her raised position, she looked out over the mass of bodies in various states of sleep and wakefulness.

The Dark Ones were still dotted around the room. Brae noted she was not the only woman to have woken next to one of them.

There was no sign of Marschand.

Grainger approached with a steaming cup in his hand. Her mouth watered.

To her surprise, he hunkered down and placed the ceramic into her hands. "Drink."

Immediately her suspicion doubled.

As if reading her expression, he grinned. He took the flagon and took sip. "It is not poison. Marschand is being compassionate for once in his pathetic life. He requested you have honey and tea to calm your throat."

"Please thank him for me," she whispered, before hesitantly sampling the steaming liquid. The warmth soothed all the way down. "Mmm," she hummed.

Grainger's mouth quirked slightly before he said, "You will launder this day."

She nodded before he left.

Brae finished her tea, plaited her hair, then attempted to stand on her sore leg. Grimacing, she realized she needed to find a moment of privacy. After carefully folding Marschand's cloak over her arm she stepped gingerly from the platform.

"Good morn," she whispered to the first awake person she passed. But as she continued her path, she garnered only hostile stares. *What have I done?* Nothing that had befallen her had been her choice.

She limped to the portcullis, where she was waylaid by a Dark One.

"I wish a moment of privacy," she explained.

Nodding his assent, he permitted her leave.

As quick as she could, Brae took care of her needs, then checked on her wound. It looked bad this morn, oozing green pus. The edges of the crescent shape were red and inflamed. She had no salve and was afraid to request some.

"My kingdom for a basin o' water," she croaked.

Brae doubled Marschand's cloak and tied it around her waist, saving her from having to carry it. On her way to the holding she decided she would return the cape the moment she located him.

Someone handed her a chunk of bread before steering her toward the laundry. Brae dove right into the task, glad to have her hands in the warm water. Later in the day, she knew she would not be so content as the water cooled. Tasks were abundant, and the hours passed quickly, giving her no time to dwell on how her life had changed. How all their lives had.

Keeping her head down and working was not difficult, since no one made any attempt to speak to her or even look her direction.

Finally, auld Myrtle came around, serving refreshment with some assistance from a Dark One, who hauled a large bucket of water for the elderly woman. Myrtle handed Brae a cup. Brae drank greedily.

"Y'ad do yourself weel not ta flaunt your position with 'em," Myrtle said out of the side of her mouth so no one else would hear.

"What?" Brae asked, frowning.

Myrtle's gaze dropped to the black cloak tied about her waist. "Ya wear it like ya think 'twill protect ya. Your own believe ya've joined them."

"And if I have, only ta save myself, what so? I saw others with 'em. As if a choice be given." Her voice was barely audible.

"Can ya name one of them now? Ya are the only one dressed as them. Ye be wearin' their colors."

She wore it only to return it. Marschand had left it in her care. What would her punishment be if she left it behind for someone else to take or lost it? It was an expensive garment.

She looked down at the offending cape, only to find it streaked with water from her carelessness. And what again if she ruined it? Frantically she looked around for him.

For some reason, Gard could not keep his gaze from straying to the girl. He told himself he only watched for her safety, but it was more than that. She troubled and fascinated him. She drew his eye and his desire. And he did not enjoy it one bit.

"She is not afraid to labor," Hudson said, as he took his place at Gard's side.

"Who?" Gard answered, distracted.

Hudson snorted. "The one you had me wait on this morn, no better than a parlor maid."

"'Twas my fault her voice be raw. And soon her smooth hands will be, too." Anger swept through him. "Who picked the assignment this day? There were other chores she could have been given."

Grinning, Hudson prodded his ill-humor further. "And what else of hers be raw this morn, Gard, no thanks to you?"

"Naught of my doing," he snarled. "And you well know it!"

"I am well aware you did not assault her yester morn, but I've no doubt she was forced to endure your ardor last eve." Hudson stifled a chuckle at Gard's frosty glare.

"And you would be wrong."

"Am I? Hard to believe, the way your eyes follow her."

"No harder to believe than I tolerate your presence year after year," he snapped.

"Don't look now, Gard. She approaches."

Gard tensed when she paused in front of him. While she stared up at him with uncertainty, she untied his cloak from around her small waist. "Thank you," she rasped.

With an air of aloofness, he took the garment then dismissed her, scanning the crowd over her head.

Brae resumed her work, puzzling over Marschand's unusual behavior. She plunged her hands into the cool water. It felt good, she realized, as she was incredibly warm. She ran her wet fingers over her forehead. Was she feverish?

"I'll take another." A familiar male voice made her tense. *Callum.*

She spun to see him hoisting a crate of linens and chanced leaving her post to speak to him.

"Callum." She touched his shoulder and he jerked as if it burned. "Callum, please let me explain. Please let me—"

"Explain?" he retorted.

The assembly quieted and watched them.

"Explain wha'?" The pain in his expression made her chest ache.

"'Twas not . . . It didna . . . I am not . . ." She did not know what to say that would not incriminate Marschand, but silence was even more disastrous. "We can work it oot. We can . . . 'Tis not as bad as ya think."

Dropping the crate with a resounding thud, he then rounded on her. "Not as bad as I think? Do ya ken how long I have waited ta be with ya? How long I have waited ta make ya my wife?" His voice lowered so only she could hear him. "How long I have waited to make love to ya?"

"Aye, Callum, I do, because I have waited, too." Brae bunched her hands into the front of her skirt.

"I have dreamt of ya. Since the minute I knew what happened between a man and a woman." His eyes filled and hers did in response. "It woulda been so sweet between us, Brae. I woulda been so good to ya."

"It can still be, Callum," she cried.

"How? How can it be? Are ya mad? Did ya forget what I saw? Ye are no longer the girl from my dreams. Ya are ruined. Used. I will never erase tha' vision from me head. Those lovely bare legs covered in your own blood. Tha' innocence to take, was mine!"

"Callum, I am not ruined. I *am* the same girl I was two days ago."

"How can ya say that? Perhaps 'tis not your fault, ya are just another casualty of siege, but it doesna change the fact that ya are hardly what ya were two days past." He shook his head. "Where were ya, Brae, when they took ya? Were ya out on the moors?"

She bowed her head.

"How many times have I warned ya?" he railed. "Ya asked fer it. Ya deserved it."

Her father had said much the same.

"Ya think I asked fer this, Callum? Because I went to gather flowers for our ceremony? That I deserved ta be ravaged just because I happened ta be there? Just because I am a girl? Do ya think any of the women asked for it, Cal? Did ya ask to be under siege? Do ya see any of us here with any choices? Any free will? Do ya not feel somewhat *ravaged* yourself at our situation? Forced ta do what ya dinna wish? Do ya think perhaps if ya'd been with me the outcome woulda been any different? Could ya have fought them all and saved me from me fate?"

His Adam's apple bobbed.

"I didna ask fer this," she continued. "*None* of us asked fer any of this. Will ya punish us both fer somethin' neither of us have any control over?"

"I canna, Brae. I canna. I'm sorry. Every time I look at ya . . . I see . . ." He shook his head.

For a moment, Brae closed her eyes, and it was as if she too were transported back to the smithy, staring down at her own blood-soaked limbs.

Brae opened her eyes to look at him, but Callum's attention was elsewhere.

In a split second, his expression altered, from grief to anger.

"And if I could ever forgive ya that in time," he sneered, "I canna forgive ya for what ya've done since. Duncan told me ya chose ta stay with *him*." He jerked his chin, to some point over her shoulder.

Hazarding a glance behind her, she connected briefly with the cold black stare of the supposed indiscretion in question. Marschand showed no remorse, no emotion at all, his eyes as well as his expression blank.

"Did ya enjoy it then, Brae?" Cal said in disgust. "Sweetness is not what ya like."

She had never seen him like this, but she knew his pain drove him to be so cruel. Once more she closed her eyes trying to shut him out as he berated her in front of all assembled. He grabbed her arms and shook her. "Well, I can give ya violence, if that's what ya prefer. And I dinna need weddin' vows anymore ta give me the right."

Brae felt a breeze and heard a scuffle as Callum's hands abruptly dropped from her arms. Upon opening her eyes, she found Callum sprawled on the ground holding his chin. Marschand stood between them.

Callum scrambled to his feet while working his jaw, his blue eyes glittered with hatred.

Other dark knights stepped in, taking Callum by the arms in defense of their leader.

"Let him go," Marschand commanded. "If you think you can hold your own against me, puppy, give it your best." He opened his stance.

For a moment Callum seemed to consider his odds.

"She's all yours," Cal replied. "Ya can have her. Keep what ya've ruined. I no longer want it. Have a nice life, Brae." Callum stormed away.

Sobbing, Brae buried her face in her palms. Marschand also withdrew. Unexpectedly, her best friend Katie appeared at her side, then wrapped her arms about her. Brae dove at her, seeking comfort. "Katie. Oh, Katie. Callum." Brae's throat closed.

"I ken, Braelynn. I'm so sorry." Katie stroked her hair.

"I canna make him understand. Will ya talk ta him Katie? Tell him how sorry I am?" Brae begged.

"I will, Brae. When ya calm doon. I'm here for ya now."

"Thank ya, Katie." Brae cried into her friend's shoulder.

CHAPTER SIX

At mid-day, Ross-shire's townspeople gathered in the great hall for the noonday meal. After a meager fair of bread and cheese, Captain Chamberlain took to the dais.

The crowd quieted.

"You have, for the most part, held to our agreement, and as a show of good faith we will allow you to return to your homes," he announced, to murmurs of surprise.

"You will continue to work for us and yourselves, as you did for your Lord Ross. As I said, we work toward a common goal."

"And wha' be tha'?" someone yelled.

"To work, to fortify, to prosper, until your permanent overlord arrives to take his rightful place as your new leader."

Another titter of unease rippled through the crowd.

Would their new defender be better or worse than Ross? And under whose authority would they live next? Scots rule, or the dreaded English?

"Cease!" Chamberlain held up his hand for silence. "Your tools and implements have been removed from your homes and work places."

Outrage overtook the assembly.

"This, as you must see, was a necessary tactic on our part, for our own safety, of course.

"Pfff, as if that'll quell us," one gentleman muttered in a low voice. "We can fashion weapons outta the simplest common objects."

A few years past, Brae would have been hopeful from his boast, but their hearts were no longer in the fight. She returned her attention to Chamberlain.

"We encourage you at this time to keep the peace between us. We mean you no harm and only strive to make things better and ease the transition of power. Your tools will be returned to you as needed so you may work under supervision. You will be compensated as before under Ross' rule. If you choose not to cooperate, you will be dealt with. And if not you, your loved ones may choose to pay the price for your disobedience."

"And who is King Edward sendin' ta replace Lord Ross?" someone bellowed.

"We are mercenaries. It does not matter to us."

"Perhaps The Bruce settin' up house within the clans," another added.

The suggestion brought the crowd to voice all at once with that encouraging viewpoint.

Can we be so lucky? Brae doubted it. Robert The Bruce would not hold them prisoner.

"Go!" Chamberlain ordered. "Return to your homes and your lives as afore."

"And what of me?" Conrad MacGee shouted. "My croft is in ashes. What am I ta do with me family?"

"You may join us here until your home is resurrected. But you must work to rebuild it, and anyone else in the same unfortunate state may partake of our hospitality. But if you stay, you will also work for your keep."

Braelynn followed the herd as people filed out of the stronghold, though she had nowhere to go. But the prospect of staying and battling to maintain her tattered innocence, night after night, held no appeal either.

With no other prospects, she limped toward home.

To her surprise, her father was puttering around outside

cleaning up what the invaders had wrought. Of course the new overlords would not yet know of the broken three-way agreement struck between Callum, her father and Lord Ross.

"Da?" she called.

His broad shoulders bunched before he turned to face her. "Brae. 'Tis good to see ya well."

"I am not well. I've no place ta go. And Callum willna see me. Now that ya can renegotiate a deal with the new overlords, ya will be able ta stay in the house, yeah? May I please come home, Da?"

"I'm sorry, Brae. Ya are no' welcome here."

"Ya mean *she* willna welcome me." Brae pointed angrily at the cottage, "And ya will go along with her ta save yourself the trouble."

He could not hold her gaze.

"'Tis true then? She is not me mother?" Brae was incredulous no one had shared this news before.

"Nay. She is not. But 'twas afore we were married, Braelynn. Her sister died givin' ya life. We married and raised ya as our own."

"But ya are my sire, aye?" she hedged.

"Aye, Brae. For better or worse." He hung his head.

"Then be my da and let me come home. I am more to ya than she. I'm your blood."

"I'm sorry, Brae, I canna. 'Twould not be good for ya here."

"And I'll fair any better oot on my own?" She could not understand him. Two days prior, he forbade her to be out alone, and now he was throwing her to it, in fear of the banshee inside the croft.

"Return to the demesne, Braelynn. They'll look after ya there. Give ya work. Protect ya."

Yes, and she knew what work she would be given by the likes of men such as Robbie Cowan. She had only been saved the previous night because of Myrtle and Marschand. She could not count on them always. Myrtle was old, and soon Marschand would be gone. If he was not already.

"Go on, Brae. Ya would have had to resort ta such no matter, now that Callum has cried off. Ya couldna have stayed here forever."

"Perhaps if Callum willna have me someone else still might. Ya could try bargainin' me ta another lad." She did not want that, but if it afforded her some time and a place ta stay she would go along with it for now.

Sadly, he shook his head. "Do ya think so, Brae? Do ya think the lads will still have ya?"

He turned his back.

"Ya'll turn me out, Da? 'Twas not my fault."

The disappointment she felt cut deep as he continued to ignore her.

Finally, Brae limped away, walking slowly through the village aching and tired. She went past Katie's, but she was not at home.

Perhaps Katie was even now trying to reason with Callum on her behalf.

She tried another friend's house, and another, but was turned away. Word had carried quickly that she had thrown in with the Dark Ones. No one would give her a safe place to stay.

Brae went to the loch and threw cool water over her face. It felt so good. The urge to bathe was overwhelming. Sadly, everything she owned was in her satchel, which had been left behind when Grainger had captured her the day before.

Destitute. No home. No money. No belongings. No kin. What was she to do? Was it only two days past she had been planning to spend the rest of her life with Callum, preparing to marry, gathering flowers of all things? It seemed so insignificant and selfish now.

Needing to find a place to sleep for the night Brae stared determinedly toward the rocky cliffs. If she had to she would sleep in one of the smaller caves, one where she could hide in the shadows and have nothing but solid rock at her back. If someone approached, they would have to come at her head on. She knew the caves well. She and Callum had explored them thoroughly, even shared their first kiss there.

As she hiked toward the caves, she passed pavilions erected strategically near the burm.

Was Marschand there? He had not been at the noonday meal. She swiped at her cheeks. Anger blurred her vision. Marching purposefully toward the encampment, she skirted the edges, watching for anyone familiar. As her luck was going lately she was apt to walk right into the clutches of a worse enemy.

Spotting Grainger, she suspected Marschand could not be far. It seemed they were always in close proximity.

Head held high, Brae strode straight into their camp.

Grainger's eyes near bugged out of his head. He rushed to her and took her by the arm. "You should not be here!"

"Where is he?" she croaked. "Where is Marschand?"

"Let me escort you to the holding," Hudson offered.

"Why? Is he there?" She jerked her arm free of his hold. "I ken how ta get there myself."

"No. He is not there. But that is where *you* should be. Or better yet, home safe with your family."

"Take me to him!" She stomped her foot, then regretted it, for a moment forgetting her injury.

"You do not want to do this. Marschand is not a man you want to rile."

Before long, she managed to attract the attention of some of the other Dark Ones and the jeering began.

"Look who's back!"

"Lookin' fer more, Lassie?"

"Can't get enough of Marschand?"

She glared up at Grainger. He avoided her gaze. In that moment, she was certain Grainger knew that Marschand had not raped her.

"He owes me. And I'd say by the look on your face that ya ken that as weel."

"That enclosure. Right there. But I warn you, if you have not already sensed it for yourself — you do not seem stupid — there is barely leashed hostility in that man. You may have escaped the smithy intact, but you may not survive that tent."

Her life had never been so ruled by physical violence as in the past few days.

Sweat broke out across Brae's forehead, but she put on a brave front for Grainger. She straightened her shoulders and prepared to accost Marschand with her own measure of ferocity. Parting the tent flap, she stepped inside. It took a moment for her vision to adjust to the dimness.

"I told you I did not wish to be disturbed," Marschand snapped.

She didn't speak, but waited for him to take notice.

The interior of the structure surprised her. It contained more furnishings than her family's croft. The devil sat at a finely carved desk where he stared at yellowed sheets of vellum.

"Hud . . ." Clearly angered at being disturbed, Marschand whipped around. The moment he caught sight of her his eyes narrowed and turned cold.

"What are *you* doing here?" His gaze darted as if he wished to escape.

"I have no where ta go."

"Go home." He crossed his arms.

"I would love nothin' more than ta go home. But I am no longer welcome. And as ya ken, my betrothed has cried off because of ya, too."

"I'm sorry that it has come to that for you. But would you have rather endured the alternative? I spared you from being violated. If I had not done what I did, you would have been. If not by me then by one or *all* the others."

"So, then am I ta thank ya?" she asked in disbelief. "No matter what did or did not happen in that lean-to, the result is still the same. Only you and I know the truth. Ta Callum and my family, I am ruined. Worthless. Callum will no longer have me. And everyone else believes me already in bed with ya."

He nostrils flared. "So, what is it you wish from me?" His black eyes darted as he stalked her and began circling.

She stiffened but kept her head up. Another wave of heat assaulted her.

"Are you here for me to take your innocence then?" He crooned.

Brae closed her eyes.

"Is that what you wish?" He leaned in close then spoke directly into her ear. "Will that make everything right for you? They all believe it to be true. Let us make it reality, will we?"

"I . . . I thank ya for sparin' me and savin' me from the others. I canna understand why ya did that. But . . ."

He brushed her earlobe with his lips. His warm breath fanned across her cheek warming her already heated skin. With a voice like velvet, he responded, "But as you said, the result is yet the same. Everyone by now thinks it. Let us make it so, *Caileag*. Come to the enemy's bed," he invited wickedly.

She swallowed.

"No?" he mocked.

"I simply need a safe place ta stay," she said weakly.

He snorted and stepped back. "And you think this is it?

You think you will be safe *here*? With *me*?"

"Ya owe me!" she cried.

"I owe you nothing. I spared you a fate you'd have never survived. Go to the holding. You will be safe there."

"As I was last eve? If not for ya and auld Myrtle, I wouldna have been."

"Cowan is no longer at the holding. You will not have to worry about him."

"And the others? Your dark knights as well as my own clan alike? Perhaps your men will leave me be, mistakenly thinkin' I'm under your protection if that's what last eve 'twere about. But what of my own? I canna be trusted in their eyes *again*, because, of you! For as much as ya didna do ta me, ya did! If nothin' else, ya owe me a safe place ta lay my head this nigh'."

By the Christ, she rambled! Why would she not go away? She haunted him. She was everywhere. Plaguing his every step.

The last thing he needed was an overemotional girl blatting in his quarters. He had no stomach for hysterical women.

But on closer inspection, he noticed the flush on her cheeks, the moisture collecting over her upper lip and forehead, the over-bright green eyes. Was she ill, or merely afraid of him, as she should be?

"You cannot stay here," he repeated.

She took a deep breath and shook her head.

"I will work. I . . . I'll do whate'er be needed. I could prepare your meals or mend your clothin'. I could . . . launder. Ya know well I can do tha'." She looked around the space as if trying to find a chore he might need doing, when her gaze landed on his saddlebags. "I could tend your horse," she said in a rush.

"I have a squire. All those things are taken care of."

Her brow furrowed, and she prettily chewed her lower lip. She glanced around again, spying the papers on the desk, she blurted, "I can read."

"You can?" he asked, skeptical.

"Aye."

"And why would they have taught you to read?" he asked of the parents who would throw her out when she possessed such a skill. And why were they willing to marry her off to a mere apprentice?

"They didna. I taught myself." Rolling a shoulder, she confessed the rest. "With the help of the young Vicar who travels through. He is verra kind and truly gifted with patience He even gave me some books ta keep." Her face fell. "But my father's wife kept them."

He raised a brow, latching onto the Vicar part of her reply. "Yes. Kind, I'm sure. And what did the young clergy demand in return for this *kindness* and *patience*?" Gard could well imagine.

"He required naught in return." She wrung her hands.

"I'm to believe the good cleric asked nothing of you?" he sneered cynically. "Out of the goodness of his pure and uncorrupted heart."

She looked away.

"Ahh. I am a'right. The reverend asked something of you. What was it? A chaste kiss perhaps?"

Her mouth dropped. "He is a man of faith, Sir. He has no need for such things."

"Aye, and I imagine he'll go through his whole life without it." He rolled he eyes then asked again slowly, "What did you give him in return?"

She sighed heavily. "I am not supposed ta tell. But on occasion I helped him with sermons for his services."

The innocence of her response surprised him. "And why would he be in need of help with those?"

"He is a verra shy man. And it helped him ta rehearse in front of me. He is accursed with a slight stammer and I helped him choose words that were less difficult for him ta say."

That sealed it, she did not belong in here with him. He needed to be rid of her.

"Please. I will do what ever needs be done," she pleaded.

She was not going easily. Narrowing his eyes, he stalked her again. He would scare the hell out of her. "I *could* be persuaded to find *something* for you to do."

With hope reflecting in her eyes she nodded.

"You would be responsible for *all* my needs."

"Aye, I will take care of your requirements." She nodded.

Gnashing his teeth together at her response, he closed the distance between them. He grabbed her roughly and crushed her softness against his hard body. She stifled a yelp, proof that his quick action had startled her. But she didn't struggle or scream as he would have preferred, instead she watched him with interest.

"You will take care of all my needs," he demanded, his mouth only a hair's breadth from hers. The plan to overwhelm and intimidate fell flat.

She had not reacted the way he had expected. *Why is she looking at me that way?* He wanted to scare her so thoroughly she would run from his encampment and out of his life. Instead, her gaze darted around his face, lingering on his mouth. He could feel the heat radiating from her body. Her familiar scent assailed him. It had clung to his shirt during the night and driven him near insane the next morning. He had been forced to change his clothing.

Shallow breaths escaped her parted lips. He could take them, crush them, do everything to her that he had not days ago, and no one would question it. He wanted to. She was ruined, as she had said, in the eyes of all but him and her. His mind and body warred. He could take her now, bury himself in her innocent heat. What difference would it make? But that would make him no better than Cowan.

He cleared his throat. "Do you understand what services I require of you?" he said slowly. He ran his hands down her spine and was pleased when she trembled. He paused shaping his hand around her shapely buttocks. He pulled her fully against him, leaving no room to misunderstand.

"Ya dinna require tha' from me," she whispered with conviction.

He snorted. "I *dinna*?" he repeated, astounded again by her answer and her reactions.

"Nay. Ya wouldna have gone through the trouble of savin' me, only ta take it now."

"Are ya really that naïve?"

"Naïve? I think ya are curin' me of that particular affliction quickly enough."

He paused taken aback by her swift rejoinder.

"Ya dinna smile often, do ya?" she commented, out of the blue.

Is she addled?

Her gaze found his mouth again. When she looked at him that way, he wondered why the bloody hell he had spared her.

Shaking his head to clear it, he released her abruptly. She was peculiar. "Smile? A soldier does not make need of such things," he snarled.

"Perhaps then that could be me chore. I'll teach ya how."

"I've no need for either. Neither you, nor humor. We are at war. You are under siege. Losing your country bit by bit, your customs, your traditions, the very damned things that make you a Scot. Don't you think you should be worrying about that? There is nothing to smile for. There is no pleasure in our existence."

"Ya are takin' those things from us," she fired back.

"I am being paid to do a job. I do nothing to you," he yelled.

"Is that how ya live with it? By convincin' yourself it isna your transgression?" she demanded, hands on hips.

Had she the nerve to question his comportment? "I need a conscience about as much as I need humor. Stay here. I will see if there is a place for you. I hope you don't mind beddin' down with the whores."

"Why not? That may verra well be me new vocation."

He glared before ducking out.

CHAPTER SEVEN

As soon as he had gone, Brae took a cleansing breath. The man truly unnerved her. She wiped her forehead, finding the tent overly warm.

As she walked around the space, she tried to get a sense of the mysterious man. There were many things about him that did not add up, right down to his accent that she could not quite pinpoint. He was such a contradiction. Most of the time his dialect was cultured English. Other times, he spoke as she. Or perhaps he was simply mocking her. Yet his surname hinted a French ancestry.

There was a thick inviting pallet on the floor. Why had he not slept here and allowed his minions to oversee the hordes at Ross?

A pack sat open on the floor. Clasping her hands behind her, she glanced into the bag. To her disappointment there was nothing but more black garments.

Brae moved to the desk. Dare she hazard a peek? Her own curious nature won out. She peered down at the papers Marschand had been reading when she came in.

The first was a map of the surrounding shires. Ross, Cromarty. Of course, that would make sense. She pushed the top document with her pinkie finger to see what secrets the vellum underneath might reveal. She scanned it quickly for names. Wallace. Longshanks. Comyn. Bruce. MontClaire.

MontClaire? Why was that familiar to her?

"What are you doing in here?"

Brae jumped at the strange voice, right before she was

seized by a man she had not encountered before. She had not heard anyone enter.

"Answer me, wench!"

"I . . . I'm here with Marschand."

"Marschand?" He scoffed. "Now I know you lie." His fingers bit into her upper arms. "Whom are you spying for? Who sent you?"

"No one," she croaked, frightened. How did this keep happening to her? She could not even scream.

"I will make you talk. I can make things quite unpleasant for you."

The stranger moved his hands from her arms to her neck, pressing his thumbs firmly on her voice box. "Who are you here for?" he asked again, increasing the pressure.

"For me!" Marschand's deep angry voice rattled the canvas. Brae sighed in relief. The man's eyes snapped at the devil's tone. He released his hold on her at once.

The man turned stiffly. "Marschand. I'd no idea. No one told me you'd taken a woman. You must trust her very much, leaving her alone with your correspondence." His words belied his obvious distress at being caught in this misunderstanding.

Marschand's dark gaze met hers in accusation. She never should have told him she could read.

"I apologize for accosting your woman, Marschand." The man bent his head in contrition and skirted around Marschand as if he were afraid of him. Marschand did not make it easy for him either, blocking the exit with his big body. The man nodded again in respect, then bolted from the canopy.

Brae faced Marschand, unable to look away. He was furious. His jaw ticked, as he hunted her, yet again.

Right before he reached her, he bent and pulled a dirk from his boot. She had been on the wrong end of that blade already.

"Please. I didna see anathin' of import." She backed up.

His lightening speed caught her off guard. Marschand was on her in an instant, pulling at her plaid. Once again, she fought him.

Leashed violence. Grainger had warned her.

Marschand subdued her easily. His dirk in one hand, he used the other to loosen his leather belt.

"Please," she cried. "I didna . . ."

"Stop fightin' me!" he growled.

Baring her legs, he encircled the leather just above her knee.

"Wha' are ya doin'?" she asked, frightened not only by his anger but his actions.

"Ya willna go another minute wit'oot bein' armed. I canna be wit' ya all the time." He panted with exertion and ire. "I am tired o' tryin' ta keep ya safe. Ya are jus' too temptin' ta all 'twould seem."

In the dim light, his eyes glittered with intensity. He snarled as he worked. She could not breathe properly with him so near. He was undeniably an incredible looking man. So different to Callum in every way. Even in her fear, she wanted to reach out and tame the unruly hair that brushed his collar. Her fingertips itched to touch his beard and feel for herself if it was rough or soft.

One last yank, and he snugged the belt. He cut off the excess leather, then slid the cool blade between the strap and her flesh, somehow without slicing her.

Suddenly his words and his enunciation penetrated her consciousness. It finally dawned on her. Was that what she had been detecting? Her heart started to pound, almost painfully.

Forgetting her fear, she gripped his chin. His eyes rounded, in shock of being touched she could only assume. But she did not care, she was too excited about her discovery.

"Be ya Scot, then?"

He blanched, from the allegation or her contact she was not sure.

"Nay." He swatted her hand from his jaw then braced to get up when he stopped. He pushed her skirt higher uncovering the gash she had sustained in the smithy. The wound was now totally surrounded by a crimson ring, spreading across her skin at an alarming rate.

"Ah, Christ! Is tha' from me?" he asked, horrified. He did not wait for a reply. "Good God! Of course 'tis." His mouth hardened. "Who did ya have tend it?" he demanded. "The butcher?"

For the now, Brae ignored the mean-looking cut. "Ya see, when ya are conflicted or upset, ya drop your disguise. Ya are not what ya pretend ta be."

"Whom did you have tend this?" he asked in succinct refined English.

"I tended it myself," she replied.

He ground his teeth.

"There was no one at home. I couldna control the bleedin'. I had no choice," she said. "'Tis festered? Aye?"

"Aye. No wonder you are so warm. Why you shivered all night long. You are fevered." He placed his cool palm to her forehead. Brae was shocked by his gentleness. It belied the power and tension radiating from every ounce of his being. Her eyes fluttered at the pleasure of the simple chilly touch.

He removed his palm and circled a finger lightly around the perimeter of the redness on her thigh. The sensation sent tingling sensation to parts of her body that she was not even aware were capable of producing that kind of reaction.

"We need to get the poison out." Leaping into action, he roared, "Hudson!"

Pre-emptively, Brae tossed the tartan over her legs.

"Gard." Grainger's response quickly signaled his nearness to the pavilion.

At the entrance, they put their heads together and spoke quietly.

"Bring food and drink as well," Marschand called, in afterthought.

"Yes, Sir." Grainger answered.

"When was last you ate?" he asked.

"At the midday meal."

"Where have you been since then?"

"Lookin' for a place ta sleep this night."

He hunkered down next to her and placed his hand to her forehead, once more.

"Why did you not say something? Ask for help? Why did you not get it looked after properly?"

"I must be feverish. Ya are actin' like ya possess real feelin's and emotions. *Soldiers dinna need those*," she tried to mimic him by lowering her voice. "But ta answer your question, if ya havena noticed, my little shire is under siege and I have been put to work and too concerned about my own personal safety ta worry about havin' that looked at."

He scowled. "You had opportunity to tell me."

"When?"

"Last eve."

"And what would I have said?"

"How about ya stabbed me and it hurts," he said, deadpan.

Was he joking? For the life of her she could not read his expression.

"Ya stabbed me and it hurts," she repeated quickly avoiding his gaze, unsure if her insolence might cause her more harm. She took a chance, poking his anger.

Out of her peripheral vision she noticed his mouth did that thing that made her think he was amused. A smile, by no means, his mouth seemed incapable of making quite that shape.

"'Tisna funny." She smiled in contradiction to her words.

Grainger entered with a tray of food. "Here is the wine."

"And the other?" Marschand asked impatiently.

"I'm working on it."

Marschand nodded. "Carry on."

"Yes, Sir." Grainger left again.

Marschand placed an arm around Brae's shoulders and the other under her knees. "Come. Onto the pallet, with ya." He picked her up.

She inhaled sharply, fisting her hand into his shirt, holding on.

"I willna hurt ya," he pledged and set her down on the luxurious bedding. He piled pillows behind her. "You will be more comfortable here for what we are about to do."

She made a face, not looking forward to what was to come.

"Do not cease being brave now," he said. "That you placed a stitch into your own flesh at your own hand is quite an accomplishment. I have had my skin sewn many times, and 'tis painful. I cannot imagine trying to do it for myself."

He poured a cup of wine and handed it to her. "Drink this."

She was about to refuse it before she remembered the pain. And she had been in varying degrees of it since. "Thank ya." She took a sip.

"You will remove your skirt," he said, straightening to his full height but averting his gaze. It was a command from a man used to having his word obeyed without question.

"'Tisna two pieces."

"Would you have something suitable in that?" He pointed to her carpetbag.

"You have my case? How did ya get it?" Thrilled, her

heart leapt to have it and the gem safe as well.

"Hudson went back for it."

"How sweet of him." She blinked. "But would ya have kept it?" she asked.

"Nay, it would have been returned to you."

"I dinna even ken what's in it. My mother . . . my father's wife packed it afore she threw me out."

Marschand brought the bag to her and she went through it. She hauled out a chemise less sheer than some of the other garments.

"That one," he said gruffly.

She blushed.

"I will give you a moment to change." He ducked outside.

After a quick change, she sat on the pallet and covered her near nakedness with her dress.

No longer finding the accommodation over warm, she found her teeth were chattering. She picked up the cup of wine and took another sip. It warmed her insides, but the liquor was not as good a heat source as her companion had been the night before. Marschand had quelled her shivering better than a rip-roaring fire. Brae shook her head. Why would she think of that? *The fever – it must be.*

Marschand opened the tent flap hesitantly before re-entering. For a moment he stared at her, making her fidget under his intense regard.

He cleared his throat. "Hudson."

Grainger followed with another tray of steaming liquids and wooden bowls. Brae pulled her plaid up a little higher, using it as a shield. Funny that she was more uncomfortable about Grainger seeing her than Marschand.

Grainger set the tray on the floor near the pallet. Both men knelt at her side.

"Show me," Marschand commanded. "What needs be done?"

Grainger touched the edge of her shift. Marschand growled. The noise stayed Grainger's hand.

"Well, may I see it?" Grainger snapped. "I'm not completely confident I have the proper medicines or implements."

Marschand did not respond but continued to glower.

"Gard. For goodness sake, do you wish my help or not? I thought she was none of your concern? You are being particularly possessive over naught."

Gard's lips tightened, and his jaw ticked. "Lift your hem," he said, in a harsh tone.

Brae did not want to show Grainger. It was bad enough Gard would see. But with all that he had seen and done—and not done—to her in the last few days, somehow oddly she was more at ease with him. The lesser of two evils perhaps, though she knew by his reputation the other man could not possibly be as bad. It made no sense.

No words were spoken, but they seemed to come to some understanding.

"Go!" he ordered Grainger.

"But . . ."

"Go," Gard said in a clipped tone. "I will take care of it."

Grainger watched him stonily, and then pointed to the different mixtures in each of the bowls. "Use that first to cleanse. Then that. Finish with this one to promote healing."

Marschand nodded.

"You must extract all the poison, Gard. It is imperative. You cannot simply assume that you have it all. You *must* be sure."

Marschand inclined his dark head in understanding but was no longer concentrating on his comrade but squarely on her. Hudson stood and made for the exit.

"Remember to keep clean. Pour wine over everything. The instruments. The wound. Even your hands."

"I've got it."

Grainger shook his head as he ducked out.

Marschand removed his overcoat and rolled up his sleeves, exposing his forearms. He looked different with a crisp white overshirt, blindingly white against his dark trews. She was so used to seeing him entirely in black.

"Ya are wearin' white," she said.

"Aye." He washed his hands with water. "Do you notice everything?" he scoffed.

She took another sip of wine then shrugged. He made it seem like a bad thing.

He poured a measure of wine over his hands, letting it run into an empty basin. He gritted his teeth, then dried his hands with the rough-looking rags Hudson had provided. Brae imagined the stuff stung every nick he may have on his work-worn hands.

"Ready?" he asked, taking the cup. He drained the remainder into his mouth before re-filling it for her. She was impressed, he drank it like water.

"Drink," he ordered.

She took a sip.

"May I begin?" he asked.

"Now ye act the gentleman? To now, ya have never asked me afore ya did anathin'."

Clearly impatient he made a frustrated sound.

"I'd rather tend it meself," she said shyly.

"You did. And you made a muck of it," he retorted. "Now raise your hem and let me—"

"But I didna have the proper—"

"Lift your hem." He paused between every word.

When she made no attempt to move, he lacerated her with a look that she imagined intimidated most men. But surprisingly she was not afraid and did not think it was the wine giving her false courage. He had vowed not to harm her and for some reason she trusted that.

In one quick jerk, he pulled her dress from where she held it over her partial nakedness. Sometimes the speed with which he moved startled her. Ever so slowly, his gaze traveled over her legs. Her body warmed by degrees under the blatant perusal.

The last thing Gard needed was this woman barely clothed in his bed. His body was very aware of her nearness.

Her legs were long and shapely. His fingers itched to caress them. Why was this so difficult? She was not the sort of woman who interested him. He liked a tough and hearty woman. Not soft and feminine. One he could take his lust out on and send on her way. He was not a kind or gentle man, nor was he the type who took his time. Women were essential for one reason and one reason only in his opinion. This one would need gentleness. Softness. Time. Lots and lots of time, to explore and discover all the hidden places that would make her moan his name.

Tearing his gaze from her legs, he noted she was staring somewhere over his shoulder. Her cheeks had pinkened with embarrassment. No, she was not the sort of woman who could handle a man like him. He tried to concentrate on the task ahead and not her lovely body parts.

Dragging a candle closer, he bent his head to inspect the wound, though he was more distracted by the cool bumps spreading over her skin.

"'Twas deep, yeah?" he asked, wishing she had consumed more before he began. He touched the bottom of the cup reminding her to drink.

She sipped, then answered, "Aye. That's what made me decide to put a stitch in the center, thinkin' it might seal best there. I knew I couldna endure sealin' the whole of it. I'm not tha' brave."

He hung onto her every word, realizing he enjoyed her brogue immensely.

"I only managed that wee one, then I will admit to ya, I must have fainted. The next thing I knew the bleedin' had stopped. For the most part, at least."

"You know, I meant to cut my own hand, at the smithy," he explained.

Her eyes widened as it dawned on her.

"Oh aye, but I kicked."

He nodded. "At my insistence." He nudged the cup and she drank.

"I thought for a moment . . ." she confided.

He could well imagine what she had thought him capable of. Little did she know he could inflict that kind of torture and much worse and feel no remorse whatsoever.

He touched her leg, and she gasped. Was her reaction more pain, or apprehension?

"Drink," he barked. The more she drank, the less afraid of him she would be, he reasoned.

"What is all tha'?" she asked staring at the bowls.

"Herbs. Rosemary and verbena, boiled." He indicated the steaming trough. "Hypericum." He pointed to some leaves running red juice from their stems.

"And this looks like yarrow, yeah?" she asked, pointing to the yellowy powder.

"Aye. Hudson says to leave it for the last."

"What is the bowl o' stringy things? They look like snakes." Her nose wrinkled prettily.

"Thread. Hud recommends soaking them afore sewing. He insists it softens the fibers and lets them slide more easily. Less resistance."

She rolled her eyes. "Och. Aye. That's a good trick. 'Twas the worst part. It burned. I swear I can still feel it now. And that?" She indicated another steaming cup.

"I believe that is willow bark tea. Steeped for you to consume for the pain."

"Afore or after?"

"I'm not sure." He frowned. Healing was outside of his knowledge.

"I thought *this* was for the pain." She lifted the cup.

"It is." And to lessen her apprehension of him.

"Where are ya from? *Are* ya French?" She squinted.

She was too smart. He wished for the hundredth time he had never met her. "Do I sound French?" he replied.

"Nay, but your name is French."

In an attempt to distract her, he poked at her leg. She flinched. The day in the smithy he had suspected the blade had gone in deep. He was angry with himself for not following up.

"Drink," he commanded.

She took another sip. "Could it be Marschand is not your real name then? Like the rest of your disguise, it isna real?"

"It doesna matter what my name is." He did not wish to prolong this. Not only did he not want to tend the wound and cause her more pain, he did not need to be in her scantily clad presence any longer than necessary.

"It *doesna*?" Accentuating the word, she made him aware of what he had said.

"Do I *sound* Scottish?" he challenged.

"Aye. At times ye do." She nodded.

"It's bein' around *you* people. It makes one emulate you."

"I dinna believe ya. I think ya are tryin' to hide it. Ya are pretendin' to be what ya are not."

She was too perceptive by half. He needed to rid himself of her company before she unearthed all his secrets.

"I think you are drunk and imagining what you wish to believe."

"And why would I wish ta believe tha'?"

"I dinna ken. Ya are soused and no' makin' sense," he said in a perfect brogue.

She smiled—an action she did so easily, even in the dire straights she found herself in.

"You forget why I am here. I can be anything I need to be," he said in cultured English. "Whatever I am paid to be," this in Welsh. "I can make you believe whatever I want you to believe," this spoken in Gaelic. "I will let you see what I want you to see." Finishing in fluent French, then quickly translating the last again in Gaelic so that Brae would understand.

She watched him wide-eyed, transfixed on his lips. She moved her mouth in different ways, like she was mirroring his face as he spoke. He raised a brow at her comely display.

"How are ya able to do tha'? Your mouth moves in an entirely different way as when ya speak English. How can ya just stop the brogue like tha'? There is no possible way even practiced tha' I would be able to speak without my accent."

He blinked. "Drink, *Caileag*."

She took another sip and her cheeks shone, indicative of the alcohol finally taking affect.

"Wha' be yor name?" he asked her.

She smiled before she answered. By the little glint of mischief in her eye he assumed she was about to have a bit of fun at his expense.

"It doesna matter wha' me name be." She giggled.

He felt the corner of his mouth quirk but would not allow himself the pleasure of a real smile. "I heard the young pup call ya Brae." Nodding, she smiled softly. She really was lovely.

"Aye, 'tis Braelynn."

"Braelynn." Her smile slipped when he repeated it rolling the *r*. She shivered. More chill bumps appeared upon her hot skin. "I'll have the whole of it," he demanded in an authoritative tone, one he used on his men.

"Braelynn Galbraith." The sultry rasp to her voice did things to him.

"Braelynn Galbraith," he echoed in a perfect burr.

Again, she watched his lips. Then she searched his gaze, clearly seeking answers he would never give. She could look all she liked, she would not find them.

"Be ya numb enough for this, Br-ae-lynn?" Stretching out her name, he enjoyed the experiment of it on his tongue.

"What needs be done?" Her eyes appeared glazed. He dreaded what came next, knowing her sparkling emerald green orbs would soon fill with pain.

"Firstly, we need to get that string out." He dropped the brogue, and if he wasn't mistaken, she seemed disappointed. "Then we need to get the contamination out."

She drained the cup, no longer grimacing with every sip. "I am ready."

How could she trust him after all he had put her through? Unintentionally, he had changed the course of her life by trying to save her. And he knew naught how to fix it.

"Second thoughts, Monsieur Marschand?" she asked, her eyes shining in the candlelight.

"I *am not* French," he said, with a lift of his brow.

"Your name is," she chuckled.

"Aye. We've already established that."

He pulled the taper closer and raised the hem of her shift. Placing his hand under her leg, he coaxed her to bend her knee. He then had her lean it against his chest.

For propriety's sake, he assumed, she placed her hand atop the shift between her legs, keeping it from rising any more.

Perhaps she was not as naïve as he presumed. Or she was distrustful of the devil that lurked within him.

Did she realize what a seductive display the pose had on a man of questionable character? She was far from safe in his presence.

Gard did not want to dally any longer. He needed to do what was necessary then get the hell away from her. She was too tempting. Her smooth creamy white leg in his hand. Her see-through chemise only added to her allure, leaving little to his imagination. Her hand between her legs created delicious images he did not need dancing in his continually rampaging thoughts.

He released a harsh breath, it whistled between his teeth.

"Is it tha' bad then?" she asked.

His thoughts being elsewhere, he was confused by the question.

"The wound," she reminded.

After lightly running a finger over the stitch, he gently plucked at it. "I believe you've pulled it too tight. I am not sure how to release it without cutting it, and I may slice your skin again if I do." That was the last thing he wanted.

"Wha' if we soak it?" she suggested, with a shrug. "Bathe it in the rosemary water. Mayhap 'twill soften the thread? Loose it? Is that not what Grainger migh' recommend?"

"Mayhap. 'Tis worth a try." He plunged a rag into the steaming water. "Is tha' too hot?"

"Nay," she said after testing it. Positioning it on her thigh, he held it in place. Rivulets of water ran down her leg. He was mesmerized by the trails the droplets took.

"Feels wonderful and warm," she said—the words went straight to his groin.

"Are ya cold?" he asked, his attention drawn to the sheerness of her shift and her breasts. To his shock, her body reacted to his gaze, adding to his suffering.

"Nay, I am na cold anamore," she responded quietly, relaxing against the cushions piled behind her.

Gard poured himself some wine then gulped it. Replenishing the mug he handed it to her.

"I dinna think I should have any more. I feel a little strange."

She wasn't the only one. He was feeling light-headed himself, and it had naught to do with the drink. He reached for a piece of bread, then passed it to her.

"Thank ya," she said accepting it but releasing the hold on her shift. He forced himself to look away. It wasn't easy.

Brae picked bits from the crust and delicately placed piece after piece on her tongue. She finished with the bread, drained the cup, and set it aside. Tucking her knee against his chest, she said, "I am ready. No more stallin'. Do it."

He placed his hands on either side of her thigh and willed himself with a soldier's discipline to tamp down the raging need she stoked in him. There was much he would like to do with her in this position and have her say those words to him in an entirely different context.

Instead he removed the cloth from her leg and ran his finger over the tight suture.

"Has it softened?" she asked.

"Nay," he choked, still running his finger lightly over it.

So innocent. Yet the images flashing in his depraved mind were hardly ingenuous. And also wreaking havoc on his longsuffering body.

Gard reached over his patient. He undid the casing he'd fashioned as a makeshift scabbard, still strapped to her other leg. "I will have a proper sheath made for you, so you do not do yourself more injury."

"Thank ya."

"Furthermore, I will teach you to wield it."

She smiled slightly, warming him inside a little, an unfamiliar sensation for him.

"And ya will wear it always. Ya willna ever be wit'oot it.

Na matter. Even when I'm aroond." *Especially* when *I'm* around," he amended. At the moment, *he* was her biggest enemy. She simply had no idea how close he was to taking what he'd saved her from to begin with.

She cocked her head slightly, in confusion.

"Take a deep breath," he directed.

She did, and he quickly ran the sharp tip of the blade over the thread, cutting it cleanly. A fresh drop of blood dripped down her leg as he pulled the thread out of her skin. Her lips parted and her eyes widened, but she did not make a sound for which Gard was thankful. He was unsure what he would have done if she had shrieked. It was bad enough when tears formed on her lashes then ran trails down her cheeks. "I'm sorry." He had done nothing but apologize to her from the moment he crashed into her life. It was not a common word in his vocabulary.

"'Tis not your fault—"

"Aye, 'tis."

She sighed and grew serious. "Well, initially, but with good intent. And 'tis my blame it has gotten this bad."

"I must remove the infection now." He pinched her skin and shuddered at the stuff that oozed out. He had expected tears, hysterics, perhaps screaming. Every other female he had ever been forced to suffer had cured him from seeking out their company for anything other than physical gratification.

"Auh. 'Tis a lovely shade o' green, yeah?" she said.

He shook his head. "Ya surprise me."

"I do?"

"Aye, I expected ya ta cry and pout like a spoiled English court chit."

Smiling, her eyes sparkled. "We Scots are heartier than tha'."

"Aye," he agreed. "I ken."

"Is that what ya thought? Well, ya probably did get the idea tha' I was a screamer from our earlier meetin'. And I will admit, at home, alone, I did. Cried like a bairn. Righ' afore I had a fit o' the vapors." She waved a delicate hand in front of her face before she broke into a genuine smile.

He watched her mouth form a bow. He felt his own mouth quirk in answer. What was she doing to him?

"How auld are ya?" she asked.

He sobered. "It doesna matter. I could tell ya anathin'. How auld are ya?" He worked in and out of dialects and accents now. Trying to keep her from guessing the truth about him.

"A score," she answered as he continued to manipulate her leg.

He snorted. "I dinna believe ya."

"Ya dinna have ta, it doesna matter." She teased. "I could tell ya anathin'." Her eyes danced as she continued to smile, tossing his own words at him playfully.

No one teased him. Who would dare? Hudson antagonized him for his own perverse pleasure, but no one had ever joked with him. No woman ever stayed in his company long enough to converse, let alone needle him. He had never wanted them to. Nor had they.

He drizzled more of the rosemary and verbena concoction over her leg, attempting to clean it. So far it had been unsuccessful. As soon as he thought the poison was beginning to clear, more contagion appeared.

"Ya have been ta the king's court then?" she asked.

The sly little fox picked up on something else about his life that he'd let slip. He slowly raised his gaze to meet hers, pinning her with his stare while wondering at his carelessness. This was his punishment for conversing. He'd revealed important details and she was much too observant.

"I have been to many courts," he said so haughtily her

nose should have frosted.

Her eyes lit. "Ahh, wha's it like?"

"'Tis tedious."

"Oh, tell me. Are the ladies beautiful in their silk gowns and jewels? Are the men dashing and courteous?" Her eyes shone with interest.

Beautiful in their silks? No. She was simply beautiful sitting here in his bed with no more than her shirt and the sweet blush upon her cheeks. But his answer was a typically jaded response. "Silks and jewels? Is that what matters to all females?" His eyes and tone were meant to be cold, but she did not seem to notice.

She laughed, catching him off guard again. "Ya have seen me wardrobe. Not a silk in the lot. And I dinna own any jewels."

She is not like others.

"I guess my books were me jewels. And Callum possesses none to my knowledge, either. But tha' willna be now."

He cleared his throat. *Aw, guilt. Another unfamiliar emotion.* "I need to bring in Hudson. I cannot do any more for you." He began to rise. She stayed him with her hand.

"Nay. Please. I prefer you ta see ta it. 'Tis one thing for you ta see me thus."

"And why is tha' better?" She had no idea how he saw her. There was nothing chaste about those images.

"Because . . ." Her forehead furrowed, and she blinked rapidly. "I just feel like we've been . . ." She shrugged as she struggled to explain. " . . . through somethin' together and I . . . trust ya ta see . . . I canna explain it. 'Tis different with ya."

It was his turn to blink rapidly. She baffled him. "I am in need of his skill. 'Tis too important not ta be sure. I'll be wit' ya the whole time. I willna allow him see or touch anathin' more than the wound. I promise ya this." He would not permit it. Gard held her gaze until she agreed. Then he bellowed for Hudson, who promptly stepped into the shelter.

Chapter Eight

Marschand covered her with one of his throws. She pulled the blanket high, and inhaled his scent, finding it strangely comforting.

"It willna cease seepin' infection," Marschand explained.

Grainger's features lit in surprise the moment Marschand started to speak.

"Dinna fret, Monsieur Grainger," Brae said. "He only speaks thus ta comfort and distract me as he works. Dinna have a care. No secrets have been revealed."

"Monsieur?" Grainger repeated, raising a fair eyebrow.

"Oui," she laughed. "Monsieur Marschand isna French, but his name be. And ya are with him, therefore ya may or may not be French as well."

"Do I *sound* French?" Grainger asked, much the same as Marschand had.

They were so alike. Perhaps opposite in looks, but the very same in manner and training, it would seem.

"Nay, but ya can be whate'er ya need ta be."

"Aye." Slowly, he turned to Marschand. "You have made her quite intoxicated, Gard."

"I am no' drunk, Sir. Feverish, mayhap. But I am feelin' less pain than I have in two days. 'Tis respite, no' drunkenness."

"You say he is speaking as a Scot to comfort and distract you?" Hudson asked.

"Aye, is tha' no' sweet?"

"Aye. Three things I have never known him to be, comforting, distracting, or sweet."

"Just have a look," Marschand demanded with growing impatience.

Grainger knelt and cleansed his hands in the wine. Marschand adjusted the blanket, holding his hand over her thigh just above the gash. Grainger seemed overly amused by Marschand's fussing.

Turning his attention to the nasty cut, Grainger prodded and squeezed, finally lifting the flap of skin.

Brae kept her eyes on Marschand's face as he watched his man. His look was severe. She wanted to reach out and smooth the lines of worry from his face. *Mayhap I am drunk.*

Hudson cleaned the wound again with the rosemary, but he shook his head. "I'm going to have to open it up. It has begun to heal and close here on the outside but also up there" — he pointed — "inside, and I believe there may be infection behind where it has begun to heal. That is why you keep extracting more infection. As much as the stitch did to staunch the bleeding, it has hindered curing."

Marschand's mouth tightened. Suddenly, Brae felt the need to apologize. "My main concern at the time was haltin' the bleedin'.

His jaw ticked.

"Do it, then, Monsieur Grainger," Brae said. She held her hands out toward Marschand.

Grainger snorted as Gard stared at them.

After securing the coverlet in place, he took her hands, perhaps grudgingly so. He then perched on the pallet next to her.

Hudson prepared to pour some liquor over her leg but Marschand stopped him.

"Let her drink first." He was being overly kind, not at all the ruthless warrior he would have her believe.

Grainger passed her the cup. Reluctantly, she let go of one

of Marschand's hands. She drank deeply then passed the cup to Marschand. He finished it in one tip of the mug, then tossed it aside to rejoin their hands.

Grainger poured the liquid over her thigh.

She held Marschand's gaze, though her eyes watered from the sting of the alcohol.

"I am no' cryin'," she said before biting her lip.

"I ken." Marschand nodded reassuringly.

"Try not to move, lass," Hudson instructed, cleaning the blade. He promptly sliced deep into the meat of her thigh.

Brae tightened her grip on Marsch's hands. Her mouth opened on a silent cry. She felt him tense.

"Talk ta me." She held on to him tightly, hoping he could distract her from the pain. Her leg trembled. "Tell me about court."

Grainger sent Marschand another hard stare, which he ignored.

"Uh. I dinna know how ta describe it. I am na good at re-tellin' tales. Court is monotonous as I told ya."

"The ladies?" she prompted.

"Aye. The ladies. They are overdressed, over-powdered, o'er-perfumed, o'er-rouged bits of o' fluff wit' no substance. Only there ta be seen. By the men as well as the women. I swear they dress more for the other ladies than they do for the men," he mocked. "Unless, o' course they are tryin' ta imprison a man, then they dress ta entice and entrap. Throwin' o'er one for the next more prosperous—or is tha' pompous—or one possessin' a loftier title. 'Tis nothin' more than a contest of sorts."

"Tha' is not a jaded vision at'all," she teased.

Grainger chuckled as he administered.

"And the men, Monsieur Marschand?" She waved her hand.

"Dinna call me tha'." In a flash, his eyes blackened, along

with his mood. "The men are boorish, there ta line their pockets by makin' deals on the backs of the one's who do the real work. 'Tis also a contest of artful gamesmanship and cutthroat politics. There be too much food and too much wine. 'Tis o'er indulgence at its worst. 'Tis not as grandiose as ya seem ta think."

She tried to imagine him at court, dressed formally. Would he tie his hair or leave it free? Would he wear black? *Of course, he will.* He would never wear colors, she thought fancifully, as if she truly knew him.

Grainger glanced curiously between Brae and Gard.

Once the bacteria had been extracted and her blood ran free and clear, Grainger said, "I will need to close it. Most others would pack the wound full of healing herbs, but I do not agree with this practice, having found it prolongs and sometimes hinders healing. I like to use the blood-let method, but even that can be tricky."

Marschand shot him another stern look.

Grainger raised a placating hand. "I know what I'm doing."

"Are ya a physician, Monsieur Grainger?" Brae inquired. "Ya seem verra efficient and confident."

Something passed between the men before Grainger answered, "Nay. I just do what needs be done. I am normally Gard's cut man after battle. I'm merely better at it than most."

"Do ya get cut often, Marschand?" She smiled innocently.

"Nay, mostly I do the cutting."

She opened her mouth to reply that she was quite aware of that fact when he pointed a finger at her while still holding her hands.

"Dinna say it," he ordered.

She giggled. Grainger chuckled again as he threaded a needle.

"Give her more to drink, Hudson."

"I am o'er warm," she said. The last thing she craved was more to drink. "I dinna think I want anamore."

"'Tis the fever," Grainger said.

"She is lookin' pale." Marschand gave her hands a little squeeze, and it did strange things to her.

"She's flushed, Gard. 'Tis a number of things causing her distress."

All of a sudden she was having a difficult time following the conversation.

"But I would prefer she no' feel the pain."

Was that genuine concern she detected?

"Is this the wound *you* created?" Grainger's eyebrows rose.

"You told him?" Brae accused. It was as she'd suspected.

Marschand did not answer her but replied to Grainger's question. "Aye, regrettably. 'Tis deep, yeah?"

"Aye. 'Tis. But did you notice the shape of it, Gard?"

"Nay, I was concentratin' on not hurtin' her." He leaned over to have a look.

Brae peered down at her leg, too, but saw nothing more than her original assessment of a half-moon.

Grainger broke into a confident grin. Marschand glowered.

"'Tisna more than a crescent moon," she announced as Marschand's fingers tightened fractionally on hers.

Grainger guffawed.

With a jerk of his chin, Marschand gave another silent command for her to drink.

Brae drained the cup, taking a deep breath at the end. She hoped it was the last of it. She felt very strange, almost weak. Dreamlike, her vision blurred.

"I am ready, Monsieur Grainger." She half-smiled at his amusement.

"I believe you may address me as Hudson, lass. We are about to become intimate friends. 'Tis a very personal thing to probe into another's creamy white flesh."

"Just do your job," Marschand snapped.

But Brae spoke to Hudson as if Marschand never had. "You may call me Brae."

"He may not," Marschand denied.

She lifted her chin, giving him a bleary stare. "Why not?" The alcohol hit her all at once and her eyes fluttered. "We are about to . . . come intimate friends," she said slowly.

Hudson snorted.

"Ye are no' aboot ta become intimate wit' him!" Marschand growled.

Confused now, she could not seem to keep hold of her thoughts. "I am o'er warm," she repeated, her eyes flickering.

He eased her onto her back, then fit the blanket around her. "Begin." She heard Marsch's deep voice. She was comforted to still feel his hands on hers.

The hot prick of the needle bit into her thigh and the burn of the thread slid through her flesh. She remembered that part, but somehow Hudson made it tolerable.

"Squeeze my hands," Marsch instructed from far away.

"Don't go," she begged.

"I'm not goin' anawhere. Dinna cry. I'm here."

"Not your responsibility, eh, Gard." It was Hudson's voice. He sounded amused again. But she could not grasp what was funny.

"I will see ya in hell, ya bastard!" Marschand responded.

He certainly sounded Scottish right now. Strange, how badly she wished it were so. Why did he not stay that way?

Extreme heat and fatigue weighed her down. She was only vaguely aware of the tugging of the thread gliding through her flesh, or the comfort of Marschand's hands.

When she opened her eyes, he was there, guarding her just as he'd promised.

Gard, she thought, hazily, perhaps fancifully, given the man's severity. His forename was not a familiar one. More a nickname or an appointment. *'Tis appropriate. Gard. As in guard.* He had been her protector since the moment he pounced on her at the smithy.

"I want ya ta be," she whispered reaching up to touch his beard as she'd been wanting to. It was both rough and soft. She should have known that it would not be one or the other. As with everything else she'd learned of Gard in the short time she'd known him, he was all things. Unique. Not one or the other.

Gard avoided Hudson's gaze while prompting Braelynn.

"Ya want me to be wha'?" He needed to know.

"I want ya to be one o' us." She stroked his beard. "I want ya to be a Scot."

Hudson was no longer smiling, but Gard ignored him as he stared down at her.

"I told ya afore, I can be whate'er I need ta be," he murmured.

Her eyes fluttered. "Then I need ya to be here for us. Ta save us. Ta save *me*. I am tired of war and I am tired of siege. I just need ta feel safe again. I need ya ta be."

Eventually, her eyes closed, and her hand fell limply away from his cheek. Her body relaxed into stillness. Gard's heart began to pound.

"She's fine." Hudson assured him calmly. "She's fainted. Or given way to the excessive amount of spirits you've plied her with."

Some of the tension left Gard's body. At least in oblivion, she could not feel the pain.

It felt strange to Gard to be counted on for support or comfort. No one came to him for those things. He did not know how to give them. He thought he was incapable, but found he liked the feel of her hands in his. He slid his thumb from side to side over her skin.

"She's been through much in the last few days, Gard," Hudson commented. "She lost her home, her family, her betrothed. Her innocence—in a fashion—not to mention the emotional furor of all those things, now this. She's done well, actually. But we need to finish this up and break the fever, then she should make a full recovery."

Hudson made another stitch. "'Tis funny, though. I heard the same speech from you on the journey here. Did I not? Sick of war. Tired of siege. You want to finally claim what is rightfully yours and settle down in one place."

Discounting him, Gard stared down at her, keeping hold of one of her hands while smoothing her hair away from her face with his other. Her complexion was flawless. She looked so young in sleep.

"She is comely, yeah?" Hudson said.

"Aye. Verra," Gard answered without thinking.

"I told you this would happen to you one day, old friend."

Gard was horrified. "'Tisna what ya think."

"Aye. 'Tis exactly what I think." Hudson laughed at Gard's discomfort.

"I feel . . . guilty, obligated for what I've done ta her. I've ruined her life. I wish we'd ne'er come here."

"You *had* to come here. But why did you feel secure enough with her to drop the guise, Gard? Is that not dangerous? We know nothing about this girl and what she might be capable of. She's obviously intelligent. What if once she recovers she feels the need to use what she's learned against you as revenge?"

Gard kept a close eye on Hudson as he concentrated on his task, placing another precise suture into her tender skin. "She wouldna dare. Besides, I dinna believe she will recall much of this night. The fever is high, and the wine, she is obviously not used ta tha'."

"You didn't answer my question. I know that you speak to pass on vital information, not wasting your breath on what you consider useless conversation. You do not speak of yourself nor do you consider anyone else. Why did you feel you could allow her to see the real you?"

"Are ya near done there?" Gard asked, switching subjects. He could not answer the question and did not know why. From the beginning, she had seemed to suspect something was not as it should be. And he was not an actor, not always capable of keeping up the charade. It helped that he did not normally converse with people. It had not been a problem until now. She was much too observant and had pounced on the fact that he could not maintain the façade when under extreme duress. "Wha' do we need to do to break the fever?" Gard asked.

"We can either bundle her in layers of coverings and let her sweat it out, or we can undress her and bathe her in cool water." With an innocent expression, Hudson watched for his reaction, certainly never happier than when he could get under Gard's skin.

"We will do no such thing. Are ya done there?" Gard asked impatient for Hudson's departure.

"Near done. Two more should do." Hudson handed Gard a wetted cloth. "Bathe the moisture from her face."

While they tended to the girl, Hudson could not help but dig at Gard some more. "And do you recall the ramblings of that old crone we met at Auburn's Inn, Gard."

"The prattling of a crazy auld cockeyed doxy. Leave off, Hudson."

"I don't think I can. 'Tis very close to this exact situation. You can no longer dismiss it as just blather. As I recall, and I am just rewording because I was deep into my cups—"

"And deep down the throat of some woman who wasna your wife, as I recollect." Gard pointed out, nastily.

Hudson ignored him. "Christ! I swear sometimes you are a woman, Gard."

"I'm not sure anyone but you would dare accuse me of such." Gard glared.

"You are a soldier. A killer. A liar and a thief. How you can hold it against me that I sought out another woman to ease my sufferings—"

"Aye, but I would ne'er betray—"

"Aye," Hudson cut him off. "That's easy for you to say, since you have vowed to never take a wife. Try being away months and years on end and see if you can rely on your morals to make it through, night after night. Morals . . . look who I speak to! Now let me finish." He knotted the thread and cut it. "The old crone said—a woman will come into your life. She will bare your mark upon her person. She will change the course of your existence. *This* woman bears your mark."

Gard frowned, ignoring the tingle of sensation that shot up his spine. What Hudson did not seem to remember— being into his cups and due to the whore he was with—there was more to the old hag's prophecy. She had predicted that by his own hand he would inflict the crescent-shaped insignia on an unsuspecting female. Unfortunately, the old crone's foretelling had not gone far enough to reveal the victim's name, but however unintentionally, he *had* etched Mistress Galbraith with his very own dirk. "Tha' is excessive. There is na woman with my mark."

"Save this one." Hudson pointed. "And I have never seen you take such care of anyone or anything, as you do this girl."

"I feel obligated because I am the one who hurt her. Can ya not understand tha'?'

"You inflict worse on a daily basis—"

Gard cut him off. "If there is any truth ta tha' prophecy, it is tha' I have forever changed the course of *her* life. Not my own. Take your things and be gone. I will tend her from here."

"Get the fever down. Try and keep fluids in her. You may have to force it down her throat. Helps if you plug her nose, forcing her to swallow. I will have some water sent. No more wine. Although it is good for the pain, it also takes fluids away. I will set someone to making some broth. She will need nourishment to recover from the weakness." Hudson directed with gravity. Gathering the supplies, he headed toward the exit. He turned back around. Gard had already taken position, standing sentry over Braelynn. He looked down at her concerned, but more so angry that he felt anything at all.

"I will be near, if she needs anything."

"She will not. I am here."

Hudson unsuccessfully stifled a chuckle before walking out, yet Gard could think of nothing humorous about Brae's situation.

Chapter Nine

Gard assembled as many throws and blankets as he could, then covered her, preparing to sweat her fever away.

While he watched her sleep, he consumed more wine from her cup. She remained still as death for the first few hours. He forced water down her throat and checked her breathing constantly to allay his own fears, while trying to rest when possible. Last eve he had not slept well, with her snuggling into his chest for warmth, nor the sennight afore, traveling to Ross.

Brae was in and out of consciousness, at times asking to be left alone, others begging for him not to leave. After another hour of fighting to keep her covered, Gard gave in and joined her in the bed. Perhaps a stupid if not dangerous decision, but his need for rest outweighed the other.

Gard pulled the mountain of layers over them, and she fought it, trying to throw them off. He growled covering her with his body. "Ya will quit fightin' me, Braelynn."

Brae's fever-glazed eyes opened, and she calmed. He expected fear or another struggle. What he was not prepared for was the smooth little hand laid against his cheek or the touch of her soft lips as she pressed them to his.

Gard did not reciprocate. Nevertheless, his body roared with new energy and anticipation. He had to reach down deep within himself, dredging some willpower, a soldier's discipline not to take what he so desperately craved.

The innocent kiss was sweet. Untried. When was the last

time he had been kissed? And with such gentleness? When was the last time he had *wanted* to kiss? Could he dare take the chance, just kiss her and not take advantage of her or the situation.

He levered himself over her. To his surprise she shifted and opened her legs to accommodate his weight. He groaned at the salacious contact. *Lord, she is not going to make this easy.*

Gard centered himself between her thighs and gave in to the small pleasure of a simple kiss. She tasted of wine and innocence. An irresistible combination.

"Ahhh." She opened her mouth on a sigh. Gard took full advantage, and swept his tongue inside, taking total possession and control. Slow, deep, intoxicating kisses made his head spin. He didn't spare much time for such intimate love play.

She tipped her hips, bent her knees, then rubbed her softness against his hardness. Gard growled at the unexpected action. He did not have the willpower to resist this. He wanted to weep, so conflicted was he. She was fragile and ill. He could not take benefit from her. She would never be his. Nor did he want a woman, particularly one like her. But, he was not strong enough to remove himself from the pleasure she offered.

Taking her with him, Gard turned onto his back, giving her the top. He would endure her uncontrived ardor. If she was as inexperienced as he expected, without his instruction, she would lead them nowhere.

Yet little Miss Inexperienced rotated her hips, driving him mad. He gripped her nice round backside, attempting to calm her harried gyrating and slow his wild desire. He threw his head back and moaned at the exquisite pleasure-pain ripping through his long-suffering body.

She lifted her head, depriving him of her plump lips. Unfocused, she stared down at him. Heat rolled off her from the malaise.

"Ya are the devil, aren'ya?" she murmured. "Ya've used your evil powers ta lure me." She didn't give him time to answer. It was she who was tempting and testing him.

Taking his face in her hands, she splayed her fingers through his beard. Stroking upward, she raked into his hair. "If ya are, I dinna care. If lovin' the devil be wrong, I dinna wanna be righ'." She dropped her lips to his and ravaged his mouth. She writhed twisting her young supple body atop him, driving him beyond reason. He was so close to losing his composure.

Once again he rolled, placing her underneath him, and he assaulted her lips. Suddenly her body lost all substance. Losing consciousness, she left him bereft yet grateful. She had saved them both.

Gard turned onto his side and cradled her against him with her head on his shoulder. He took her hand and placed it flat against his chest, giving himself something he had not even been aware he had been missing. This close intimacy with another. He was incredibly uncomfortably aroused, yet he willed his body to calm.

The heat from Brae coupled with the extra bedding made him sweat profusely. Her breathing was harsh but shallow. Her heart pounded rapidly against his chest. His fervor gave way to concern. Why was the fever not breaking?

"Hudson!" he bellowed.

"Gard." Standing at his post just outside the structure, Hudson answered immediately when summoned.

He entered but could not see Gard or the patient for the mountainous coverlets.

"Where are you?" Hudson asked.

"In here, with her," Gard replied, his voice muffled.

"Ahhh," he said, smiling over the blanket pile. But his amusement didn't last when he saw the look of dread on Gard's face.

"Why is the fever not breakin'? She just keeps gettin' hotter. Her breathin' isna good. What am I doin' wrong?"

Hudson pulled back the covers to Gard's growl of disapproval.

"Oh, give over, Gard. I've seen it all afore." Hudson set his hand to the girl's head. "She's clammy, sweat-soaked, hot and yet cold." He placed his fingers to the side of her neck, counting her rapid pulse. He shook his head, not liking what he was seeing. "The sweating-out is not helping. Sometimes 'tis one or the other. Hot or cold, that tames it. We need to cool her down, and we need to do it now."

"And what will happen if we are too late?"

Gard would not appreciate the truth in this instance. "I'll have the men go into the village and locate a tub."

"Do we have time to wait?" Gard asked.

"I cannot be sure."

Gard bounded from the bed, then pulled the girl into his arms. "Cover her," he demanded. Hudson draped a throw around her. Gard strode toward the tent opening.

"Where are you taking her?" Hudson followed.

"The loch."

"But everyone will see. Don't you think you've damaged this poor girl enough?"

"Do ya think I'm concerned at this moment about her ruined reputation? If she doesna live, wha' the hell will any of it matter?"

Hudson grabbed more blankets, then rushed after them.

It was just before dawn. Gard strode purposefully toward the water. There was scarcely enough light to distinguish where they tread. Brae lay limply in his arms, unaware that her very life might depend on this cool dip they were about to take.

Mist hovered over the murky pool, as if even the vapor thought the water too cold to touch. But the bitter chill didn't seem to bother Gard. He waded in deeper and deeper until all but Brae's head was submerged under the water. His bare shoulders caught the light of the rising sun.

For the longest time, Gard simply remained still, holding the fevered girl in the frigid pond. Then he began to sway from side to side, cradling her.

"She's not wakin', Hud?" Gard suddenly began to shiver. His teeth hammered together so hard, Hudson could hear it on the riverbank. "She hasna moved."

But before Hudson could reply, Gard bent to her ear. Though Hudson felt like he was eavesdropping on an intimate moment shared between two people, he strained to hear.

"Braelynn. I wish for ya ta wake now. I want ya ta be well. The way ya were afore the devil came and ruined yer life. I need ta move on. And I canna leave with ya unwell."

Hudson looked on in utter disbelief. The whole scene held a dreamlike quality. No one would ever believe war and life-hardened Gard Marschand was capable of handling anything tenderly or whispering soft words to comfort and sustain. Let alone to a woman. He had *one* use for them. And gentleness was not in his nature. Yet he held this girl as if she were delicate glass or the most precious treasure.

Although Hudson had been known to torment Gard good-naturedly that one day, he would meet a woman who would turn his bleak and dismal existence upside down, he had never truly believed it.

A small gasp echoed round the loch. Braelynn's eyes fluttered, and she began to tremble violently. "Dinna leave me," she said, winding her stiff arms around Gard's neck. "P-p-please. Be here for me." She began to cry softly as she tried to climb from his grasp. Gard struggled to keep ahold.

"Come now, Gard or you'll both catch a death of cold," Hudson called.

Gard moved awkwardly toward shore, his limbs rigid. Hudson rushed to wrap them both in a blanket and kept his arm around Gard's shoulders, lending his own body heat to the cause.

By the time they reached the encampment, the troops were beginning their morning chores and the cooking of the morning meal.

"Have ya gone and killed her then, Marsch?" Ferguson yelled.

Ignoring the insolent young subordinate, Gard ducked into his quarters with Braelynn in his arms.

"Give her over to me, Gard," Hudson demanded, following him in.

"Nay!" The bitter chill had made his lips blue.

"Listen to me. You need to remove those wet clothes immediately. Or you will be no use to this girl. I will not touch her. I'll sit with her bundled warmly by the fire if you will allow it. If not, I will stay here with her until you can take care of her yourself. But you need to get warm. 'Tis crucial."

Gently, Gard attempted to pass Braelynn over, but she would not let go. "Dinna leave me," she begged.

"Brae. Listen to me." Astonishingly, Gard spoke to her in Gaelic. It seemed to calm her. "I need to get warm. I'm freezing. I will be as quick as I can. And when I return, we'll snuggle back down under the covers, yeah? Would you like that?"

"Aye." She petted his bearded cheek.

"Then let me go and allow Hudson to hold ya while I'm gone."

"Hurry back to me," she returned, in the same dialect.

Gard leaned in but hesitated. Again, to Hudson's complete shock, Gard kissed Braelynn's forehead gently before releasing her into Hudson's care.

Hudson secured his grip and waited for further orders. None came, but for once, when Hudson looked his friend in the eye, there was so much more than the black void he was used to seeing. For the first time since he'd known him, there was life in Gard Marschand.

CHAPTER TEN

Gard hurried to change into dry clothes.

While Hudson held Brae, he bowed outside. "Stuart!" he barked. "Toss some rocks on the fire and get them in my bed as soon as possible."

"Aye, sir!"

On his return, one of the men passed Gard a cup of hot liquid. He drank it down without tasting it.

Upon entering the lodging, he quickly rummaged through Brae's pack in hopes of finding something suitable for her to wear. He had no idea how he would manage to get her into anything dry. But for her own safety, she needed to be clothed in some form if she was going to be anywhere near him. And for the foreseeable future, she was his burden.

"Place her on the bed," Gard ordered Hudson, as he fought to control the tremors that coursed through his body.

Hudson did as instructed. "She has not moved since you left. Let me aid you. She will be no help."

"Nay. Leave!"

"Gard, you cannot even feel your fingertips, can you?" Hudson reasoned.

"I will manage."

Hudson sighed heavily. "I'll be close by if you need assistance."

"I willna. How is tha' broth comin'? We will both be in need of it when she wakes."

"It will be ready when you require it."

105

With trembling hands and clumsy fingers, Gard rushed to remove Brae's wet shift. Just peeling the blanket away warmed him by several degrees at the sight of her. The gauzy material might have been invisible for the protection it afforded her. But now, plastered to her cold wet skin, it left nothing to his imagination. Her nipples—puckered against the fabric—begged for his touch.

Gard shoved aside his longing and tried to concentrate on removing the wet chemise. Pulling the dirk from his boot, he sliced up the center and down each arm, rendering the garment useless. She lay completely exposed to him. He closed his eyes, but it did not help—he could still see her. The image would be ingrained in his mind for the rest of his sorry life. He stifled a groan and fisted his hands to prevent himself from reaching out to her. He fought with what was left of his conscience and control.

No one would ever know if he touched her. Not even her.

Gard took a deep breath as a tremor ran through her body, spurring him to finish the task and get her bundled up again. He selected one of his own black shirts from his pack, and although it swam on her, it covered her lovely body.

Once he had positioned her in the bed, he crawled in beside her. He drew her against his trembling frame. He wasn't sure which one of them was colder. Closing his eyes, he commanded himself to sleep.

Gard dozed intermittently. It took hours for the shivering to cease, and even after the convulsions stopped, just thinking about how cold he'd been produced the same reaction.

Every time he roused, he checked on Brae's condition. Gradually, she warmed, not suffering the same uncontrollable tremors that had plagued him. He attributed that to her high temperature and her state of unconsciousness. Her heart rate was slow and steady. Her breathing had returned to normal, no longer labored from fever. He believed she was just sleeping now. It put him more at ease and he was finally able to rest. He was exhausted.

But in the night, when she turned her ardor on him once again as he slept, Gard easily thrust his tattered conscience away, and reveled in what she so freely offered.

Brae shivered so hard she jolted herself awake.

After gathering the covers closer, she sought the incredible heat source beside her. She turned into it and inhaled the familiar scent.

A strong arm pulled her closer. She sighed contentedly.

Safe. Warm. Tender. Gentle. Gard. She was confused, her brain foggy. When had she begun to think these things of him? Those were not her initial impressions of him at all. He was cold, calculating, dark, evil—could very well be the devil himself.

Yet he had been present through the entire ordeal. Whenever she had roused, he was there with a soft touch and a comforting word. Or a kiss from his warm beautiful lips.

Brae's eyes flew open. *A kiss?* She must have been dreaming. Marschand was none of these things. Not gentle or tender. Nor safe. Yet she felt protected.

She snuck a quick peek up at him.

He *was* indeed handsome. She would give him that.

Dear God, what am I doing in his bed? In his arms? The last thing she remembered was Hudson tending her leg. Then all of a sudden, she'd been overwhelmed by warmth and sleepiness.

Brae closed her eyes and tried to sort through what was real and what was not. She could almost imagine Gard in a dreamlike way, his full lower lip descending to hers. But that was as far as she could remember. Was it real? And why could she not relive it? Why did her imaginings stop there?

Damn it! It was just beyond her reach. Could it have really happened? No, she decided. It couldn't have. She would remember being kissed by a man like him.

Gard stroked softly up her arm. His caress made her shiver again, but for an entirely different reason.

"'Tis a'righ', Braelynn."

Dear Lord! The brogue was back.

"Rest. I'm here."

The words rumbled deep in his chest, under her ear. She was comforted and secure. She snuggled into his embrace loath to ever leave.

Gard startled awake.

Someone was inside his dwelling. Who would dare? Anyone who served alongside him knew better than to sneak around, else end up dead.

He tried to gain his bearings. He was on his stomach, with one arm outstretched across Brae. His palm firmly cupped her perfect breast. His fingers twitched as he came to the realization. Which caused Brae to wake with a start, too.

She gasped, and her eyes popped open. She moved quickly about to knock his unwelcome hand from her person. But Gard rolled quickly, covering her mouth. "Cease! We are no' alone," he warned. She stilled.

Where was his dirk? He was never without it. The dagger was always in his boot or strapped on him. But the circumstances were much different than he was used to. He wore nothing but a pair of tight-fitting trews. Another reason he slept alone, he reminded himself. Better to be prepared and only responsible for oneself. But he was not alone, and his main concern was Brae.

Where the hell is Hudson. Why was he not at his post? Or worse, was he at his station and some evil had befallen him?

The tapers still flickered. But the early dawn filtering through the canvas provided Gard enough light that he was able to locate his weapon.

"Fantainn." Gard whispered in Gaelic, instructing Brae to remain where she was as he slipped soundlessly from the under the covers.

Brae held her breath. A scuffle ensued nearby, followed by a yelp of pain. She experienced a moment of panic, fearing for Gard's safety. She pushed the covers out of the way.

Marschand held none other than Robbie Cowan by the hair. He gave it a good yank, exposing the young man's throat, and pressed the tip of his dirk to his jugular.

"Caisg!" she croaked and jumped from the pallet, belatedly remembering her leg injury. "Stop! Ye'll kill him!"

"'Tis my intent," Gard snarled.

She was shocked by the savagery in his expression. The man who had tended her so gently was gone, replaced by the devil part of him. In that moment, he was more savage than he was man.

Had it really been a dream? It was all a confused illusion in her mind, of kisses and gentleness. But it could not have been from this man with murder in his eyes.

"'Tis no less than he deserves." Marschand's voice chilled her. "What are you doing in here, Cowan? Do you wish for me to end your sorry life? You try me time and again."

"Ferg said she was 'ere. I didna believe it. I had ta see fer meself?" he panted.

"And you would risk your life to all but see that she be here, knowing that I would be here as well?" Marschand bellowed.

Brae was well aware how disturbed Gard was and what a short leash he had on his anger. Cowan had made a big mistake in breaching Marschand's refuge. He would see that as a crime punishable with death.

"Remove the blade from his neck," Brae asked softly. "Please."

His nostrils flared, but he slowly lowered the blade.

Robbie Cowan assessed her. His overexcited gaze traveled up her bare legs. It was then Brae noticed her state of undress—in nothing more than one of Marschand's oversized shirts.

"Och. Who woulda guessed when we saw ya on the moor tha' ya would so enjoy the brutality of a man like Marsch. Tha' ya couldna bring yorself ta leave his bed—"

Marschand punched Cowan in the jaw, knocking him prone in the dirt.

"Hudson!" Marschand bellowed before striding to the bed. He threw a blanket at her and barked, "Cover up."

Yes, she must have dreamt it. There was no softness in Gard Marschand.

Gard grabbed Cowan by the scruff and dragged him to the tent opening, where he tossed him out carelessly.

"Hudson!" he hollered again. When there was no reply he turned in Brae's direction. He was bare-chested. His muscles flexed as he roamed the space like an animal.

He picked up a discarded shirt, then pulled it on as he exited, leaving her alone without a word or backward glance.

Now that the panic had receded, Brae felt weak and slightly nauseous. How long had she slept with Marschand?

She rummaged through her bag for something more appropriate to wear. She felt quite naked in Marschand's voluminous shirt.

Unaware of how much time she might have, she hurried to wash the dried blood from her legs. An oversight on Hudson's part, she assumed, from after he'd cleaned and stitched her wound. Most like Marschand had not allowed it. She could not remember.

A short time later, Marschand stumbled in with his arms around Hudson's shoulders. Blood poured down the side of Hudson's face.

Marschand tossed him on the pallet.

"Wha' happened?" Brae asked rushing forward.

"I found him in the brush," he explained. "Out cold. I knew when I summoned him and he did not answer that something was not right."

Brae took one of the clean rags and placed it against Hudson's head.

"Thank you, Brae," Hudson said, trying to sit.

"Do not call her that." Gard pushed him down. "Keep still."

"Wha' happened to ya, Hudson?"

"Do not call him that," Marschand snapped.

She ignored him. Perhaps he could order Hudson around, but not her. "Who did this to ya, Hudson?"

"I believe I just said—" Marschand interrupted arrogantly.

"I believe *Hudson* gave me permission to address him thus. And ya may have authority o'er him, but ya dinna o'er me." She glared at him, unsure as to why she felt such anger toward him. It was not his fault that she had dreamt him to have a whole other side to him than truly existed. And she was quite disappointed to realize he was not what she'd concocted in her fevered mind.

Hudson chuckled before answering. "I believe, *Mistress Galbraith*, I was struck from behind and dragged into the brush."

Brae's eyes rounded. "Was it Cowan, then?"

"He will die at my hand," Marschand vowed.

Brae shivered at his words.

"We do not know for sure that it was him." Grainger

111

placated.

"Who else would it have been?" Marschand roared. "Stands to reason. He eliminated you from your post, and the next thing Cowan is slithering through my hut like the gutter snake he is."

"I didn't see who 'twas." Hudson's tone changed. "You will leave this go, Gard."

"I will not." He punched his palm.

Hudson grabbed Marschand's wrist. "You will leave this be, Gard. Soon enough he will no longer be our problem."

Marschand's gaze shot to Hudson's hand.

One by one, Hudson loosened his fingers and removed his hold slowly, as if afraid the beast might chew it off.

Brae stood, then headed for the exit.

"Where do you think you are going?" Marschand barked.

"Ta get some water to clean Hudson's wound."

Marschand stood. "You cannot go out there! Do you not realize *you* are the reason Cowan is skulking around knocking out my second?"

"Yer second?" Brae blinked.

Marschand snatched the bowl from her grasp. "I will get it." He stormed out.

Wide-eyed, Brae turned to Hudson.

"How are you feeling, Mistress Galbraith?" he asked, cordially.

"Much recovered, thank ya. A little weak and dizzy. I canna seem to quit tremblin', but better." She walked to his side and picked up the cloth.

She was about to dab his wound when he said, "I thought Gard was going to catch a death of cold, for the both of you, standing out there in the loch at dawn."

"Standin' in the loch?" She cocked her head.

"Do you not recall?"

"No, I dinna recollect much." Except for Gard's lips seeking hers. She blushed furiously at the course of her thoughts.

"He did not leave your side and would not allow anyone else to tend you."

"Why were we in the loch?" she asked.

"The fever rose dangerously high. And we couldn't risk waiting to locate a tub. So he took you to the loch and cooled you. Himself as well," Hudson added, with a chuckle.

She remembered being scalding hot. Then extremely cold. And warm insistent lips. She shook her head slightly. Why could she not banish that thought? It was like experiencing a vivid dream but forgetting the content soon upon waking, yet all the next day being bombarded by elusive teasing snippets. She imagined bare shoulders rising above her, but the memory evaporated before she could get a hold of it.

"Why would he do tha' and no' have one o' the men toss me in?"

"I have pondered that myself. Gard is not . . . uh, generally concerned over the welfare of others. Especially, uh . . ."

"Women. Aye, I've gleaned tha' much. He isna verra personable." She wrinkled her nose.

"Aye, that's Gard. Not very personable."

"Did I hear ya are a married man?" she asked, steering away from the devil.

"Aye."

"Is he?" she asked quickly before she lost her nerve.

Hudson snorted. "Nay. No one woman would put up with him. Nor, he with she."

"Do ya have bairns?"

Hudson displayed his palms. "Nay, we have not so been blessed."

"Perhaps tha' will happen fer ya soon."

He did not respond.

"Ya did say Robbie Cowan willna longer be your problem ere long. It made me think tha' perhaps your services may no' be in need after our new overseer arrives."

Hudson narrowed his gaze. "You do not miss much do you, Mistress Galbraith."

"She does not," Marschand answered, as he re-entered with water.

Brae rose to take the bowl from him.

"I have it. Sit," he snapped.

"But I would tend Hudson as he did for me."

"You may, but you have also been ill. I would have you sit. What else might you be in need of?" He was brisk and all business.

"She should eat, Gard. Or at least drink a cup of broth," Hudson recommended.

"Tend," he commanded her. "I will return."

Sitting next to Hudson, Brae washed away the blood from the side of his head and face.

"How's it look, Miss Galbraith?"

"'Tis no' too deep. But head wounds do like ta bleed, do they no'? Makes things look much worse than they are."

"Aye, you are aright."

Marschand returned again with a tray of steaming liquids. Hudson took the opportunity to poke at his friend. "Is it deep enough that you may need to stitch it, making it necessary for you to become intimate with me, Brae?"

His eyes danced as he tried to tame the grin that threatened, as he unmercifully tormented Gard.

"Your creamy white face and my fist are the only things that will become intimate," Marschand growled. Taking Brae by the elbow, he forced her to stand.

"Go over there and eat," he commanded, dismissively.

"But I am no' finished."

"Aye, ya are." Turning his back on Brae, he knelt, taking her place at Hudson's side.

"I thank you for your kind and gentle attention, Miss

Galbraith. Your touch is soft, your bedside manner and nurturing is something a man will never forget . . . Ouch!" He squawked when Gard probed the wound.

Brae drank some hot broth while Hudson continued to terrorize Marschand. "This is a change is it not? You tending me?"

Marschand did not respond.

Brae finished her soup and poured some for Marschand. If he had not left her side, as Hudson had informed her, then chances were he had not taken time to eat either. Approaching the men, she unthinkingly laid her hand on Marschand's shoulder. Slowly, he lifted his gaze to hers. For some reason, she found the action totally disarming. She handed him the cup without a word. Turning to Hudson, she said, "Do ya have a headache?"

"Aye. Slightly."

"Do ya feel light-headed?"

Hudson smirked, and placed his palm to his chest. "Only when you smile."

Brae chortled, yet she wondered what it would take to make Marschand smile. Hudson was handsome in his own right, but Marschand would have a devastating grin, if he only knew how to work it. "Aye, and I've not heard tha' one afore, Sir Grainger."

"And you'll not hear it again." Marschand jerked Hudson to his feet. "Get up. You are well enough to vacate my quarters."

"Is tha' wise?" she questioned, perhaps stupidly by the thunderous expression Marschand sent her. "Head injuries can be complicated," she said in a rush. "He should be watched. Woken evra few hours or so."

"You are questioning me?" Gard rounded on her, eyes blazing. "How do you know so much? I thought you were nothing more than a wife in waiting."

"Aye. I guess tha' I was. But my mother . . . my father's wife tended numerous injuries for not only my da but also our neighbors. My sire is a bricklayer and suffered many a mashed finger and a fallen brick or two on the head. I have seen enough gashes ta know tha' much."

He ignored her. "Find my dirk," he said coldly.

Brae shrank.

"You will remain here, and you will be armed. Have I not been clear?" Marschand glowered.

"Oh, aye. Verra." She located the weapon.

"Anyone comes in, besides me, kill him."

Hudson, with Marschand's help, turned to leave.

"Monsieur Marschand?" Brae called.

He sighed impatiently in response.

"Does Hudson have a third?" she asked.

"What?" He frowned and shook his head with an angry jerk.

"Ya said earlier tha' Hudson is your second." She grinned, unable to keep a straight face. "Does *he* have a third? Because he should no' be alone for a time."

Hudson snorted, and Gard thrust him from the shelter.

CHAPTER ELEVEN

In a temper, Gard stormed inside, without Hudson. After pulling on his cloak, he slid a small dirk into his boot and tucked another more lethal gut-hook blade into the waist of his trews.

"I have four men stationed around this structure. You will remain here until I return."

Brae nodded, twiddling with the folds of her skirt in an outwardly nervous habit. Was she afraid to be left alone? That too would be his fault. Every time he left Braelynn to her own devices some catastrophe befell her.

Gard did not relish the thought of being separated either, but he had no choice. Moreover, he did not like the fact that it bothered him at all. Further reason to be rid of her as soon as possible. *Starting now.* He ducked outside.

"Where are ya goin'?" she asked in a small voice.

Had she the nerve to follow him!

He did an about-face and glared, not used to anyone questioning him.

"I am needed at the holding." He slapped his gloves against his thigh.

"May I no' accompany ya?" she asked. "Or sit wit' Hudson while ya are gone? Instead o' bein' alone?"

He scowled, a gesture which made most men cower, yet she continued to beseech him with those damned soulful green eyes. It would resolve the perplexing roiling in his belly if he were to simply take her with him. He would not be bothered by the worry of not knowing if she was safe in his absence. The realization angered him as well.

"Are you well enough to ride?" he barked.

She tried to conceal a smile but could not keep the delight from her eyes. "Aye, let me jus' get me slippers." She disappeared into his quarters.

She was a confounding woman. He had no idea why she wished to continue in his surly company, his mood souring by the minute.

"Bind your hair," he bellowed through the canvas.

By the time she resurfaced, Gard was mounted, and quite satisfied that his directive to tie her glorious hair had been observed. Alas, it did not dilute her appeal, as he had hoped.

The moment Brae neared, Gard reached down. She placed her small hand in his and he pulled her onto the horse, side-saddle — her two legs over one of his.

She winced, presumably from the pain in her thigh, then she fidgeted in his lap. Gard grimaced at the tightening in his groin. Positioning his arms around her, he took the reins and coaxed the horse into a canter.

After a few minutes of riding in silence she glanced behind them and asked, "Ya ride alone?"

Gard did not answer in an attempt to curb her incessant need to converse. He had divulged entirely too much in her presence already.

"Ya arna afraid o' attack?"

She had not taken his cue.

"No one would dare," he replied at length.

"Aye, tha's wha' I used ta think as weel. 'Twouldna happen ta me."

His thigh tightened under her knees.

"Why are ya needed at Ross?"

"Hudson was to be in charge of the indenture petitions. Someone must be there in his stead."

They rode in silence the rest of the way until they entered

the bailey of Ross. Using the brogue he reserved only for her, he inquired, "Is your leg painin' ya?"

"Nay, 'tisna bad," she answered, too fast.

Not only had he noted her limp, but he had seen firsthand the devastation they had wrought. Between the initial injury, the muck she had made of it tending to it by herself, and the ensuing infection, he would be amazed if it did not scar.

Gard reined in his mount, and the well-trained animal came to a stop. Gard slid Brae to the ground, then jumped down after her.

For a moment neither of them moved. Brae's stare lingered on his lips so long they tingled at the memory of how she had kissed him with utter abandon. Gard gritted his teeth at his body's swift reaction.

"Ya will remain at my side," he said, gruffly.

Brae jerked her gaze from his mouth, as though she might also be reminiscing. But he believed her recollections were vague at best.

The better part of the day was spent hearing petitions, most of which were agreed upon according to the same arrangement as held with Ross, carrying over to the new command.

Unable to focus elsewhere, Brae watched Marschand, who sat in Lord Ross' overseer's chair. He listened to the bids and resolved the odd civil complaints over the transition of power.

He was commanding, holding himself with such cool self-assurance and imposing authority she was captivated by his fairness and his intelligence. The man belonged in the leader's chair, she realized. Ross would do well to have a man such as him as their overlord. She almost wished he would stay.

He'd once told her he could make her believe anything.

He appeared completely at ease and comfortable, perhaps even bored at the task. Yet Brae knew he was none of those things.

"Mistress Galbraith?" She was startled when his deep voice cut through her reverie.

Brae met his stare.

"Can you scribe as well as read?"

"Aye."

"You will record as I instruct," he said.

Thankful for something to do, she rushed to do his bidding.

For hours a steady stream of folk passed by, and Brae documented his will.

During a lull in the proceedings, someone called her name. "Mistress G-g-galbraith?" Turning, she found the young vicar waving madly.

Wishing to speak to him, she deferred to Marschand for permission. He nodded, suspending the hearings for her. She thought it was very kind, until she realized he had followed closely on her heels.

Brae was mortified by the look of horror on the vicar's face as she approached with the devil dogging her steps.

"Vicar Dufferin," she greeted. "Wha' brings ya ta Ross?"

His soft brown gaze remained startled as he pried his attention from her large companion.

"I-I-I was summoned ta p-p-perform a m-m-marriage," he stammered.

"Ah. Tha's grand. E'en under the most dire o' circumstance life continues, eh?" Brae smiled.

"Aye. So 'twould s-s-seem. I was s-s-surprised ta see ya were no' in attendance."

"Oh?" She frowned. "Why is tha'? Was it a couple I migh' ken?"

Marschand cleared his throat and moved so close she perceived his body heat.

"Och, excuse me manners. Vicar Dufferin." She gestured with her hand. "Monsieur Marschand." Turning slightly, she peered up at her domineering shadow. "Marschand. Vicar Dufferin."

Marschand glowered. "You will cease presenting me as *Monsieur*. I *am not* French."

"And wha' would ya have me present ya as?" she demanded, losing patience.

"Overlord Marschand of Ross, would be fitting," he replied, arrogantly.

"Oh, aye, o' course, *Lord* Marschand," she stressed. "The vicar . . . from the house of God."

The corner of Marschand's mouth twitched. She was aware the vicar watched their exchange with great interest.

To her shock, Gard wound his hand around her hip in a possessive display. All the while, he continued to stare menacingly at the young cleric.

Gard extended his free hand.

The vicar winced when Marschand took hold. Brae patted the hand Gard still had at her hip and he eased up, releasing the vicar from his vise-like hold.

Vicar Dufferin cleared his throat and addressed Marschand as if she were not there. "L-l-lord M-m-marschand. I-I-I have a tome I wish ta p-p-present ta, M-m-mistress Galb-b-braith." His stammer worsened as his anxiety grew over Marschand's overbearing behavior. "I-i-if, tha' w-w-would be a-a-acceptable ta ya, S-s-sir."

"You may. Mistress Galbraith is in need of some new reading material as of late. Your gift would be much appreciated, Vicar."

Dufferin reached into the pack slung over his shoulder, then handed the volume to Marschand instead of Brae.

"Thank ya," Brae said as Marschand passed it to her.

"Who was it tha' ya joined in wedlock, Vicar?"

"'Twas your f-f-friend, K-k-katie."

"Katie married? Who? I wasna e'en aware she'd received an offer." Brae felt less than a good friend, too concerned with her own marriage preparations and then this misfortune with Marschand. She had even asked Katie to intervene on her behalf with Callum without considering what might be going on in Katie's life.

The vicar shifted from foot to foot. "Oh, dear. I-I-I thought ya kenned."

"We need to continue, Mistress Galbraith," Marschand said abruptly, exerting pressure on her hip.

"Oh, Vicar." Auld Myrtle shuffled into their little assemblage. "Glad I caught ya afore ya left. Ah, Brae. How be ye, lass?"

"Well, thank ya," Brae replied.

"I have no' seen ya since we put the run on the red-haired dark one." Pride shone on her grizzled face before she turned a shrewd gaze on Marschand.

Gard straightened to his full height, towering over them.

"I see ye are still in *his* company." Myrtle's nose wrinkled in distaste.

"I believe Mistress Galbraith was put into my care, at your dictate," Marschand retorted.

"I dinna believe ya take the dictate of anaone, dark one. But more mistake me," she said. "Tha' was afore I was made aware 'twas ye tha' attacked and ruined our poor Brae afore the red-haired fiend took his wound. Had I kenned, I woulda used me other blade on ye."

Brae braced her back up against Marschand's broad chest, trying to hold him at bay as she anticipated his step forward. Instead, he leaned over her, mere inches from Myrtle.

"It is for the reason that you have defended Mistress Galbraith in the past, that you are being tolerated, old woman.

Do not test me further. That fact will not save you a second time."

Myrtle had the good sense to retreat before speaking again. "Are ya threatenin' me, dark one?"

Marschand pushed Brae as if she created no obstacle at all.

Myrtle faced him in defiance. "Ye would terrorize an auld woman? Aye, ye would," she answered. "Do ye cut off the tails o' puppies and boil innocent bairns fer enjoyment?"

Gard studied his fingernails, feigning boredom, yet Brae sensed the tension roiling through him. "As if I have not been accused of such afore, auld woman."

"Humph!" Myrtle snorted. "Ye e'en appear as one would imagine the devil hisself might present ta the world. Ye *look* like evil incarnate."

The vicar stepped between them, which brought him into closer proximity to Brae. Gard scowled at the cleric.

"T-t-there's no need fer aggression, Lord Marschand," the vicar said, then swallowed audibly. "T-t-the good p-p-people of Ross-shire only s-s-seek ta protect their own in this t-t-time of tumult."

"As do I," Marschand growled, leaving that particular statement open for interpretation.

Brae frowned in confusion.

"Mistress Galbraith, let us return to our task," Marschand said, in authoritative voice that left no room for argument. Directing her by the hip, they turned as one.

"Ah, wait." Brae paused. "Who did Katie wed?"

"Oh, Braelynn." Myrtle tsked and grasped Brae by the elbow. "She married Callum." Myrtle never was one to beat around the bush.

Marschand growled, low and animalistic. It didn't sound like he appreciated the news any more than Brae did.

Brae wavered. Her vision tunneled. Gard tightened his

hold on her. She leaned into his strength.

"Callum?" She let out a humorless laugh. "Katie. Married. Callum." She shook her head in disbelief.

"Aye," Myrtle said. Concern flushed the old woman's face. "And although I am sorry tha' ya are feelin' loss, ya should no' be, Braelynn. He was no' the man fer ye. And now tha' he is hers, I can say it. Ya need a strong man at yer side. One who is confident enough in his own right ta let ya be wha' ya have the potential ta be. Callum woulda smothered ya and made ya no more than yer sire. Ya are better than tha'. At least ye were." Myrtle sneered at Marschand. "But perhaps yer benefactor will provide such a man fer ya once he is done wit' ya. I think he owes ya tha' much."

"I warned you once, woman!" Gard replied sternly.

"How could they have done this?" Brae cried.

"Och. 'Twas no' by their choosin'. Her father insisted on it when the two were caught in a position tha' demanded the union," Myrtle explained.

Brae inhaled sharply. "Ohhh." She whimpered as the scene played out in her mind. She turned into Gard, burying her face in his shoulder. "'Tis ma fault," she mumbled against his chest. "I asked Katie ta talk ta Callum for me. Ta make him understand. How could they do tha'?" she sobbed.

The old woman narrowed her hawk-like gaze. Gard returned it, with one of his own, over Braelynn's head.

It was not Brae's fault. It was his. Everything awful that had befallen her in the last few days lay squarely with him. And it just kept getting worse. Awkwardly, Gard gathered Brae into his arms.

He bowed his head into her hair so no one else would hear and whispered in Gaelic, since it seemed to comfort her,

"The auld woman be a'righ'." Strangely he found the dialect soothed him, too. "He was not the man for you."

Brae lifted her head. Her lovely green eyes were two shimmering pools of sorrow. "How can ya say tha'?"

"Because he wasna worthy o' ya if he could be turned so easily ta another."

"Easily?" she snapped. "He has waited our whole lives ta claim me and in one moment he believed me ruined, and if tha' wasna bad enough he was made ta believe tha' I *chose* ta stay wit' ya."

"As I said, ya didna have a choice at tha' time. If he could na see tha', he doesna deserve ta have ya. And in a way, ya did choose me. Ya came ta me."

"For a safe place ta stay."

"But wha' does tha' tell ya, Braelynn?" The sound of her name upon his lips rattled him. "Ya jus' said it. Ya came ta me, fer a safe place to be. Why would ya do tha'? Because already ya are convinced tha' I can keep ya tha' way. Ye didna go ta him. An' e'en if ya did, he turned ya away, obviously. E'en though ya consider me the enemy, ya still came to me. Ya trust me. At least to a point, ye do."

"I had na choice but ta come ta ya," she repeated.

"Aye, by tha' time ye did. There are always choices, I wasna threatin' ye by tha' time. Ye could've gone anawhere else." The growing need to shield her was absolutely intolerable. Yet so was his deepening desire. He needed distance.

He dropped the brogue along with any semblance of consolation. "Now dry your eyes and be my scribe. I tire of this. I wish to return to the garrison afore full dark."

She wiped her face, but the tears in her eyes remained. "May I have a few moments o' privacy?"

Gard experienced a moment of suspicion. Did she think this was her chance to escape him? She'd be stupid to try. Why should he care? That much needed distance could be within his grasp. However, like it or not, for the foreseeable future, she was in need of his protection. And he *would* release her, in his own time and on his terms.

"You may. But you will not tarry. I am in need of your services. Myrtle," he bellowed.

Auld Myrtle shuffled over.

"You will accompany, Mistress Galbraith."

"I will, but only because I wish ta see ta Brae. No' because ya so demanded it."

"As you wish," he said, still getting what he wanted. *The old woman has spirit.*

"Do you have my dirk?" Gard demanded of Brae.

"Aye," she whispered.

He was not convinced she heard him, so lost in her own thoughts. He could not let her leave until he was sure she could defend herself. Sliding his hand over her thigh, he patted her down, until satisfied she was armed.

She gasped, and her eyes flashed.

He was unapologetic. "I will not have you unprotected."

"And who will protect me from ya?" she snapped.

"I will," he snarled through his teeth. "As you well know. I willna hurt ya!" He said the last for her ears alone.

"Ya already have," she sobbed, then rushed away. Myrtle tottered after her.

Gard closed his eyes and absorbed Brae's accusation. She was right. He had hurt her. Irrevocably.

CHAPTER TWELVE

Brae saw to her needs and washed her face. Then she and Myrtle strolled in the direction of the keep when unexpectedly she came face to face with Callum.

"Brae," he said, stiffly.

"Callum," she greeted in passing, desperate to put distance between them.

"Brae," he called after her.

She closed her eyes and paused but did not turn around.

"Why dinna ye leave her be, Callum MacCrae," Myrtle said. "Dinna ya think ye've done enough?"

"Ya have heard aboot Katie and me then?"

"I have. I need ta get back," Brae said, taking another step.

"Ya need ta run ta your master?" Callum sneered.

"Aye, I do. And ya need ta return ta your wife." Brae held her head high and returned to Marschand's side.

He studied her carefully, and although she was sure it was obvious she'd been weeping the entire time, she worked extremely hard to maintain a calm façade.

Marschand took up the Lord's seat. "Next," he bellowed, signaling for the proceedings to resume. "State your names and the task for which you wish to petition."

"Callum MacCrae," Cal boasted.

At once, Brae knew Marschand recognized the man standing down front.

Next to Cal stood her father. Fresh tears threatened.

"Guillium Galbraith." Her father's voice sounded gruff

and weak with age, or life. At this point Brae wasn't sure which.

Marschand leaned toward Brae. "Be he your sire, sweet?"

Brae wondered at the sudden endearment, but murmured, "Aye. But he willna longer claim me as such."

Marschand focused on Callum with the blackest intimidating stare, bringing the tension in the room to a fevered pitch. Pure and simple tactics from a man used to plotting defensive campaigns.

Callum returned his regard defiantly, hatred blazing from his being.

Marschand's mouth hooked into a malevolent grimace, by no means a grin. "Well, well. We meet again, puppy. 'Twould seem you have burned your bridges. How does it feel to have to come to *me* and beg for position?" He patted his broad chest.

"I beg fer nuthin'!" Callum spat.

"Then you may leave." Marschand turned to the side, dismissively. "Next!"

"Ya canna do tha'!" Cal hollered.

"Aye. I can." He straightened to his full height, an entirely intimidating act, coupled with his bulk and menacing scowl. He neared Brae's former fiancé and sire.

"And you . . ." Marschand angled his chin toward Brae's parent. "Have you naught to say? Will you have this infantile snipe ruin your chance to gain my favor?"

"Oh . . . I . . ." Guillium Galbraith stuttered, wringing his hands. "I . . . we . . . had an agreement with Lord Ross ta reinforce the retainin' wall."

"Is that so?" Marschand drawled.

"Aye. 'Tis." He nodded.

"But I am not Lord Ross," Marschand challenged.

"And ye are no' the only one here ta make the decision," Callum interrupted. "Chamberlain is in charge here. E'en o'er ye. We will petition him!"

"Look around you, snippet." Marschand placed himself perilously close to Callum, looking down his nose, so Callum was forced to peer up at him. A most threatening posture, in front of the other townfolk. "Do you see anyone else but me?"

With his arms wide open, palms up, Marschand gestured about the room, until he singled out one of his men. "Ferguson!" he barked.

"Aye, sir." Ferguson stood at attention.

Marschand turned his interest toward Callum, but continued to address Ferguson. "Step forward," he commanded with such quiet vehemence Brae heard Ferguson inhale sharply.

"Perhaps you might inform the young doubter here as to who be truly in charge."

"Chamberlain be third in command, here fer the Ross siege, at our Lord's behest."

"An who be your lord, Ferguson?" Marschand prompted.

"You, My Lord Marschand." Ferguson inclined his head.

"At ease. Take your post."

Falling in, Ferguson released an audible exhalation, as if he had been holding his breath the entire time. "Aye, sir."

"Now that we understand one another," Marschand clasped his hands in front, "I will explain to you what I expect. Lord Ross was content to let time pass him by. His defense measures and reinforcements were rudimentary, at best. I expect more from the people who are under my employ to strengthen what is *mine*."

By the way he spoke and carried himself, Brae actually believed that Ross-shire was now Marschand's and that Ferguson's admissions were more than just for show. Marschand turned his attention to Guillium Galbraith.

"I do not think a man who could toss his own flesh and

blood into the street, with no protection and no coin simply because he believes her to be no longer useful to him, is the kind of man that I would appoint to labor on my behalf. It shows disloyalty. Perfidy."

Her father bowed his head at Marschand's words.

"And you." He turned his attention to Callum, towering over him. "A *man* . . ." he sneered, "Who would turn on his woman for an injustice committed against her through no fault of her own, then just as easily crawl into the bed of another with no care for either, is not a man I would trust to fortify my holding. Demonstrates betrayal and capriciousness."

"*You* made me turn her aside!" Callum yelled. Spittle flew from his mouth.

"I *made* you do that?" Marschand mocked. "My! Perhaps I am even more powerful than even I consider myself." He puffed out his chest for a second before his expression turned severe. "Did I hold a dirk to your throat? Did I threaten your life? Did I coerce you in any way to make such a choice?"

"Ya ruined her. How is a man to o'er look tha'?" Callum glared.

Marschand turned, speaking directly to Brae. "I did not ruin her," he said.

He confessed her innocence, for all to hear. Although she knew no one would believe his words, she could not look away. He was formidable.

"Look at her," he demanded. When Callum made no move to do so, he shouted. "Look at her!" The sound of his booming voice cracked the silence startling everyone in the room. Callum jumped. His gaze snapped to Brae.

"Does she look ruined to you?" he asked Callum. "Is she not just as lovely as she was a fortnight past?" Callum's shoulders drooped. "Is she not?" Marschand pressed.

"Aye," Callum admitted.

"Aye," Marschand walked behind him. "She is. And it will eat at you for the rest of your miserable life, MacCrae, that you chose to turn your back on her. And which of your associates will stand up proudly and claim her now that you have foolishly cried off and married another? How about young Duncan? Who at least demonstrated enough manhood to make an attempt to save the lovely Mistress from the enemy? *He* is more man than you. *She* needs a man. Not a boy, prone to sulking fits and tantrums, when life does not go his way."

"Duncan will do jus' as me," Callum mumbled. "He will not be able to overlook the fact tha' she has been wit' the likes o' you."

"Ahhh, and there's a fact, aye?" Marschand finally grinned, but it was the most diabolically evil thing Brae had ever seen. "Perhaps she no longer desires you, after she's been *with the likes of me*," he boasted.

Gard leaned forward so only MacCrae could hear him. "And I can assure you, she *likes* me. Every way she can take me and as often . . ."

Anticipating some form of physical eruption, Gard easily caught MacCrae's fist when he swung.

Gard chuckled. "You will have to be better than that." He gave a hefty push, sending Callum off balance.

Some of Gard's men moved forward to capture Callum, in case he tried to retaliate against their leader. Unconcerned, Gard waved them off. He didn't need aid. Not against the likes of Callum MacCrae.

"And what of you, Guillium Galbraith?" Gard demanded. "Does your beautiful daughter appear useless to you? Is she not worth more than a mere bride price, Sirrah? She is more than a bargaining chip?"

"Aye. She is." Her father bowed his head.

"And how do I know that you do not simply agree with me just to gain my favor?" Gard asked. "Would you take her back?"

Brae's eyes widened.

Guillium hesitated.

"Sadly for you, that choice is no longer yours. She no longer belongs to you. And as for your petition, 'tis not *my* favor that you will need." Gard walked to the Lord's chair. "You will need to seek Braelynn's." He turned to look at her. "'Twill be her decision whether or not you deserve her forgiveness." He sat and folded his hands, prepared to wait. "'Twould seem she is *not* worthless to either of you. What say you, Braelynn?" He dragged out her name seductively. "Do they deserve our forgiveness?" He watched her casually, as if they were just having simple conversation between them and not surrounded by a room full of people hanging onto their every word. "Can we forgive them for what they have done to you?"

While reaching for Brae's hand, Gard focused on Mac-Crae. Gard turned her wrist and placed a kiss in her upturned palm, before laying it over his chest and holding it there.

The pretense produced the desired affect. MacCrae was seething.

As he had hoped, Brae took his lead and played the game with him. While peering into his eyes, she stroked his lapel lightly, lending to the intimate appearance.

"I will yield ta your knowledge in this. I have no further quarrel with either of them. They have each done me a kindness, unbeknownst ta any o' us at the time, by leavin' me in your generous care."

Well done! He squeezed her hand.

"Wha'e'er will make ya happy, My Lord, will in turn please me." A zing of awareness shot up his spine. He found he liked it when she referred to him thus.

"I believe we will be charitable, my sweet. Your sire, has a wife, yeah?" Brae nodded, her focus never wavering from his face. "And so now, does the young pup. They are both in need of our benevolence. What was it Lord Ross agreed to pay?" Gard asked of Guillium and MacCrae.

The two men responded with conflicting sums.

"They are an honest pair, aye, Brae?" Gard chuckled.

"S'would seem," she replied.

"Scribe half of the lower amount that they have just provided, my sweet. That will be their bond."

She smiled. "Aye, My Lord. Tha' seems a fair and wise solution."

Gard kissed the back of her hand before he let her go.

"Ya canna do tha'," Callum exclaimed.

"Aye. I can. Scribe it, my lovely, and let us quit this place, yeah?"

"Aye, My Lord," she purred.

Brae wrote it down as he'd instructed. When she had finished, Gard closed the ledger with a flick of one finger. He then stood and presented his hand with a flourish. Brae took it.

"Do you have your precious tome from the smitten vicar?" Gard asked.

"Who be the vicar smitten wit'?" she asked guilelessly, picking up the book.

Gard shook his head and tugged her along.

Brae laughed. "Who?"

They walked out to the bailey. Stuart held the readied mount.

Without preamble, Gard seized her hips and was about to lift her onto the horse when Brae was beckoned.

"Brae?"

Gard raised an eyebrow in question.

"'Tis Katie. Callum's new wife," Brae informed him. Her eyes glassed over, which angered him.

"Brae. Can I speak ta ya?" Katie asked in a small voice.

Brae looked to Gard.

"'Tis up to you," he said.

"I dinna think I can," she said, tears falling. "No' yet."

Gard boosted Brae up onto his steed, then addressed the young lady. "I believe you have talked enough Madame MacCrae. All your friend asked of you was to make simple words on her behalf, and look where it has gotten you. Go home to your husband, Madame." Gard vaulted up behind Brae and turned the horse toward camp.

CHAPTER THIRTEEN

In his quarters, Brae and Gard shared a meal of pottage and stale bread.

When they were through, Brae asked, "May we check on Hudson?"

"I will see to him while you ready yourself for bed." Gard stood, dusting crumbs from his fingers.

"Am I ta bed down with the camp whores then, My Lord?" Brae asked.

Only half jesting, if he read the intrepid expression right. "You will bed with me," he said, and ducked out, but not before alarm lit her features.

If all went well, she would be asleep by the time he returned.

After dropping in on Hudson, Gard headed for the loch, to cleanse his body and cool his raging desire for the woman warming his bed. Visiting the camp whores held no appeal. Not when he knew what was waiting for him. When he closed his eyes, he saw only one woman. It was time to get out of Ross. But what of his burden? Returning Brae to her family was not an option, and he had successfully driven her betrothed into the arms of another. Indeed, she was better off without MacCrae. However, it was imperative he find a safe place for her to go, so that he would not worry about her once he was gone. And far enough away that he wouldn't be tempted every second. A convent was the only place he could think would be safe. At least from him.

Viciously, Gard dried his head. "Worry! Christ!" What the

hell was wrong with him? When they rode out of Ross-shire, he would never again allow himself to think of Braelynn Galbraith, let alone fret over her welfare.

He would leave on the morrow. He would inform Hudson in the morn.

Freezing, Gard made a mad dash to his dwelling.

Thankfully, his charge was tucked under a mound of coverlets.

In silence, he crawled into bed and was relieved when his companion did not move.

"How be Hudson?" she asked.

The sound of her voice made him jump.

"I didna mean to scare ya." Brae said, turning toward him.

His flesh, still cold from the swim, absorbed her heat. Brae's unique feminine scent combined with the freshness of her clean shift wafted about them.

"He seems fine," he said in short.

"Be he complainin' of headache?"

"Aye, slightly. He maintains 'tis mild though. Dinna fash yerself o'er Hud. No more talkin'. Sleep."

His surly tone had the desired affect. Brae rolled away.

Gard kept his distance and turned his thoughts to the days ahead. Eventually Brae's breathing evened out into the gentle rhythm of sleep and Gard was able to doze off, too.

In the middle of the night, Marschand's hand found her breast. Brae woke with a start, then she froze. Yet strangely, other parts of her body warmed.

With a mumble Marschand turned in his sleep. He tossed one bent knee over her abdomen and snugged his hard body to her hip.

For the longest time, Brae remained still and debated how

to extricate herself without waking the sleeping lion. She'd seen enough of men in the last few days to know they had but a short leash on their baser urges and didn't need much provocation to act on them—if they needed any at all. And Marschand had been in an unpleasant mood when he had returned that evening.

Before Brae could devise a plan, Marschand's lips moved against her neck. Chills coursed over her body, and those elusive dreamlike memories that had haunted her throughout the day danced in her head. *Hot kisses. Bare skin. Heavy breathing.*

His fingers moved softly in a circular pattern over her flesh, causing ripples of sensation to radiate from her breast to places farther down. The reaction of her body to his touch mortified Brae. Was she really much different from Callum that she could enjoy another man's touch on the heels of losing her betrothed? Could she, too, be turned that easily to another? Had she not loved Cal as much as she had thought?

Marschand stroked her nipple to hardness. He ground his hips against her and growled low in his throat, and she felt it rumble through his chest. The noises were reminiscent of the ones he had made in the lean-to. The memory made her shiver.

Marschand tensed and roused.

His fingers twitched on her breast. Like a boy caught with his hand in the candy box, he splayed his hand out flat and eased it away. Then systematically he removed himself from touching any part of her body. He rolled to his side, then got out of bed.

On his way by his pack, he grabbed a shirt. He pulled on his boots, then departed, leaving Brae embarrassed and alone. Hot tears of shame splashed down her cheeks. She burrowed further under the covers and cried herself to sleep.

The next time Brae stirred, Marschand had still not returned.

During his absence, she had taken the opportunity to wash and dress while she had some solitude. She had even tried to clean her hair with the limited bit of water in the basin. After a good combing, she left it down to dry.

To pass the time Brae tried reading the book the vicar had given her. But she was unable to keep her mind on it—reading the same sentence over and over again.

The morning dragged on. No one checked on her. No food came.

What if he isn't coming back? She did not care for the thought and went to the flap of the tent. There was a soldier posted on either side. She spoke to the closest one.

"Could ya tell me which enclosure be Lord Grainger's?"

"Tha' one yonder." He pointed "But ya are no' ta leave."

"Am I ta starve then as weel?"

He frowned. "Naw, o' course, no'."

"Then I will check on Sir Grainger, and after that I will find meself somethin' ta eat."

"But I dinna think Marsch will want ya walkin' aboot."

"Then I suppose ya should accompany me," she said, stepping out in the direction he'd indicated.

She tapped on the canvas. "Monsieur Grainger," she called. "'Tis Braelynn Galbraith. May I enter?"

"Aye, Mistress Galbraith, please."

Crossing the threshold, she expected to find him abed. Instead, he sat at the desk, with Marschand standing over his shoulder. Her stomach flipped at the sight of her formidable guardian. Her skin tingled at the memory of his touch.

"Excuse me, I dinna mean ta interrupt. I jus' wished ta inquire as ta your condition." She directed her attention toward Hudson, unable to bring herself to look at Marschand. Her blazing cheeks betrayed her again.

"How good of you, Mistress Galbraith. I was just telling Gard here that my vision is somewhat compromised."

"Och, nay. Tha' isna good, Hudson. How so?" Brae asked, concerned.

He turned to face her. His eye was black and blue, and swollen shut.

She gasped and placed her hands on her hips. "Did ya do tha' ta him?" she accused, jumping to conclusions.

"Did *I* do that to him?" Marschand thundered. "Why would you think that I did that to him?"

"Because ya are unpredictable, prone ta fits of fury o'er nuthin'. Ya are hot and cold."

"And she has only known you mere days." Hudson chuckled. "But no, Mistress, he did not do this, this time. I lost my balance in the dark last eve. I fell. I woke up this morn, my face in the dirt."

"Is the ill-balance an affect from the knock on the head do ya think?" Brae neared.

"Could be. Or just my own clumsiness. But I am still suffering a slight headache and dizziness."

"I'm sorry," she said.

"Do not apologize to him. 'Tis not your fault," Marschand snapped.

"Aye, 'twas. Robbie Cowan hit him ta see if I was wit' you. And I'm permitted ta say I am sorry jus' because I dinna enjoy another's pain if 'twas no fault o' me own." The man was a complete pain in her backside. He saw things only one way. His.

"What are you doing here anyway?" he stormed. "Going to a strange man's tent unattended. I never gave you my consent to leave my quarters."

"I told ya why. I was inquirin' as ta yer second's health. And you are the only strange man's tent tha' I go. And if my welfare was left ta you, I would starve ta death. And furthermore, I am no' alone, your dog oot there followed me, more afraid o' your reaction than me safety, I'm sure."

"I have not broken my fast as yet, Brae," Hudson invited. "Come sit." He set out bread and cheese.

"Thank ya," Brae uttered, accepting his hospitality. She took a seat.

"My pleasure."

"We do not have time for this," Marschand ranted. "We have work to do before I go."

Sadness suddenly filled her. Not for his departure, surely. After what he'd done to her life, she should be glad for it, but instead she was in a constant state of confusion over him.

"Are ya all goin'?" she asked softly.

"Nay, I'm sorry. I'm sure you would prefer us to leave as a whole," Hudson answered.

"Then he is ta leave on his own?" Brae inquired, careful to keep her focus on Hudson for fear of the rejection she may see in Marschand's eyes.

"Aye. Well, with his men that is."

"Are ya na one of his men?" Breaking off a crusty piece of bread, she waited for his answer.

"Aye, but as you can see, I would not be good to have at his back at the moment."

"Ya will be stayin' on then?" Hope flared.

"Aye, for a time."

The prospect and fear of being alone prompted her to ask, "May I stay wit' ya, when Marschand leaves, then?"

"No. You. May. Not!" Marschand erupted. "And quit speaking as if I am not here." He began to pace.

"Ya see wha' I mean? Hot and cold. Ya willna permit me oot o' yer sight, then ya want me as far away as can be. Ya want me safe, but then ya leave me unattended. Ya are goin' to leave, and I have na where ta go. But ya willna permit me ta stay here wit' him. Wha' am I to do, Lord Marschand? Ya have all the answers, tell me tha'?"

He took a deep breath. "I will set you up at the demesne."

"Not with Cowan running around," Hudson interjected.

The reminder stopped Marschand in his tracks.

"I will take Cowan with me." The distaste in his tone was obvious.

Hudson stared at him, then said matter-of-factly, "You cannot do that. You will kill him."

"I canna stay at the holdin'. Me own people dinna trust me anamore. I wouldna last a day," Brae said, more to Hudson than to Marschand. "And after yesterday, I am na sure tha' Callum wouldna try ta do somethin' in retaliation. He was furious."

"He wouldn't dare," Marschand said ominously.

"Ya willna be here ta stop him. Ya truly pushed him yesterday. I have ne'er seen him tha' angry afore."

"I was defendin' *you!*" He thundered.

"I ken tha's wha' ye were intendin', and I appreciate ya tryin', but if ya expect me ta stay here, tha' was the wrong way ta go aboot tryin' ta re-ingratiate me inta their good graces."

The men exchanged a glance. Marschand's mouth hardened, his eyebrows furrowed. Brae wondered if she had angered him or if he was actually considering some things she had said.

There was a tap on the canvas.

"Enter," Hudson called.

"A messenger has arrived with a missive from . . ." Hugh Chamberlain came to a stop as he glanced around the tent. "Oh . . . I . . . uh perhaps Mistress Galbraith should return to Marsch's quarters."

Brae knew she'd been dismissed. Without a word, she exited, leaving the men to their business.

Marschand's guard followed.

Gard paced as Hugh handed Hudson the missive.

Hudson pulled it close to his face, then away. "I cannot read it."

"What do you mean? Is it in code?" Hugh inquired.

"No, I cannot see." He gestured to his eye. "The good eye is bleary. I cannot focus. Besides, this message has been wet at some point. The ink has run, the words blend into one another."

"Well, you know I cannot read it," Hugh said.

"Gard? Can you decipher any of it?" Hudson asked.

Hudson had been teaching Gard letters and simple words, but their lessons had been few and far between. Gard looked but could not make sense of it, only able to pick out the odd word. The cursive puzzled him. Frustrated, he tossed it on the desk.

"What will we do?" Hugh asked.

Gard stopped pacing for a moment. "Mistress Galbraith can read."

"No," Hugh blurted. "We cannot risk it."

"But can we risk not knowing for the few days it will take for my eye to heal sufficiently so that I can read it?" Hudson interjected.

"We will call on the vicar," Hugh said, heading for the exit.

"Nay." Gard dismissed the idea. "'Twill take time to send for him."

"Do you trust her, Gard?" Hudson asked, leaning forward.

Gard considered for an overlong moment. She had kept all his secrets so far, from the detail that he had not actually attacked her in the smithy, to his alternating accents, to all the hints about his identity he and Hudson had let slip. Yet she'd made no attempt to inform her clan that something was amiss.

"Aye," he answered. It was difficult for him to place his faith in anyone. There was no choice.

"Fetch her," Hudson agreed. "If 'twere only up to me, I would have her translate it."

Gard waited for Hugh. "Two votes against one."

After some consideration, Hugh nodded his assent.

Gard stalked across the compound, then entered his quarters.

Braelynn sat curled on his pallet reading the book from the vicar. She stared up at him in surprise.

"Come." He held out his hand. She put the book aside. Taking his hand, she walked with him across the clearing to Hudson's canopy.

At the desk, Gard pulled the chair out for her. Hudson sat across and Hugh stood as far away as possible. Gard hunkered down in front of her. He looked into her eyes.

"I . . . we . . . are in need o' yer help," he said in a low voice. "But I must ask ya for your complete honesty and absolute secrecy. Ya must no' repeat anathin' ye are aboot ta learn ta anaone. May I extract such a vow from ya?"

She searched his gaze. "Aye. Ya ken I will keep your secrets. I have 'til now. I have na one ta tell. Wha' do ya need?"

He handed her the sheet of vellum. "We need you to read that to us," he said, dropping the brogue as he stood.

Her eyes widened. "Ya want me ta read your communication?" She shot Hudson a glance.

He gave her a reassuring nod. Chamberlain watched her stoically.

Peering down at the sheet she remarked, "Oh, My Lords, 'tis extremely difficult ta decipher. The strokes are so thick and smeared."

"Take your time, Brae." Hudson sat forward, his elbows on his knees encouraging her. "'Twas difficult for me as well at first. Sometimes holding it closer or further away can help. Or, 'tis going to sound strange, but try to unfocus your eyes for a second."

"Oh," she said in surprise. "Tha' does work."

Gard knew the exact moment Brae noticed the seal. Her eyes widened fractionally, and her expression turned apprehensive. "'Tis the seal o' the Guardian."

Gard's lips tightened. He should have known. She was far from ignorant of the political climate.

"We know who it is from," Hugh barked impatiently.

Brae's gaze never wavered from Gard's. "But I thought the Guardians o' Scotland had been disbanded years past?"

"Read the bloody text," Hugh chafed. "We do not need or want your annotations."

Gard growled and shot Hugh a black look. Hugh was quick to offer an apology.

Brae concentrated on the message and began to recite, haltingly at first as if trying to ascertain the wording. *"'Tis with . . . a heavy . . . heart . . . That I . . . regrettably am charged with the unenviable task to . . . in . . . form all Nobles of the Peerage that with . . . the . . . ."* She shook her head and rubbed her eyes a moment, then resumed, *" . . . help and Grace of God, departed . . ."*

As soon as the word *departed* left her lips, Gard jammed his fingers to his forehead, anticipating the rest.

" . . . from the House of Plantagenet, Edward His High in Majesty King of England, Lord of Ireland, Duke of Aquitaine, has succumbed — Oh, dear God!" she exclaimed. Gard knew she was absorbing the significance these events might have on her country. She shot another look of shock to Gard. He scraped at his beard with his hand in aggravated fury. She continued. *" . . . in death at Burgh By Sands in England on the border of Scotland, this the passing seventh day of July in the year of our*

Lord this One thousand three hundred and seven the Prince Of Wales . . ."

Gard covered his face. Dread settled in his gut.

" . . . at the present currently in succession. Further thee nobles of the peerage may be in demand to appear together in summit onto London to attend to and to swear fealty unto their new Sovereign presently. I await your instructions. Long may he rest in peace. Long live the king. Yours, forever-in faithful service to the cause. Sons of The G of S."

For Gard, time stood still. The ground under his feet tilted. His knees weakened, and he suddenly felt too big for his skin. Gard covered his mouth to keep the roar in his head from bursting from his mouth.

Hudson's voice came to him from somewhere far away. "How many times must we go through this?" Hudson's tone was deep with emotion. "First Balloil, then Comyn. The Bruce, now this?"

"He will do this ta me again! In life!" Gard raged. "And death!"

"We don't know that," Hugh interjected.

Unable to keep his anger contained, Gard exploded, "Ya ken tha' aberrant heir malefactor willna uphold Longshanks' pledge ta me. He will surely deny knowledge of it. If he be e'en aware of it." Gard shook his head in disbelief. "After all we have done. *The things* we have done." His stomach churned. "'Twill end in naught!"

Hugh rounded on Brae. "Why is it she does not seem shocked by your sudden and undeniable lapse into brogue, Gard?"

"She be the least o' ma worries." He could not wait to be rid of her. This newest development reminded him of his need to keep focused.

"Let us at least continue this discussion in private," Hugh insisted. "I believe you have imparted quite enough onto eyes and ears that have proven no loyalty."

Brae stood and placed the sheet on the desktop, then headed for the exit. Yet before going through, she stood toe to toe with Hugh Chamberlain. "I am a Scot, Lord Chamberlain," she said proudly. "Loyalty therein be proof." She left them to plot their next course.

In spite of the new and calamitous circumstance, Gard admired her pluck.

"What mean she by that?" Hugh asked.

"She is a Scot, therefore she is eternally loyal to Scotland," Gard explained humbly.

"Aye and look where your steadfast loyalty finds you," Hugh fired back.

Hudson stood quickly, anticipating a clash about to ensue.

Gard ignored them both and instead stalked outside.

Many would contest the idea that he had been steadfastly loyal to Scotland after the things he had done to regain his right. To anyone looking in, his allegiance would be questioned. He had played both sides of the border trying to regain his due.

Marching straight to the makeshift enclosure housing the animals, he mounted his horse, foregoing the time to acquire a saddle. Viciously, he kicked the animal's side and rode from the encampment.

CHAPTER FOURTEEN

Brae paced every square inch of Marschand's quarters. What did this all mean? Were these Dark Ones here on the orders of King Edward the deceased, or some other unknown enemy? Brae was so engrossed in the possibilities she was startled when Marschand's squire entered. She recognized him from their previous foray to the holding.

"Ye should be doin' Lord Marschand's wash o'er the loch wit' the other whores, preparin' fer the departure o' their Lords," he said, nastily.

Brae blinked at the disparaging comment. But what else would he think? She had slept within his master's quarters these past nights, and the men had witnessed Marschand's attack upon their arrival.

Brae rifled through Marschand's pack and gathered up the garments she could find. After collecting her own apparel as well, she headed for the water.

The other women were there as the squire had said.

With trepidation, Brae approached. She pulled up a little slice of ground at the edge of the loch. The women ignored her for the most part, deep in conversation, but Brae felt their eyes on her.

Braelynn dipped the first of Marsch's shirts into the cold water.

"Yah, migh' wanna hitch up yor skirt there, fresh one."

Brae looked at the lass across from her who spoke. She had her dress hiked so high that most of her leg was in view, for all to see. There was no chance Brae would allow that.

She looked at the girl next to her who had her garb tucked haphazardly in bunches around her waist. Brae pulled the material up to just below her knees and tied a loose knot. "Thank you," she said to the girl.

"Eww, ye are a polite 'un, aren ya? Ne'er thought ta see Marschand wit' a lady." Making fun of Brae, she performed a mock curtsey.

"Aye, I know what you mean." Another with an English accent spoke. "Marschand is not one for finery." They giggled.

Brae's nape prickled at the implications of their words. *Do they all know him in that way? Intimately?* The thought angered her.

"Ye are a quiet one as well, then?" the first girl spoke again. "Save, he isna one fer conversation either. Is tha' why he picked ya? Other than the obvious?"

"Other than the obvious?" Brae echoed.

"Aye, yor pretty face and yor desirous figure?" another replied, wiggling her hips.

Brae's cheeks blazed with heat.

"Nah," the first one answered for her. "Looks dinna matter ta Marschand. He has only one use fer a woman. No pleasantries. No tenderness. There is no play in tha' man. He doesna e'en kiss, that one. Jus' in and out, na chitchat."

Brae shook her head trying to stave off the awful feeling skittering down her spine. She was on the verge of tears, and she could not understand why. She was beginning to understand her new lot, she supposed. Perhaps that was what gnawed at her. She was not used to the crude chatter or this type of woman. If Marschand was departing, what was going to happen to her? Would he leave her at the holding to fend for herself? Or would she be left at camp, to make one up for the campies who were accompanying the Lord's entourage?

Hauling Marschand's shirt from the water she wrung if out savagely, taking out her anxiety on the fabric. 'Twas all his fault!

And Marschand does kiss. Damn him! At least he had in her dream. She bit her lip to keep her tears in.

"Aye, for the longest time, I thought Marschand didna speak at all. So fierce," another of the women added.

The girl next to Brae moved, placing her hand down into the mud. Groaning, the young woman grasped her side, in obvious distress, as she tried to rise.

Brae dropped the tunic then helped the girl to her feet.

The lass looked into Brae's eyes as she clung to her. She could not be any older than Brae. "Thank ye," she murmured.

"Ya are hurt," Brae whispered. "Let me fetch Lord Grainger for ya."

"Nay." She stayed Brae. "I will be fine. Jus' a hard nigh'."

"A hard night? Is tha' righ'?" the first girl spoke again. "Did ya get the brute las' eve, Bronny?"

"Aye." She breathed as if just that simple act hurt.

"Why dinna ya sit here." Brae lowered the girl to the ground. "I will do your wash."

"Nay, I canna ask tha' of ye."

"Ye didna ask, I'm offerin'. Ye just rest and I will take care o' it, after I am through with Marschand's. Aye?" Brae could not understand why the others were not helping her.

"Thank ye. Ye are verra kind. Where did Marschand find ye?"

Brae looked away. "Here at Ross."

"Ahh. He's ne'er taken a woman. Ye are no' wha' none of us would imagine he would choose."

Brae shrugged, re-dipping the chemise she'd dropped into the cold water.

"I'm Bronwyn, though they call me Bronny. Tha' be Islay." She pointed to the first one who'd spoken to her. "Tha's Penny." She indicated the girl whose accent was English. "And tha' one o'er there, be Wyn."

"'Tis a pleasure ta meet ye," Brae said.

Islay snorted. "Ya do possess some fine manners there," she scoffed, again. "Ya are no' in some salon somewhere. Do ya think Marschand will keep ya and tha' ye are better than the rest o' us?" Islay said with contempt.

"Nay. I dinna think anathin'. I'm jus' tryin' ta make do wit' wha' be fer the now," Brae answered.

"Humph," Islay uttered, beating the fabric she held on a rock.

"Wha' be yor name?" Bronny asked her.

"Brae."

"Well, I'm sorry tha' ye have been dragged inta this life, Brae, but I am thankful tha' ye are here this day, ta help me." She stretched on the slippery bank, then grabbed her ribs, wincing.

"Wha' happened to ya?" Brae inquired, almost afraid to know.

"Robbie," she said, in short.

Cold dread cramped Brae's stomach.

"I can tell by the look on yer face that ya ken all aboot Robbie Cowan," Islay called over. "Ye'd better harden up, 'cause when Marschand be done wit' ya Robbie will use ya up."

"Bah," Penny chimed in, as she placed a basket on her hip. "She must be tougher than she looks to spend this many days in Marschand's company and still be able to stand, let alone do his wash, her own, and Bron's, too. Marschand is not delicate by any means." The group of women nodded in agreement.

Brae took her rage out on his clothing.

It took her hours to finish up. Only she and Bronny were left at the water's edge when Marschand finally approached.

Out of her peripheral vision, Brae saw him, coming but was too infuriated to acknowledge him. Yet it frustrated her that she was not quite certain what exactly she was angry about.

"Are you planning on taking all day?" Marschand admonished.

"She be helpin' me, Lord Marschand," Bronny explained.

He looked down at Bronny, reclining in the muck as if she were nothing less than a pest.

"I be almost finished, Lord Marschand," Brae said, pulling a pile of his shirts onto her arm. They were heavy. Her hands and fingers had lost all feeling an hour past, making it difficult to wring out the thick material.

Without a word, Gard reached to take them from her. Surprised, she looked up in his face. His eyes were black as night and his visage a mask of barely contained rage.

"Thank you," she said.

Brae picked up Bronny's wash. She, at least, had a basket for her burden. "Where do ye hang them?" Brae asked her.

"I will take ye."

Brae set the basket down and helped the girl to her feet. Bronny swayed against her. Brae had to brace her feet apart to keep them both from falling into the mud. Bronny met Brae's gaze. Brae could not help but tear up at the girl's obvious pain. Silent understanding passed between them. "Thank ye, Brae," she whispered.

The clotheslines were bound between two trees. A small fire burned beneath.

To Brae's surprise, Marschand helped her hang the laundry. She could not imagine this was a chore he often worried over. The man was a conundrum. It was obvious he was furious, yet he took the time to tend to the mundane task.

When they'd finished, Brae turned to Bronwyn who stood not far with a look of amused amazement on her young face.

"I thank ya fer yer help this day, Brae."

"Ye are most welcome."

Without warning, Marschand grabbed Brae's arm, spinning her in the direction of their quarters. Her feet skipped across the ground as he propelled her.

He pushed her through the canvas.

His anger was unsettling, but she had other things on her mind. "Does Bronwyn have a man?"

The lines on his face deepened in a scowl. "Wha'?"

"Is there a Lord here tha' looks after her?"

"I do not know to which one you refer."

It would seem Marschand could use the women when he needed them but had not bothered to learn their names.

Brae frowned and stopped her hands from going to her hips. "The one we just left. Does she have a keeper?"

"I do not know." Dismissing her, he turned toward the desk.

"Please, wit' yer permission, may I take Hudson to her? She was brutalized las' eve and I am concerned fer her well bein'. I think she may have a broken rib."

"We have our own worries to attend, Miss Galbraith. The welfare of one whore does not concern me."

Unbidden tears filled her eyes. "She could be me!" she said fiercely.

His head snapped around.

"When ye are no longer here ta protect me, tha' *will* be me." Tears rolled down her cheeks. Acceptance was not comforting, she realized.

"I will not let that happen to you," he vowed, through clenched teeth.

"And how are ye goin' ta stop it? Ya willna be here."

"I will teach you to wield that dirk as I promised."

"And am I ta slay everaone who approaches me then? I still have ta survive as weel. I canna bite the hand tha' feeds me, now can I, or stab it as it were? *I will be* one o' those lasses when you're gone. And ye canna stop tha'. I dinna care who ye think ye are. Ye are no' all powerful ta keep them at bay in yer absence. The threat o' the great and powerful Lord Marschand willna keep the likes of Robbie Cowan from breachin' the fore. If I have learned anathin' in the last few days, it is tha' sense doesna trump desire in some men."

The anger in his expression doubled. It scared her. Not waiting for his decision, she flew through the tent opening and ran across the expanse to Hudson's tent. She tapped the canopy. "'Tis Braelynn Galbraith," she called, then glanced over her shoulder, only to find Marschand approaching.

"Come." Hudson's voice cut through the canvas.

She darted inside.

"What can I do for you, Mistress Galbraith?" He smiled but his gaze focused over her shoulder.

By the tingling of awareness cooling her neck, she knew Marschand had just stepped in behind her.

"We need to stop meeting like this," Hudson teased.

"I would ask a favor," Brae said in a rush.

A look of surprise crossed his face. "Oh?"

"Will ya accompany me and attend Bronwyn."

"Attend Bronwyn?" he asked, his earlier hilarity fled.

Obviously, *he* knew to whom she referred.

"She isna weel. I think she may have a broken rib. Will ya please see ta her? I am concerned for her health."

He stood, then gathered a black leather bag. "Show the way, Miss Galbraith."

Her shoulders drooped. "I'm sorry, I dinna ken the way. I jus' met her at the loch."

Hudson presented his arm. "We'll find her together."

Brae kept her attention affixed to the ground as they bypassed a glowering Marschand.

Outside Brae asked, "Ye are a physician, aren ya, Hudson?"

Much like Marschand, he did not respond to her questions.

Hudson led them to some shabbier looking pavilions further away from the main encampment. He lifted the tent flap and Brae stepped forward, but Marschand caught her elbow.

Brae tensed, having not heard him follow.

"You will not enter," he said, increasing his hold.

"But . . ." she pleaded.

"Hudson will take care of it. You have ended your obligation. You will attend me now. You will *not* go there."

Oddly, she had the feeling he was not referring to the tent.

CHAPTER FIFTEEN

They ate another meal of stew and stale bread.

Brae jumped every time his squire entered, then her features fell in disappointment.

"Hudson will report to me when he is through."

"Aye. O'course." Brae ripped off a piece of bread and dunked it in gravy. "How soon do ya leave?" she asked.

"On the morrow," he replied briskly.

"Where will I go?" She looked up at him from under her long dark lashes.

"You will go to the demesne," he responded.

For once, she didn't argue.

"Are you finished?" he asked.

"Aye, thank ye." Brae began to stack the serving dishes.

"Leave them, the boy will be along. Come, I will teach you to use the dirk."

"'Tis fairly straight forward, is it no'?" she said.

"Nay. It is not. An attacker will be stronger, faster, more savage than you. His determination will be more than yours. You will have to be more cunning to make up for your lack of strength." He pulled her to her feet. "Do you have it on you?"

"O' course." Automatically, she covered her thigh, where he imagined the dagger was strapped.

He was pleased.

"Remove it."

She blinked. "Ya told me ne'er ta be wit'oot it."

"I would prefer neither of us run afoul of it. Discard it for the now."

With a lift of her skirt, she then slid the dirk from the leather band surrounding her creamy thigh. She placed the blade on the pallet.

"Remove the leather as well," he instructed. He swallowed convulsively at the sight of her long shapely legs.

Gard cleared his throat. "You will wield to kill, Braelynn."

Her eyes widened.

"You cannot simply wound a man, you must aim for the kill. An injured man is like a wounded animal. First, he will be angry that you wounded him. Then he will seek his revenge, and he will punish you and probably turn the weapon upon you, *after* he is done with you. You cannot give him the chance."

Gard handed her a wooden rule from his desk to act as a dirk. "Now, if he should approach you head on, most like his arms will come from above or mid-level." He demonstrated. "You must go underneath and aim upward." He jumped her.

She did as instructed and ducked under him, aiming the makeshift blade toward his ribs.

"Excellent. The ribs, the stomach are good places. The heart will be instantaneous, the throat as well. Aim here."

When he placed his thumb to her jugular, her gaze flashed to his. He tried to maintain a delicate touch, belying his ferocious nature.

Slowly he scanned her face, halting to focus on his hand at her throat. He stroked lightly over her neck. Her eyes fluttered when he swept his fingers over her breastbone before surprising her with an unprovoked attack. He had her flat on her back before she knew it, smothering her with his weight, out-muscling her with his strength. Confiscating the wooden blade from her with ease, he flung it away.

"Now what will you do, Braelynn?" He continued to

overpower her, then raised her heavy skirt.

Meekly, she fought, flailing and kicking, as she had in the lean-to.

"Come, you must stop me. My resolve is stronger. I'll get what I want and take it because you are not powerful enough to fight me. My will to get inside you is stronger than your instinct for survival." Deliberately, he tried to incite her so that she might turn her anger into something useful. She made all the same mistakes again, ending in the exact same position as she had in the smithy—her dress up around her waist and Gard with his granite-like hips thrusting between her soft thighs.

"Will you let me do it to you again?" he taunted.

All of a sudden, she went completely still. "Ya willna hurt me," she whispered, her doe-like gaze searching his.

"Dinna be too sure." He spoke as a Scotsman. For some reason it seemed to disarm her when he did. He would use all the tricks to show her how deceptive an opponent could be. "I told ya ta keep tha' dagger on ya fer a reason." He thrust his hips. The action shoved her up the pallet. "Your first mistake was lettin' me so easily convince ya ta relinquish it. Do ya think I possess any more control o'er my cravings than Cowan does? I *am* goin' ta take wha' I want from ya, Braelynn. Stop me."

"Your word. Ya willna hurt me. I trust tha'."

Is she daft?

"Well, ya shouldna," he roared, diving for her neck. Their impassioned mock-battle had him acutely aroused. Viciously, he seized her hips, his fingers biting into her enough to make her cry out. The sound snapped his tenuous control. He was no longer playacting. He wanted her.

Surging against her, Gard tugged at her bodice and exposed her voluptuous breasts. He lowered his head and raked his teeth over her bared flesh.

Brae slapped at him. When that did not work, she tried to jab him in the ribs. Her attack did not affect him at all.

"Wha'? Lovin' the devil isna longer righ'?" he crooned, smothering her breath.

She had no idea what he meant by that, but before she could think, he closed his mouth over her breast, and she cried out again, for a whole different reason. But it still scared her. In frustration, she slammed her palms onto the pallet. By chance, the dagger bounced against her fingertips. Stretching, she frantically searched for the weapon. Finally she wrapped her hand around the handle. Brae aimed for Marschand's throat, pausing when she felt resistance from his skin.

He froze.

"Very good," he murmured wickedly. He stared up at her from her exposed breasts. Her chest rose and fell very near his full wet lips. If she had gained the upper hand, why did she still feel like he had all the power?

"Are ya willin' ta use it, Brae? Will ya end my life ta save your own?" His obsidian orbs flashed with eagerness.

"Ya arena threatenin' me life." *Why must I sound so weak?*

"But I *am* threatenin' your person. Ya wouldna survive this, Braelynn. Ye are too delicate ta come back from someone invadin' your body wit' force."

Like Bronny.

"Ye have already done evrathin' *but* tha' ta me," she accused.

"Tha's it, be angry. Use your anger. Draw strength from it." His eyes glittered dangerously, shining like onyx. She had seen that flicker of fire enough to know he was up to something else. Leisurely, he licked her nipple. Her lips parted on a silent moan. The fear in her fled, only to be replaced by that strange all-over tingle that only he could create in her. A burst of hot pleasure shot from her breast and flooded her lower body with delicious heat. All the while he continually ground his hardness against her thigh. She should be outraged — scandalized by his actions. But the sensations he unleashed were too good and left her wanting more.

"Stop me, Brae," he whispered, his warm breath sent chills over her.

To her utter shame, her nipple tautened even more. The change did not go unnoticed. With deliberate slowness he used the very tip of his tongue and circled — his brazen gaze never leaving hers.

"Caisg mi," he repeated, then closed his sinful lips around the sensitive nub. "Och, Brae," he groaned.

If he honestly wanted her to stop him, he should not speak to her in Gaelic for it only added to his appeal. She dropped the dirk, then laced her fingers into his thick dark hair. Her body relaxed under him. God forgive her, she did not want him to stop.

He raised his hand, then squeezed the opposite breast. With calloused fingers he mimicked the same torturous gesticulation as he continued to lave her flesh. Brae shut her eyes and let the all-consuming sensation take her away.

"Gard, do you know . . ." The sudden sound of Hudson's voice made them both freeze. "Oh! Sorry about that." He turned his back to them.

Rage mottled Gard's face. His mood changed with the wind. He pulled her bodice into place before moving off her, flinging her skirt over her legs as he did so.

"Ya e'er think ta knock afore ya enter," Gard fumed.

"I apologize, Gard." Hudson cleared his throat. "Mistress Galbraith."

Her cheeks flamed in humiliation.

"Forgive me. I'm not used to you being in this kind of circumstance, Gard." Hudson seemed sincere, but his eyes danced at their shared awkwardness. "I will leave you."

"What did you want?" Gard's deep angry tone seemed to echo.

"I sought to inform Mistress Galbraith that Bronwyn is well and requesting her company if it please you, Lord Marschand." With obvious glee, Hudson continued to prick Gard's temper.

"May I?" Brae moved from the pallet.

"Nay. Ye will no' go inta tha' filth."

"And why no'? You do!" she said, irritably.

Gard made a slow cold assessment of her, churning her up inside.

"How does it make her any less than you? Jus' because you sleep up here and she doon there. When you go there ta do, as ya need, in the meantime. As I see it, your filth isna better or worse than hers. Any o' them, for tha' matter."

Marschand grabbed her arm roughly. "Ye will cease!"

"Gard," Hudson cautioned, stepping forward.

In frustration, Brae stamped her foot.

Gard's grip tightened. His mouth curled unnervingly before he snarled, "Wha' I do or do not do be no concern o' yours."

"Gard!" Hudson said more sternly, circling them.

"And nuthin' I do is any concern o' yours," she retorted. "After yon morn, I will ne'er have ta endure your overbearance again. I dinna need yer permission ta visit anaone or go anawhere. Ye are no' my keeper, or my sire, or my Lord! Unhand me!" She tried to wrest her wrists from his viselike grip.

Perhaps she should not taunt the animal within him, but he had humiliated her time and again. His nostrils flared and his eyes blazed. His fingers bit into her forearm.

"Gard!" Hudson barked, then clamped Gard's shoulder.

Abruptly, Gard released his hold.

"Go!" Hudson bade her.

In all haste, she made for the opening.

"Nay," Gard roared.

The sounds of a scuffle between the two men reached her ears as she hurried to put distance between them.

She scarcely made it to the other side of the encampment when Marschand caught up. He swung her up onto his shoulder as if she weighed next to nothing. She shrieked and kicked at being manhandled yet again.

Gard marched across the clearing, ducked into the enclosure, then slung her onto the pallet. He yanked up her skirt. Brae knew what he was up to. Replacing her dirk. But Hudson had no idea and tried once again to intervene.

"Damnation, Gard, leave her be. You don't want to hurt her, and you are going to. You will never forgive yourself."

When Gard ignored him, Hudson lunged.

Gard jabbed his fist into Hudson's jaw. With a thud, he dropped to the dirt.

Nonplused, Gard cinched the leather around Brae's leg, then jammed the dirk into the makeshift sheath. She was shocked he had not cut her.

When he was finished, he flipped her plaid over her legs. Furiously, he stared at her, his chest rose then fell rapidly, from the exertion.

Brae returned his steely regard. "If ye are done humiliatin' me, I would quit you," Brae panted.

"Go! Afore I hurt ya," he roared, throwing his hands up. She flinched.

Not needing to be told twice, she fled, though guilt followed for leaving Hudson to face Marschand's wrath.

She had almost reached her destination when she realized two of Marschand's sentinels shadowed her steps.

She tapped lightly on the canvas. "Bronwyn?"

"Aye, come, Brae."

Brae entered the dimly lit dwelling to find Bronny abed. Brae knelt at her side.

"I thank ye fer sendin' Lord Grainger ta me. I feel ten times better. He bound my ribs, and the support is like heaven."

"Are they broken, then?" Brae asked.

"Lord Grainger says nay, they're but bruised. He's banned me from any activity for a bit. Suits me jus' fine."

"And wha' of Robbie? Will they jus' let him brutalize ya like this and do nuthin'?"

"There is nuthin' ta be done," Bronny replied, matter-of-factly.

Aghast, Brae shook her head.

"'Tis no different than when Marschand hurts ye. There will be nuthin' ye can do. It just is."

They talked for a while before Brae excused herself.

Wandering slowly toward Marschand's quarters, she heard him raving long before she neared.

"Why would I do that?" Marschand ranted.

"You really don't have a choice, Gard," Hudson replied. "I cannot accompany you in my present state. I will be of no use to you, neither to have your back nor to do what needs be done. I will stay here, and when my eyes get better, I will be able to resume my tasks. And Hugh will remain and hold Ross. 'Tis the next best solution."

"I cannot be traipsing around the country coddling the lass, not to mention keeping her safe, or keepin' meself from violatin' her. 'Tis a full-time job. I do not want a woman!"

She had a sinking feeling it was she about whom they spoke. Though reluctant to, she tapped on the canvas.

"Come," he roared, shaking the structure.

As soon as she stepped through, Marsch turned his back on her.

"Are ya a'right, Lord Grainger?" Brae inquired.

"Aye, I'm fine, Brae. Just my headache has doubled along with my vision. My jaw's a bit sore." He cupped his chin, working it from side to side.

She glared at Gard and mumbled, "And ye wonder why I think ye capable o' violence."

Stiffly, he swiveled in her direction, then pinned her with an icy frown, but he directed his remark to Hudson. "You worry about Cowan, but you think I will not kill *her*?"

"My hope is you will do your best not to, since we are in need of her talents," Hudson replied.

Resignedly, Gard closed his eyes and shook his head. "Pack your meager possessions, Miss Galbraith. We leave with the sun."

Leave?

So many emotions bombarded her at once. Leave Ross-shire? Her parents and home? But anger took precedence over all of them.

"I dinna think so," she announced.

Gard's shoulder's bunched. "Dare you nay say me?" His voice was low, controlled.

Once more, Hudson moved between them.

"Ya canna do this ta me," she argued. "Ya canna jus take me from me home, ma family, ta do as you want. I am na yours."

"Aye, I can. And I will!" he boasted, hands on hips.

"I willna go. Ya canna take me from ma family."

"Aye, the same family who threw you out with no care for your well-being. Look around you, Mistress Galbraith. You have no family. You have no fiancé. You have naught."

"I have naught because o' you!" she cried.

"And you will have even less if you do not accompany me. You have only me, Miss Galbraith. You would do well to accept my generosity."

"I will na do anathin' for you for nuthin'. If ya want me for somethin', then ye will pay me a wage. And when ya are done wit' me, ya will leave me somewhere safe, where I can . . ." She paused shaking her head as she tried to think. "Where I can tell people I am a widow. Ya will set me up in some small safe little village where I can live me life wit'oot the disgrace ya have brought ta me here."

"On your own?" Gard snorted. "You will not last on your own, Mistress Galbraith. But who am I to care. If that is what you so wish, it is yours. When you have fulfilled your obligation to me, I will set you free, to die alone in some little village, if that is your want." He focused on Hudson. "You will make sure she is ready, or I leave without her." He stalked out.

Brae released a breath she did not even know she had been holding.

"Wha' is it tha' I must do?" she implored Hudson.

"Since I cannot accompany the troops, you will be needed to read and perhaps respond to our communications. Your continued concealment of our secrets would be to your best interest. But you must keep your skills to yourself. No one but Gard must know that you have these talents. You will travel under guise as his woman. That is what the men will be led to believe, as well."

Brae closed her eyes and bowed her head. This was what her life had become.

Chapter Sixteen

B rae slept, thankfully alone. Marschand never returned. She was awakened with noise of the camp stirring.

While she still had privacy, she took the opportunity to wash, then dress.

While she had slumbered, someone had delivered her dry clothes from the line. The bundle sat atop her carpetbag. When she picked them up, something fell at her feet. She bent and retrieved the leather sheath Marschand had promised. She strapped it on. It fit perfectly and was far more secure and comfortable than the leather belt.

Brae folded the clean clothes and added them to her bag. She tossed in the discarded belt along with the book from the vicar. She was unsure if she was permitted to take it but did so anyway. If she would never return to Ross or Cromarty, she would regret that she had left it behind like so many other things, including the other tomes she'd lost. Not to mention her father or lost love. She would not even get to say goodbye. But as Marschand had stated so coldly, they had already forsaken her. There was nothing left for her here.

"Mistress Galbraith?" Hudson called from outside the structure.

Before Brae answered, she skimmed her hand along the lining of her satchel to ensure the gem from Gaveston was still secure. Satisfied that it was in the safest possible place for now, she responded, "Aye?"

"Be ye ready?" he asked, as he ducked inside.

"Aye. Is there anathin' I was supposed to pack up for *him*?"

"The squire will put things to rights in that regard. The canvas is about to be dismantled and stored for the journey. Will you join me to break your fast?" Hudson hefted her bag, then presented her with his arm. Brae slid hers through his.

The moment they emerged into the barely dawning gloom, Hudson handed her belongings to the squire. The boy's scowl was enough to indicate he was not fond of the idea of her traveling with them.

By the fire, Hudson shared flatbread and cheese. Marschand was nowhere in sight.

There was a chill in the air. She was not sure how long or how far they would travel, but her wardrobe was sorely lacking. If they still traveled come the cooler months, she would be ill-prepared to fight the cold. Brae pushed the thought away. For now, she had other things to fret over, one of which was how long would she be forced to suffer Gard Marschand's unpredictable company.

"May I bid farewell to Bronny?"

"Aye, I will escort you there."

The second Brae and Hudson rounded the last of the pavilions, Marschand did, too — ignoring them he strode by as if they were not even there.

Where had he passed the night? With Islay?

Marsch has only one use fer a woman. No pleasantries, no tenderness, no play in tha' man. He doesna e'en kiss, that one. Jus' in and out, na chitchat.

Resentment filled Brae again when Islay's words assailed her, though she was doubly cross because she did not know *why* it bothered her so much to think of Marschand with the other women. She gave herself a mental shake, ridding her thoughts of anything Marschand. She hated him for wherever he had been last night. She detested him for what he had done to her life. And she loathed him for whatever he was yet to inflict on her.

Hudson waited outside while Braelynn took a few private moments with Bronny.

"I'm sad ta say farewell, when we've jus' met," Brae said, kneeling at the bedside.

"Oh, aye, I as well," Bronny smiled.

"I'm losin' friends and family all over, 'twould seem."

"Miss Galbraith," Hudson called. "We musn't tarry."

"I must go, Bronny. I wish ya well."

"Wait, Brae, afore ye go." Bron gripped her hand before she could rise. "I ken Lord Marschand took ye from the village an' all and ya may not be privy to some of the techniques we lasses use ta prevent certain *things* from happenin' — if'n it hasna already — ta keep the men from passin' certain diseases or ta stop his seed from takin' root . . ."

Dear Lord! Brae's cheeks flamed with embarrassment but she sat in rapt attention while Bron imparted what she thought — bless her heart — was some much-needed guidance. It was not Bronny's fault. She, like everyone else, thought Brae was sharing Marschand's bed. Like a good friend, Bronny only sought to protect Brae from things she might not know about. Who knew there were tricks to prevent such things? She had never really given much thought as to how women like Bronny or Islay were not continually with child.

When Bron was finished, Brae left her company in haste.

"Are you a'right, Miss Galbraith?" Hudson asked, jogging to catch up.

"Aye."

He frowned. "Did she upset you?"

"Nay."

He took her arm and slowed the pace. "May I have a moment, Mistress Galbraith?"

Pausing mid-step, she faced him. He took a deep breath. "Brae. I do not know you well, and in the few days we have, I've noticed that you can stand up to Gard when he is . . . uh, overbearing. With that, I feel obligated to reiterate to you as I have in the past, that although he will take much, he will only take *so* much. He is not gentle or kind in any way. Some say he is not human. I would hate for you to push him into . . ." he hesitated, carefully choosing his words. "I would hate for you to be hurt. Do you understand what I am trying to say?"

Brae turned her head to find Marschand glowering from atop his warhorse.

"Aye, he is a savage beast!" Brae replied. "I am truly aware o' tha'. And 'twould be in my best interests jus' ta do as I am told and no' prick the sleepin' monster inta violence."

Hudson nodded gravely. "Aye."

"I thank ya for your counsel Hudson, but ya dinna have ta restate anathin'. I'm painfully aware o' wha' he is capable of. From the moment he pounced on me, I didna need your warnin'."

She walked away from him and toward the mounted beast awaiting her.

Acting the gentleman, for now, Marschand extended his gloved hand. Brae took a deep breath and joined hers to his—another decision that would change her life, she was sure. He hefted her into his lap.

Hudson squinted up at them. "And one more thing. Those sutures must be removed three days hence."

With a nod, Marschand kicked the horse into a canter—no fare-thee-well or pleasantries wasted on his comrade.

Brae craned to see around Marschand, watching her home disappear, getting smaller and smaller until she could no longer see it at all. She had never been farther from Ross than to Cromartyshire. She had left everything she loved behind. Her father, Callum, Katie. Her books. Sorrow seeped down her cheeks at the realization she might never see Ross again or the people who had meant something to her. Anything could happen on the road. Anything could happen with this unpredictable man. Brae might not return, and even if she did, she would no longer be the same innocent girl who rode off this day. Alas, she was not even the same girl she'd been just a few days past.

They rode all day, barely stopping to eat or see to their needs. Marschand's attitude was hostile. He was not talkative, but neither was she. She was angry with him and saw no need to converse to make time pass.

Gard tried his best to ignore her tears, thankful instead she was not chatty. He was in no mood to regale tales of court to keep her entertained.

Just after midday as the sun rode high in the sky, heating his shoulders, Brae relaxed against him and dozed. At least in sleep, she was no longer crying. No doubt she was not used to such hard riding, if she was even capable of riding at all. Nobles learned to ride—her lot learned to care for them.

He peered down at her. She would get a pain in her neck if she stayed that way. Shifting, he eased her head into the crook of his arm. With a subtle compression of his knees, Gard silently commanded his obedient steed to slow the pace. The men around him did the same, falling back.

Christ, she looked so young in sleep. How on earth had he gotten himself into this mess? He should have known returning to Ross would be a disaster, as had every other thing associated with it since he had left.

The day they had captured Ross, he had only meant to protect Brae from the others, never realizing it would become a full-time position. Why was he the one to be punished for such a selfless act? How on earth was he supposed to sleep with her night after night, and not take her? He was not that strong—as he'd found out—and definitely not that good.

As he pried his gaze away from her bewitching face, his body came alive with the thought of her, the feel of her, in his arms. Perhaps he would not have to subject himself to her at all. Now that Cowan was no longer a threat, placing her with the other women was a better option. Beyond her translating and responding to his correspondence, that would be the extent of their interaction.

Brae awakened.

Marschand did not acknowledge her but kept his focus on the road ahead.

Still half-asleep, she admired his handsome profile. Without a doubt, he was of Roman or Norman decent, with the straight nose, classic strong jaw line hidden under the dark beard, and overlong hair. Yet his extraordinary dark eyes could cut right through a person. How could she detest him as a human being, but think him so incredibly easy to look upon?

"Where do we go?" she asked as she sat up. "Dinna ya think I at least deserve the courtesy o' kennin' where ya take me?"

"London," he said, in a clipped tone.

"I have ne'er been oot a Scotland." Suffering from a cramp in her backside, Brae adjusted herself.

"Will ya stay still, fer Christ's sake!" he demanded.

"There isna need ta curse. I am stiff."

"So am *I*," he seethed, through gritted teeth.

"Perhaps ye should let me down, and I will walk. I have

na more desire ta spend time in your company than ye o' me."

"Ye have na idea." Halting the horse, Marschand then slid Brae to the ground. Not sparing her another glance, he rode on ahead.

Two horsemen paused behind as she slowly put one foot in front of the other, working out her achy muscles.

She recognized them as the two sentries who had been tabbed to follow her at the encampment.

The fair-haired one, with the twinkle of devilment in his blue eyes, reminded her a bit of Callum, both in looks and of a similar age.

Brae shielded her eyes and peered up at the rider. "Are ya bein' disciplined for some slight? Bein' tasked with watchin' me canna be the most enviable task."

"Nay." He smiled down at her. "Are ye bein' punished?"

"Nay, 'twas my choice ta walk."

"As 'twas me choice ta watch o'er ye."

Brae shaded her eyes. "Ye lie."

He laughed. "Aye, as do ye. Wha' be yor name, Marschand's woman?"

"Certainly no' tha'," she retorted, kicking the dirt.

"Dinna let *him* hear ya say tha'," he warned.

"He doesna care. I'm Braelynn. Wha's your name?"

"I am called Llachlan, they call me Llach, and this be MacBain."

"Jus' Bain." His companion spoke for the first time.

"Where be ye from?" she asked, picking up the pace. The conversation helped the boredom.

"We both hale from Skye," Llach replied.

"Ahh, I hear 'tis beautiful, aye?"

"Aye," he agreed, pride evident in his tone.

"Have ya been ta London afore?" she asked.

"Many times. Have ye?" He shifted atop his horse.

"Nay."

"Ye'll like it. Plenty o' people and a bounty o' merchants. Mayhap Marsch will buy ye some silks."

"Wha' are ye gettin' her hopes up fer, Llach?" Bain broke into their exchange. "She's na goin' ta see anathin' but the inside o' his tent from the flat o' her back."

Brae inhaled sharply and hurried her step. Her eyes stung from unshed tears.

"Why would ya say tha', Bain?" Llach whispered harshly.

"Wha'? Speak the truth?"

Llachlan pulled alongside her. "I'm sorry, Braelynn. Bain has the sense and the manners o' an ox."

"Unfortunately, ox or no', he be a'righ'." She swiped at her cheeks.

To her surprise Llach jumped down. Taking the horses' reins, he walked beside her. "Well, if Marsch willna buy ye a trinket, I will."

Self-consciously, she laughed. "Ye dinna have ta say tha'. It doesna matter. I dinna need trinkets. But I thank ya fer your generosity."

"He doesna promise ye this oot o' the good o' his heart, Mistress. He jus' wants wha's left o' ya when Marsch be done," Bain said from atop his horse, before he spurred it on ahead of them. "He seems ta like whores," he added over his shoulder.

She squeezed her eyes shut for a split second. *When will I learn?*

"Tha' be no' true, Braelynn. I dinna wish anathin' from ye. I have a lass."

"In Skye?"

"Nay, at Ross." He patted his mount's nose.

"Oh." She was disappointed again. He was probably one of the Dark Ones that she'd seen waking with the women of Ross the morning after the siege.

"Ya know 'er. 'Tis Bronny. I canna thank ya for coming ta

172

her aid. She didna confide in me tha' she was in need. I wanted her ta join us this trip, but she is no' well enough ta ride. I will kill Robbie Cowan one o' these days."

"There be a list o' people who would do so afore ya. He is a terrible man. I canna believe Lord Marschand has continued ta let him breathe. Marschand doesna strike me as a man who would suffer the likes o' Robbie Cowan under his command."

"Aye. But Robbie is related ta John Comyn, and Marsch made some deal through John when he swore his fealty ta Edward ta reclaim his—"

Llachlan's words were cut short when Marschand seized him by the scruff of the neck. Having circled around, they had not detected him sneaking in, speed and stealth on his side.

From atop his steed, Marschand lifted Llach right off his feet. Dangling, he choked and gurgled.

"Marschand! Caisg! Ma's e do thoil e!" she cried, beating on his thigh with her fist. "Stop. Please."

He dropped Llachlan into the dirt.

Not waiting to see if his man was all right, Marschand grabbed Brae by the front of her dress, then dragged her up onto the horse into his lap. Unconcerned about gentleness, he urged the animal into motion.

Barely harnessed fury radiated through his tightly coiled body. The tension transferred to her and manifested in more tears.

"Why do ya feel the need to humiliate me time and again?" She tried to straighten her dress. "Is it no' enough for ya ta have all these men thinkin' tha' I am your . . ."

"Ya are," he roared. "Ya are mine, and ya will comport yerself as such."

The vehemence in his voice shocked her, along with the realization that he was not angry with whatever Llachlan was about to confide regarding Marschand's personal crusade—whatever that might be. Instead, Marschand was furious with her for conversing with Llach.

"Ya mean to tell me there are rules ta actin' the whore?" she spat.

"Ya are no' a whore. They see ya as me mistress."

"Aye, because there be much distinction." She craned her head, to look him in the eye. "And we both ken, I am no' either o' those things," she refuted.

A nerve in his jaw jumped. He inhaled sharply and kicked the horse into a run.

In a panic, Brae fisted one hand into his cloak and dug the other into his rock-hard thigh. She held on for dear life as they flew past the others.

At breakneck speed, he raced into a copse of trees. Wind whistled by her ears. Without warning, Marschand stopped the charger.

Before Brae could think, he dragged her from the animal, then flung her against the trunk of a tree, the force knocking the breath out of her. Her vision tunneled for a fraction of a second before the mad man sandwiched her between the tree and his firm body. The tree's rough bark bit into her shoulder.

Marschand grasped her chin in a bruising manner.

"I can remedy tha' any time I wish."

It took her a moment to catch up to what he referred.

"Ya have no idea wha' I could do to ya. Wha' I've already done ta ya. Wha' I want ta do ta ya, evra second ya are near. I can have it any time I want it, and ya couldna stop me. I can make ya my whore righ' now." He shifted. His erection prodded her lower abdomen. He forced her chin higher, his lips hovering just out of reach. Even over his anger and her fear, she wanted nothing more than to taste his lips.

Damn you!

She was highly unpredictable. He wanted nothing more than to scare her—have her realize once and for all what he was capable of doing. Yet she stared at his lips as if she wouldn't mind.

"Dinna tempt me," he raged. "Ya wouldna survive me either. I am na kind. I dinna ken how ta be, I dinna want ta be. I take. Ye are no' strong enough for the likes o' me. 'Twould be violence evra time. Do ya understand tha'?"

Her gaze searched his.

"'Twould be rape evra time. Ye wouldna want it. So quit lookin' at me as though ye would."

To his utter shock, she touched him, her cool tentative fingers stroking his beard. Her luminescent green eyes shone on the verge of tears. She brushed lightly over his bottom lip with her thumb. "But I remember," she whispered. "When I was racked with fever, ya kissed me. It wasna violent. Ya can be kind. Ya *have* control o' it e'en though ye think ye dinna. Or we wouldna be standin' here righ' now. Ya warn me. Ya try ta scare me, but *I* ken the truth. Why do ya pretend ta be wha' ya are not in *evrathin'*? I remember your kiss."

He crushed her supple lips, cutting off her words, invading her mouth with his tongue.

He gripped her hips and ground his hardness against her stomach, longing to be inside her.

"Ya were dreamin' in your fevered state if ya think there is anythin' kind in me," he growled into her mouth, as he bunched the material of her skirt, pulling it up. He explored her soft skin. "If ya thought I was gentle or gentlemanly in any way, your thoughts are illusory." And when she remembered all, she would know with certainty there was nothing *good* in him.

"Wha' else do ya remember?" he taunted. He nipped her

chin and neck with his teeth, just enough to pinch.

Tears sprang to her eyes.

He ignored them. "Did I touch ya?" he mocked. "Did ya act like ya werena the innocent one touchin' me in return?"

"I dinna recall tha'. I jus' remember your lips."

"Ya kissed me back," he exclaimed. "Ya opened your lovely legs for me. Ya invited me in."

What little self-discipline he still possessed deserted him. He body-slammed her to the ground, on her back. She gasped. Her breath left her in a rush, but he did not care— just one thing on his wicked mind. With a knee, he parted her legs, then settled between them.

All gentleness gone, he seized her thigh.

"Ow!" she cried out, and recoiled, swatting at his hand. Belatedly, Gard recalled the wound.

This woman bares your mark . . .

Hudson's words reverberated in Gard's lust-fogged mind.

Gard scrambled away from her. She would bear more than his mark if he did not gain control of himself. Discipline always deserted him in her presence.

Gard hauled Brae to her feet, then swatted her skirt down. He pushed her through the thicket.

The rest of the troop had carried on ahead, except for his squire, who held his dancing warhorse. And to his vexation, Llachlan of Skye also remained.

Gard thrust Brae in front of Llachlan's horse, then he vaulted onto his own. Without a backward glance, he left them in the dust.

Hot tears of shame coursed down Brae's cheeks. She dared not face Llachlan, knowing what he thought had just occurred between her and Marschand in the trees.

Bowing her head, she straightened the neckline of her dress, only to discover the conspicuous red streaks on her flesh from the devil's teeth.

Behind her, Llachlan's boots hit the hard dirt with a thud. Without a word, he gently lifted her off her feet, then set her atop his horse.

Then he leapt up behind her, placing his arms around her to take the reins. "I apologize, Braelynn. I didna mean ta anger him. I ken better than tha'." The regret in his voice was genuine.

"'Tis no' your fault. I do nuthin' but elicit his wrath, for evrathin' I do makes him angry. Thank ye for waitin'." She sniffled.

Regaling her with tales from Skye, Llachlan attempted to lift her spirits.

By the time they had caught up with the company, camp had been set up for the night.

As soon as Brae rode in with Llach, Marschand dragged her from the horse, then pushed her into his tent. Fortunately for her, he did not accompany her within. The furnishings were sparse compared to those at Ross. Tears threatened as she thought of home.

Brae rolled out the pallet, then unfolded the throws for sleeping. She was unsure if she was to unpack Marschand's belongings. Was that her responsibility or the squire's? She did not wish to anger Marschand any more than she already had. His punishments were disturbing and his volatile moods unsettling.

The squire entered with a plate of flatbread and cheese.

"Thank ya," Brae murmured.

The boy stared at her with ill concealed hostility.

"Am I ta unpack the Lord's things or is tha' your task?"

"He doesna care for his things bein' touched."

Brae nodded as he left. She wondered if the bread and cheese were her whole meal or whether there would be something hot and more substantial to follow. Certainly soldiers who had been in the saddle all day needed more sustenance than bread.

After she had eaten, she glanced around searching for something to do. The thought of waiting for Marschand to return, especially in his present temper, put her on edge.

The mouth-watering smell of meat cooking over the fire lured her to the entryway of the pavilion. Her stomach growled. Surely it would be permissible for her to help with the evening meal. She took a step outside.

"I wouldna." The voice to her right belonged to Bain. "Marschand be in bad humor."

"And Llach?" she asked, worried he was not at his post. Had Marschand taken out his misery on Llachlan for aiding her?

"Here, Braelynn."

The men had switched places. She heaved a sigh of relief but retreated inside.

Brae was not given anything else to eat. Instead, she sprawled out on the pallet and cried herself to sleep.

For a second night, Marschand did not join her.

Brae slept until the noise of the camp rising woke her.

She dressed, then packed her gear and waited for the canvas to come down and the day's travel to begin.

She was unsure whom she would ride with, Llach or Marschand. Or if she would have to walk. She could not march too far without eating. She was starving.

Half and hour later, Brae waited outside where Marschand's lodging had stood only moments before.

"Did you eat?" Without a sound, Marschand appeared at her side.

She jumped. "Nay."

"Why not? Do you think if you do not consume, that in death, you will escape me?"

"Nay, it had no' occurred ta me, but it is somethin' ta

keep in mind. Thank ya for the suggestion."

His lips tightened.

"As usual I am no' allowed ta leave your quarters, but no one brings me food. And you are off doin' wha'e'er it is tha' ya do. I'd think ya might be nicer ta the one ye need ta rely on."

His dark eyebrows knitted. "You grant yourself too much importance."

Unable to help herself, even after Hudson's warning, she said, "Ye ne'er ken when I could miss a word or reword a message or jus' plain no' read the whole o' it. Puttin' ye in a bad position." She challenged, returning his scowl. "Ya migh' want ta think aboot tha' the next time ye be dolin' oot your punishments. I can be vindictive, too. 'Twould seem ya have a whole lot more ta lose than I do." She tried to walk away, but he snaked his hand out and grabbed her braid, hauling her backward.

His black eyes glittered as he yanked on her hair so hard, she had no choice but to face him. "Why do you not learn?"

"And why *dinna ye* learn? I think I jus' made meself perfectly clear." Slowly and deliberately, she reached downward in hope that neither Marschand nor anyone else would detect the measured movement.

"And *if* you are of no use to me," Marschand countered, "then I *have* no use for you. Do not bite the hand that feeds you, Mistress Galbraith, is that not what you once said?"

"*No one* feeds me, Marschand, be tha' no' wha' preceded this particular argument?"

"And perhaps the withholding of food may continue, Miss . . ." He stopped speaking when the blade from his own dirk cut into his skin. A trickle of blood ran down his neck.

His mouth quirked, and his eyes lit from within.

He was the most confounding man! If she did not know better, she'd think he was proud of her. "Ya see, Marschand,

I am learnin'. Soon ya willna be able ta push me aroond."

"Ye need ta be willin' to use it, Brae." With lightening speed, he took hold of her wrist and applied enough pressure that she was forced to drop the blade. "Or I will continue ta push ya around all I wish." He ground his hips into her, leaving her no doubt as to what kind of pushing he meant. "But it was a splendid attempt." He winked. The action surprised her. "I did enjoy the bloodletting. Ruadh!" he yelled to his squire. "You are neglecting your duties. Mistress Galbraith has not been fed this morn."

The boy glared before trudging off.

"And ye dinna think he will spit or somethin' far worse in my fair after bein' set down," Brae vented.

"He wouldna dare," Marschand boasted.

"Mayhap no' ta you he wouldna, but he has no like for me."

"Good. I'm glad to know there is at least one male in this camp not sniffing at your skirt."

"Na one is interested in ma skirt now tha' they believe I have been wit' ya."

His aristocratic nose wrinkled. "Aye, and tha's why Llach of Skye be pickin' ye off the ground when I am done wit' ye, eh?"

"He's jus' bein a gentleman."

Marschand snorted.

"He has a sweetheart," Brae defended.

He grunted again. "Be she here?" He pointed at the ground.

"Nay."

"Then he doesna have a sweetheart," he sneered.

"Ya canna convince me all men are like tha'," Brae argued, hands on hips.

"Hudson is the most loyal steadfast man I ken, and e'en he canna honor his vows."

Ruadh approached with a hunk of bread in hand. He thrust it at her. Brae reached out to touch it, but Marschand grabbed it, then raised it toward his mouth. The squire's eyes widened. With the morsel halfway to his mouth, Marschand paused.

"May I eat this?" he asked of his squire in a firm, low voice.

"Nay, Sir. 'Twas no' meant fer ye," the boy said, his Adam's apple bobbing.

"You will prepare her food as if it were meant for me. You may never know when I might take it right out of her mouth and put it in mine own. Do you understand me, Ruadh?"

"Aye, Sir."

Marschand tossed it to the ground at the boy's feet. "Now, you will eat it."

The boy's gaze darted, and his lips trembled. He hesitated then bent to pick it up. He swallowed audibly before opening his mouth. He closed his eyes and cringed, taking a bite.

What did he do to it? Brae's stomach rolled.

"Marschand, dinna make him," she whispered, feeling sorry for the boy.

"He was about to have you consume it," he pointed out.

"I ken, but . . ."

"'Twill be a lesson. For both of you."

She blinked in question.

"*He* will learn not to tamper with what is mine. And *you* will learn that you are not the only one I dole out punishment on." Crossing his muscular arms, he watched the squire eat every last crumb.

"You will go wash your hands and you will prepare a portion for Mistress Galbraith properly, or you will prepare to return from whence you came. I will not tolerate your treachery yet again."

"Aye, Lord Marschand," the child muttered.

"First you will apologize to Mistress Galbraith."

His lip curled. "I am truly repentant, Mistress," he intoned, as one would expect a boy of his age being forced to apologize for something he was clearly not remorseful for.

Marschand moved with his incredible speed that unnerved her. He clouted the lad on the side of the head with such force the thud resounded off the trees. Brae closed her eyes, unsure what to do. If she defended the child, she might make the situation worse for both of them. Marschand was so unpredictable she was afraid he would see her interference as another affront to his authority. Or perhaps he would turn around and strike her as well. Or worse.

"You will apologize with sincerity," Marschand demanded, his voice deep and malevolent.

"I apologize fer me behavior, Mistress Galbraith. It willna happen again," he said gasping, trying valiantly not to cry in front of his master.

Brae had no problem letting her tears fall.

"Go wash and begin again," Marschand decreed. "And quit your sniveling. Be a man."

Marschand focused on Brae as the boy scurried away, head bowed.

"I *hate* you," she enunciated.

The corner of his mouth ticked. But more surprising yet, his eternally black eyes were a startling light brown. "Ye are learnin, Brae."

CHAPTER SEVENTEEN

Gard pulled Brae up onto his horse without giving her a choice to walk on her own or ride with Llachlan. Gard was not fond of Llachlan from Skye following her. He was a big, strapping, good-looking easy-going lad. A perfect match for the bonnie Mistress Galbraith. And a Scot to boot, which Gard knew she favored above all others, all but melting when he let his own brogue free or when he spoke to her in Gaelic. But it was Llach's strength and ability with a sword that overrode Gard's other qualms. If need be, he could keep Brae safe in Gard's stead, and that was all that mattered.

For the better part of the morning, the group rode long and hard, eventually pausing for another piece of bread. Fortunately, this time they stopped near a fresh-water stream where they drank their fill.

With Gard's permission, Brae took the opportunity to dip her feet in. She even went as far as to wash her arms and face thoroughly. The other women followed her lead, while some of the men dove right in.

Gard settled near the bank. Brae watched the others longingly. After a moment, she rolled her sleeves down and waded out of the water, hesitating when she found him watching her.

"We will ride into Inverness on the morrow," he said, as she passed. "We will stay indoors. You may bathe thoroughly then and have a decent meal. Sleep in a real bed."

When she lifted her gaze to his, he saw her anger, but realized it was now laced with gratitude.

"You should be clean when we remove the thread."

An expression of panic crossed her delicate features, then quickly disappeared. She nodded and walked away.

Brae dried her feet and had just pulled on her slippers when a loud wail rent the air.

Ruadh burst from the trees, swatting at his arms and head. Sprinting to the pond, he then plunged headfirst under the water, a swarm of bees trailing him.

For a lengthy period, he stayed below the surface, then dragged himself out, looking like a drowned rat. The older men laughed as he stomped away removing his wet shirt.

Like a good squire, he went about his duties, readying Marschand's horse.

A lover of the moors, Brae had been on the stinging end of a few insects afore and remembered how painful it could be. She recalled a helpful trick her stepmother had once used.

With a handful of packed mud, Brae approached him.

"Ruadh," she called.

He swiped at his cheeks before turning. He glared pure hatred.

Strange—for such a little man, she suffered the same kind of uneasiness as when she approached Marschand.

"Let me put some o' this on your stings" She showed him the mud in her hand. "'Twill take the fire oot."

"I dinna want yor help," he sneered. "Get tha' away from me." He ducked.

She made to leave but then waited until he returned to his task. When he did, she smeared the sludge across several of the red welts.

"Wha' do ye, ye crazy witch?" His gaze darted. He lowered his voice. "Are ya tryin' ta rile him so as he'll hit me again? Is tha' wha' yor aboot? Did ye like the sigh' o' me bein' beat by him? Do ye figure if he's punishin' me he will leave ye alone?"

"Naw. I was jus' tryin' ta help the pain," she explained.

"I dinna want a Goddamn thing from ye," he stormed.

Taking the handful of muck, she placed it on the saddle of Ruadh's horse in as neat a pile as she could, so that he would notice it before he took his seat and not think she had positioned the mud there out of spite.

Later that afternoon, Brae noticed that Ruadh had several globs of the poultice caking his face and arms. She had known if he would just try it, the burning bites would ease for him. She tried not to smile—he continued to avoid her gaze.

They rode again for hours before finally stopping to set up camp for the night. The men had snared some rabbits on the trip and cooked them as the tents were assembled.

As directed, Ruadh brought her some meat and another hunk of bread, though he did not utter a word. An apology sat on the tip of her tongue—regret for not only his misfortune with the bees, but also what had happened with Marschand. However, she had no idea how to broach the subject, so decided it was best to leave him be.

Brae wondered idly why they called him red or Ruadh, when his hair was black as pitch. Much like . . . Marschand's. Thoughts collided in her head. *Is the boy his?*

Her stomach clenched. She did not like the idea of him having a child. And worse, she did not care for her response. Why should she be concerned? But was that why Marschand assumed he had the right to discipline the child with violence?

Absently Brae gnawed on the end of her thumb as she puzzled it out. Right or wrong, father or not, that wouldn't stop Marschand from thinking he had the authority to strike anyone he wished. And who would be foolish enough to nay say him?

Curse his wretched hide! Gard Marschand made her feel so many things she did not want to or could not explain. She detested the way he churned up her emotions and hated *him* more and more every second she was forced to suffer his churlish company.

The shadows grew long, yet Marsch did not return. Though grateful she did not have to spar with him, she was also restless. Brae spotted the spirits Ruadh had placed out for his master.

There was no better time than the present to remove the sutures from the wound, thus eliminating any reason that would necessitate Marschand's touch on the morrow.

Brae undressed, leaving only her shift on. Before she started, she cleansed the area around the cut with the hard liquor, then she drank a measure to help numb the pain.

Pulling the taper near, she began the painful task of removing the foreign matter from her skin. Using the tip of Marschand's dirk she severed the knot Hudson had tied. She gritted her teeth and picked each stitch out carefully. The thread burned like a fiery brand as it slipped from the fleshy tissue.

Several times she had to stop and restart, drinking more in the meantime.

When she'd finally finished the gash throbbed, but the numbing effect of the alcohol helped.

One more time, she cleansed the wound, as well as the tip of the blade. She slid the dirk into the sheath strapped to her opposite thigh. She then disposed of all the nasty fragments of thread.

At last, Brae settled on the pallet. However, she was slightly nauseous, from the drink or the ordeal she was not certain.

Drawing the taper closer she examined the tender pink moon. The scar was not as bad as she'd imagined, and with time, it would fade even more.

Brae blew out the candle, then snuggled under the covers. Breathing deeply, she inhaled Marschand's scent that clung to the bedding.

In no time, she drifted off to sleep.

In her dreams, she was back at Ross.

Groggily, Brae awoke as grainy images of an unfamiliar banner of red and blue waved proudly over the Ross-shire holding before disappearing from the cobwebs of her mind. She rubbed her aching temples as the gold moon in the center of two lions evaporated into the fog of imaginings.

"Are ye dead?"

Brae opened one eye to find the raven-haired squire standing over her with a bucket of water.

"Nay, but you will be if ya throw tha' on me," she warned, pulling the blanket up.

"Tha'll be the day tha' some whore slays me," he retorted.

"I am no' a whore! And if ya call me tha' again, ya will be slain."

Anticipating the child would not be able to keep his filthy mouth shut, Brae wrapped her hand around the hilt of the dirk, resting under her pillow.

"Whore!" he taunted.

She flung the covers over his head, then jumped off the pallet.

Clumsily, he flailed with the heavy coverlet over him. He managed to uncover his face, but she seized his shoulders, then pressed the dirk to his throat. "I said, ya willna call me a whore again!"

"Ye are crazed!" he screamed.

"Aye, I jus' migh' be. So ya better do as I tell ya from now on, or I'll slit your throat jus' as soon as look at ya. I wouldna struggle if I were ya!" she cautioned. "Ya dinna like me and I dinna like ya either. We have na choice but ta find a way ta exist together. But ya willna disrespect me. Do ya hear me?" With her arms around his shoulders, she applied more pressure.

From nowhere, Marschand, with his unnatural speed and stealth, appeared beside them. "Why are you trying to murder my squire?" he asked, calmly.

Brae was about to enlighten him, but she did not want the child to be punished. "'Tis between him and me. He kenned wha' he did, and now he's mindful o' wha' will happen if he does it again," she exclaimed. "I have dealt wit' him, and ya will not. I extract tha' promise from ya now, Lord Marschand, or I dinna let him go."

Marschand raised an eyebrow. "You do not wish for me to reprimand him?"

"Nay."

"I will not," he vowed. "Now let him go." His fingers twitched as if he were about to intervene.

She waited a moment before releasing him. The boy struggled with the blanket before turning on the adults, wide-eyed. "She be crazed!"

The corner of Marschand's mouth quirked. "Perhaps." He shrugged. "But did you learn your lesson?"

"Aye. *She be crazed!*" he repeated, his dark eyes large in alarm.

"Aye." Brae brandished the blade and circled the squire. "And demented people are unpredictable, so ya may wanta watch your mouth aroond them."

"Go." Marschand waved, dismissing the boy.

"Go?" Ruadh echoed in surprise.

Marschand nodded.

"Ya willna discipline me then?" he asked, incredulous.

"I will not. Now go, afore I change my mind."

The squire scurried from the dwelling.

Brae straightened. Marschand's gaze roamed over her sheer shift, reminding her of her state of undress. He gripped her wrist and applied pressure until she had no choice but to drop the blade. It made a thud as it hit the dirt.

"Why are ya threatenin' me squire?" Marschand demanded. "Wha' did he do ta ya?"

"I told ya. 'Twas between him and me, and I handled it. Jus' like ya taught me."

His gaze turned hawk-like. "Did he try somethin'? Because if tha' be the case, I canna let it go. He must be punished."

"Ya promised me ya wouldna," she accused.

"Ye ken better than ta trust me. I will do as I wish. And if he messed wit' wha' be mine, at least for the now, he will be dealt with." Once again, his gaze drifted over her body "Though I can see why he would be tempted."

She might as well be naked, for the look he gave her. "He didna mess wit' me," she replied in disgust. "He's but a boy."

Mere inches from her, Marschand grasped her chin, forcing her to face him.

"Wha' *did* he do?"

Her focus shifted to his full lips as he enunciated. "He called me a name," she explained. "I didna care for it. He willna disrespect me. Ya do enough o' tha'. I dinna deserve it from him."

He traced her mouth with his thumb, parting her lips. "And wha' did he call ye?"

"He called me a whore," she said with righteous indignation.

To her shock, Marschand's mouth moved in a semblance of amusement, and he chuckled.

"I'm glad ye find it so humorous!" She moved away from him and picked up a day-dress, then held it in front of her as a shield.

"He says but wha' he believes," Marschand said, dismissively.

To her utter vexation, her eyes filled. "Aye. Tha's wha' evraone now believes, thanks to ya." Her lip quivered. "But 'tis no' the truth, and ya ken it."

"'Tis of no import. Get dressed. You hold up the day's progress."

"Moody. Disagreeable. Humorless," Brae chuntered, once he had ducked outside. *And an absolute bastard.* That was Gard Marschand.

She dressed hurriedly, half-afraid the men would lower the canvas regardless of her state of dress.

When she emerged from the tent, Ruadh thrust an apple in her hand. Tired of the stale bread, she was grateful for something different. Brae ate the fruit quickly, right down to the core, which she saved for Marschand's steed.

As she waited to discover what the arrangements were for the day, Brae tested out her leg, finding it quite tender. She hoped she would not have to walk. Every time her thighs touched, she experienced discomfort.

"Gud Morn, Braelynn."

"Gud Morn, Llachlan. 'Tis a beautiful one, is it no'?" The sun warmed her shoulders.

He squinted up at the sky. "Aye. 'Tis. Will ye ride wit' me this day?"

Marschand joined them, interrupting her reply. "She will ride with me."

Llachlan gave a quick nod and backed away. Marschand mounted and then extended a hand to Brae. When he yanked her up, she reacted to the pain as her legs came together.

"'Tis past time to remove the thread, aye?" he said.

Brae wiggled her bottom, seating herself securely, in his lap.

Marschand's nostrils flared and he inhaled sharply.

It was on the tip of her tongue to inform him that she had taken care of it, but she thought better of it. She did not want to give him any reason not to stop at the inn. She could survive without a good meal and a proper bed to sleep in, but she would *not* go another day without bathing.

Instead she answered simply, "Aye."

As they traveled, Brae listened to the soldiers converse around them. Marschand did not interact with his men, and if he did it was only to bark out a command or impart his next directive.

Still suffering a slight headache from imbibing the night before, Brae relaxed against Marschand's chest. As the sun warmed, Marschand's unique scent surrounded them. Soon she was drowsy and content. Absently, she toyed with the wrinkles in the sleeve of his shirt.

"Ya are wearin' white again," she said idly, wondering about his choice of colors, or lack thereof.

"Aye. And ya are wearin' blue," he replied.

Brae peered down at the muted green on blue Galbraith woolen cloth. "Ya are verra observant, Lord Marschand," she teased.

"I wouldna say tha'. 'Tis jus' blue be a favorite o' mine and I notice."

Surprised, she glanced up at him. This was the first time he had voluntarily shared something of a personal nature without provocation. She had never considered that a man like Marschand would have a preference for something so simple as color. She would use the opening to learn more about him.

Brae settled down once again, relaxing against his solidity, but angled herself so that she could see his face. "Is blue a family color then?"

His eye twitched right before he looked down and away. His gaze darted rapidly yet focused on nothing. She found the action disarming, though she was certain she had angered him. Again.

"Why are ya always so irritated wit' me for gleanin' things? Would it be so awful for me ta ken somethin' aboot ya?"

"Ye dinna need ta ken anathin'. 'Tis none o' your business. And it angers me because I dinna understand why I'm constantly careless wit' ya."

"Careless?"

"Ya ken more aboot me than most o' these men. And some of them have been wit' Hudson and me for years. I dinna share me dealin's wit' anaone."

"Is tha' no' lonely?" she asked, no longer simply playing with the material of his shirt, but caressing his forearm beneath.

"Lonely?" he repeated.

"Aye. Ya have na one save Hudson who recognizes the real you. Ya canna confide or consider a problem wit' anaone, or simply get a fresh perspective from another."

"I dinna need those things," he scoffed.

"Aye. I remember. Ya are a soldier. Ya dinna need what other men need."

"Wha' do ya ken aboot wha' other men need," he snarled, shaking her fingers from his arm.

She sighed. "I dinna wish ta quarrel wit' ya. I am tired o' sparrin' wit' ya aboot evra little thing." Crossing her arms, she closed her eyes, shutting him out. "I simply asked if yor favorite color has some special significance. As if I could glean all your deep dark secrets from tha'."

For many minutes, they rode in silence before he said quietly. "Aye. Blue is a color associated with my lineage."

Though he had once again curbed his brogue and spoken the last as an Englishman would, she could not help but smile over the small revelation.

CHAPTER EIGHTEEN

With the sun setting low in the sky, they rode into Inverness.

Marschand lowered Brae to the ground and then dismounted.

He barked orders to the men before taking Brae by the elbow and escorting her into the inn. The sign above the counter read *Auburn*.

"Lord Marschand. 'Tis good ta see ye again," the gentleman behind the desk greeted. "How many o' ye this time?"

"A score." Marschand threw a velvet bag of coins onto the scarred wood.

The man wound his wrinkled hand around them covetously before turning his attention to Brae. She must look a sight. The innkeeper smiled. "Be this yor lady wife, Lord Marschand?"

"Nay." He pushed her toward the corridor. "We will be in need of a meal. I want hot water for a bath. And a flagon of wine."

"Aye, Lord Marschand. Righ' away. Take the room ye had the las' time."

Down the short passage, Marschand opened a chamber door. The furnishings were not opulent by any stretch of the imagination, but it was better than the tent and pallet. Brae walked to the window and observed the men milling about outside. Marschand lit tapers throughout the room.

Ruadh burst in with Marschand's pack and dumped it hastily on the floor. Marschand threw him a coin.

"You will behave yourself," Marschand warned.

The boy grinned, gripping the coinage tightly in his palm. "I will," he replied as he ran down the passage.

"Why do ya call him the Red when he is clearly no'?" she asked, trying to satisfy her curiosity.

"His sire had flaming red locks."

She nodded, oddly relieved—Marschand was not the boy's father. "Where be his sire now?"

"Dead," he stated matter-of-factly.

Brae frowned. "Oh. I am sorry. Wha' happened ta him?"

"Why are you apologizing again? What matter is it to you? You did not know him."

"Have ye no' sympathy in ye at all? A person can feel empathy for another e'en na kennin' 'em. And moreover, show some compassion for a child who mus' carry on wit'oot his parents. Forced inta the care o' the devil who abuses him."

He lifted an eyebrow. "Would this be the same child whom you feel such compassion for that I saved you from slitting his throat? Is that not abuse?"

"I explained tha'," she said in exasperation.

"Aye, 'tis a'right' for you ta abuse him, but I'm the devil when I try to teach him manners and respect."

"Manners and respect? Ye canna teach anaone such things when ye dinna possess them yourself."

His mouth ticked. "Ya really are learnin', Mistress Galbraith."

After a knock on the door, several boys dragged a wooden tub into the room, followed by a bucket brigade.

With longing, Brae watched as jug after pail of gloriously clear water was emptied into the vessel.

As the water neared the brim, Brae suffered a momentary worry Marschand would not grant her some privacy.

But as the lads exited, Marsch said, "I will leave you to

bathe, but I will return shortly to remove the sutures. If you wish to be clothed when I do so, do not linger. I will use the water after you, and I do not wish it to be cold."

The second Marschand closed the door, Brae hurried to disrobe.

With a sigh of pleasure, she submerged herself in the warm water. With some harsh lye soap, she washed her body and then her hair.

Brae reclined, draping her long wet hair over the side of the tub. She closed her eyes. She would just take a minute and bask in the lavishness of being clean again.

With a tankard of ale, Gard stood near the fire and watched his men, drink, eat, and grope the wenches. His gaze landed on his wide-eyed squire. The lad's mouth was full of some greasy morsel, yet his curious gaze remained affixed on the abundant cleavage of the whore in Bain's lap.

And the lovely Miss Galbraith believes I exploit the child.

Ruadh would not be a boy for long, by the look of him.

Gard surveyed the serving girls. He should simply pick one and quit distressing over the naïve opinions of the young naked girl bathing in his chamber. His groin tightened at the thought.

One of the lasses sidled up to him, leading with her ample bosom. "Be it righ' tha' ye came wit' a woman this time, Lord Marschand?" He recognized her as the girl who had serviced Hudson the last time they had traveled through.

He watched her coldly. In truth, she disgusted him.

"Be on yer way, gel." The old crone appeared out of nowhere and edged in between them.

Gard straightened. The grizzled old woman unnerved him.

"Marschand 'ere has na interest in ye. Get ye gone."

The serving girl's mouth hardened, and she moved on to

the next man.

Gard took a long drink. The hag peered up at him, pulling her knitted shawl around hunched shoulders.

"So, ye have found her, aye?" She gifted him with a gap-toothed grin.

The cold fingers of fate grazed his spine. Looking down his nose, he cast his coldest stare, but her repellent smile only widened.

"It is she. She bears yor mark. Ye put it there yorself." Her aged eyes glistened strangely in the dim light. "Ye can deny it all ya like. Lord kenned ya are an obstinate man. But ye canna let tha' stubborn pride get in yer way this time. Ye will ne'er reclaim wha' ye seek withoot her. Ye mus' let go o' yor auld ways. Open yor black heart. For if ye dinna, ye will lose evrathin'."

"I have already lost everything." He sniffed "They cannot take more. There is nothing left."

"Ye be wrong. Ye will soon come ta realize tha' fact. Soon ye will ken that wha' ye have made yor life's purpose ta reclaim will mean nuthin' wit'oot the one who bears yor mark. For she be the key ta evrathin' ye seek."

Ignoring her nonsense, Gard gestured to the innkeeper.

Within seconds he placed a flagon in his hand. Gard nodded his thanks, then strode down the corridor toward his chamber.

Before barging in he placed his ear to the door. It sounded like she was scurrying around as if the devil chased her. He pushed the door open, harder than he meant to, it banged against the opposite wall.

Brae jumped and tried to gather the sides of one of his shirts together. The brief glimpse of her nakedness was enough to make his hungry body roar. *God's blood, she'll be the death of me.*

"Red didna bring me bag," she said in a rush. A pretty blush pinkened her cheeks. "I borrowed your ..." Her words died on her tongue as his gaze made a slow insolent sweep of her body. But when he reached her delicate ankles, his focus settled on the familiar dark blue cloth bag with gold tassel drawstrings lying on the floor.

"Is tha' all ye do?" he accused — for the moment, his anger overrode his lust.

"Tha' fell oot when I jerked on your shirt." She bent to retrieve it. He used his speed to beat her to it, snatching the sack from her fingertips. The motion sent some of the contents rolling across the scarred wooden floor.

Brae picked up the item which had clipped her toe, while Gard gathered the other articles.

"Unnaturally cold," she whispered. She examined it closely. "Ohhh, 'tis breathtaking," she exclaimed. "Wha' is it?"

Yes, the precious stone was beautiful, but the curiosity in her eyes would only lead to more speculation on her part. It was the last thing he needed. More intrusive questions.

Unbeknownst, to Brae, she held the last article that linked him to his lineage. And according to the old doxy, the one who bore his mark would lead him to his rightful place.

His skin prickled.

Brae's expressive eyes lit with wonder as she peered through the gem. "Ye are blue, Lord Marschand." She giggled lowering the treasure. The smile fell from her face as he continued to stare at her. "'Tis a seal, aye?" She turned it over. "Em, Cee?" she questioned, placing it in his outstretched palm.

He was well aware of the ornate script, with its flowing swirls, curling and twisting the M and the C intimately and eternally together.

"'Tis a *nobleman's* seal, yah?" she asked. "Hidden under that enormous gem?"

Without answering, Gard seethed as he returned his belongings to the sack. Not because he thought she had been thieving. He was incensed the old woman had insinuated that he needed to rely on anyone to regain what he'd bled the last twenty years of his life for. He didn't *need* anyone. Especially this girl, who would not leave him in peace. Braelynn was everywhere. All around him. In his thoughts. In his quarters. In his clothes!

These past nights, he had stayed away because he could not trust himself around her. He could smell her even when she was not near. She even invaded his dreams.

And she dared to say that *she* hated *him*. Hate? She did not know the meaning of the word. He lived and thrived on hatred. It fed him. It kept him going. He despised her. He did not want her for anything other than the obvious. He could not wait to be rid of her. The old crone was demented. Her foretelling naught but bunk.

Anger. Hate. That was what he needed to focus on, the constants in his life. The things he could rely on always. He would lie, murder, cheat, steal and apparently rape to regain what was his. He would do anything.

"'Tis none of your concern." He tossed the bag carelessly into his pack and thrust his flagon toward her. "Drink."

Brae wrinkled her nose, not wishing to drink after last eve. She still had an ache in her head. "I would prefer na to. I dinna feel all tha' weel. I can do wit'oot it this time. As a matter o' fact, I—"

"I will find ya somethin' else then." He left, without giving her a chance to enlighten him.

She eyed the dark blue bag sitting atop Marschand's pack. The gem attached to the seal in Marschands's possession was conspicuously like the stone Gaveston had bequeathed into her care.

Could Marschand be the rightful owner that he'd spoken

of?

She quickly laced her borrowed shirt, then tried to tame her hair with her fingers, since her comb was also in her missing carpetbag.

Marschand returned carrying a tray of food and a steaming cup of brew.

"Drink tha' and eat, while I bathe," he ordered.

"Wha' is it?" She sniffed the tankard.

"I dinna ken. Jus' drink it," he said as he pulled his shirt over his head.

His dark hair stuck up in different directions. Brae averted her gaze and took a sip.

"Eeew. Be ye tryin' to poison me? Tha's awful."

"Jus' get it doon, then wash me shoulders." Water splashed softly as Marschand stepped into the tub.

Her eyes widened. "I willna."

"Aye, ya will or I willna pay ye a wage for services. Because ya havena provided any."

"I ne'er agreed ta such duties. Ya brought me along in Hudson's stead ta read your communications. Tha' be all."

"I dinna remember hashin' oot wha' was expected o' ya. Ya promised me the world at Ross. I wish for ya ta wash me, and ya will do so."

"I dinna think tha' was one of Hudson's duties," she argued.

"Hudson had me rear in another way. Ye are no' capable of protectin' me back, so ya will wash it instead."

"I willna." She'd been so concerned about covering her nakedness that she had not replaced the dirk upon her person. When would she learn? She inched toward the sheath.

"Dinna bother. I will be on ya afore ya get there. Jus' do as I tell ya and we can forgo the figh' we both dinna wish ta have." He looked deceptively relaxed and sleepy in the warm water, yet she still tried to gage her chances. Feigning compliance, she took another sip of the nasty brew, then set it down on the table and swiped at the taper stick, knocking it to the floor.

"Oops," she said, bending slowly to retrieve it.

When Brae made the rapid lunge toward the weapon, Marschand hurdled the tub rim, clearing it with the ease of an animal leaping toward its prey.

Before Brae even knew what hit her, she was flat on her back.

The wetness from Marschand's naked body seeped through her clothing, saturating her skin as he stretched her out on the floor. He blinked slowly, meeting her gaze.

"No, apparently, I ne'er will learn," she stated. "Now get off me." She bucked.

"Not until ya agree ta wash me. We can lay here all nigh'." He lowered his lips to her neck, then grazed her with his teeth as he pressed his bare hips against her. "I'm thinkin' I prefer this option ta the washin'."

Brae manoevered her knee between his legs. She drew it up quickly, but he was faster. He shifted his hips away from her but gripped each thigh. His thumbs dug in. She cried out at the pain when he pressed on the sore wound.

He grunted. "We should see ta tha' while the threads be still soft from your soak." Easing his hold on her opposite thigh, he sat up, not the least bit concerned at his nakedness. She used the opportunity to scramble out from under him.

"Ya should have your bath afore the water turns cold," Brae recommended.

"I would have tha' task done first." He rose, in all his splendid glory. Brae focused above his head.

"It has been done, ya dinna have ta worry o'er it," she said quickly.

He narrowed his gaze. "Ya canna put it off, jus' because ya dinna enjoy the pain. Hudson said three days. Come, drink some o' tha'." He pointed to the cup. "And we will take them oot. And then we can both forget the whole miserable matter."

"It has been done. I dinna need tha'."

He sighed in impatience. "Braelynn! I am tired o' fightin' o'er evra little thing wit' ye as weel. Let us be done wit' it." He approached. She shied away.

"'Tis done. See?" She lifted the end of the shirt high enough for him to see but careful not to lift the material any higher than was required.

He blinked. Then snatched her up and drove her onto the bed. He scrambled to his knees, pushing the fabric with his hands. "Who did ya have help ye do tha'?" he asked angrily. "If 'twas Llachlan o' Skye, I vow I will . . ."

"Na one, I had na one tend it," she said in a rush, while swatting at his hands. "I did it meself."

"When?" he snapped.

"Last eve." He had to believe her, no one had entered his quarters while his men stood sentry.

His scowl deepened. "I said I would help."

"I dinna want your help." Brae crossed her arms.

"More like ya fear my touch."

"Ya are forever manhandlin' me."

"The only reason we stopped here was so ya could bathe afore we remove the sutures. We made the detour for nuthin'. Ya have cost us precious travelin' hours." He slid into his trews, then snatched up his shirt, before storming from the room.

Brae took a deep cleansing breath. Dealing with Marschand was exhausting. Brae stretched out on the bed, then covered up.

Half an hour later, Marschand stormed into the room and threw her carpetbag down.

Groggily she raised her head.

"The men are too far gone. I have ye at thank for tha'. Now we will get another late start, for they will all be sufferin' the after effects o' too much drink." He drank a hefty amount of dark liquid from the decanter. "Wha' be wrong wit' ya? Ye look jus' like them."

"Ya have drugged me," she accused sleepily.

"I didna ken wha' was in it. The auld woman said ya would feel no pain. Tha' is wha' I wanted. I didna wish to hurt ya anymore. But 'twas all unnecessary, given that ya went ta such extraordinary lengths so tha' I wouldna touch ya."

He sat on the edge of the bed and stared down at her. Then he eased his hand into her hair, reminding her of the night that he had cared for her at Ross.

"Ya are the devil," she whispered.

"Aye," he murmured, as she closed her eyes for the last time. "Tha's the one thing we agree on."

CHAPTER NINETEEN

Brae woke with a foggy brain but soon became aware that she was not alone. Marschand was curled around her, his face snuggled at the side of her neck, one knee cast across her body, and his large hand covering her breast possessively.

When she tried to ease away, he stiffened, then opened his eyes.

For a moment he and Brae stared at one another.

Methodically he disentangled their limbs.

Brae hopped out of bed. She slipped behind the privacy screen and dressed quickly.

When she had finished, Marschand was already clothed and sitting on the edge of the bed, yet she had not even heard him move.

Easing onto the stool in front of the round looking glass, Brae began to comb out her hair. Through the mirror she made eye contact with Marschand. It felt odd to have him watch her.

The mattress rustled as Marschand gained his feet. His image grew closer in the glass. Without a word, he took hold of the comb. Using tender strokes, he brushed her long tresses. No man had ever done so before. And the woman she had believed was her mother had been so rough Brae had often ended up in tears while she tamed the knots.

Marschand was astonishingly gentle. He was never what she expected. One minute he was hurling her to the ground or bellowing at her. The next he was placid, touching her in ways that no other person had. He was a stranger but had been more intimate with her than people she had known her whole life. This was the man she had dreamed of at Ross. Or had it been a delusion? If he was capable of this gentleness now, while she was fully lucid, mayhap it had been real.

Just as abruptly, he tossed the comb onto the top of the chest. "Bind it," her ordered, then he left the room.

When the squire did not appear, Brae took it upon herself to pack up their belongings. She had taken extra care folding Marschand's garments. But when he returned, he still inspected the bag.

"I didna take anathin'. I ken you'll want ta be leavin'. Are the men set?"

"They are sluggish at best," he said in disgust. "We will wander through the merchants as we wait for them."

Marschand hefted the baggage. Brae followed him down the hall and out of the inn. The sunlight was so bright, she shaded her eyes.

A few of the men wandered about in various states of dress and illness, a number of them standing, some leaning, others still with their heads hung over shrubbery.

"You will be ready within the hour, or I go on without you. And you know what that will necessitate," he told them in no uncertain terms.

Marschand shook his head, then gripped Brae's elbow, and rushed her away.

Waiting until they were out of earshot, she asked, "Wha' does tha' imply?"

His jaw tightened. "What do you think it suggests? Do you believe that I will have them all strung from the nearest tree afore we leave?"

"Nay. But I ken ya weel enough ta realize tha' there will be some kind o' consequence or penalty."

"'Tis as simple as they will not be paid for a job left undone."

She nodded.

They walked slowly past loaded carts and stands. Merchants called out to Marschand. He either ignored them or gave them a black stare.

"I am aware of a vendor just a few steps further who will be of interest to you."

They stepped around a curtain. Brae's breath caught as she stared at stacks of volumes, vellums, and manuscripts. In awe, Brae smiled. "May I look?"

With an imperceptible nod, Marschand agreed.

So that she would not be tempted to touch, Brae clasped her hands behind her.

There were tomes of poetry and sonnets, songs and hymns, prayers and psalms.

"May I assist ya?" the clerk spoke to Marschand, ignoring Brae as her fingers itched to touch the bindings.

"Perhaps," Marschand said in a low voice. "When the lady has made her selection."

The vendor's eyebrows dove. Folks were often surprised that she could read.

"May I touch?" she asked the vendor.

The bookseller started to shake his head, but Gard jingled a cloth bag of coin.

"Of course, please, browse ta yer hearts content, Milady."

Carefully she picked up a volume. "Roman de la Rose."

"Oh. Ah, I do not consider tha' appropriate for the lady, My Lord."

"Oh?" Gard frowned.

"Nay, 'tis a work of . . . experienced entertainment, shall we say. Your lady does not look like one who would enjoy such, uh . . . wickedness."

Brae's cheeks heated, and she replaced the book, then

chose another. "Llyfr Taliesin," she recited.

"Welsh," Marschand said.

"Aye, The Book of Taliesin," the book vendor explained. "Ye would like tha' I believe. 'Tis mostly sonnets and poems. The originals were written in Welsh, but tha' particular volume has been translated many times in many different languages."

She glanced inside the book and then to Gard in disappointment. "'Tis French. Ya would have ta read it ta me. Or teach me French?" she asked hopefully, keeping from the shopkeeper the little-known fact that Gard could not read.

"We've no time for me to teach you the language."

"You could have read it to me in its original state as well," she murmured, recalling the languages he had spoken when they'd first met.

"I have a Gaelic version," the shopkeeper said, while rummaging through a wood crate. "The ink is most like still wet on this one." He laughed at his own jest.

Brae beamed with excitement.

"You surprise me yet again," Marschand spoke in a low voice. "You act as if I were about to give you jewels, not some loosely translated text of some eccentric bard's dreaming."

"The tomes are worth so much more ta me than trinkets. The baubles will ne'er take me ta the places tha' these can."

"Here 'tis." The vendor handed it over. "Be some Arthurian and mythological poems and legends in tha' as weel."

Brae opened it reverently. "Pendragon?" Brae asked in wonder.

"Aye." The bookman winked.

"Do you wish to have it?" Marschand asked.

"Aye, but I'm sure 'tis too much."

"Cost be no concern. How much do you desire for the translation, sir?"

"Well, this be an uncommon tome for which I paid dearly ta have translated."

Gard did not wait for him to name a price but threw the sack of coin at the man. It thumped into his ample chest and he caught it greedily. He emptied the contents into his hand. His eyes widened.

"'Tis enough, I trust," Marschand said.

"Aye, My Lord Marschand," he said in appreciation. "Is there anathin' else I could interest ye in?

"Be there anything in addition befitting the Lady?" His dark eyebrows rose.

"Aye, I will throw in this work of Psalms and hymns. Ya will like tha', Lady Marschand."

She gasped at the man's misguided assumption.

"Wrap them up," Marschand commanded without correcting the mistake.

"Aye, My Lord. With pleasure." He rushed to bind the parcel.

When he was finished, Marschand gathered the bundle and took Brae's arm. They continued to walk the gauntlet of merchants.

"Be there anything else you are in need of, Mistress Galbraith, that you are without?"

She looked toward him astonished.

"We left Ross in a hurry. And your parents were less than hospitable with your belongings, I have noticed. If there is anything you require we will purchase it now. I will not stop again in a village until we reach the border."

"Nay. I thank ya. I am no' lackin' anathin' now tha' ya have been so generous as ta purchase the tomes." She was extremely appreciative of his generosity and relieved to be in the company of the Marschand who was kind.

"When we reach England, I will purchase a new wardrobe for you."

She was delighted at the thought, until he finished his comment.

"You will not be seen in my company wearing *that*."

Discomfited, Brae peered down at herself and thought she was dressed respectably. There were no holes in her dresses or worn patches.

"Even if you are naught but my whore," he finished.

Hot tears of shame threatened. The gentlemanly Marschand had evaporated. Why had she let herself think that of him when she knew better? 'Twas impossible for him to keep the mask of kindness in place.

"Come along. We've wasted enough time here." He strode on ahead. Brae followed at a slower pace, having no desire to walk next to him.

The troops were loaded and ready to leave by the time they returned. Some were mounted, and others were readying their chargers.

Bain prepared Marschand's horse.

"Where is the black little red?" Brae asked, scanning the men for the young squire.

"I dinna ken wha' ya ask?" he replied. "Ya speak riddle."

"Ruadh? Why is he no' preparin' Lord Marschand's mount?"

"Ah, the little whelp drank hisself sick. He's still abed. Marsch be leavin' him behind."

Brae looked around for Marschand but could not find him. "Where be Ruadh? Show him ta me," she implored.

"Wha' fer? He's nuthin but a bloody nuisance, anawho."

Without warning Marschand, seized Bain by the collar. "You will not spew obscenities in the lady's presence again. Now apologize for your ignorance."

"I'm s-sorry!" he choked, as Marschand strangled him with his own shirt.

Though Brae was troubled by Bain's current circumstance, she was more concerned for the lad. She took the opportunity to escape and ran straight for Llachlan.

"Where be the boy? Do ya ken? Ruadh?"

"In the stable. But ya dinna want ta see him, Braelynn. He be in a mess."

"I dinna care. Please. He shouldna be alone."

Llachlan sighed, hanging his head. "Come."

He led her to the dimly lit paddock. It smelled of moldy straw and vomit. The boy was curled up in a ball, shivering, surrounded by puddles of his own filth.

"Oh, dear God," she exclaimed. "How could the lot of you let him be like this? Do none o' ya watch over him? How could ya let him drink such vast amounts? He's just a child."

Brae knelt next to him. "Oh, Dubhán, wha' have ya done ta yerself?" She placed her hand to his head—he was sweaty in spite of the quivering.

The child snarled, then gripped his head. He cringed as silent tears fell down his temples. "I am Ruadh," he corrected in a whisper. "No' Dubhán!"

"Ye are black, Dubhán, no' red, and I believe I can call ye anathin' I want at this particular moment and ya canna contest it." She looked to Llachlan. "Ya will find me a bucket o' water, a blanket and some fresh clothin' fer the lad."

"Aye, Mistress."

"And ye, young Dubhán, are goin' ta get a lecture tha' will blister your ears when ya are feelin' better."

"I dinna have ta listen ta ye. Ye are nuthin' but the master's whore and I willna . . ."

Cutting off his rant, Brae dragged him by the ankles out of the mucky stall that he'd fallen into. He howled, then grabbed his aching head.

"First o' all, I told ya ne'er ta call me tha' again. Would ya like a reminder o' tha'?" She tapped her thigh where Marschand's dagger was housed.

"I dinna want anathin' from ye," he protested.

"Well, ya dinna have a choice. I am goin' ta help ye whether ya want it or no. Do ya wanna be left behind?"

"Left behind?" He cracked one eye.

"Aye, Marschand be threatenin' ta leave ya if ya are no' ready. Now come, let me help ya get cleaned up."

"Bah, 'tis probably better off. Let him leave me. He doesna care if I am aroond anawho."

"Now, Dubhán, tha's jus' Lord Marschand's way. He doesna care aboot anathin' save his own agenda. But I dinna believe tha' he doesna want ya around. He doesna care if *I* am here. But ye are a part o' his regiment and have jus' as much ta do wit' the runnin' o' it as anaone else. Your duties ta your Lord are verra important. Ya have a coveted position tha' other boys your age would envy greatly. So ya need ta hurry afore ya lose tha'."

"Let him leave me. I dinna care. I hate his innards!" he blustered.

"You do, do you?" Marschand's deep voice interrupted their banter.

Simultaneously, Ruadh gasped, and Brae jumped at Marschand's silent appearance.

Llach entered with the bucket of water and blanket Brae had requested. He set it down near the youngster. Brae wet a cloth and tried to clean Ruadh's face.

Both the Lord and the squire erupted.

"What do you think you are doing?" Marschand barked.

"Dinna touch me!" Ruadh gritted his teeth as Brae mopped his sweaty brow.

"I'm tryin' ta get this child cleaned up so tha' he may accompany us on the rest o' our journey," Brae said.

"Leave him! He knows what's expected of him, and if he is not prepared to leave, he will be left behind. It's quite simple."

Marschand took Brae by the elbow and forcibly assisted her to her feet. "You will not fight me on this, Mistress Galbraith, or you *will both* regret it."

Marschand turned her toward the exit, then dragged her from the stabling.

Frantic, Brae glanced over her shoulder at Llachlan.

His mouth hardened and he shook his head almost imperceptively. She accepted it for the warning it was but it didn't stop her.

She waited until she and Marschand were far enough away from all the men. "Ya canna leave tha' child here by himself." She attempted to snatch her arm from his bruising grasp, but he held strong. "He was obviously put inta your care by his sire for a reason. Dinna shame the man's memory or your promise ta him by leavin' the boy ta fend for himself, alone, with na coin and na home and na one to look after him. Anathin' could befall him if we leave him."

"You are completely unaware of the situation, and I *can*, and as you know, *will* do whatever I please."

"Please dinna leave him," she begged.

"He is not ready to depart, and I am not delaying one more moment. You have both held me up. If I didn't need you, I would leave you behind as well. *You* could look after him. It sounded as if he would appreciate that," he said sarcastically.

"Please, Lord Marschand." She tried to appeal to him on an authoritative level. "Wha' are ya teachin' him now? Ya speak of loyalty and dependability when ya take people inta your employ." She remembered what he'd said to her father and Callum at the keep. "What of the men who watch your back? Would ya treat them this way and then expect them ta be as devoted, when ya would so easily turn on them?"

He snorted. "He is my squire, not my second nor a soldier. He be of no importance. I could have him replaced before we leave here, perhaps by one that does not hate my innards."

"Find me one person tha' has spent e'en one hour in your company tha' doesna hate your innards," she retorted.

The corner of his mouth twitched. "Why Braelynn, do you hate my innards as well?"

"I think ya have two different people livin' inside ya. Ya are part human, part demon, and the longer the demon rules the more ya become it." She shook her head. "Ya dinna wish ta be it, surely."

"I think you have been reading too many tales," he retorted. "You live too long in another's mind, living their ideas and dreams. You lose your own self in fiction. I am not a demon. I am not the devil. I am just a man." He pulled her against him.

The action no longer scared her. She was acutely aware of every solid nuance of his body. "And ya have lived too long seeking retribution," she said. "Letting the lust for revenge kill evrathin' in ya tha' be human."

"You know nothing of what I seek. You know nothing of my revenge. And you know naught of what I may have been afore. Perhaps I have always been this way."

"I dinna believe tha', or the other side of ya tha' I have witnessed wouldna be there. Ya would be cruel all o' the time. The child only feels the same way as me. He only hates ya because ya abuse him."

Llachlan cleared his throat.

Marschand kept a firm grip on her but flicked a glare at Llach.

"If 'twould no' displease ya," Llach hedged. "I will stay wit' the boy this day and we will meet up wit' ye on the morrow when he is weel enough ta travel."

Marschand swung his irritated gaze to Brae. "Would *that* please you, *Milady*?" he drawled.

"Will ya allow their return wit'oot repercussion?" she asked, boldly.

"Aye," he said, but bared his teeth.

"And can I take tha' *aye* as your solemn word. Given that the las' time I extracted such a promise, ya said ya migh' punish him regardless o' wha' ya vowed, if ya saw so fit?"

His gaze bore into her, but the clarification did not come.

Brae bowed her head. "'Twould please me, My Lord," she acquiesced in a soft voice.

He released her so abruptly she staggered to keep her balance.

"Mount," he barked. The men scurried to obey.

"Thank ya, Llachlan. Ya are a good man." She patted his chest in passing as she hurried to Marschand's side.

Marschand gripped her hips. She inhaled as she prepared to be lifted onto the awaiting horse, but his mouth found her ear. She froze. "The child has every right to hate me. I be the one who murdered his sire." And with that unexpected confession ringing in her ear, he lifted her onto the horse, then bounded up behind.

CHAPTER TWENTY

They rode in silence until finally he said, "You wished to know more about me, Mistress Galbraith. Now do you wish that you did not? You have been unusually quiet."

Her thoughts went in every direction. There must be some explanation. 'Twas self-defense, an accident, some kind of mishap. The man was abusive, and Marschand saved the boy from him. But even that explanation did not ring true. She had been witness to Marschand's mistreatment of the boy.

"I think ya try to scare me, as ya frequently do. The big bad murderin, rapin', siege-wagin', child abusin' devil, or wha'e'er else ya may be. But *I* remember ya takin' care o' me."

"You do not remember me taking care of you, for if you did, you would not doubt what I tell you. I am not trying to scare you. I am what I am—all the things you have just described, and the ones that you have not as yet recalled."

"Why are you speaking English to me now?"

"I am what I am," he said with a shrug.

"Ya are no' English, and ya will ne'er convince me ya are. Ya play games."

"None of this is a game," he said in a grave tone. "Not to me."

The sound of horses' hooves bearing down on them at a great rate of speed sent Marschand into a defensive stance. He wrapped himself around Brae as the men closed in around their leader.

215

"At ease. 'Tis only Aidean Ferguson."

Marschand eased away from Brae and turned slightly to glance over his shoulder.

Breathing heavily from a hard ride, Ferguson pulled level. "I talked ta Llach, he said ya werena far. I rode like hell to catch up."

"You will mind your mouth around the lady."

"Aye, My Lord. My apologies, Mistress. Lord Grainger bid me catch-up to ya and give ya the news. Robbie Cowan left camp. We dinna ken where he went."

"Perhaps he finally ran out of lives," Marschand replied, coldly. "Any one of us has wanted to slit his throat on any given day."

"We thought tha' at first as weel. There is na body and his belongings are gone. He's gone off on his own, Sir. Grainger wanted ya ta ken so tha' ye could be more vigilant, especially wit' Mistress Galbraith wit' ye."

"And why would that make me extra vigilant?" Gard's gaze narrowed.

"Cowan attacked another girl," he said grimly.

"Nothing new there," Marschand responded, matter-of-factly.

"The lass said he'd been callin' her Braelynn, the whole time he ravaged her. He was brutal this time. More than e'er. 'Twas horrible ta see her like tha'. There were excessive amounts o' blood smeared all o'er her legs. She looked jus' like Miss Galbraith did when ye attacked her."

Brae trembled. Marschand eased his arms around her.

"She bled ta death, Sir."

"That's enough, Ferguson." He held Brae tighter to him. "You may either continue on with us or return to Ross."

"I have a written message for ya from Lord Grainger. He would like me to return if ya have a communication in answer."

Marschand took the note, tucking it into his shirt.

"Ride with us then until we get to where we will stop for the night. I will read the missive then and decide if there will be a response."

"Wait," Brae called to Ferguson as he turned his horse to ride with the other men. "Who was it? The lass?" She had the most horrible feeling it was Bronwyn, and prayed it was not. Then she sent up a second prayer in repentance, as she'd just condemned some other poor soul if 'twas not. She pleaded one extra blessing for the sainted Llachlan.

"I dinna ken her. She was new ta our camp. Perhaps she'd joined us since we came ta Ross. I didna ken her name. Ya may have kenned her from your town folk." Brae sighed in relief that it was not Bronny. She shivered again imagining the woman being brutalized and called by her name.

Marschand dismissed him with a nod and Ferguson fell in with the other men.

"Who was in charge of the look out?" Marschand demanded. "Ferg was down on us before we knew. We would be dead if it had been an enemy. You will be more alert and more cautious or there will be repercussions. You are not new at this. I will not tolerate such incompetence."

"Aye, Lord Marschand," the men said in unison.

"Llach was ta be watch this day. I guess we didna think ta appoint someone else in his stead, when he volunteered ta stay with Ruadh."

"You must be better than that." He kicked his horse into a trot. "*I* need to be better than that," he said, more to himself than to anyone else.

He was incredibly hard on himself, taking all failures or lessons as a personal affront. In comfort, Brae wound her hand around his. His nostrils flared, but he did not push her away.

Marschand set a hectic pace. They rode hard, even eating

dry bread in the saddle.

Brae worried over Llach and Dubhán. How would they ever catch up?

Ever since Ferguson had joined, them Marschand had been watchful, more than usual. His body was rigid with tension. He had not spoken in hours.

Every bone in Brae's body ached, every muscle screamed for relief. Tired of holding up her own head, she leaned into Marschand, closed her eyes and dozed.

Much later, the temperature plummeted. Even with her eyes closed and the heat of the sun still warming her body, she sensed it. "Ya may wanta think aboot findin' a place ta set up camp," she murmured. "A storm be brewin'."

"And what makes you think so. The sun be warm. The sky blue. Not a cloud to be seen?"

"Ya have been away from the Highlands too long then, if ya canna detect the gale tha' comes this way. Did ya no' just feel the clime change? Our travel on the morrow will be slow, if at'all."

"Perhaps we do not have such storms in France," he replied, expressionless.

"Ya are no' French. But if ya dinna wish ta listen ta me ya will be settin' up camp in a torrent."

"'Tis why I have been pushing so hard this day. I wish to get to the protection of Beinn Nibheis."
"The Ben at Lochaber?" Brae straightened so fast she almost clipped him under the chin.

"Aye." Gard was ever surprised by Braelynn's knowledge, from her understanding of the political mood to her ability to read and write, and for one who had never been beyond her own little shire, she knew her geography. Her mind's bounds seemed limitless. He had never met a woman as apprized of so many different topics as she. *Are most women this intelligent?* Generally, he did not spend much time in their company to know. Nor had he wanted to.

"'Tis no' the weather worse near the Ben?" she asked.

"Aye, sometimes it can be, but where I take you affords us much protection from the elements. The Ben, as you call it, links to Càrn Mòr Dearg, creating dual U-shaped valleys. We will be safe and dry there."

"Valleys? Are ya sure ya wish ta be down low?" She peered up at him, then skyward.

"Aye, the caves and overhangs will protect us if the wind decides to buffet. We will not get swamped."

It was astounding. They were carrying on a mature conversation without sparks flying around them — with her spitting venom and him losing control. In addition, he was quite enjoying the discussion and the feel of her in his arms. She leaned against him like he was an overstuffed armchair in some fine lady's parlor. Her legs dangled limply over the sides of the horse in a trusting and comfortable posture.

Spontaneously, he ran his lips across the top of her hair. He had no idea what compelled him. He just did it.

Brae cocked her head and stared at him in surprise, but her gaze was soft. "Have ya just admitted ta me tha' ya sprouted from these verra Highlands, *Monsieur* Marschand?" She smiled teasing.

The corner of his mouth quirked in response. "I confess ta nuthin', *cailin*," he murmured.

She reached out and smoothed her thumb over his bottom lip. "Ya be learnin', Gard," she whispered.

The sound of his given name coming from her lips did things to him. A strange and sudden sense of loss flooded him, knowing their time was drawing to a close.

Impulsively, he curled his hand around the back of her

neck, raising her head as he lowered his. Her gaze darted around his face before he covered her parted lips.

Thunder cracked above their heads, jarring them.

Carelessly, Gard dropped her upturned chin as he raised his other hand. "Make all haste, men!" He kicked his horse into a sprint. The rumble of hooves beating the dry ground filled the air as they raced toward the Ben.

Once there, Gard left Brae in the mouth of a deep cave as he helped erect the tents. They did not raise the normal amount. Most of the men, and the scant number of women, took cover under the cavernous overhangs.

By the time he entered the cave, he was soaked through. After building up a fire in the arch, he stripped off his wet clothes, leaving only his tight-fitting trews.

Brae gathered his garments as he dropped them and laid them out to dry.

One of the men set a grate laden with skinned hare over the flames. The smell of cooking meat filled the cavern making Gard's mouth water.

Gard handed Brae the missive from Hudson, then poured them each a dram. He sat in front of the fire. Brae settled at his side. "Are you hungered?" he asked.

"Aye. Ravenous."

Gard turned the meat. "Decipher the message."

With great care, she unrolled it. "'Tis again the seal o' the Guardians," she said. "Ya got it wet," she accused, when he did not respond.

He sent her an intolerant frown. "'Tis rainin'," he stated.

She giggled. "I warned ya 'twould."

"Ya are fortunate it did," he said and took a sip of ale.

"Oh? Why is tha'?"

"Ye left me without a squire. I had every intention of inflicting *his* duties on you."

"Ya did?" Her head twitched.

"Aye."

"Wha' made ya change your mind?"

"The rain. I did not want you out in the cold."

She raised an eyebrow, in disbelief, he was certain. "How *gallant.*"

And she was right. Chivalrous, he was not. "All my luck, you would become ill, and I would be forced to care for you."

"'Tisna *my* fault tha' Dubhán isna wit' us," she disputed.

"*Dubhán?* Ye are now calling him Dubhán?" His lips tightened as he assessed her. "Black," he translated.

"Aye. Ruadh be no' appropriate. For one, he is clearly dark, hence the Dubhán. As weel his father was red, he is no'. And he be no' his father. He deserves his own identity."

"Thank the good Lord, he is not his father. Nevertheless, it is your fault that *Dubhán* is not with us."

Green eyes blazing, she rounded on him. "Ya were the one tha' had evra intention of leavin' him behind. How is tha' my fault? You flipped him the coin and bade him *behave.* Tha' was your permission in his eyes ta do as the full-size lads were doin'. Ya kenned he would. And the men allowed him ta get inta tha' condition in the first. Mayhap ya even contrived the whole of it in the hopes tha' he would get so soused tha' he would be in no condition ta accompany us, and *then* he wouldna longer be your responsibility. Bein' tha' yor rules be so rigid."

"And how would that benefit me? I would be out a squire, as I am this evening, having to tend my own horse."

"Ya said ya could replace him afore we left. Again, how is tha' my mistake?" she argued.

"But you are the one who requested both, your lovelorn Llachlan from Skye, and your newly dubbed, Dubhán, be absolved of any punishment if they were to rejoin us. I do not need two."

She threw her hands up. "Oh, ya are the most exasperatin' man I've e'er met."

"I was thinking the same of you," he retorted.

She snorted. "*I* am the most exasperatin' man ya have e'er met?"

Not about to argue the fact—the exasperating, part at least—he nodded "Aye. Ya are. Now translate."

Brae angled the missive toward the light of the fire and began, *"My Dearest Friend and Comrade Gard . . ."*

"It doesna say tha'," he growled.

"It doesna?" she repeated, with a swagger.

Oh, she was going to make sport.

"Hudson does not begin his missives in that way."

"Ya are a'right. It starts, *My Dearest Friend and Comrade Gard and the lovely Mistress Galbraith.*"

"Ye lie and ya will read it properly or suffer the consequences."

"Are ya truly threatenin the eyes tha' read to ya?"

"Brae-*Lynn*," he enunciated slowly, then gritted his teeth.

"A'righ'. But it really does commence with *My Dearest Friend and Comrade Gard, Vigorous soldier and noble friend, As you know I have sent young Aidean Ferguson to inform you of Robbie Cowan's latest calamity.*"

"Calamity. I would refer to it as murder," Gard interjected.

"Aye," Brae agreed, then read on. *"The strangeness with which the poor departed soul retold of his rantings before she passed led me to fear for Mistress Galbraith. I believe Cowan has followed you. Stay vigilant and alert, as I know you will. I have alerted the proper authorities as to this newest development and await their judgment."*

Brae turned to him and opened her mouth. But before she could bombard him with questions, he had no intention of answering, Gard held up his hand cutting her off. "Dinna ask. Ya ken I willna tell ya."

With a sigh, she continued, *"I also would inform you, word has reached us that the Plantaganet usurper — and if this message is intercepted — long live the king"*.

Brae frowned and blinked rapidly several times.

"You are unfamiliar with his sense of humor." Gard supplied. "Continue." He pointed.

"I would inform you, word has reached us that the Plantaganet usurper, has stayed to the North and has made no move to return to London as of the present, while his poor departed sire's body, heads south toward Westminster despite his dying wishes detailing of his heart to the Holy Land and his bones to be carried in his ongoing quest against Scotia. You may quit gritting your teeth now, Gard."

Gard glared at Brae wondering again if she was reading the exact text or adding her own commentary.

"'Tis wha' he writes, no' me," she explained. "Hudson kens ya too weel." She shrugged, then persisted. *"It has also been rumored that the Successor has by now sent for the Gasconian Knight to be reinstated. And yes, I feel your revulsion."*

Anger roiled inside Gard.

Brae narrowed her gaze. "Wha' be revoltin'? And who be the Gascon Knight he refers ta?"

In frustration — not necessarily aimed at Brae — Gard slammed his fist into his open palm.

Smartly, Brae persevered, *"You may slow your rapid progress, my friend. At this rate, you will reach London afore him. I am also in need to inform you that several of the good citizens of Ross-shire have decided to strike out on their own and seek opportunities and protection with other clans. Hugh and I are not in agreement with this course of action, but he is the commander in this undertaking in your stead, or so he would wish to remind me, and he has granted them leave, which I think may come back to haunt him, and or you, and us. You would be happy in the knowledge that we did come to blows over this matter and blood was spilled on both parts. With bated breath I await your instruc-*

tion if you so intend it. Yours, in faithful service to the cause. JHG, EOR, Sons of the G Of S."

Even after Brae had finished, her attention remained fixed on the missive. It raised his suspicions, particularly after her threat to keep things from him.

"Is there more?" he prompted.

"Nay."

"I do not believe you."

"There isna' more for ye," she clarified.

"You will share it, regardless," he commanded.

"He sends his best wishes tha' I be endurin' this . . . trip," she explained.

"Read it!" He turned the rabbit yet again, eliciting a loud growl from her empty belly. "You will read it true, or you will not eat," he threatened.

"Dear Mistress Galbraith. I hope this message finds you whole and hale. I also share in your pain, Braelynn, I am truly aware how complicated and wretched your companion can be. But try as you may not to annoy him. He is of shoddier quality when angered. All sympathies and God Speed, Mistress."

Gard sighed and rolled his eyes toward the damp rock above.

"I dinna why he feels the need ta inform me o' this o'er and o'er. I am well aware o' your dual personalities."

"Aye, hot and cold. That be me," he muttered. "Is that all?"

"Just the normal farewell. But not signed Sons of the Guardians for me," she added.

Once more her way of reckoning astounded him.

"Are ye each born the son of a Guardian?" she asked, straightforward.

"You will heed Hudson's warning, Mistress," Gard reiterated.

Heedless of caution, Brae continued on her ever-present quest for information. "You, Lord Grainger and Lord Chamberlain, all sons of, hence your righ' ta use the Guardian's seal? Are they Scot as weel—Hudson and Hugh—pretendin' not ta be? As do you?"

Removing the meat from the skewer, Gard began to pick it apart, stuffing large pieces into his mouth, all the while keeping eye contact with her.

Brae licked her lips.

Good. He'd finally made his point. He would not share information or the food if she did not cease her questioning.

"Do ya wish ta reply?" Brae asked.

"Nay. I have nothing new to impart. You may destroy the missive."

Her eyes widened. But at his nod, she tossed it into the fire.

"Are you finished interrogating me?" he asked, at length.

"Aye."

He tore off a piece of meat, then handed it to her.

"For the now," she said as she placed the morsel into her mouth. "Oh, tha' is good." She closed her eyes, savoring the meat.

"You know what troubles me?" Gard asked, suddenly, without thinking.

Damn her! He could blame her for this as well. He had never before been compelled to discuss his thoughts with anyone but Hudson.

Ya have na one save Hudson who recognizes the real you. Ya canna confide or consider a problem wit' anaone, or simply get a fresh perspective.

Though her expression turned to one of surprise, she responded in an even manner. "Nay, wha' plagues ya?"

"Hudson sent you on this journey in his stead because he could not, or so he led me to believe, he was unable to read or scribe because of the injury to his eyes, yet he has written this message." His anger grew as he reasoned it out. Could his friend have set him up? Sent the girl with him just to drive him insane and execute some perverse joke on him?

"Naw," she said, in a dismissive tone. "Hudson didna scribe tha'."

"How do you know?"

"I recognize the writer's cursive. 'Tis by the vicar's hand tha' missive comes."

He accepted this and calmed somewhat. "'Tis not prudent on either of our parts. Hudson or myself. We have involved too many outsiders into our fold. 'Tis dangerous."

"The vicar willna break his vows o' confidence. I ken o' his discretion." She attempted to ease his concerns.

"And what of you?" He turned his gaze on her. "Do you know what happens to those who glean too much valuable information, Mistress Galbraith? Even inadvertently? Sooner or later they run out of usefulness and since they possess so much important knowledge that may be harmful to another, they need be silenced. Do you appreciate what I tell you?"

"Aye. But there isna way for me not ta learn things as long as I am forced to cipher your communications."

"'Tis unavoidable. But you will not question me. You interpret entirely too much with your over-clever mind. Do not let that be your ruin, Mistress."

"None o' this was o' my chosin'. Neither me ruin, or ta be in your service."

"And because of that you may feel in time that retribution is your only recourse."

"Ya think I will use wha' I learn against ya?" She recoiled.

"Aye. Ya will." Of that he had no doubt.

"And whom will I use this ta gain favor with, and exact my revenge on ya?"

"You will learn that in time. But I will not permit you to gain anyone's favor. You are mine for the now, and you will remain loyal to me. And as for revenge, you will gain yours when I achieve mine."

He ripped off another piece of meat and handed it to her.

"Eat, drink and get ye ta bed, Mistress Galbraith." He peered out unseeing, into the darkness as the rain pounded down. "I believe travel on the morrow will be arduous."

During the night Gard had taken up a corner of the blanket. The fire had died down and the dampness seeping from the cold stone along with the rain prompted Brae to seek his body heat.

Sometime later, Brae awoke in his arms, her head on his chest.

Gard stirred beside her.

Brae could not stop thinking about their almost kiss while atop his horse, or how much she wanted Gard's firm lips on hers again.

The touch of his bare skin under her cheek did crazy things to her. What would he do if she pressed her mouth to his warm skin? Would he pounce? Or would he be the tolerant Marschand? She could never be sure. She could not risk her curiosity getting her into trouble again. Yet she sat up slowly, pulling the blanket to her chest as she did. The covers slipped, baring Gard's chest.

His dark intense gaze followed her every move, perhaps warily so. He remained eerily motionless, animal-like in his stillness.

Tentatively, Brae reached out and skimmed her hand over his stomach. The muscles there contracted.

Gaining confidence when he did not immediately snap, she continued a cursory exploration over his chest, tangling with the dark coarse hair sprinkled over his sternum and well-defined pectorals.

Finally, her fingertips brushed the beard covering his strong chin. Her fingers felt cool when she touched his warm bottom lip.

With lightening speed, Gard captured her wrist, but she did not flinch. She'd braced for some sort of reaction.

His dark eyes glittered, dangerously.

Brae caught her lip between her teeth, waiting. Goosebumps erupted all over her body.

But to her disappointment, he shifted away, removing himself from their pallet. He grabbed a dry shirt and slipped it on before disappearing into the pre-dawn light.

Brae held her tears. She wondered if she would ever know what it was like to be with a man. Callum was gone and now married to her best friend. She would never know him in that way.

Marschand did not want her, for any length of time, or without brutality. At some point, he would probably use her as he did the other women, but it would not be what she wanted.

What do I want?

Surely not Gard Marschand. Aghast at the course her thoughts had taken, Brae shook her head.

He was a horrible man.

How could she let herself think of lying with him? What was wrong with her? What inside her had changed that she could even consider such a thing?

Brae wanted a husband to love and to love her in return—the opposite of what her parents had—and she'd thought with Callum she could achieve it. They'd loved each other, or so she'd thought. But how could either of them have turned so easily to others if that was the case—Callum to Katie and Brae to the devil.

Brae covered her face with her hands. "Ye've gone and lost yer mind," she mumbled. That was it, all the things that had befallen her had addled her brain. She did not wish to lay with a man like Marschand.

"Nay, of course, not," she dismissed.

But as she dressed, she could not keep her mind from straying to the devil in Gard's clothing.

CHAPTER TWENTY-ONE

A constant drizzle made travel miserable. Even with his cloak surrounding them, both Gard and Braelynn were saturated to the skin.

Gard had sent Ferguson back to Ross without a response to Hudson's message. Although he did rather strongly advise Hudson that any future correspondence should not include or refer to Miss Galbraith.

Gard had not shared with Brae the other bit of news that Ferguson had divulged. Something Hudson had consciously omitted from the missive. It would seem the young woman Robbie Cowan used in Brae's stead, was not the only murder Cowan perpetrated before he had departed Ross-shire. Brae would be devastated to learn Robbie had also exacted his revenge on auld Myrtle for wounding him at the holding, while protecting Brae. His vengeance—blades through the center of each of her hands and feet, left to bleed out and die alone, pinned to the dirt floor in her own home.

If he had anything to say about it, Brae would never learn of this.

"Why are ya pushin' so hard?" Brae asked. "Accordin' ta Hudson's correspondence, their new king is no' even in residence yet, if tha' be where we go. Why canna we reside at an inn or have stayed in the caves while the heavens open up?"

"You will not question me," Gard responded.

She sighed while trying to burrow further under his cape.

"Will ya cease your constant thrashin' and movin' against

me. Or ya are goin' ta end up on your back," he warned.

She settled against him, her lush bottom perched against his hardness. Though she'd stopped squirming, it gave him little comfort.

"Do ya think tha' Llach and Dubhán will be a'righ' ridin' just the two o' 'em?"

"Ye fret over things that are not your concern. Though your incessant worry over Llachlan of Skye is quite thoughtful. His pretty face has made a fair impression on you. What *would* his sweetheart think of your attraction to her lover?"

She pulled her head from his cloak and turned to look him in the face. "My feelin' for . . . Oh! Ya think jus' because I hold concern for him and Dubhán tha' it mus' be a result o' nefarious feelin's? I will admit he isna bad ta look upon, but he isna . . . y . . . uh . . ." she sputtered, "as fine as . . . er . . . Callum."

A pretty blush colored her cheeks, making him wonder what she had been about to say.

"He looks just like MacCrae, now that you point it out. Is that your fascination then?"

"I am na fascinated. And wha' concern be it o' yours? Are ya next goin' ta accuse me o' havin' feelin's for the black ya call red?"

"Now he be better looking than either of them, if you ask me."

"Na one did. And why do ya think tha'? Because he is dark like you?"

"O' course," he boasted.

"Ya are insane as well as exasperatin'." She settled back down under his coat. "And wet," she grumbled.

Marschand chuckled. Several of his men glanced over at him in a peculiar manner—perhaps not used to his amusement.

231

Llachlan and Dubhán caught up the next day.

Brae was delighted. Marschand on the other hand, was as usual abrupt with the pair of them, giving no indication that he was pleased by their safe return.

The following sennight consisted of the same pattern— traveling, stopping, setting up camp, repeat. Often, when Marschand was not maintaining a blistering pace, he allowed Brae the small freedom to walk about on her own. Today she was especially thankful for the respite, as she and Marschand had been sparring all morning.

As she strolled among the men on horseback, her thoughts, as always, turned to *him*. Since they had camped in the caves of Beinn Nibheis, Marschand had taken to sleeping next to Brae every night. They often awoke limbs entangled and in some painful state of unrequited arousal. Marschand inevitably deserted her at that point, leaving her to wallow in confusion.

Did he seek out one of the other women? The idea made her chest ache. Yet they were nothing to one another. She had to keep reminding herself of all the reasons she was supposed to hate him.

It was another drizzly day, which only added to her melancholy.

When the rain eased, Marschand called a halt to the procession. They paused to eat and stretch.

Brae wanted to be alone. She missed her moor at home in Ross. What she wouldn't give to get lost in the heather. She'd taken for granted the time she had been free to do as she pleased.

Dubhán handed her an apple. "Thank ya," she croaked, trying to hide her tears.

"Wha' is wrong wit' ye?" he snapped. "Be ye ailin'?"

"Nay."

"Gud, cause I willna tend ye if ye be sick. Tha' be no' my chore. And I dinna owe ye fer lookin' after me when I was ailin'."

"Nay, ye dinna. Ya owe Llach," she pointed out.

He scrunched up his face, then left her.

Brae sat at the edge of the pond.

"Did I hear me name?" Llach dropped beside her. He bent his knee, placing his arm over it in an outwardly casual stance. "Are ya arigh', Braelynn?" he asked with concern, but she could not handle his kindness. 'Twould only make things worse.

"Aye, I'm fine. Ye did hear your name. 'Twould seem Dubhán is most grateful for your assistance."

Llach snorted. "I dinna think *Dubhán*" — he smirked at her nickname for the boy — "be capable o' gratitude."

"Humpf," she scoffed. "I am more and more inclined ta believe Marschand be his sire."

"The lad woulda been better off if tha' were the case."

Brae frowned, surprised, what with Llach and Marschand's tenuous rapport.

"Believe it or no', Braelynn, there are worse men than Marschand."

As if he could sense they were speaking of him, Marschand appeared. He glowered at Llach until he stood, ready to take his leave. "Mistress." Llachlan nodded formally as he turned. "Lord Marschand."

Without acknowledging Llachlan, Marschand sat next to Brae.

At the end of her patience, Brae hung her head. "Can ye no' leave me in peace for two moments?"

"I often think the same of you." He looked out over the greenish water.

"I get it, ye dinna wish ta be in my company ana more than I yours," Brae snapped.

"Ye seem particularly *prickly* this day," he chided. "What be your burden?"

Unable to control herself, Brae burst into tears.

His eyes widened. "Ye are especially weepy this day also, even for you."

"I dinna cry in front o' ya," she contested.

"Nay, you weep into my chest when you believe me to be asleep," he said.

She crossed her arms. "I dinna."

He sighed and stood, then extended his hand. "Come. Walk wit' me."

Against her better judgment, she took it. He helped her rise. Just as quickly, he released her when she fell in beside him.

Marschand led her into the forest. Normally when he took her into the trees, it was not a good outcome.

They walked silently until they were out of earshot from the men.

"You will tell me why you are so inclement this day," he ordered.

"'Tis the weather," she replied. "Makes one gloomy."

"It has eased. Now you will quit your crying."

"O' course. 'Tis jus' tha' simple," she mocked.

"Now you will concentrate on your anger and hatred for me and cease your sniveling."

"Tha' I could do. I've an over abundance o' tha'."

"Excellent. I canna abide your tears."

To her utter horror, the small admission made the sorrow more acute.

He stopped walking, then turned to face her, taking her by the shoulders. "You will tell me what is troubling you and I will fix it."

"Ya canna fix it."

"Wha' be wrong, Braelynn?" The brogue nagged at her.

"Perhaps I miss me home and me friends . . . my sire. Can ya fix tha'?"

"I dinna believe tha'. Ya will tell me the truth." His dark gaze bore into her. "More like ya miss your old tomes and your moor." He hitched up her chin. He slid his thumb over her wet cheek. "Ya will tell me."

Fresh tears overflowed her lashes.

"Dh'innis mi." *Tell me.*

"Today was ta be me weddin' day," she confessed.

His lips tightened, his pupils dilated. "And wha' aboot tha' be makin' ya sad? Ya should be thankin' God, *as well as me*," —his voice rose— "tha' ya were saved from marryin' a man o' such faithlessness. Ya should be angry wit' him for betrayin' ya so easily. Not mournin' this day as a loss."

Her lips twisted. "I dinna ken wha' me problem be. I can see his side, though. I am na sure tha' I would want him now tha' I ken he has been wit' Katie."

His forehead wrinkled. "'Tis different for a man."

"But why? Why is it tha' it is widely accepted men do as they please, but when a wife strays she is a whore or she is punished or killed for it? I dinna see tha' as a'right. I wouldna like my man ta be faithless."

"But ya would be unable ta stop it as weel. Are ya now thinkin' tha' he woulda stepped oot on ye as weel? In time."

"Aye. I guess I am wonderin' aboot tha'. But mayhap therein lies me problem this day. It willna be any different wit' anaone else. And the longer I stay wit' ya, the less chance I have o' e'er kennin' wha' a decent marriage woulda been for me. I willna manage a good man. All the things I yearned for are no longer within me reach. I wanted love. And wha' if I ne'er ken wha' tha's like? I want tha'."

He mopped her face. "I will make it righ', Braelynn. I will make it up ta ya. When this be all o'er, I promise ya, I will provide ya wit' wha'e'er ya require ta make ya happy."

She searched his gaze and smiled softly. "I almost believe ya."

"Trus' me this once, Braelynn."

She wanted to, but he'd proved to her time and again that he was more dangerous when she let herself do that. She nodded slightly to make him believe she had accepted his vow.

After wiping her cheeks one last time, they started toward the others.

Brae touched his arm. "Can I ask ya somethin'?"

His jaw tightened. "Ya ken me weel enough by now ta ken I might' no' answer."

"Aye, but ya ken me weel enough ta ken by now tha' I will ask ya anyhow." She stopped, making him turn to look down at her. "Wha' would ye have done? In Callum's stead?"

She could see him struggling as he thought.

"If 'twas you . . ." Gard's eyebrows knitted. "And I were he . . ."

Anger roiled. He'd thought he had visited the depths of which his anger could reach, but for some reason the very thought of another man touching Brae made him see the blackness within him more vividly than his need to reclaim his birthright. "I would have killed the bastard wit' me bare hands."

Her eyes widened. "I expect nothin' less than your violence and rashness. But if it had been your woman who had been attacked, after ya had made short work o' the villain, wha' would ya have done wit' her?"

He could not hold her gaze.

"Would ya have left her? Or would ya have in time accepted tha' it wasna her fault? Would ya have been able to overcome it and return ta her bed?"

He shook his head. "I dinna ken. I dinna ken wha' I would . . . I have ne'er felt tha' strongly aboot a woman afore ta care if she'd been violated. Or ta care how many beds she'd been in."

Sadness clouded her expression. She nodded and turned to meet the others.

Yet Gard did not move, his thoughts in turmoil, not only from her question but from the depth with which she had made him feel. He did not want to feel, nor could he afford to. This was never in his plans. He needed to be rid of her and quickly.

"Lord Marschand!"

The call snapped him from his reverie.

The rain had ceased, and if he were not mistaken, the afternoon would bring intermittent bursts of sunshine.

Brae stood beside his charger, feeding the remnants of an apple to the animal. It wasn't the first time he'd caught her doing so.

Gard prepared to mount. He spanned Brae's tiny waist. As was their habit, she positioned her hands atop his, and poised to give the little hop that she executed to help him propel her onto the horse's back.

Instead Gard placed his lips close to her ear. "Ya be spoilin' the beast."

She turned her head. His lips grazed her cheek.

"He deserves ta be pampered. No' only is he beautiful, he isna used ta carryin' two, he be o'er worked."

"Ya concern yourself wit' the strangest things," he mumbled against her.

"Ya count on him, ya should appreciate him."

Of course, he respected the steed. He shook his head — she was being absurd. Again. "Leap, Brae." He boosted her up.

Before Gard joined her, he rummaged through his bundle.

Then he vaulted up behind her. She settled against him as if she were a missing part of him. That, too, was becoming routine.

Gard raised his arm, and as a group they set off.

"The sun be tryin' ta shine," Brae said. Her head bumped his chest with the tread of the animal.

Brae shifted. "Ow. Wha' have ya got in your shirt?"

"Retrieve it," he suggested.

She frowned but did as he asked. She cocked her head to the side when she discovered the tome.

"Leugh ri mi." He demanded she read to him.

"But the others might hear," she said.

With a wave of his hand, the other men slowed and drifted farther away from them.

"They are far enough away and will assume I read to you."

She eased open the cover. Gard peered over her shoulder. "Hudson has been instructing me, but he has not the patience."

"*He* has na the patience? I find tha' hard ta believe."

"Ya question me?" he mocked, then shrugged. "To tell the truth, there is not time."

"Tha' I believe."

Brae wondered why a nobleman's child had not been taught to read. She was positive that he was a noble, but why had this skill been overlooked?

Reading slowly at first, she pointed out the relationship of similar words, focusing on the simple ones.

"The script be fancy, aye?" he commented.

"Mmm." She attempted again to engage him.

"Just recite, Brae."

She read for an hour or more before tiring. She stretched.

"Ya ken, ridin' all day makes me more weary than when I put in a full day o' chores for me ma, I mean me father's wife."

Gard made another gesture with his hand and the men closed in around them.

"Why do you do that? Say your ma then retract?" he asked.

"The day ya took me, I found oot tha' the woman I thought was me mother is not. I guess tha's why she found it so easy ta throw me away. I was ne'er hers."

"And your sire? Why is it, do you think, that he could turn you out?"

"She isna easy ta get along wit'. He would jus' find it simpler ta do as she says than figh' wit' her day after day. 'Tis why I loved ta roam the moors so much. Jus' ta escape her when me chores were done."

"And what kept you busy throughout the day?"

"Normal evraday tasks. Laundry, bakin', mendin' and the like." They were silent for a spell. "And wha' keeps ya busy throughout the day, *Monsieur* Marschand?"

"Nice try, Mistress Galbraith."

She was quiet again, then asked. "When ya are done wit' me, will ya tell me?"

His primitive gaze met hers, the lift of his dark brow the only response.

CHAPTER TWENTY-TWO

When the contingent reached the border between Scotland and England, they set up camp on the Scottish side and waited for the Prince of Wales to return as the new king.

Marschand had granted Brae the freedom to leave his quarters during the daylight hours, which helped battle the boredom of camplife. She gained favor with some of the other men, helping out with chores, especially the cooking, and even taking requests for certain favorite dishes the lads were homesick for.

July turned to August, and another message from Hudson arrived delivered by Aidean Ferguson. The new king had abandoned his father's campaign and was headed south. Hudson ended the letter by suggesting Gard meet him at Richmond Castle, while Hugh Chamberlain continued to hold Ross.

On the move again, they crossed over into England, heading to North Yorkshire.

It was a pleasant day, and Brae was relieved to be on the road moving toward something—if not her freedom, at least they were making forward progress.

As the powerful warhorse carried them toward Richmond, Brae leaned against Gard and read to him. He liked the stories of Arthur, but she always made him endure a sonnet or two as well. Today she read a Welsh poem from *The Battle of the Trees.*

"I have been in a multitude of shapes, before I assumed a con-

sistent form . . . I have been a sword in the grasp of the hand . . . I have been a shield in battle . . . disguised for nine years . . . a combat though small . . ."

Brae's throat tightened, emotion from the words crashed over her.

"What is it?" he asked, in a husky voice.

Had he too found significance in the verse? "Nuthin," she sniffed.

But Gard tucked his head against her shoulder. His lips brushed her neck, and he coerced her in Gaelic to share her thoughts. "Dh'innis mi, Braelynn."

Curse the man. He knew just how to persuade her. She turned to look at him. "It be you," she said as tears breached her lashes.

He blinked.

"Have ya not been listenin?" She referred to the text, line for line. "Ya have been a multitude of shapes, just like it reads, a man wit'oot consistent form, hidin' what and who ya truly are. Twistin' yourself into whatever ya must to fit, wha' man ya need ta play at any given time." She intertwined the words of someone else's fancy and shaped them into the context of his life as she saw it. "Ya have taken up the sword ta figh' against those who have taken from ya. Ya have been a tear in the air, for I ken ya ache for what ya have lost, a mere droplet in the bucket of the vastness of what ya suffer. At times ya must feel so small in comparison ta the ones ya pursue. Ya have been a course, just as it says, on a mission, an undertakin' tha' will be your life's labor until ya achieve what ya are missin', or ya will die tryin'. 'Tis all ya ken anamore."

Gard swallowed hard, experiencing an unfamiliar prick behind his eyes.

A soft breeze blew little tendrils of her hair across her

mouth. While she continued to speak with such passion, he was transfixed, as he always was, by her language and the depth with which she perceived the words.

"Ye are the eagle, the sea, the banquet. The sword in the hand, the shield in the battle, the string in a harp, strung so tightly, I fear 'twill break ya. Disguised for nine years, the stanza goes, but I would guess at least a score ya have been wagin' this war, yet ya willna speak of a combat though small. Ya have done and been evrathin'. Do ya not see yourself in these words, Gard?"

When she spoke his forename, it punctuated the meaning of the verse and made it even more personal.

It was as if she knew him and understood what drove him. These things she thought of *him*? He was stunned. She was supposed to hate him. And should, for the violence he'd inflicted upon her, together with the misdeeds he was yet to commit. It was inevitable. Why was she crying at words not even meant for him?

She was too perceptive not to see the truths even though he withheld the details of his life. Nevertheless, she was correct in her assumptions. He would fight until death. Her concern that he would bend himself so far that he would break astounded him. Why would she care if he did? Why did these words that reflected him move her so? She had made him sound noble and strong, as though all the crimes he had committed—and was yet to—had been honorable and irreproachable. She had no idea the lengths to which he had gone, and was willing to go to, in order to achieve his purpose. In the end, there would be no absolution for him.

They searched each other's eyes. She seemed to understand him more than anyone else ever had. Even Hudson did not recognize the depth of his anguish. But she did, in this moment, know him.

She stroked his beard. "If things had been different," she

whispered, "If ya were not so hard and cruel, turned bitter by what has befallen ya? Wha' kind o' man would ya have been?"

Ah! So the sentiment was not for him. She was mourning a man who did not exist. The man that *could* have been, but not the one before her.

With a jerk of his head, he shook away her touch. He had been in her soft company too long. Her nonsensical whimsy was wearing off on him.

"Perhaps I would be the same abhorrent bastard I am today," he responded, nastily.

Brae's expression faltered. She turned facing forward again.

"Read," he barked. The horse tossed its head, sensing his master's distress. Gard controlled the animal easily while Brae whispered reassurance, stroking the steed's neck.

"I dinna wish ta read to ya anamore," Brae said.

"I suggest you earn your keep."

She remained silent.

"Fine." He huffed. "How about this for a verse. The devil of Fife ruined your life."

She inhaled sharply and tried to face him, but he squared his shoulders and used his arm strength to stop her from turning around.

"Ya are from Fife?" she exclaimed.

Exasperated, he rolled his eyes heavenward. "Not everything I say is insinuation as to where I am from or who I am. I conjured a nonsensical couplet. Now if you do not wish to endure more, you should most likely begin entertaining me."

She flopped against him, headbutting his chest with intent, he was certain. Then she continued softly reading of the oak, the bluebells, the chestnut and the pear trees, of battalions and of Christ and the great purifier of Brython. And she spoke of the hero. However, this time she made no comparison between the champion and Gard. No, he was the antithesis of such conquerors.

"I was enchanted by the sage . . . I played in the twilight . . . slept in the purple . . . I was truly in the enchantment . . ."

"You enjoyed that verse," he said, brushing her ear with his lips.

She trembled. "Aye."

"I can see you there," he said. "In the enchantment of your violet moor, laying in the soft grass, with your hair unbound flowing all about you as you lay flat against the green. As gloaming closes in, you wish to remain in the heather and not return to the life beyond the burm."

Brae was warmed by his words and surprised he could express himself in such a way. "How did ya ken tha' I liked tha' passage?"

"Your voice changes when you take pleasure in the words."

She had not been aware he was that attentive where she was concerned.

He avoided her gaze, staring off into the trees.

'Twas strange how they were coming to know each other in such intimate ways. Like she knew he favored dark meat, with a dram after the meal, not during or before. That he preferred to have his arms out of the blankets when he slept, while she pulled the covers right up to her neck.

Sometimes he had nightmares. She tried her best to calm him and he would cling to her. They never discussed the reasons, and in the morn he acted as though it had never happened—as he did with many things that occurred between them in the night.

She had learned he did not mind her touching his belongings, 'twas Dubhán he did. The chore to pack up Marschands's possessions for travel was now hers. She knew he enjoyed brushing her hair and that he liked to be clean. He often came to bed with wet locks, smelling of fresh clean cold water.

She knew that he desired to learn to read, yet he would not be pushed. He would do so in his own way and his own time. He *was* learning, though. Sometimes his lips moved when he tried to decipher the words before she recited them.

Once in a while, after supper when he had consumed a few drams and was more relaxed, if she teased him enough, he would let his guard down. Then he would give her a *semblance* of a grin or the odd chuckle that looked so awkward without an accompanying smile. She knew that his desire to reclaim whatever it was he had lost ruled his every breath, his every other thought, and every decision he made.

And she had learned something of herself as well. Brae wished that one day Gard would breathe for her. But that would never happen. Gard Marschand, or whatever his real name might be, had no use for her or any woman. He did not want one. But she could no longer see her days without him.

God help me, I am in love with the devil.

"Oh, dear Lord!" She gasped as the realization hit her full force. She almost dropped the book. Gard juggled to catch it.

She felt as though she had just been doused in ice water. The emotions bombarding her dwarfed any sentiment she had held for Callum.

Why was she so stupid with this man? He could destroy what was left of her if she let him.

"What is it?" Marschand snapped. "Are ya ill?"

Looking down at the ground from the height of the stallion, Brae experienced a sickening sense of vertigo. She shook her head trying to clear it and ward off the cold feeling of foreboding and horror seeping into her cognizance.

Gard cupped her shoulder. But she dared not face him.

He would know!

"Wha' is it?" he demanded.

"Please, may I walk?" she choked.

His nostrils flared, but he lowered her to the ground. Her feet had barely touched the earth when he kicked the sides of his horse, leaving her in a cloud of dust.

Seconds later, Llach's shadow fell across her. "Be ye aright', Brae?"

Unable to speak, she merely nodded.

CHAPTER TWENTY-THREE

They crossed the Yorkshire Dales.

"Oh, 'tis lovely. I didna expect it to be so beautiful." Once more, Brae sat tall in Marschand's lap, gaping at the amazing landscape.

"Did you think only your beloved Scotland was beautiful?"

"Well, we are born and bred ta believe the worst o' the English, as they in turn do us. I guess I always imagined 'twould be brown, barren, and leafless." She chortled. "Rather narrow-minded o' me, eh?"

"Rather," he repeated dryly. "The land be attached, the borders all but invisible. 'Tis the same land strung together. Stands to reason 'twould be just as breathtaking as your Highlands."

Still gaping at the spectacular landscape, she had to agree.

On horseback, Bain and Llachlan closed in.

"We will reside at the inn this night," Marschand instructed. "The merriment will be kept to a minimum. Pass that along."

"And ya willna allow Dubhán ta partake in anathin' more strong than diluted doon mead," Brae added. Though she had no authority to issue such a dictate, Marschand nodded his approval.

"Aye, Lord Marschand." The men rode on ahead, eager to reach their destination.

More slowly, Brae and Gard rode into the village. "Wha' be the name o' this shire?" she asked.

"Leyburn."

"Have ya been here afore?"

"Aye." Marschand halted the horse, then passed the reins to Dubhán. The boy watched with an openly optimistic expression as Marsch dismounted.

Gard reached up, and Brae let herself fall into his arms. He set her on her feet but kept his hands about her waist.

"When we convene on the morrow to depart this shire and you appear on time and unsick, then and only then will you receive coin, Dubhán," Marschand announced.

The boy's head swiveled from Marschand to Brae.

"This be *yor* doin'," he sneered at Brae.

"Ya will thank me on the morrow when the other men come ta the table wit' sore heads and gapin' mouths o' wrought."

"Bah! I curse the day we ever seen the likes o' Ross!" he complained loudly as he turned the horse in a large circle heading for the livery.

Brae peered up at Gard. "There be alotta tha' sentiment," she said.

"Do ya curse the day we stormed Ross?" he asked, sliding his hand into her hair.

An affirmation was on the tip of her tongue. She cursed the day he had ruined what she thought she wanted her life to be. But she would not lie to him. "Nay," she whispered. "Not anamore."

Using his other hand, he reached around and released the leather thong binding her hair. He ran his fingers through her long tresses, smoothing the waves. "Do ya curse me?" He continued to stare into her soul, bringing her earlier misery over her outrageous feelings for him to the fore.

She shook her head, not trusting herself to speak or she might embarrass herself further by blurting out her strange new fondness for him.

His forehead creased. "Well, ya should."

Luckily, just when she started to think of him as human, he was quick to dispel any such idea, with a cruel dose of reality.

Without warning, Marschand turned on his heel. Dragging her by the arm, he marched her down the line of vendors away from the inn.

"Where do we go?" she asked, skipping to keep up.

"You will be in need of that wardrobe now. I take you to the seamstress."

"Oh, no. May I no' bathe first I have the filth o' weeks upon me," she pleaded.

"You do not look or smell foul." He sniffed.

"I wash evraday, " she retorted.

"I ken," he replied with a self-satisfied frown.

"But 'tis no' the same. I dinna get the luxury of immersin' myself as ya do."

"A'right. But you will look through the glass and tell me if you approve of anything you see."

Outside the dressmaker's storefront they paused. Brae admired the garments displayed on a makeshift clothesline. A beautiful blue gown caught her eye. The over-wide sleeves were trimmed in gold, the waist cinched loosely with a simple braided belt of the same color.

"Aye. That one," he said in agreement, though she had not spoken. "I can see your face in the glass. You like that one, as do I," he explained, as if he truly read her thoughts.

"The sage-green kirtle and skirt wit' the cream-colored bliaut is lovely, too," she murmured.

"Aye, would look good with your eyes and your coloring."

She blinked, again somewhat stunned by the trajectory of his thoughts.

In the corner of the exhibit was another dress in a deep

red, near brown, it was so dark. It featured voluminous skirts with horizontal pleating under the bust across a snugly fitting bodice. The sleeves fitted closely from shoulder to elbow, fell like sweeping wings, then draped dramatically, coming to sharp points, nearly brushing the floor. The garment was also belted, but with black corded silk.

After escorting Brae to the inn, Gard ordered her a bath, then left her in peace.

When Marschand returned, Brae was sitting in front of the looking glass combing her hair into long sheets. Once more, she had pilfered one of his shirts.

"You are not dressed," he accused.

"I am loathe ta put on my things. They are all in need o' a good washin'."

From behind, Gard pulled a parcel and placed it on the bureau in front of her. "Open it."

Inside Brae found a simple cream-colored bliaut. "'Tis lovely. Thank ya."

"Don it, then I will return you to the dressmakers. She will do the alterations this night, so they will be ready when we leave on the morrow."

Once he had exited, Brae unlaced the borrowed shirt then reverently pulled the soft new material over her body. She had never owned such a fine garment. She peered into the glass, not recognizing herself. The pleats perfectly fitted under her breasts, and the scooping neckline, although lower than she normally wore, was still comfortable. She looked all grown up.

Marschand knocked once, then entered, stopping short to assess her. He nodded as if he approved. He went to his pack and rooted through it, finally coming up with a length of material.

He wound it loosely around her waist, letting it fall to

drape her hips. He knotted the middle, level with her mid stomach, allowing the length to fall almost to her ankle.

"'Tis tartan," she said, slowly, studying the green, and blue check on red, not recognizing the clan.

"Aye," he said, in a clipped tone. "Breacan."

"'Tis *your* blue?" she asked, not really expecting an answer.

He blinked in that slow archaic way, concealing his thoughts.

"Come," he said abruptly, and escorted her to the seamstress.

There, Marschand barked orders.

"Anything of her choosing, as well as the three in the window. The blue and gold. The red. The green. Including slippers, underthings and whatever else it is she may need, even if she is not aware that she is in need of it."

"Understood, Lord Marschand."

Brae felt inadequate and out of her element. Apparently, there were things *ladies* wore that she was not aware of.

"I will return."

Brae experienced a moment of anxiety. Foolishly, she grabbed the tail of Marschand's cloak.

Marschand glowered down at her.

"Ya are no' stayin'?" she asked in a meek voice.

"Nay. I will leave you to this." He snatched her grip from his cape. To her surprise he held onto her hand and stroked the ball of her thumb. "Ya will be fine here, Brae," he said quietly for her ears alone. "'Tisna place fer me. I dinna the first thing aboot this. Get whatever ya need. A'righ'? Llachlan and MacBain o' Skye be right ootside. Go now. I will return." Giving her hand a squeeze, he was just about to the door then said, "She will be in need of a wrap as well."

She spent the next few hours. She tried on almost everything in the place at the seamstress' insistence, but she did not wish to take advantage of Marschand's generosity even if the dressmaker had no reservations about it. She picked out enough clothing for five days, and two simpler dresses to work in, as well as slippers and a cloak.

Marschand returned as promised before dusk. Brae was dressed in the cream-colored dress he had provided earlier.

"How did we do?" he asked the seamstress as he fussed with the length of cloth he had placed around Brae's hips.

"Excellent, Lord Marschand. My girls and I will hurry through the alterations this night. Your lovely wife be the perfect size in almost all areas. 'Twill not take as much work as I thought to rework her selections. We just may sleep afore dawn."

The dressmaker left them alone.

"You did not bind your hair."

"I didna have time afore ya hauled me here. Besides, ye dinna say so."

"I should not have to. Come."

They left the shop and Marschand presented his arm, like a real gentleman. Brae sent him a sidelong glance before placing her arm atop his. They walked toward the inn.

Marschand acted the proper English gent he needed to portray here. She wondered how he of all people could convince anyone he was a refined man with perfect manners. He was dressed the part, and quite differently than she was used to, although still sporting dark colors—a black tunic with a surcoat over a crisp white linen shirt, and tight-fitting chausses over dark hose, covering his muscular legs. He would look good in any form of clothing. He was impressive, imposing. Handsome in a dangerously exotic way. No balloon pants for that man.

To her surprise they did not go straight to their room. He took her into the dining area, and they were led immediately to a round table. Random patrons dined, but Brae could not find any of Marschand's men.

Servers appeared and placed trenchers of meat-filled pastries and puddings, steak and kidney pies with thick crust, lastly a flask of wine and a jug of mead.

With her mouth watering, Brae tested one of the golden-brown pasties. Her eyes rolled as she chewed the delicious morsel. "Awww, Gard, 'tis heavenly."

He shook his head, but also took a sizeable bite.

Brae stared across the table at him. His hair had been trimmed, his beard groomed.

"You are gaping, Mistress Galbraith. As if wearing this costume is not enough, you must make me ill at ease as well?" he charged.

She giggled. "Ya have ne'er been ill at ease a day in your life, Lord Marschand. Ya could wear burlap and ya would still be the most impressive yet daunting man in the room."

"Was that a compliment?" he asked.

"I am no' sure. If ya think intimidation and menacin' are virtues, ya can take it as praise, I suppose."

His black eyes gleamed and she knew that if he was capable of smiling, he had just done so.

"I was more addin' another piece to the Gard Marschand riddle," she said, then sampled some of the kidney pie.

"And what have I divulged this time." He sipped his mead.

"Ya referred ta your English clothin' as a costume. Therein leadin' me ta believe tha' ya are no more English than I am, or ya wouldna have used tha' particular disparagin' remark. So, now those are two nationalities tha' I have eliminated. Ya are not French, nor are ya English. *Thank the good Lord*," she said the last in a hushed tone.

"You will not need for me to reveal my secrets, you will have pieced it together all by yourself, before you leave me."

"Ya mean when *you leave me*," she whispered. Another

foolish wave of soft emotion where he was concerned threatened. Brae dug her fingernails into her palm to keep herself from returning to the misery.

"What difference?" He shrugged.

She ignored him. "If ya must ken why I stare, I was missin' your hair. It no longer curls over your collar."

"You do not prefer it shorn and kempt?"

"'Tisna concern o' mine," she said, trying to maintain the distance he'd established between them. But she preferred his hair overlong and unruly. It suited the rest of him.

"You look different as well in your English clothing." His gaze flicked over her.

"'Tis also not my choice ta dress as they do. 'Tis your dictate. Do ya prefer me thus?"

"Nay, I would prefer you on your back, but for your own good that will not be. Nor is it acceptable for an English gentleman to speak of such things."

Brae gasped.

"Close your mouth, Mistress Galbraith."

The dining area started to fill. Several gentlemen tipped their caps to Brae in greeting. She returned a small smile and a nod. But when she refocused her attention on Gard, he was furious, if the tension in his clenched jaw meant anything.

What have I done now?

"Come." He extended his palm, then directed her to their room.

"I will give you a moment to change for bed," he said shortly.

Brae was quick to slip on a nightgown.

To her disappointment, the tub had been removed. Even cold, she would have reused the water. Lord knew when she would be given the chance to bathe again.

She hopped into bed, then covered up.

Time ticked by and still Gard did not return.

Where did he go?

The longer Brae thought about it, the more upset she became. Was he with someone? Tears filled her eyes. It made her stomach ache to think of him with another woman. She had no right to feel this way and certainly did not want to, but she couldn't help herself.

Gard would never keep her. Once Hudson rejoined the troop, there would be no reason for her to stay.

Brae chewed on her thumbnail.

Unless I make myself indispensable to him in some other way.

Those mornings when they awoke with their limbs intertwined, she knew he fought his lust. Sometimes while he was just waking, he ground his hips against her. His hard body had awakened a hunger in her, too.

Supposing one morning while he wrestled with his desire, what if Brae turned to him and pushed the issue? Would he stay? And not seek out another to slake his need?

She was bombarded by thoughts and images of his naked skin sliding over hers. She wanted that. Her face warmed, along with several other body parts.

"What are ya thinkin'," she berated herself. "'Tis ludicrous! Gettin' in bed with the devil!"

Besides, he had warned her he was not a kind man, and that if they ever came together as a man and a woman, he would treat her brutally.

Was she truly willing to live her life that way, for as long as he would have her? In such turmoil, she gnashed her teeth together and tried to keep the tears at bay.

The door burst open with such force that it slammed the opposite wall. Marschand held a red-faced Dubhán by the scruff.

"Are you hard of hearing or just stupid!" Marschand hollered, tossing the lad into the center of the room.

Dubhán skidded across the floor at the force.

Wide-eyed, Brae knelt on the bed, afraid for the boy.

Marschand was seething. The veins in his neck corded.

"Answer me!" Marschand demanded, legs splayed, as he towered over the boy.

"'Tis *her* fault." Dubhán waved at Brae. "*She* talked ya inta leavin' me wit' na coin."

"*She* has a name, and you will respect her by using it. And Mistress Galbraith had naught to do with my pronouncement. What would make you believe that I would let a woman make my decisions for me? I had all but determined you would not be given the opportunity to hold me up a second time. You had no need for coin. I paid for your meal and a place for you to put your ungrateful greasy head for the night, and you repay me by thieving from our host?"

Brae's stomach roiled.

"Weel, then ya gave me na choice. 'Tis *your* doin'," Dubhán spat.

Brae covered her mouth—how did he dare such audacity?

"'Tis your sire's doing," Marschand replied in a sinister tone. "You grow to be just like him. He was nothing more than a thieving bastard his whole sorry life, and look where that ended for him."

Please keep your mouth shut, Dubhán. Brae wrung her hands.

"Tha' ended for him at the end o' your sword!" the boy spat out. "Tha's wha'! And ya are no better than he and ya ken it!"

Marschand's expression mottled, and he raised his hand.

"Nay!" Brae flew across the room and braced herself against Marschand's chest. But in his rage, he shoved her violently by the shoulder. She tried to remain on her feet but skidded across the floor. As she fell, her cheek clipped the corner of the night table and everything went black.

The next thing she knew Llachlan hovered over her. "Brae! Brae? Are ya awake then?"

"Gard?" she murmured.

"Nay. 'Tis Llach."

Brae tried to open her eyes again.

"Be she a'righ'?" Dubhán stood just off Llachlan's shoulder, dancing from foot to foot in nervousness.

"Gard?" she repeated.

"Naw, Brae, 'tis Llach," he said again.

"Nay, Llachlan," she said with impatience. "Where is he? Where be Marschand?"

"He ran off when ye dinna wake!" Dubhán supplied. "He picked ya up real gentle. Like I've never seen him treat anathin', so careful he was. And I never saw the look on his face as he had. He laid ya on the bed and bade me fetch Llach."

"He was gone when we returned," Llachlan finished. "Why did he hit ya, Brae?"

"He didna," she protested. "He all but pushed me oot o' his way for gettin' involved in somethin' tha' isna me concern."

"He was aboot ta punish me an' she stepped in," Dubhán explained in a rush. "Why'd ya do tha'? I deserved wha' I was aboot ta get."

She ignored him. "How bad is it?" she asked Llach.

Llach winced. "Ya have a nice egg upon your cheek."

"Let me up. I am well," Brae complained when Llach tried to keep her down. "Please leave while I dress. But Llach, dinna go far. I will need ya."

CHAPTER TWENTY-FOUR

Swiftly, Brae pulled on the cream dress, then opened the door.

"Come," she demanded, and Llach fell into step behind her. Dubhán ran on ahead of them. "Where would he go?" Brae asked Llach.

"I dinna really ken. He isna one ta socialize wit' the rest o' us."

"Would he be wit' a . . . wit' . . . would he seek another's company?"

"Nay. I dinna believe he would. He has ye."

She rolled her eyes. No, he did not, but Llach was not aware of that fact.

Dubhán ran toward them, showering them in dirt as he skidded to a stop. "He be o'er at the livery. Pacin' like an animal. He be spookin' the horses."

"Thank ya, Dubhán."

"Aye, Mistress." He bobbed his dark head.

She almost smiled. Mayhap the whole debacle had had a good outcome after all.

As they neared the stables, Gard came into view, treading up and down the fence line. Brae knew he would hear them coming.

"You may go," Brae said to Llach and Dubhán.

"Brae," Llach started. "I dinna think ya should face him alone."

"I'll be fine. He willna hurt me," she reassured. "I thank ya both for your assistance. Please leave us."

They left but looked back at her frequently.

Brae took a deep breath, not knowing what to expect or how to approach Gard. She waited until Llach and Dubhán were out of sight.

"'Tis cold," she said, tremulously.

"Go inside," he said, his voice harsh.

"Not wit'oot ya."

"Why do you not learn?" he snapped, whirling on her.

"I am learnin'. And so are ya. 'Twas an accident. I ken ya didna mean ta hurt me. Ya were upset. I tripped o'er me own big feet interferin' in somethin' tha' wasna my concern. Ya have warned me time and again, and I will endeavor to do better. Now come." She held out her hand.

He glared, and she was afraid he would reject her. Other than this ploy, she had no idea how to persuade him inside. "Come, Gard, I'm freezin'." She shivered for good measure.

All of a sudden, Gard bowed his head, his dark locks fell over his forehead, and he placed his hand in her outstretched palm.

Immeasurable relief flooded her.

Holding hands, they strolled to the inn.

In silence they traversed the corridor.

Llach stood at the end dimly lit of the hall. Brae sent him a small reassuring nod, which he returned before turning away.

Once they had reached the room, Brae suffered several awkward moments, now that she had lured him within. She wanted to change but was loath to ask him to step out while she did, for fear he would leave again.

"I will jus' be a moment," she said as she ducked behind the privacy screen.

When she resurfaced, Gard reclined on the mattress, his hands behind his head. Warily, Brae slid in next to him. She wanted to speak but had no idea what to say.

Instead she eased near him. He remained stalk still. After a long while she fell asleep.

Gard woke with dawn's early light. His first thought was Brae. The events of the preceding night came rushing to the fore.

Slowly, he turned to find her sleeping next to him. Some unfamiliar emotion swarmed his being—one he did not wish to examine.

Instead, he eased up on one elbow but grimaced at the purple welt swelling her cheek.

Self-loathing simmered in his gut.

Last night, by the stable, when Brae had reached for him in forgiveness, he had never experienced such relief. But in the same instance, he had also been enraged beyond reason that he seemed to require her absolution. It was unacceptable.

Desperation dogged him. He had to be rid of Braelynn, and soon, before he hurt her any more. Their time was running out. Once they reached Richmond, he would no longer need her. As promised, he would pay her, then make arrangements and have her set up in some small hamlet. Hudson would know where.

Remorse washed over him. Gard pressed his lips gently near the contusion. Hesitant, he reached over, then ran his thumb lightly over the swelling.

In sleep, Brae's forehead creased slightly. Gard had never been one to kiss, finding it useless play that wasted time and energy. But he found himself frequently kissing this girl.

Wincing at the contact, Brae opened her eyes. Her soft lips curved, and her lovely green eyes lit from within. How could she possibly be happy to see him?

Her eyes fluttered closed, but he continued to watch her.

She was beautiful to him, even more so now than the night at Ross when Hudson had tricked him into admitting so.

Before he knew it, he was moving over her. Her eyes snapped open as he levered himself above. She searched his gaze and shifted under him, ready to accept his weight. Her hands came to rest at his waist, and when he captured her lips, she welcomed him. He slanted his head and coaxed her mouth open.

While their tongues dueled, Brae explored his body. She was more timid than the other time they had been together like this.

Unable to endure the sweet torture, he abruptly rolled off, dragging a whimper from her. He made the mistake of looking at her. Normally, he left when things progressed to this point, frantic to put distance between himself and her allure. Her lips were puffy from his aggressiveness, her skin scraped red by the coarseness of his beard. Her cheekbone inflamed, from his lack of control.

By the soft confused expression on her young face, she wanted to continue. *Damn her!*

"Dinna look at me like tha'," he cautioned. "I *will* hurt ya. Last night shoulda proved tha'. Ya have seen wha' kind o' man I am, time and again. But, ya still let me touch ya. And ya still look at me like *tha'*. I'm *not* the man from your romantic verses those useless bards would have ya suppose in prose. I *am* the devil!" he yelled, and she flinched. "Ya said it yourself. Now see it and accept it, for ya canna change it. And I willna let the darkness that is in me ruin wha' is Braelynn Galbraith. Ya are better than tha', and the longer ya stay aroond the likes of me, the less I see o' her."

Fuming, Gard grabbed his pack, then made for the exit.

Behind him, Brae inhaled sharply, as if she were about to speak, but thankfully she restrained. He closed the door between them.

Gard Marschand had her tied in knots. In one breath he promised never to hurt her, in the next vowed it was a foregone conclusion.

Brae argued with herself while packing Gard's belongings.

"Let *me touch ya,*" Brae mimicked. "As if I have a choice!" She had no way to stop him, nor would she. "Enough, Braelynn! He is na gud for ya."

However, it was unsettling that he said the more she stayed with him, the less he saw of her. Yet day-by-day, the less she saw herself, without him.

She took out her frustration on his chemise, then turned to her bag. It was near empty but for a few personal effects. What had Marschand done with her clothes? She had naught but the cream dress to don. She did so, but she forewent the sash Gard had fashioned out of the unidentified cloth. Instead, she folded it neatly and placed it in his pack.

There was a soft knock on the door. "Come."

To her surprise it was Dubhán. He came laden with a tray of porridge and warm cider.

"Thank ya, Dubhán," she sing-songed.

"Aye, Mistress."

Brae chewed the inside of her cheek to keep from beaming at the change in his manner.

"Are ya excited ta finally reach Richmond this day?"

She was amazed he had initiated conversation. He had never done so before.

"Oh, aye. Do we?" she asked, suffering mixed feelings about the conclusion of the journey. With Hudson's return, Marschand would no longer need her. "I didna realize we were so close."

"Aye. Ya will meet Lady Richmond." His eyes glowed.

"Oh, aye, and Hudson's lady wife, as weel," she answered, but he sent her an odd frown. "I look forward ta tha'. Be she English, Dubhán?"

"Aye. But I dinna hold tha' against her. Tha' be no' her fault."

"Nay, of course naw," she agreed, smiling at the clearly smitten young man. Brae's anticipation mounted. The Lady Richmond must be quite something, garnering such favor from the sharp-tongued squire.

Dubhán fidgeted. "Be tha' enough fare for ya ta las' the day, Mistress? I'm na sure Lord Marschand will stop. He be in a temper ta get there this day."

In a hurry to be rid of me!

"Aye, thank ya, Dubhán, ya are verra kind. 'Tis more than enough for me."

He moved toward the door. "Mistress Galbraith," he said in a low voice, yet he kept facing away.

"Aye, Dubhán?"

"I am truly wretched aboot wha' occurred last eve. I never meant for ya ta be injured."

"I ken tha', Dubhán. 'Twas jus' an accident. Lord Marschand didna mean ta hurt me."

He turned to look at her. By the bleak expression on his young face, he was not convinced the incident had been pure mishap.

"I dinna ken aboot tha', Mistress. He may have turned on ya for interferin' after he punished me e'en if ye hadna struck your head. We've no way o' kennin' wha' he was aboot. He may or may not be a thief like me sire, but he owns the same temper tha' canna be tamed. I thank ya for steppin' inta prevent the thrashin', but I would ask ya not do so again. I can take it, Mistress. I dinna"—he pointed toward her cheek, then shook his head—"like ta see ya thus. And dinna for certain e'er step in front o' me when the men be aroond. Gor!" He rolled his eyes dramatically. "They'd ne'er let me hear the end o' it. They believe me ta be a pissant a'ready. Oh, s'cuse me." He apologized for the coarse language.

"I willna, *Ruadh*," she promised, using his old nickname. But in truth she would intrude on his behalf in a heartbeat.

He blushed. "Ya may continue ta call me Dubhán, Mistress. I find I like it better, anyhow."

Brae grinned as he exited.

She was still smiling at the open door when Marschand appeared out of the gloom of the hall. For some reason she knew he'd heard every word.

Brae held up her hand. She did not want him to punish the boy. "He didna mean . . ."

"You should listen to him, if you will not heed me. Even the boy knows my true nature. I hope you are ready to leave."

"I would be if I kenned where ma clothes have gone."

"I took them over to the dressmaker and had her clean and mend them. I thought you might like your old things for when you return to your own life."

She averted her gaze so he would not see the hurt. "Tha' was verra thoughtful o' ya."

"Aye, that's me. Hot, cold, and thoughtful."

She ignored his sarcasm. "Let me jus' have a couple o' spoonfuls of the gruel Dubhán brought me and I will be ready."

He nodded, while she sat in front of the food, then took a bite.

"Your hair isna bound."

With her mouth full, Brae picked up her comb and held it over her shoulder. She was not sure what he would do, but was pleased when he took it, then sat behind her.

To her surprise he not only brushed her tresses but braided them as well. He then bound the braid with his own thong. He would not be needing it—his hair was too short now to be tied.

He sat back and met her gaze in the glass. She turned slowly in his direction but hesitated. Never knowing what to expect, she often felt like she was facing a wild animal. She raised her hand slow and touched his newly trimmed and civilized beard. "Ya look more tame, but ya seem more savage. Ya are no' playin' the part the costume demands. Ya are strung tight."

With a gentle touch, he traced her swollen cheekbone, and even though it hurt she used every ounce of willpower not to grimace.

"We reach Richmond this day," he said. "Your obligation to me will be fulfilled, and my submissiveness or wildness will no longer be your worry."

Sufficiently rebuffed, she asked, "If your destination be London, how am I ta return ta Scotland?"

He scowled. "You wish to return to Scotland?"

"O' course. 'Tis my home. Where I belong."

"But not to Ross?" he questioned.

"Nay. No' Ross." Saddened, she lowered her hand from his cheek and stared at the floor. Ross was no longer her home. There was nothing left for her there.

"I will find a suitable place for you," he pledged as he stood.

Without delay he hefted their packs and they headed for Richmond-shire.

CHAPTER TWENTY-FIVE

The closer to the shire they got, the more tense Gard became. Brae felt the anxiousness in every ounce of his being.

Atop his steed, Brae reclined against Gard's chest, appreciating each minute of his touch. This would be their last ride.

It was nearly dusk when the massive castle finally came into view.

"'Tis Richmond, Brae," Gard murmured.

Brae peeked from inside Marschand's cloak. He had wrapped her up as the sun grew low, and she welcomed his warmth.

"Oh, I imagine it be truly magnificent in the daylight," she raved.

"Hudson would be happy to hear your praise."

"He would?" She frowned.

The call went up, announcing their arrival.

"MacBain! Ride ahead," Gard ordered. "Inquire as to whether Lord Grainger has made his appearance as of yet."

"Aye, Lord Marschand." Bain galloped ahead.

The further into England they traveled, the less Gard lapsed into brogue—to Brae's disappointment—even when they were alone.

Before long, Bain returned. "The Earl be in residence."

"Carry on," Marsch bade him.

"Tha's fine," Brae said. "But is Hudson here? He didna find oot wha' ya requested."

Marschand did not respond as they rode through the gates.

A crowd appeared to greet them, Hudson among them. Brae was excited to see him again.

Before Marschand dismounted, Hudson reached for Brae. Without thought, Brae leaned down and let him pull her from the horse.

"Mistress Galbraith. How good to see you whole and hale." He smiled, embracing her.

"'Tis good to see ya as weel, Hudson." She hugged him in return.

"You survived traveling with *him*, I see. No joy by any means, as I well know," he added, dryly.

"His bark be worse than his bite," Brae said, taking a step back so she could look up into his handsome face.

His gaze narrowed on her bruised cheek.

"Unhand her," Marschand said from behind. He yanked Brae's elbow and tucked her into his side.

An uncomfortable moment passed as the men eyed each other.

Hudson was the first to look away. "Come. Lady Richmond is in great anticipation of your arrival."

"Oh, dear. I look awful." Brae dusted her clothing. "My new dress is covered in filth from the road."

"You look lovely, Mistress Galbraith. In English clothing, no less. Gard thinks of everything." Hudson patted her hand. "You do not look like you have just endured miles with *him*, let alone the road. Please." He gestured her forward.

It was then Brae wondered why Marschand had gone to the trouble of purchasing English clothing for her. She would not need the garments returning to Scotland. Perhaps just a bonus of their bargain.

They walked into a well-lit vestibule teeming with servants, directed by a beautiful blonde woman dressed to perfection. "John, you will direct Gard's men to the barracks," she said facing them.

"Of course." Hudson nodded. "Constance, come meet, Mistress Galbraith."

The woman smiled stiffly while observing Brae with a critical eye. "'Tis a pleasure to meet you, Mistress Galbraith. John has done nothing but sing your praises since the moment he returned home."

Brae shook her proffered hand. "'Tis gud ta meet ya as weel, Lady Richmond. John?" she whispered the last, turning to Hudson in confusion.

"Aye," Gard said from behind. "The Countess Lady Richmond refers to her Lord and husband John Hudson of Brittany. The Earl of Richmond."

Brae's eyes widened. "Oh! My Lord Richmond." She had been addressing him so informally all this time. She fought the urge to curtsey. She frowned at Marschand, speculating again at his own secrets.

"Ya *are* English," she said, focusing on the earl.

The Earl dipped his head formally.

One more footnote in the endless riddle of Gard Marschand slid into place.

"You must be worn out from your travels *and travails* of being on the road all these weeks." The lady Richmond paused and her gaze touched on Gard, who bristled.

Mockingly, Gard dipped his dark head. "Lady Richmond," he greeted.

"Gard," she said, with obvious disdain. "Follow me, Mistress Galbraith."

Lady Richmond was clearly English, born and bred. Brae tagged along.

"You will put her with me," Marschand called after them.

Lady Richmond's spine straightened, and she whipped

around to face him. "You are not married to the woman. You will not sleep with her here. You may disgrace her all across the land, but I will not condone it, or support it, in my own home."

Gard nodded, but extended his hand toward Brae, all the while keeping his dark gaze leveled on the attractive lady. "Then we will darken your door no longer, Lady Richmond."

Brae took his hand and he directed her toward the foyer.

"Enough," Hudson barked. "Neither of you will deprive Brae of a bath and a bed to sleep in." He took her arm and escorted her above stairs while his wife and his friend squared off.

"Should we leave them tha' way?" Brae asked.

"Constance will concede. Gard is not someone she can push."

"Ya have a lovely home," Brae said as they climbed the stairs. "As castles go." She smiled, teasing him.

He returned her grin but sobered as he observed her cheek. "Did he do that?"

"'Twas an accident," she said truthfully.

"He has abused you?"

"Na more than he has since the moment we met. But our time be at an end. Is it not? 'Tis all o' no matter now."

"Here, Brae." The earl led her into a richly furnished chamber. To Brae's pleasure a copper tub sat in the center of the room.

"I will have the water drawn," Hudson announced.

"Thank ya, Lord Richmond. I guess, we willna longer be on intimate terms, eh?" she joked.

"We will forever be intimate, Brae." He laughed.

"You will not," Gard barked from the doorway.

"Why not?" Lady Richmond said nastily from behind Gard. "My Lord husband has been *intimate* on numerous occasions with several different women on his travels, so it would seem." She rounded on Gard. "I imagine I have you to thank for that."

"Oh aye, I held a dirk to his throat and commanded he fornicate as was my wish. You are inordinately familiar with my perversions, Lady Richmond," Marschand replied, stonily, as though he was used to her preposterous accusations.

"No wonder you spoke so highly of *Brae*, John." The lady gestured in Brae's direction. "Do you share *her*, as well then? *You* and the heathen?"

Brae inhaled sharply. Marschand straightened and for a moment Brae worried for Lady Richmond's safety, but Hudson was quick to lunge across the space and stand between them.

Brae did not wait for explanations or rebuttals. She crossed the space and twined her arm in Gard's. "I believe we are in need o' other accommodations, Lord Marschand. I dinna wish ta stay here."

His mouth quirked. Without delay, he escorted her belowstairs while the earl and countess screeched at one another.

Brae assumed Gard would have the men erect their quarters and they would rest outside as they had these many weeks. Instead he led her to one of outbuildings.

"Be careful. The stones can be slippery," he warned.

He steadied her up the winding stairs. At the top, he shouldered the stuck old door. "'Tis not the opulence of the castle, but 'tis preferable to sleeping on the ground."

In the fireplace, he built up the flames.

"'Twill be warm momentarily. I will find your bags and return."

Minutes later, Llach, Bain, and Dubhán trudged up the stairs with their packs and Marschand's pallet. They left wordlessly.

Brae approached the fire extending her hands to the warmth.

Eventually, Marschand returned with food and drink. They sat before the fire and ate.

"Ye have na like fer the Lady Richmond?" Brae asked.

"She has no like for me."

"I dinna why, ya be such a charmin' and agreeable gentleman," Brae teased.

"I am in agreement," he replied, his dark eyes gleaming in the firelight.

"She has na like for me as weel," Brae added, nonplused. "How did she and Hudson meet?"

"'Twas arranged, as nobility does."

"Are ye arranged?" Brae blurted before she thought better.

He snorted. "I said nobility."

"Aye." She agreed. "Ya did. So are ya?"

She had already decided that he was of the aristocracy.

"I haven't thought past regaining my due. If I am able to accomplish that, I will most like be able to make my own arrangement. Or not, if I so choose."

"Ye dinna wish ta have a wife? Not ever? Ye will be in need o' heirs."

"I am not in need of a wife to produce heirs," he replied, with a lift of his eyebrow.

"Naw, o' course na. Ya make yer own rules."

"Aye. I do. Ya be learnin'."

They bedded down for the night.

Cozy with the fire and his warmth, Brae slept soundly, until she wakened to hot insistent kisses. He teased her mouth with his tongue. When she parted her lips he swept inside, taking possession.

Shifting her legs, Brae welcomed him. He braced his well-muscled arms on either side of her, saving her from the bulk of his weight. He ground his hips against her, awakening her own need.

How was it he could resist her all through the day, but in his sleep or upon waking, he could not?

Brae allowed her hands to roam, emboldened when he did not immediately refuse her touch. A growl rumbled deep in his chest. Slow and deliberate, she ran her finger around the waist of his brays, following the line around his hip, to his hard stomach.

He batted her hand, then rolled from her.

Breathing hard, he perched on the edge of the pallet. Brae sat up behind him, staring at his broad shoulders, wanting to touch him.

Why would he not just take her? Was it her? He had need but could not bring himself to be with her?

"Wha' am I doin' wrong?" she asked in a pathetic voice.

Marschand bounded to his feet. "Ya are here!" he snapped, before donning his shirt.

While he laced it, he took several deep inhalations. "You will wear the green this day," he said before departing with a slam of the door.

Brae washed with a bowl of water that Dubhán provided. She then dressed, in the sage-green kirtle and skirt with the cream-colored bliaut, as directed. She had no glass to know, but she believed she could face Lady Richmond today and not feel inferior.

After, she tidied their meager possessions and rolled up the pallet, just in case Gard wished to travel this day. Her spirits sagged with the thought.

Next Brae tried to tame her hair. She wished for some pins to fashion a style similar to that of the countess, but another braid would have to suffice. To add an extra bit of sophistication she twisted each side close to her ears before braiding the length intricately in a loose fishbone style.

She was just tying it off when Marschand returned. "You take too long."

"I didna ken I had a time restraint," she said, pulling the ends of the thong tight. She faced him. The look in his eyes warmed her.

"I have no glass. How looks the plait?" she asked.

He circled, before taking her face in his hands. He was not gentle, his fingers bit into her jawline. "Ye look gud enough ta eat," he growled, then nipped at her lips before making his way down her neck, raking with his teeth.

She winced. "Caisg! Ye are hurtin' me." She moved her head to the side.

He froze. His jaw tightened as he swept his hand across her neck and décolletage as though trying to erase the results of his aggressiveness. He set her away from him.

"Hudson awaits your company to break the fast," he snarled, presenting his arm without looking at her.

He helped her navigate the dew-dampened steps

The castle swarmed with people going about their chores.

Gard led Brae to the earl's table and pulled out a chair for her, seating her next to Hudson. Gard took the other side.

"Good morn, Mistress Galbraith. I hope you slept well, and I would like to assure you that this eve's accommodations will be better."

"There be na need Hudson . . . er, uh, My Lord Richmond," she amended. "We are happy where we are, are we no', Lord Marschand?"

Hudson looked to Marschand.

"Aye, we are happy where we are," Marschand answered, stuffing a biscuit into his mouth.

Hudson snorted. "Gard . . . and happy. Seems a contradiction in terms."

"Aye, as is the phrase marital bliss," Gard retorted.

"Where be the lovely but enraged Lady Richmond this fine morn, Hudson?"

Hudson snorted. "I've no idea."

Brae listened to their exchange while nibbling a flatbread.

"What made you confess your transgression?" Gard asked, rudely.

"You," Hudson said, stirring his gruel.

"Me?" Gard frowned.

"I assumed she could not be any less disappointed in me than you were." Hudson took a sip of warm cider, then said, "Evidently, I was mistaken."

"She will get over it. Or she won't. What importance be it?" Gard said callously.

"Aye, that is how you would view it. You cannot imagine yourself in that situation because you have no intention of putting yourself there."

"Aye. Mayhap you should have listened to me."

"I never listen to you."

"Therein lies your problem."

"Oh, will ya two cease. Ye are worse than the women." Brae stood. "Migh' ya show me aroond yor English castle, Lord Richmond?"

"Aye. That would be very nice, Mistress Galbraith."

Hudson rose and took Brae's arm. Gard growled, but followed behind.

Hudson took great pleasure in showing off his castle and reciting the rich history of the earls of Richmond.

They finished the tour by strolling in the gardens.

"Brae!"

Stunned to hear her name, Brae turned, only to find Bronwyn waving madly.

"May I, Lord Marschand?"

He nodded, moving to stand next to Hudson.

"Bronny? Wha' do ye here?" Brae squealed.

"Some o' the folks o' Ross left wit' Lord Chamberlain's blessin'. I followed in hopes o' meetin' up wit' Llachlan."

"Have ye?"

"I havena located him yet. We were told tha' he stayed wit' Lord Marschand's squire for some reason."

On the walk around, Brae had seen Llach and the others on the training field with Hudson's men.

"May I, My Lords?" Brae asked again.

On their go ahead, Brae scrambled up the hill, unladylike she was sure, but did not care. She bellowed over the wall. "Llachlan!" His face lit when he saw her. "Llach. Come here." She gestured.

Brae shoved Bronny behind her while he loped over.

"I have a gift for ya," she shouted as he neared.

"A gift? Fer me?" He grinned in his easy way.

Brae pulled Bronny from behind her.

Llach let out a deafening whoop and scooped a giggling Bronwyn into his arms.

"How are ya here?" he asked, kissing her cheeks. She explained as they walked off arm in arm.

Brae smiled, her heart swelling as she watched them go.

Still caught up in the couple's excitement at seeing each other, she tangled her fingers with Gard's without even thinking about it. It was not until she noted the all-knowing expression on Hudson's face that she realized the mistake. Yet she was pleased when Gard did not reject her, even giving her hand a small squeeze while avoiding Hudson's grin.

They walked farther into the grounds. Hudson pointed out his cherished roses. Brae smelled every one. The men spoke in low tones while Brae explored. She strolled up the path and came face to face with Callum and Katie.

"Brae?" Katie said in surprise.

Brae's heart began to pound and her cheeks heated.

Katie reached out, but Brae recoiled.

Katie bowed her head and her eyes filled. Callum stared with utter contempt.

"Well, if it isna Lord Marschand's whore," Callum taunted.

Brae's mouth tightened, and if Katie had not been her cherished friend once, she would have had some choice words in response.

"Where is he? Dropped ye when he was done wit' ya? Has Lord Richmond taken pity on ya? Be he your new bene-factor? Do the dark ones jus' pass ya aroond then?"

That was the second time in as many days that someone had accused her of such.

"Ye are even dressin' the part now, I see." Insolently, his gaze raked her body, lingering on the fading red blotches Gard had left on her skin.

"Callum!" Katie admonished.

"Did he blacken your eye for your disobedience afore he threw ya away? I assumed I would have ta resort ta such wit' ya as weel after we were wed, since ya ne'er were one ta listen."

Brae wondered if he had struck Katie yet. Just as quickly, she discarded the thought. Katie was more subservient than she—though Katie stiffened at her husband's remark.

Callum's eye twitched.

Somehow Brae knew Gard was near. She could well im-agine her dark avenging angel cut a rather impressive figure bearing down on them.

But what the couple had not realized yet was that Hudson had circled around and was even now bearing down on them from the opposite direction. Brae spotted him, over Katie's shoulder.

Gard moved in behind. In a possessive stand he wound his arm about Brae. His hand rode indecently low on her abdomen.

Where his fingers grazed made her tingle. Brae covered his hand with her own, attempting to give the impression she was used to his touch and enjoyed it.

His fingers twitched. In silence, Gard stared at Callum.

Callum finally tore his contemptuous gaze from Brae and focused on her Lord.

"Have you by now used up your welcome, MacCrae?" Hudson's deep voice rattled Brae's former fiancé. "I do believe you were warned that my hospitality would only go so far, in view of your shoddy treatment of Mistress Galbraith."

Callum straightened. "Aye, Lord Richmond. I dinna forget. I was jus' surprised ta see Braelynn, is all."

"Oh, and in your astonishment you thought to insult and demean her in my presence? Not to your advantage, that."

"No sir. I apologize."

"You will apologize to Miss . . ."

"I dinna need it, Hudson," Brae said hoping she had given the impression she had forgotten the pair of them the minute Gard had touched her. She turned into his arms hoping he would take her lead and get her away from them. "Shall we?" she asked.

Gard searched her gaze, and for a moment she was mesmerized. She thought he was about to kiss her. She stared at his lips. They curved as they would if he could smile. She had forgotten what a convincing actor he could be when he wanted to be.

"Aye, we shall." He all but closed in around her, giving them a clearly intimate appearance.

"Afterward, Hudson," Gard called over his shoulder, suggesting there would be an act and they would meet up with him after its completion.

CHAPTER TWENTY-SIX

When Brae and Gard had finished exploring the garden, they retired to their quarters.

Gard rolled the pallet out, then loaded it with pillows. "You will read to me," he demanded, while reclining on the flat mattress. "I wish we had something different to study for a change. I am tired of the Llyfr."

Brae headed for her pack.

"Look in mine," Gard suggested.

She rummaged through. "Ohhh, Gard!" Her face lit up. "How did ya get them?" she exclaimed unearthing several tomes.

He wondered if she had even realized she had used his name. She did it so infrequently, and only when she was not angered with him.

"When Ferguson left, I bade him inform Hudson to retrieve them from your father. And when Ferg made the announcement, your smitten vicar was there and had some others to add to your collection."

She smiled as she stacked them on the pallet for him to see.

He felt strangely contented to witness her delight. She was close to tears.

"I ne'er thought ta see them again. Thank ya."

"You will thank your lord properly."

Her smile slipped. Confused, she shook her head. "Properly?"

"Aye." He tapped his cheek with his index finger.

She leaned in and kissed his cheek. "Thank ya, My Lord Marschand."

"Ya are welcome. 'Twas worth it."

She smiled softly.

"Read me your favorite." He patted his chest. She retrieved a book, then placed her head on his chest. Gard wound his arm around her and rested his hand on her stomach as she read from cover to cover.

"The meal time should be near. Are ya hungry?" Gard asked, sitting up.

He reached into his pack and pulled out the velvet bag of jewels. With reverence he removed the seal and set it aside.

"I will leave these here for Hudson's safe keeping." He jingled the sac, then placed the rest of the treasures in the inside pocket of his surcoat. "If things do not go as I plan, I do not want them falling into the wrong hands."

He picked up the seal, and using his dirk, he pried the blue jewel free. He set the insignia aside, then dropped the cold gem into Brae's palm. "For you."

She blinked and shook her head.

"Dinna fash yourself. Ya will receive coin as weel for your service. But I saw how ya were dazzled by it when ya laid eyes on it afore."

"I canna accept tha'. 'Tis too much, I havena done much ta receive such an amazin' gift. I am na e'en sure tha' I have done enough ta receive much coin. I read but two missives."

Brae tried to return it, but he would not accept it.

"Take it as payment for the life tha' I took from ya. This way ya will be a verra *wealthy widow* tha' the fellows will flock ta. Ya can have your choosin'."

Instead of the gratitude he had expected, her eyes filled.

He thumbed her tears, but they fell faster than he could swipe at them. "Why do ya do this?" he asked, confused.

279

She turned away from him.

"Braelynn."

He waited for her to face him.

"Dinna tell me ya will miss the manhandlin'?" he said softly.

"Was tha' a jest and a semblance of a smirk, Lord Marschand?"

"Aye, 'twas," he admitted.

"Then me work be done," she said, with a sad smile.

"Then ya will accept me gift."

She bit her lip. "Wha' is it?" she asked, holding it up to the light as she had before.

"'Tis topaz."

"Where did ya get it?"

"I dinna ken where it came from. They were already a pair. I received it this way."

She slid the gem under their pillows. "Do ya think 'twill be safe there while we go ta supper?"

"Aye." He retrieved the seal and was about to place it into his inside pocket when she ran her finger over the initials.

"Tha' be you. Yah?"

He paused and considered not giving a response. With that bit of affirmation along with the new information she had gleaned of Hudson's identity, would she piece together the significance?

In his own warped way, perhaps he wanted her to. "Aye," he confirmed.

"I hope ya reclaim evrathin' tha' was taken from ya," she said.

He believed she was sincere. "And I hope ya find wha'e'er it be ya are lookin' for, too, Braelynn."

"Wha' I be lookin' for?" Puzzlement etched a wrinkle between her brows.

"The thing tha' guides ya. The thing tha' makes ya get up

oot a bed in the morn. I could see ya bein' a teacher. A governess. A keeper o' tomes for the smitten vicar or a smitten vicar elsewhere, since ye dinna wish ta return ta Ross. Ya could e'en be a scribe, one day."

"A female scribe?" she said, dubiously.

"Aye, why no'. Or perhaps ya will jus' settle doon wit' the husband ya seem ta require ta obtain your contentment. And ya will make bairns." For some unidentified reason, his stomach tightened.

Her eyes filled again.

He gripped her chin. "Mayhap if ya decide wha' ya require afore I depart, ya will let me ken and I will provide it for ya." He stood, ready to head for the door. "Ya clean yourself up and I will take ya doon for supper, yah."

"Gard," she called, before he left.

He closed his eyes from the strange burning pain behind them as she called his name. "Aye?" Pausing, he opened his eyes and turned to face her.

"Wha' directs ya? Wha' makes *ya* get up in the morn? The need ta repossess wha' be yours?"

"Aye."

"And when ya have achieved tha'? Wha' will be your reason?"

He blinked. "I dinna ken," he answered gruffly and made to leave, but she stopped him again.

"Gard?"

"Aye." His voice was deep with emotion he couldn't name.

"If ya glean your reason for after ya regain wha' ya lost, and afore ya leave me, ya will let me ken, yah?"

Again, he had no answer for her, so he let the door swing shut.

Brae removed the stone from beneath the pillow and observed it closely. She ran her finger over the flat side. If she was not mistaken, the smooth part would line up perfectly with the edge of the same gem she had sewn into her bag. They were one and the same.

What was she to make of it? How did Gard and Gaveston fit? And what significance was the topaz to either of them? And what of the M C engraved on the seal?

Brae slipped the treasure safely into its hiding place, while other thoughts invaded her racing mind.

What was her reason for rising in the morn, he had asked.

In the beginning, right after the siege, her motivation had been pure survival. Particularly after she had sustained the injury to her leg. And if not for Gard, his care, and the trip to the cold loch, she might not have survived. And then, for a time, she had relied on unadulterated anger to sustain her. But now? Why did she rise? Tears sprang anew. She knew why. She rose for *him*. Her reason was Gard.

CHAPTER TWENTY-SEVEN

The next morn Brae awakened to raised voices outside their door.

"I cannot. You do not know what you ask!" Gard shouted.

Brae tried not to listen but couldn't help it. She sat up pulling the covers with her.

"And *I* cannot leave right now," Hudson replied. "The heir apparent has not even made London as of yet. What good would it do for both of us to be camped outside the palace waiting to petition the king? Which I guarantee you, teems of others will be waiting to do the same. I promise you, I will have your back, when the time comes, but for the now, I need to be here with my wife."

"You will choose her over me?" Gard retorted with incredulity.

"For Christ's sake, Gard, I am not choosing her over you. And I had this same goddamned conversation with her when I left to follow you. She accused me of choosing you over her. I am sick to death of both of you. I have half a mind to snap up Brae and run off with her . . ."

His tirade was cut short and Brae heard scuffling, followed by grunting. Something weighty hit the door with a thump. Then all fell silent.

Brae sat up straighter but was startled when Hudson spoke again.

"You need to take her with you so that we can communicate."

"I canna, Hudson. Ya have no idea wha' your askin' o' me. I cannot take her with me. I need to get rid o' her. I canna spend anamore time with her. Do ya understand?"

Brae teared up at his words. She was in love with him and he could not wait to discard her.

"Why? What is this sudden need to be rid of her? She is smart. She is not hard on the eyes. She sleeps in your bed. She puts up with your sporadic bouts of insanity and violence. And don't think I did not see the bruise upon her cheek."

"'Twas an accident. I dinna mean to hurt her."

She recognized the regret in his voice.

"Strange, she said much the same in your defense. You have spent more time in this woman's company than I have ever known you to spend with anyone, myself included. And she does not seem to want to kill you, which is more than *I* can say, and you want to be rid of her? Why? She seems like the only one on this earth who can tolerate you. And you know what else, Gard? You don't want to kill *her,* and *that* speaks volumes."

"She has na choice but ta endure me. It is not as if she desires it. And who said she doesna want ta kill me. Surely *she* did not."

He sounded like a little boy kicking his toe in the dirt explaining something he would rather not. Brae wanted to yell through the door that she would choose to stay with him if he would only allow it. If he would only give her one slight indication that he was capable of feeling even a third of what she did for him. She merely wanted to be with him.

"Have you bedded her?" Hudson asked.

There was silence.

"You haven't!" Hudson exclaimed. "Have you! My God, man. You are inhuman! How have you been able to manage that and stay sane?"

Sane? Brae was not so sure of that.

"It has not been easy," Gard admitted. "I nearly take her every morn."

Brae's lower stomach twinged.

"And what stops you? I walked in on the two of you at Ross."

"I have done enough to her."

"You don't care about anyone else's feelings. You never have. That is what precipitated this argument between you and me. What makes you spare her?"

"Perhaps she wouldna have me. Did ye e'er think o' tha'?"

"Again, I ask what stops you. You could force her at any given time. As you say, she has no choice here."

Another hush paused the conversation.

"You don't want her to hate you! My God, man! When did you ever care about what anyone thought of you?"

"She does hate me. And I dinna care if she does. I dinna want her. I dinna want anaone. I dinna have time for any o' this." He began to sound desperate. "I cannot take her any farther, Hudson. You need to keep her here. And if that is not acceptable to your angry lady wife, then I will leave it up to you to find a place for her somewhere else. Some little town somewhere, where she can live safely alone for a time until she finds a husband. Or better yet *you* find her a decent man. Perhaps a man of piety."

Brae rolled her eyes.

"I cannot do that right now. I have my own life to worry about. For once I am going to put myself first before you, Gard, and you will just have to understand it. When you need me, I will be there, as I always have. But for once you must act the comrade and let me do what I feel I need to do."

"Fine. Do what you need to do. Kiss your wife's bloody feet and be quick about it. I need you at my back."

"And I will be there," Hudson repeated.

"I will leave Brae with you," Gard said.

He had no intention of letting her return to Scotland. Anger filled her.

"I do not think you should do that," Hudson responded.

"And why not?" Gard demanded.

"I cannot watch her full time. And I do not have enough of my own men, or any that *you* trust, to guard her, especially if I set her up in some far-off town somewhere. I cannot leave a contingent there with her. And you forget one very important thing."

"Cowan," Gard said coldly.

"Aye. Cowan still lurks, and by what I witnessed, he is more savage than ever."

Silence reigned so long, Brae thought they'd moved away.

"I will take her," Gard said. Brae almost shouted with delight. It might not be forever, but it was a reprieve.

"Now about the other matter. What possessed you to bring MacCrae here?" Gard sounded irritated once more.

"That was entirely Hugh's doing. He was the one who sent them here. All of Ross-shire's people that he granted leave to—he suggested they come here and assured them of my generosity. Can you imagine? I will repay him for this. The ones I cannot find a place for, I am sending to Kyme. I will keep the best and send the rest to his holding."

"Excellent idea. Send MacCrae and his other half there. I will not have them here if by some small chance we are able to return. I will not allow Brae to suffer them further."

"I would do so, Gard, but not now."

"You will nay say me?"

"Did you not notice his lady wife's condition?"

"I do not notice her at all. She pales in comparison. What condition?"

"She is with child. She was quite ill when they arrived. I

will do as you command, but I would request that I be allowed to keep her here until she has the child. I believe she is going to have a difficult time, if she carries to term at all."

Brae gasped. Katie was expecting a child, so soon after they had wed? It had been many weeks.

"Did you tend her yourself, upon their arrival?" Gard asked.

"Aye. She was not well. For a little while there, I wasn't certain she'd recover. I think MacCrae pushed too hard to get here. But with no travel, some good food and lots of rest, she may just deliver a healthy babe in time."

"Do as you see fit."

Brae heard footsteps moving away.

She dropped her head, feigning sleep by the time the door swung open.

"You will rise, dress, and pack our things. I am certain you are in no need of explanation for I am confident you overheard every word."

Not waiting for a reply, Gard closed the door behind him as he left her.

Brae did as asked, feeling lighter than she had in ages, just knowing she would spend more time in his company.

Before they departed, Brae sought out Bronwyn to bid farewell, but was pleased to discover that she and Llach would be joining the caravan.

While Brae waited for Gard's men to prepare for their departure, she wandered about Hudson's rose garden with Gard's permission. Every once in a while, she looked over her shoulder to find Gard watching.

To her vexation she was confronted with Callum's mean spirited company yet again.

Gard stood near the gate, conversing with Hudson, when

Brae's former fiancé approached. Gard crept closer, staying out of MacCrae's line of sight and waiting to hear what vileness he spouted this time.

"Where be your lover, Brae? He ne'er leaves ya alone fer long," Callum sneered.

"Oh, I'm sure he be near. He doesna care ta be far from me, nor I him."

Good Lass! She was not about to let the bastard get to her.

"For the now. He will soon tire o' ya, and then ya will be labeled a whore fer the rest o' your days."

"I can live wit' tha'. His company has been well worth me time. And I will be well compensated if no' sadly deprived o' his companionship."

"I be thankin' me maker nightly tha' I didna marry ya. Not only were ya not the woman I thought ya ta be, ya are obviously barren as weel."

Gard waited for her reply.

"Barren?" she chuckled. "Oh, Callum. Are ya so naïve? Did ya no' ken tha' there be ways o' preventin' such things? Had ya kenned, 'twoulda save ya from an unhappy marriage, aye?"

To Gard's mortification, Brae had truly developed a broadened education since she had been in his company.

"Who said I wasna happy ta marry, Katie?" Callum argued.

"Ya were in love wit' me just the day afore. I ken ya better than anaone Cal, and I ken ya still do. Your eyes linger on ma face and . . ." She paused looking down at her scooped neckline. " . . . and the rest o' me. Just like ya used to. Ya could not have fallen in love wit' her after one beddin', Cal. 'Twas a romp o' circumstance, not a lifetime in the makin'."

"Listen ta yourself, Brae. Ya sound like a whore." He sneered. "Katie be a good and decent girl, which is more than I can say for ya. She will make a good wife and she will deliver me o' a healthy son. Did ya ken she is already growin' wit' me child?"

"Aye, I noticed. But I dinna envy her."

"Don't lie ta me Brae. I ken ya better than anaone, too. Ya desire a child above all else?" His eyes glittered. "Ye were hopin' a child would result from our first couplin' after we wed. Could it be, ya take such precaution as ta not let the devil's seed take root within ya, kennin' the moment he finds oot, he will no longer have use for ya and he will throw ya ta the gutter? Or is it him tha' has na wish for the likes o' you, just a dirty whore, ta be the mother o' his heirs. He will find a real lady for tha'."

"Things change, Callum. For the now, I have no use ta drag a bairn aroond wit' us. We are findin' too much enjoyment in each other ta worry aboot another. I wouldna wish ta split me time between him and some squallin' brat." Brae dragged her fingers slowly over the great expanse of flesh exposed by the low cut of her dress. MacCrae's gaze followed them covetously.

Gard acknowledged pride at how well Brae was handling MacCrae—a good little actress in her own right.

She continued. "We are travelin' all o'er and I am seein' and doin' things tha' would ne'er have been possible if I had settled for ye. I woulda ne'er been privy ta all the wonderful things he be teachin' me. Gard gives me things and shows me things tha' ya dinna e'en ken exist."

"Ah, 'tis Gard now, is it?" Callum's mouth hardened.

"Aye. 'Twill always be Gard."

She spoke with such conviction and emotion, a shiver shot up Gard's spine. He had tolerated enough of their exchange.

MacCrae's look of revulsion doubled when Gard sidled up to Brae. "Ahh, there you are, my sweet," he murmured. He wound his hand into her hair and gave a gentle tug, forcing her to look up at him.

His breath caught when she met his gaze, her soft expression one of submissive longing. Gard fought the urge to devour her right then and there.

Establishing his possession, Gard placed his hand over the expanse of bare flesh exhibited by the neckline of her new clothing. He was pleased when the bold touch raised coolbumps on her warm skin.

True to form, her gaze affixed on his mouth, and Gard thought for once to take advantage of that fact and give MacCrae a dose of envy he would not soon forget. "Be ye ready to depart," he asked, then licked his lips.

In reflex, she mirrored the action. Gard's body tightened.

"Aye, My Lord," she replied, breathily.

"I'm grateful that you have decided to continue our journey together instead of staying on here at Richmond," Gard said, hoping she would take his lead and continue torturing her former betrothed.

"'Tis *my* pleasure, My Lord," she purred. She raised her hand and played at his collar. "I am most gratified tha' ya wish ta continue as weel. I have become quite infatuated wit' your . . ." She traced the line of his shirt. " . . . company." She smiled slightly as she stared at his lips.

"'Tis to our mutual pleasure, then. You will thank your lord properly for prolonging our expedition." He took her hand and placed it near his mouth, indicating a mere kiss on the cheek would not suffice this time.

With a gentle touch, she traced his bottom lip.

His flesh prickled under her rapt attention. Her shallow exhalations buffeted his chin. She tilted her head slightly, rose up on her tiptoes, then pressed her lips to his, in what he was anticipating being a chaste meeting.

He grabbed her head so she could not pull away, but to his shock, that was not her intent at all. Instead she treated him to an earth-shattering kiss. He was taken aback by not only the intensity but his own powerful reaction to it.

MacCrae and the good people of Richmond faded into the background as Gard concentrated solely on the beautiful woman kissing him senseless.

Hunger consumed him. She was burning him alive. Before he knew it, he had taken over the direction of the kiss, mindless of anything else. Including Brae.

"Gard, ya are hurtin' me," she gasped into his mouth.

He froze and immediately forced himself to relax his grip, but it wasn't easy.

Brae brushed his mouth with hers, attempting to reengage his lips once again, but Gard refused to continue. He would take her right there in the courtyard if they did.

"MacCrae is gone," Gard panted.

Brae blinked several times then. Her face suffused with color.

"The pretence served the purpose," he said callously.

For a split second she could not mask the hurt in her expression.

But Gard had no time for mollycoddling. He stepped away from her. "'Tis time we departed. We have wasted enough time here."

He allowed her a quick farewell to Hudson before they were off.

CHAPTER TWENTY-EIGHT

Travel was arduous, as were Gard's moods.

Most often Brae rode with him and read. Yet the days they endured the trip in silence, Brae now knew enough not to prick his volatile temper.

The nearer they drew on London, the more the tension in him increased. His frame of mind grew ever darker. The brogue was all but forgotten, even when they were alone, and his treatment of Brae turned worse by the day. Something had changed during their time at Richmond, the progress she had thought they had made there all but forgotten. He had made it clear he no longer wished to travel in her company, but it was more than that. He seemed furious with her most time.

The apprehension in Brae multiplied as well. Gard would go to any lengths to regain what was his, and she was afraid he might lose his life in the process.

Brae pushed the troublesome thoughts aside and tried to concentrate on what she did have. The friendship with Bronwyn helped pass time on the days that Gard would allow them to walk together, but he'd also made it obvious he was not fond of the new camaraderie.

Bronwyn did most of the talking, which Brae was grateful for — anxious she might reveal her lack of experience, thereby leading Bronny to discover the truth concerning her association with Gard. Bronny was not shy in any way. Brae now not only knew particulars about Llachlan she had no business knowing, but also details about what happened between a man and a woman that left her red faced and uncomfortable. Thoughts which inevitably only led her to carnal imaginings of her handsome yet surly benefactor.

Unable to keep her attention elsewhere, Brae watched Gard, straight-backed and alert in the saddle, a natural leader. He was arresting to watch, almost animal-like at times in his stillness, speed, and caution.

"Ye can take yer eyes off o' him fer a moment, ya ken. He isna goin' anawhere," Bronny teased, while they walked among the men on horseback.

Brae shrugged her shoulders. "I am na watchin' him."

Bronny laughed. "A'righ'. The same as his eyes dinna follow ye when ya arena lookin' at him."

"Perhaps tha' is where my eyes be, but I am na thinkin' aboot him," Brae denied.

"I'm but teasin'. Except I'd be more apt ta believe ya if your cheeks werena flamin' red."

Brae averted her gaze, instead staring straight ahead.

"I ken how ye feel, Brae. There isna need ta be embarrassed or ashamed aboot wha' ya feel for him. We've all developed feelin's at one time or another for the men tha' visit us. I ken 'tis different for ye since 'twas no' your choice in the beginnin', and there mus' be somethin' different aboot ye for Marschand, since he has kept ye longer than any o' us thought he would. And for you, him bein' your first."

Brae digested that. "Do ya think tha' makes a difference, him bein' . . . me first?" Yet, in reality he wasn't even that.

"Oh, aye. Ye will remember tha' forever. Whether 'tis good or bad. 'Tis bad and hurts for all women the first time, whether ye were taken by violence or wit' your childhood sweetheart in the barn, or ye are lucky enough to last 'til yor weddin' nigh'. It only gets better, as ya ken. 'Twas a rough start for ya, but he has more than made up for it, aye?" She elbowed Brae. "I saw ya two kissin' in the garden. 'Twas a wonder he didna pull your skirts up righ' there and then. I saw Callum MacCrae storm off in a thundercloud as weel." She chortled. "And Islay said he doesna e'en kiss. I was almost in need o' Llach after witnessin' the two of ye together." Brae did not know what she meant by that. "I kenned Islay was a liar."

"Wait. Does tha' mean *you* have no' been wit' him?" Brae asked, needing to know.

"Nay." She shrugged.

"But at the loch, ya agreed wit' her. Made me believe the lot of ya had warmed his bed, at one time or another?"

"I did. Sorry, I misled ya. I jus' wanted ta give it ta Islay. I wanted her ta think tha' he had been wit' me. Wit' all the rest o' the girls. She likes ta laud it o'er the rest o' us when she has been wit' one o' the lords."

Brae's stomach turned, and her chest ached at the thought of Gard lying with Islay, or with any of them. And she was angry with Bron for misleading her. Besting Islay was one thing, but lying to Brae all this time seemed cruel, especially when Brae believed her to be a friend.

"Was there a man afore Llach tha' ya had feelin's for?" Brae asked.

A far off look transformed Bronny's expression. "Aye. But he didna feel the same for me. I tried evrathin' ta make him take me wit' him. I enticed him ta me bed. I wore indecent clothes, did indecent acts, rubbin' up against him just tryin' ta drive him crazy. I tried bein' submissive, then bein' aggressive. Ya mus' ken aboot tha'. I can imagine ya need ta be assertive ta hold your own wit' Marsch. He bein' such a rough sort. Anywho, for a time it worked, but when my love finally grew tired o' me, he couldna get away fast enough."

"I'm sorry."

"Dinna be, I wouldna found Llach otherwise." Her soft gaze swung to Llachlan.

"Does he no' hate it tha' ya . . ." Brae chose her words carefully. "Ya still entertainin' other men?"

"I willna do tha' anamore. Llach and I had talked aboot it afore Robbie. I was gonna stop doin' it and just follow along wit' him. Lord Marschand doesna care as long as we dinna hold up his progress. But then Robbie stormed me tent and did as he wished wit' me. I'm feelin' quite fortunate since wha' he did ta tha' other girl at Ross."

Brae shivered. "Aye, 'twas awful I hear."

Not long after, Marschand called a pause in the expedition and allowed the troop some nourishment.

Bron and Llach sat together but Brae didn't wish to intrude.

Marschand had disappeared, as he was wont to do.

Dubhán approached with an apple and dry bread. Gratefully, Brae chose the apple and took a bite, while the young squire ripped off a big hunk of flatbread with his teeth and chewed noisily.

"Where be your lord, Dubhán," Brae inquired.

"He's scoutin' aboot."

"Why?"

The boy shrugged. "I wasna gonna ask. He be in a fine temper. Been in one since I met him," he added.

Brae had to agree. He had been wretched of late, more so than usual. If he wasn't taking it out on her, he was sharing his misery with Dubhán.

"Ye should be thankin' me, Dubhán," Brae teased.

"Why is tha'?"

She winked. "He's not takin' his displeasure solely oot on ye anamore. Evra other outburst he directs my way."

"Aye. He be spreadin' it aroond. But I have noticed tha' since ya stepped in front o' me at Leyburn, he hasna laid a hand on me. He still rants, but he hasna struck me since. How aboot ye?"

"He has ne'er struck me," Brae replied.

The lad's expression turned dubious.

"He manhandles me in evraother way, to be sure. But he doesna abuse me."

To her surprise, Dubhán sat down beside her and they chatted companionably, until a large shadow crossed over them.

"You will ride with me," Marschand said before promptly walking away.

Once travel resumed, Gard did not want to be read to and he did not want to talk. He was extremely stiff and alert atop his horse.

"Be there somethin' wrong?" Brae asked.

He sent her a dark look but did not reply.

"Be there someone followin'?"

His jaw tightened.

"Ya are obviously watchful for somethin'."

"You ask too many questions," he snapped.

"And ye ne'er give any answers."

Viciously, he gripped her hips. "And you never sit still," he snarled, through clenched teeth.

Brae remembered what Bronny had shared, of how she'd enticed her Lord, rubbing up against him.

Brae fidgeted, as she often did, stretching sore muscles or shifting to a more comfortable position. Yet this time, she wrapped each of her hands around his upper thighs for support. His muscles bunched under her palms.

Brae braced her arms and lifted her rear end off the horse. She pressed her tailbone against Gard's abdomen, then deliberately eased downward, sliding her bottom over his hardness until she was seated. Then she snuggled between his legs.

Her reward was a throaty growl. She tried desperately not to smile. Could it be that simple to tempt him? His hands tightened painfully at her waist as he pulled her more snugly against him. His manhood dug into her.

Gard's breath quickened in her ear. The sound and the heat excited her. She raked his thighs with her fingernails, and let her head fall against his shoulder.

"You play a dangerous game," he warned in a gravelly voice.

"I'm not playin' a game," she retorted.

Gard signaled to the rest of the troop with a mere raise of his hand. The horsemen either sped up or dropped back, then fanned out, leaving Brae and Gard virtually alone, but for the far-off snort of the horses.

Gard slowed the animal, then demanded, "Bring your leg over."

She did. Now both legs hung over the same side of the charger.

"Ya arena playin'?" he crooned. He ran his lips over her jaw. Cool bumps shot all over her body. "Then wha' are ya doin', Braelynn?"

She wilted when he unleashed the Gaelic.

"Ya think ya can toy wit' me?" He kissed the corner of her mouth. Turning her head toward him, she gave him full access to her lips, which he took without hesitation.

Brae wound her arm around him, not only securing her hold, but also taking the opportunity to touch him, running her hand over his broad back.

With his index finger, Gard traced the U of her bodice before covering her breast. He kneaded her flesh until her nipple pearled in his palm, then stroked the sensitive tip to a hard tingling point.

Brazenly, Brae arched into his caress, seeking more.

As he continued to school her lips, he raised her skirt, skimming his rough hand up her calf, and over her thigh. The most delicious wet heat gathered between her legs. Her body prickled with anticipation.

Expertly, he plied her with his fingers, swirling the evidence of her arousal over her folds. Instead of being outraged by his boldness, she found only eagerness. She wanted his hand there, craved it.

"Wider," he demanded, roughly parting her knees.

All of a sudden he found a sweet spot. Brae jerked at the unexpected thrill that shot through her highly sensitized body. Gard tapped the raw nerve ending several times before rounding his fingertip, abrading the crux.

A moan of pleasure burst free from her throat. He roared in response, but to her frustration, he paused the amazing stirring. Then without warning, he eased a finger inside her.

"Unh, gaw," she cried, at the startling yet welcome invasion. Unable to help herself, she bore down on his hand, trying to create more of the luscious heaviness invading her lower body.

"Do ye wan' more, Braelynn?" he tempted, removing the digit.

"Aye, Gard," she groaned, and wiggled her hips.

With slow precision, Gard penetrated her once again, only to withdraw quickly. He repeated the action over and over.

Trembling, Brae clung to him.

He kept up a slow torturous rhythm, urging her ever closer to a precipice of sensation she had never experienced before. Bending her knees, she sought the pressure of his hand as he plunged faster and deeper. He invaded her mouth with his tongue and mimicked the action.

Brae whimpered, wanting to weep at the desperation he was stoking inside her. Who knew this kind of feeling existed?

"Be ye lovin' the devil, again, Braelynn?" he murmured.

"Aye!"

"Be it wrong?" His voice was ragged yet savage.

"Nay," she panted.

"Could MacCrae make ya feel this?" he asked cruelly as his fingers came to an abrupt halt.

She cried out—bereft of his attentions, offended by his words. She and Callum had never done such things. And how could she want *this* man to do these things to her? He was so spiteful.

By the nasty twist of his lips, vindictiveness was his intent. Gard tossed her skirts over her legs.

"Now you will endure the torture you inflict on me, on a daily basis!"

With her body thrumming with unrequited arousal, it took her foggy mind a moment to catch up to his implication. Shame flooded her, tears threatened, but she refused to give him the satisfaction.

"Put me doon," she demanded, as she sat up.

Gard placed his arms around her, corralling her so she could not jump, and seized the reins. He brushed his mouth across her ear. "You will ride with me for the duration." His warm breath and the deepness of his voice shot another jolt of sensation through her. "And suffer the same discomfort you impose on me." His lips grazed her ear lobe. To her further degradation, her stomach contracted.

Readjusting the reins, Gard made sure that his inner arm grazed the side of her breast with the natural rise and fall of the beast. His words finally made sense. He was going to punish her with this newfound sensitivity. But for what was she being chastised this time? Or was he just trying to share his own misery?

He signaled for the rest of the troop to catch up.

"How do you feel, Braelynn?" he murmured. "Uncomfortable? Can you not find a place to set your backside? 'Tis most unsettling, isn't it?"

Embarrassed, now that all the men had closed in around them, she was sure they knew what he had done to her. What he continued to do to her. She felt like she was on the verge of some cataclysmic awakening and they were all about to witness it.

Brae tried to create some space between them, but Gard yanked her against him. It was obvious he was suffering aftereffects as well. She could still feel his length and the very shape of him through their clothing, branding her.

He thrust his hips and trapped his hardness between them.

"Is it the constant jarring of the horse, Brae, that keeps you restless? The endless rhythm. The ever present bumping up and down. Does it remind you of my hand between your thighs, sliding in and out of your sweet wet heat? Did it thrill you? Did it whet your appetite for more? Or can you feel how affected I am by you? Do you know how I wished ta take the place of my fingers and drive inta your . . ."

Damn him, her insides clenched in response to his vulgar words.

" . . . over and over until we both can't stand it?"

"But ye willna," she whispered harshly, her breath ragged, her head bent in humiliation. "Ya willna give either o' us tha'. Ya stop. Ya run away and hie yourself off where ya shouldna."

He grabbed her chin, hurting her jaw, and wrenched her around to face him. "I have explained that before. You do not want what I have to give you."

"Mayhap I have proven ta ya time and again, tha' I am tougher than ya think."

"Ya don't want it. Not from me. I am no good for you."

"Dinna tell me wha' I want." She slapped his hand away. "Ye arna in me head or me body. Dinna e'en try ta tell me how I feel or wha' I want. Ya, for once, have no idea." She heaved herself over the side of the horse desperate to escape him. "Now, let me doon, or let me fall." She dangled precariously. Gard's arms were the only force holding her from perhaps being trampled by the big beast.

Viciously, he clamped around both of her biceps, then heaved her up, slamming her in front of him. "I told you, you would endure this day with me, and so you will." He kept his left hand secured over her shoulder while he covered her breast with his right and kneaded her flesh, right in front of all his men. A purely possessive and humiliating act.

Closing her eyes, Brae tried to leave her body and not feel anything but unadulterated hatred for the man. To her horror, heat pooled anew between her thighs. Slowly he slid his hand over her ribs and stomach before cupping her roughly through her skirt. Her body responded to his rough treatment and she involuntarily bucked against his hand.

He chuckled evilly in her ear.

"I hate you," she sobbed.

"Ya have evra righ'," he agreed.

For an excruciating amount of time, if he was not touching her in some way, he was verbally assaulting her with words of sensual pleasure he would only deny her. Deny them both.

Somehow, she was finally able to shut him out. Her body cooled and his lecherous diatribe ultimately ceased. It gave her some satisfaction that he was still enormously affected.

"I told you, you could not toy with me and win," he grumbled in her ear.

She pushed her bottom cruelly against his erection. "I told ya I wasna playin' a game, and clearly neither one o' us be winnin'."

Like a rabid beast, he roared. Gard shifted his weight and leaned backward slightly. The steed halted at the silent command. Then without warning Gard all but tossed Brae to the ground.

She landed hard on her hip.

"I hate you, too" Marschand sneered down at her, his black eyes glittering. "The devil take you!" He cursed her before kicking the horse into a gallop, leaving her in a cloud of dust.

"The devil did take me, ye heartless bastard!" she screamed at his retreating form. Under her breath she strung together an impressive stream of obscenities.

Yet again, Llachlan came to her rescue, helping her to her feet. "Be ye a'right, Brae?"

She nodded as dreaded tears threatened. Llach placed his arm around her shoulders.

"Wha' did ya do ta anger him this time?" Bronwyn asked from atop Llach's mount.

"The verra breath I take angers him," Brae replied, shaking the dust from her garments.

"Then why does he no' let ya go?" Bronny asked callously.

"Bron!" Llach chastised.

"Well, it jus' doesna make sense. If he be done wit' her, why does he keep draggin' her aroond?"

"Obviously, he be no' done wit' her then, aye?" Llach defended. He yanked Bronwyn from his steed. "Ya can walk as weel."

"Humph." She fell into step with Brae.

Only a few steps in, Brae was certain she had twisted her ankle in the fall.

"Why does he keep ya? He doesna seem ta like ya verra much."

"Mayhap it be no' me company he wishes ta keep," Brae retaliated snidely. "He enjoys me jus' fine when I be flat on me back with me mouth closed."

"Mayhap ye should use your mouth for better things and

keep him in a better mood," she said, picking up the pace and leaving Brae behind.

Brae shook her head. Had the whole camp gone mad?

Another rider approached on horseback. The animal's nose nudged her shoulder.

"Ya can ride wit' me, Mistress." Dubhán eased alongside.

"Tha's a'righ', Dubhán. I can walk."

"Na, ya canna. I see ya hobblin' from him dumpin' ya. No need ta deceive me. We be o' the same." He held out his hand, Brae took it and boosted herself up.

"'Tis easier ta mount your horse, Dubhán," she commented, clutching him as he moved the animal forward.

"Aye, he be a tad smaller than the rest o' the fine beasts, but he makes up in heart, Mistress." The boy patted his steed's neck.

"Call me Brae," she said softly, trying very hard not to cry on the lad's shoulder.

"I'd jus' as soon call ya Mistress, or *he* will take offense." Dubhán was most likely right.

Brae could not hold her misery in any longer, and let the tears fall.

"It gets easier," Dubhán commiserated. "Soon ya will no' e'en care tha' he mistreats ya. Ya figure evra-one be the same. Ya will be mistreated all your life until ya get big enough ta figh' back, and then they will leave ya alone."

Brae's tears fell faster, not only for herself, but also in sympathy for the boy who had no options. Perhaps she could bargain him away from Marschand as part of her payment when the time came.

"Ya are lucky, Dubhán. Ya have tha' ta look forward ta. But I dinna."

To her surprise he patted her hand where it lay at his hip. "Dinna fret. One day, I will protect us both."

He was correct in one way, Dubhán was in the same mind

to protect her as she him.

Sobbing harder, she placed her forehead between his shoulder blades. She tried to restrain herself when she saw him swat at his own cheek. "I thank ya, Dubhán, but ya willna have ta do so. My time here grows slight."

They rode in silence for a time.

"Do ya have a real name?" Brae asked. "Other than the nicknames o' Red and Black, Dubhán? One your parents gave ya?"

"Aye, but no one uses it. I prefer the black now anawho."

She experienced some small sense of gratification in that.

"Kinda puts me in mind o' the Comyn's, ya ken," he said proudly, indicating his admiration for the two. "The Black and The Red. Can ya imagine wha' I could accomplish if only I had a bit o' both in me?"

"I believe ya do. Ya are strong in mind, body and will. I have witnessed it. Ya can endure and survive. And ya have somethin' *he* doesna." She referred to Gard. "Ya have forgiveness. For I have been the recipient o' it, and for tha' I am grateful. I'm proud ta call ya my friend. Ya will be a fine man, Dubhán, if ya take all the good ya can learn from Marschand and cast away the bad. Jus' like ya did wit' your sire. Take the good and do good wit' it. Scotland could use a few o' the good righ' soon."

Just when Brae thought he would not share his name with her, she felt him take a deep breath. He turned his dark head to the side so that she could see his profile.

"My name is Donnchadh," he said in the Gaelic throaty manner.

"Donnchadh?" She smiled at first. "Ya are a Duncan too, jus' as Callum's best mate." Brae blinked. She could not have heard him correctly. Duncan was a common Scottish name, but Donnchadh in the Gaelic form was not. "Donnchadh?" she repeated as her mind circled all she knew. Her memory surged to the missives on Gard's desk at Ross and the intricately entwined M C on the seal. "MontClaire," she whispered in awe. The fine hairs at her nape stood on end.

The boy nodded. Another tear dripped off his chin. "Me mother" — he paused, then squared his jaw and jerked his head toward Marschand, who rode far up ahead of them — "and *he* be siblings."

Brae gasped at the confession and shook her head in bewilderment. "Ya are his nephew."

"Aye. How grand it be, eh?" he said with contempt.

Brae finally comprehended the resemblance. She racked her brain for what she knew of the MontClaire family. Their holding had been Fife. She rolled her eyes at her own naïvety. Gard had been toying with her when he had conjured the fantastical rhyme. *The devil from Fife ruined your life.* And when she had questioned him, he had sloughed her off. The Earl of Fife, or Mormaer, had been a Guardian of Scotland, charged with the responsibility of supervising the government of Scotland in the absence of a King, before the clan MacDuib lands were confiscated by the Bishop of St. Andrews, making him the Custos of the Mormaerdom. The Mormaers of Fife were the highest-ranking nobles in Scotland, frequently holding the office of Justiciar of Scotia, and owned the right of crowning the Kings of Scotland. Dubhán's own mother had crowned Robert the Bruce in MontClaire's stead. In *Gard's* stead.

Brae almost smacked her own forehead at her ignorance. No wonder Gard had given her such an odd look when she had renamed his own nephew Dubhán when the Duib in MacDuib also meant black.

Brae was uncertain why the land had been stripped as well as the title. However, many lands and titles had been confiscated with no need of explanation or justification from the English, or the Church.

"I thought King Edward the first had MontClaire arrested, and e'en now he remains in the Tower o' London. 'Tis why Isabella . . . your mother, crowned the Bruce and no' MontClaire."

"Aye. Most people be under tha' assumption."

"Did he escape then?"

"King Edward ne'er had the real Donnghardh."

Donnghardh. Ghardh. Gard. Dear Lord!

Brae's mind worked over time at all the implications. Gard was not a mere soldier. He was from *the* most powerful and influential family outside of the king. A Mormaer was second only to the king of Scots.

This was Gard's reason. Gard MontClaire was the Earl of Fife, whether the Kings of Scotland or England acknowledged him or not. This was he.

Brae trembled in disbelief. He had lost much.

"He hasna told ya any o' it?" the boy asked.

"He is verra private," Brae replied, absently.

"But ya ken enough?" Dubhán nodded.

"I learn by leaps and bounds."

"I will say no more, for if he finds oot ya learned anathin' from me, we will both pay the price."

What could have gone on between the brothers-in-law to end in Dubhán's father's death at Gard's hand? And why was Dubhán with Gard in the first, and not in the custody of his mother?

They rode on in silence, caught up tumultuous thoughts.

CHAPTER TWENTY-NINE

Gard set a fast pace trying to outrun his demons and the woman who hounded him worse than they. Every time he touched her, berated her, or humiliated her, he regretted it, but could not seem to stop himself from doing so. Nor keep from wanting her. She had become an obsession. He woke up every morning wanting her more than the day before. He treated her horribly, but still she took it. He wanted her to hate him. It would make the intolerable situation so much easier for him if when he looked at her, he could see absolute loathing. But when he stared into the incredible green eyes of Braelynn Galbraith, abhorrence was not what he saw.

When they had left Richmond, he promised himself he would keep his distance from her. He had attempted to erect a wall between them, but she had torn it down and thrown it at his feet. And his subconscious betrayed him in sleep.

He had to repossess his life, and she had no part in it. She would fulfill his need, and then go. He was not good for her. How could he make her understand that? There were things in him he could not explain. Rage that dogged him. A darkness that drove him to commit despicable misdeeds. *Ya make your own rules.* He did what he wanted, when he wanted . . . until her.

When had his single-minded goal begun to incorporate *her*? How many times had he caught himself thinking of Brae before he made a decision or included her in plans for the future as if she would be there? It angered him beyond reason. She was not apart of the plan. He wished to take his dirk and cut her from him, viciously, permanently, from the parts and pieces of his being that she had so inhumanly wormed her way into.

At interminable lengths, they finally made London and set up camp outside the palace in wait for the Liege's grand homecoming. As Hudson had predicted, there were crowds of people already waiting to be heard, many ahead of Gard. His already dark mood plummeted. He added his name to the lists and they began their stay to be heard.

Gard and Brae did their best to avoid each other during the daylight hours. She didn't know where he spent his time, but his mood was blacker than she had ever seen. Since the day he had cast her from the horse, he had barely spoken to her. She spent her days laundering and mending for the men while chatting with them and tutoring Dubhán in studies. He would need the skill of reading, and Brae was determined to teach him. Much like Gard, though, he was resistant and stubborn, but she tried to find ways to educate him without him knowing that he was learning, making it fun for him by playing little word games.

But in the dead of night, Gard did not ignore her. He plagued her and played with her until they were both in agony. Then he would leave her with a dual dose of misery. She had no way to help herself douse the unrequited lust, and the anguish of knowing he went elsewhere destroyed her more and more each day.

Gard could barely stand to be near Brae, so aroused was he by everything she was, her voice, her smell, her hair, her skin. Gritting his teeth, he envisioned throwing her to the ground and ending it for them both. He wished this over, one way or another. Whether denied by the new king or living to fight another day, he needed to be free of her and she of him. Even now he stood on the opposite side of their tent listening to her interact with his men and teach his nephew while preparing the evening meal.

He could barely contain this overwhelming need. No one would stop him, everyone believed it was already so. Even she would not stop him. She had shown him how much she wanted him, would let him do whatever he wanted. She wanted it too, she had made it very clear in both action and word. He had awakened something very potent and sensual within her that day on the horse. He had been trying to teach her a lesson, but she had taught him whom not to toy with. It was no longer curiosity that kept her beneath him, but a need of her own that only added to his torture. She was a willing and encouraging participant now — like she had been that night at Ross.

Scrubbing his face viciously, he tried to banish the thought. She deserved better than him. He could not control himself at times, and they both knew it. He could not risk hurting her. Hudson was right. He would never forgive himself if he hurt her.

The sound of her laughter tinkled through the air. He left the camp in all haste.

As soon as Richmond joined them, he would send Brae away.

CHAPTER THIRTY

Gard's breathing labored in Brae's ear. He ground his hips against her, only his trews between them. Groans of pleasure rumbled through his chest every time he surged forward.

Brae lost herself in sensation. A burning throb deep within her heightened with his every thrust and every sound that burst from his lips. He seemed so lost this time, further involved and aroused than before. Not thinking, just feeling and riding the stir he created, Brae pulled her knees up while simultaneously gripping his tight backside, encouraging his drive.

With a feral growl, he attempted to pull away, but Brae clamped her thighs around his hips, bearing down against him, while pulling on his buttocks. The hot tip of his hard flesh met the wet heat at the core of her, searing her. She cried out and tried to welcome him.

All of a sudden, Gard flipped her violently onto her side.

A wet hot streak shot across her hip. Brae tensed.

Over her shoulder, she met his gaze. His eyes were black with fury.

He stood and snapped his shirt with rage. He threw a coarse rag at her before seizing the basin of water from the stand. He heaved the cool liquid in her direction. The bowl left his hands, then hit her in the hip with a dull thud. Water splashed all over Brae and the bedding.

"Clean yourself up!" he roared before exiting.

"Weel, I would have if ye hadna jus' tossed the water, ye

big dumb oaf!" She hoped the whole camp heard her call him names. Yet she dissolved into hot tears of shame. What was wrong with her? Why did she keep putting herself in this position with him?

Brae stood and cleansed his seed from her skin before attempting to save the pallet. There was no use, it would have to dry in the sun. How much more embarrassment must she endure at his hand?

"Mistress?" Dubhán called from the tent opening. "I've warm water for ya."

She was overwhelmed by the kindness.

She was not dressed decently. Brae reached through the flap. The squire placed the basin in her hand but held it. They could not see each other, the canvas between them.

"Be ye a'righ, Brae?" he asked, concern evident in his young voice.

More hot tears seared her cheek when the boy whispered her given name, as if he dared not say it aloud.

"Aye, Donnchadh." She patted his warm hand. "I be fine."

"He be in a temper, yah." He stated.

"Aye, I ken. I'm sorry. I will be oot shortly ta help ya take the burden o' it."

"No hurry, Mistress, there be enough o' us ta go aroond this morn. He be makin' the rounds."

She washed and dressed, but before she could help Dubhán as she had promised, Gard stormed his quarters, making the canvas shake in his anger.

Brae kept her back to him, too ashamed to face him.

He grabbed her by the arms with enough force to bruise her flesh, and he spun her around. He paused momentarily, his gaze darting about her tearstained cheeks.

"Ya willna do tha' again!" he roared.

"I dinna e'en ken wha' I did!" she retorted.

He bared his teeth and flung her away.

Losing her balance, she hit the wet pallet.

With as much dignity as she could muster, she stood, then brushed herself off.

Anger like she had never experienced burned in her belly.

Brae did not consider her actions, she ran at him with this newfound fury. She hurled herself at his chest. When he reached to steady her, she raised her hand, then struck him with all her might. The blow landed on his chin.

He reared in shock.

"I willna do it again. Because ya willna touch me again! Do ya hear me? Dinna touch me!" she screamed, standing toe-to-toe with him. She would not concede. Even if he retaliated, he would have to look her in the face to do it, and she would not cower. She slapped indiscriminately. "Dinna e'er come ta me like tha' again! Not unless ya be man enough ta finish it!"

His black eyes gleamed with fury as she struck him again and again.

"I canna take it anamore! Ya willna treat me this way! I willna have it!" Tears fell in earnest as she continued to scream like a madwoman. "I have done nuthin' ta ya, Gard, ta deserve your rough treatment, day after day." She punched his shoulder. "If I dinna seem like Braelynn Galbraith anamore, ya be a'righ'. 'Tis all your fault. Ya drag me further and further inta your murky world o' wretchedness, evra damned nigh' 'tis the same."

She slammed her palms into his abdomen so hard that he took a step backward before bracing his legs apart to accept more of her attack.

She fisted her hands and pummeled him. "Ya canna stand me durin' the ligh' o' day, but ya come ta me in sleep. Your unconscious desires me." She continued to assault his person, uncaring if he would retaliate. "Ya turn ta me. Ya put us both in a state o' bein' tha' I didna e'en ken existed." She hammered at him. "And then ya leave me! And ya seek oot someone else ta expend your want." She clenched her teeth at the pain it caused her, then she released her pent-up angst with her fists. "How do ya think tha' makes me feel? Oh aye! I ken! Ya dinna care. Ya do wha' ya wish. Ya are the great and powerful Gard Marschand and ya treat people abysmally and ya beat children and ya seize things tha' arna yours. Ya kidnap women from their homes and ya ruin their lives, but as long as ya are content bein' miserable, all is a'righ' wit' the warped and twisted world ya have created, built on anger and revenge!"

Crying openly, she punched him. "Ya willna do it ta me anamore. Do ya hear me? No more will ya turn me inside oot. Ya willna touch me again, Gard, fore if ya do I will turn your own dirk on ya. See if I dinna!"

Her fists slowed.

Gard was incensed by Brae's audacity, but he was also oddly pleased, if not extremely stimulated by the assault. Grown men did not stand up to him like she just had.

He took a moment to harness his anger. "'Twas always the plan," he explained, "if you have forgotten, for you to be able to defend yourself against me. And now that you truly hate me, you may just be able to bring yourself to do it."

"God kens 'twould be a lot less agonizin' for me if I did!" She stomped her foot, then planted her hands in the middle of his chest and heaved. While he recovered his balance, she made a run for the exit.

He was on her before she breached the opening.

One thing bothered him. "And why would it distress to know that I go elsewhere to expend my lust? I have told you time and again, and you have witnessed firsthand how cruel

I can be. You do not want . . ."

"Ahhh!" She shrieked in frustration as she battered him anew. "How many mornin's must we wake up this way? Obviously ya are wrong aboot wha' I want or wha' ya keep promisin' will hurt me. Seems as we have been doin' jus' fine simulatin' the act!"

He gritted his teeth when her words surged straight to his groin. "That is the difference!" he snapped. "We are merely simulating. You do not . . ."

Before he could even finish his thought, she clamped her hand over his mouth. "Go back ta hell!" she shouted, then spun on her heel and escaped.

Stepping outside, he watched Brae run for her life, weaving between the pavilions and the men.

Gard turned to his wide-eyed squire, knowing he had overheard their quarrel. Now that his nephew and Brae had bonded over their mutual hatred for him, Dubhán had been sticking close to the enclosure.

"Go. Find Llachlan. Follow her," Gard ordered.

"Aye." The boy scurried.

While replaying the heated argument, Gard paced in front of his quarters. What did she mean, it would be easier for her if she did hate him? She could not possibly be fond of him.

"Lord Marschand."

"Aye." Gard turned to find a magnificently clad notary who handed him a scroll.

"Your petition to see the king has been granted."

Time was at hand. For better or worse.

With mixed feelings, Gard accepted the parchment.

Braelynn had picked a fine time to flee camp. Gard needed her to translate the missive, as well as scribe one to Hudson.

Riding out of camp, Gard was forced to pick through the

crowds. People and pavilions had cropped up far and wide. The already crowded city swelled in numbers as people not dissimilar to him, tried to gain audience with the king.

Gard inhaled deeply. The place was beginning to smell like a city as well, human filth and unwashed bodies, coupled with manure and the acrid smell of smoke.

Close quarters and limited space had tempers running high. During the short ride, Gard witnessed several groups quarreling. The propensity for danger had risen along with the number of new citizens. Gard tried to quicken his progress, but the congestion slowed it.

A cold chill prickled over his neck and down his spine. His mount began to sidestep in fear and confusion, in the crowds.

Sitting straight in the saddle, Gard stretched trying to catch a glimpse of Brae over the sea of people. Brae liked to walk and would head for open ground. There were no moors in London, but there were a few grassy areas. But even those spaces seemed to be taken up by the makeshift city.

Finally, Gard reached an unblocked quarter, but he was still powerless to give his mount his head.

Scrutinizing and surveying everyone and everything around him, Gard was unable to shake the uncomfortable feeling that had taken residence in his chest. He didn't like it and furthermore did not wish to examine the cause. Nevertheless, he was most certain the sensation wouldn't leave until he found Brae.

Vendors had set up crude carts and exhibition areas just past the tent city. All manner of entertainment, goods and amusements were on display, entrepreneurs benefiting from the growing populous. Peddlers called to him as he passed, only adding to his raw nerves.

Where were they? Why could he not spot them? Thousands of possibilities ran through his troubled mind. Brae was angry. Perhaps, as he had predicted, she would use what she had gleaned from his past against him. Mayhap even now she was posting some message off to the vicar at Ross encouraging him to send the rebels for her. What she did not know was that the vicar would no longer be of any help to her. And Gard was not blind to the fact that Llachlan from Skye or his turncoat squire would do anything Braelynn asked of them, both so smitten, it irritated Gard to no end. But the English King was the only one who could cause him any serious damage at present. She was no one. The sovereign would never grant her an audience.

Viciously, Gard cast away his suspicions for the time being. Turning his concentration to finding Brae and her band of besotted misfits, another more dreadful and detestable thought slithered into his troubled mind.

Cowan.

What if Llachlan and Dubhán had been unable to catch up to her? Cowan was still out there. He could be in this mass of bodies, hiding right under their noses.

As his mind raced, he absently stroked his beard, irritated when he realized his hand trembled. Anxious, he coaxed his mount into a trot.

What had she been wearing? He vividly recalled the green as she had run from him. He had handled things abominably. He had done nothing but bungle the entire mess since the moment she'd had the misfortune to walk the moors alone.

Just then Gard spied several women roaming about, but none of them were his. Why couldn't he locate her? Why had he not caught sight of Llachlan? A head taller than the average man, his blond mane should stand out like a beacon.

Gard followed the bank of the Thames for a time before he turned to retrace his steps, confident they could not have traveled that much distance on foot.

The nagging chill renewed at his nape. Placing his hand there, he wiped as if he could erase it from his being. He had experienced this particular sensation only once before, on the day he had lost his father, and he vowed then and there to never let himself feel it again. It was fear. And it was unacceptable.

He commanded himself to discard his thoughts, to not even acknowledge them. For to do so would force him to admit that he cared. Currently, he could only afford to care about one thing. Reclaiming his name. There was nothing else. Certainly not a woman. Absolutely, not *her*.

In the near vicinity, a woman laughed.

Gard spurred his horse onward, slowly making his way past the vendors once more.

Where is she?

He could barely stand the clawing in his throat, the roiling in his gut or the heavy band that was even now tightening about his chest.

He halted the animal. Gard craned his neck this way and that. The horse danced, sensing his mounting alarm.

Like a litany, Brae's name resounded in his head, over and over. Until panic overwhelmed him and her forename burst from his lips. "Braelynn!" he bellowed. "Brae!" The animal sidestepped catching his master's agitation.

"Gard?"

To his relief, Brae stepped out from between two vendors. Llachlan and Dubhán followed.

The tension in Gard lessoned by degrees. He would have sent up a prayer of thanks if he still owned one thread of belief.

Openmouthed, Brae stared up at him. "Are ya mad?"

A lunatic he might be, but apologetic, he was not. Especially when the tactic had worked.

Reaching for her hand, he conjured a guise of boredom. "I am in need of you."

317

Brae frowned and hesitated.

"Come!" he snapped.

She turned slightly to address Llach and Dubhán, confusion still lingering in her expression. "Thank ya for your escort."

Both men nodded but stared oddly at Gard.

Brae took his proffered hand. He pulled her up in front of him. Stiff with unresolved anger, she leaned away—trying not to touch him, he assumed.

Urging his mount into a canter, he yanked Brae against his chest. She attempted to resist the contact, but he would not permit it.

Finally she relaxed against him, sighing in obvious resignation.

Gard held the reins in one hand while wrapping his free arm about her waist, holding her to him. He felt strangely light-hearted, not a common sensation for him. He lowered his chin to the top of her head as he held her.

"Wha' be ye in need of?" she asked.

"I have been granted my hearing."

Brae's heart began to pound.

While on one hand she was pleased he was one step closer to achieving his goal, on the other, she was frightened for him.

Without delay he rode to camp.

When they were safely inside his quarters, he handed her the scroll.

Respectfully, she opened it. "Ya are ta have your audience in a sennight," she announced.

Gard dictated a missive to Hudson at Richmond, and one for Hugh Chamberlain at Ross. She signed both messages with Sons of the Guardians of Scotland, as usual. But when it came time to secure the parchment, to Brae's shock Gard melted wax, then pulled the seal from his pocket.

A chill spread over her arms when Gard met her gaze before he pressed his initials into the hot beeswax.

"Another step closer," she whispered.

He blinked in that slow primordial way of his. "Aye."

"How long do ya think 'twill take for Hudson ta arrive?" She would feel much better, where Gard was concerned, once Hudson arrived. *Safety in numbers.*

Absently, Gard stroked his beard. "'Twill take a day, perhaps two, for him to receive my message. A day to prepare and another two days travel to London."

"He will be cuttin' it close. And Lord Chamberlain willna e'en be half way here in tha' time."

"Richmond will suffice," he replied confidently.

She prayed he was correct.

CHAPTER THIRTY-ONE

Gard moved to the tent flap and hollered for Llachlan, who came quickly.

"You will take this to Richmond." He handed Llach the message. "Then accompany him. Take however many you think you may need." He spied Bronwyn hovering as always over Llach's shoulder. Gard nodded his head in her direction. "Take *her* with you and leave her at Richmond on your return."

Brae touched Gard's arm tentatively. "Do ya think tha' be wise?" she whispered.

He turned angrily, ready to castigate her for challenging him yet again, but the worry on her face stopped him from exploding.

"I dinna mean ta question ya," she said as if reading his mind. "And I dinna presume ta ken wha' 'twill entail this meetin' wit' their king. And I dinna ken how dangerous or mayhap no' at'all. But dinna leave yorself short here. Ya should have strong numbers aboot ya until Hudson arrives."

Nodding, he then left the tent without comment.

Brae knew he was angry with her continued interference, but she didn't care. His safety was paramount.

Sadly, she began to gather her things.

So this would be the end. As Gard had ordered, she would accompany Llach to Richmond, and he would leave her there. She tried not to cry. She could weep all the way to

Richmond she reasoned. But to no avail — her tears betrayed her.

She did not look forward to being housed with the Lady Richmond without Hudson in residence. And then there was Katie and Callum to contend with. Brae shook her head. This next phase was bound to be unbearable — watching Cal and Katie continue with their lives, while she pined for Gard and mourned for what might have been. Brae placed her hand over her stomach. As Katie bloomed with Callum's child, Brae would be left with nothing of Gard's to take with her.

What could she do differently that might sway him to allow her to remain with him? What could she say?

While packing, Brae held Gard's portion of the topaz. If only she could use it as a talisman and pretend it had magical powers that might grant her one wish. But even in makebelieve, she was torn. Did she dare act selfishly and wish to remain with Gard, regardless of his continued ill treatment? Nor would it matter to her if he ever returned to his earldom. She would be content to live with him anywhere, in any condition. Or would she be selfless and choose for him to finally realize his heart's desire and be awarded his due?

She sniffed at her own silliness. The bauble was no more than a pretty blue stone. It held no mystical gifts.

Moving on to Gard's pack, she placed the gem inside. She did not feel right taking it. She would accept his coin if he so offered, but the gem was his. He might be in need of its value as well. Brae had the stone from Gaveston, and she had decided to sell it only if absolutely necessary.

She took one last look around, making sure she had all her things. As an afterthought, she tucked her favorite book of sonnets into Gard's pack. She considered leaving him with *The Battle of the Trees* but decided to keep it for herself so that in time she could pull it out, read it and think of him.

"What are you doing?" he snapped, upon re-entry.

"Preparin' ta leave wit' Llach."

"Oh, aye. I would imagine you would both enjoy that. But not this time. You will remain with me. At least until Hudson returns to Richmond, regardless of what happens between myself and the king."

"But I thought . . . ye told Llach I would accompany him?"

"Nay. I bade him take his whore with him."

Brae's spirit soared. *Yet another reprieve.*

"She be his woman," Brae corrected.

Gard's lips twisted in contempt. "Humph. If you wish to bid farewell to your *friends,* then you'd better hurry."

She rushed outside to find Llachlan, Bronwyn and four other men awaiting departure. A wave of apprehension hit her as her gaze landed on Dubhán who stood near them.

Brae turned to Gard. A look of surprise crossed his face as she placed her hand at his waist and looked up at him. "Dinna ya think 'twould be safer ta hire a runner? Then ya wouldna be down five more men?" He frowned, but then just as quickly, the strain in his expression relaxed.

He searched her gaze then matched her hushed tone. "I canna trust others, Brae. Not now. Particularly with my seal."

Her eyes widened. He had not only confided in her, he was also considering her counsel.

"'Tis tha' dangerous, this?" she asked.

He shrugged. "It could go either way."

Brae's gaze strayed to Dubhán. She knew Gard would not appreciate her meddling, and Dubhán could very well revert to despising her, but she had to voice her fears or forever live in regret. "Send Dubhán wit' them." She begged.

"Nay!" Dubhán, who was close enough to hear her request, disagreed. "I willna." Thankfully, he kept his voice low. "I will stay here wit' ya." He addressed Brae, his dark eyed gaze boring into her, much like his uncle. Donnchadh no longer seemed a child to her, but a burgeoning young man. She had come to care for the lad greatly.

She took his hands, trying to appeal to him. "Would ya not prefer ta be with the Lady Richmond? Ya did express a fondness for her." She tried to coerce him, using his infatuation with the countess.

"Naw. I will remain with ya."

Not wanting to expose the secret Dubhán had confided in her but needing Gard to understand the importance of her point, she appealed to Gard. "He be your heir. I would have him away from here if there be any chance tha' this may not go well for ya. He should be safely within the walls at Richmond, where Hudson will return ta assure his continued safety, if for some reason ya are unable."

Dubhán's eyes rounded and he squeezed her hands at the disclosure to their unpredictable lord.

Gard's lips tightened as he observed them coldly. "She be right. You must go."

Dubhán shook his head, and that look of defiance she was becoming used to crossed his young face. Brae took his cheeks into her hands, unable to hold the tears that filled her eyes at the thought of something happening to him. She allowed him to see how much he had come to mean to her.

"Donnchadh. Ye may be Mormaer's las' hope. If things dinna go well for Gard, ya are the las' o' the line. It canna end this way. Not after Gard has sacrificed so much ta retake it. I willna, *he* willna have ya here and risk tha' someone else discover who ya be. Ya are goin' ta be a great leader, Donnchadh. E'en if neither o' ya e'er realize the Earl o' Fife again." Her tears fell harder when Donnchadh's eyes filled.

"Jus' as Gard will learn ta rule again e'en if it na be Mac-Duib . . ." Her lips trembled as she tried to smile her confidence in this. "Ya will succeed. I have faith in your ability."

She nodded her surety, ruffling his hair. "My black-haired champion. Ya have wha' this country is in great need o'. A little Wallace, two Comyn's, The Red and The Black. And alotta determination tha' I ken ya learned from this one." She pulled at Gard's vest. "Ya go to the safety o' Richmond. Yah?"

"But wha' o' you, Brae?" he asked, worry etching his features. "Wha' if things dinna go well for him? Wha' will become o' you? If I be no' here ta protect ya, if he be unable?"

She needed to convince him. "Gard will lay doon his life for me," she said with more confidence than she knew. "And if he be incapable, then Lord Richmond will take care o' me in your stead."

He looked less than convinced.

"They willna e'en notice me, Donnchadh. I be nuthin' but his whore," she reminded him.

The boy closed his eyes and his face scrunched. "Dinna say tha'. I didna mean it." He threw his arms around her waist and hugged her.

Brae held him until Gard split them up. "Enough!" His patience had run out. "Do as your lady requests of you. Go pack your things."

Brae patted Donnchadh's cheek and winked at him, with contrived contentment. "Go," she whispered.

The boy ran off. Brae looked up at Gard, unable to convey her thanks.

He blinked slowly in response. "I am overwhelmed by the confidence you jointly possess in me," he said acerbically.

"'Tisna tha', and ye ken it. Ya said yourself ya dinna ken how this migh' play oot. Ya will feel better kennin' he be safe. 'Tis one less worry for ya. Ya can focus on the task ahead."

"And what has ever led you to believe he will receive any of it?" he asked callously, one eyebrow disappearing into the dark hair covering his forehead.

"Ya dinna drag him all o'er the countryside merely because ya enjoy his company. I ken ya better than tha'. I'm proof o' tha'. And ya only keep me aroond for me role. The boy has one, too. Ya may no' treat him as any person would approve, but he is your blood, and ya willna let your title pass to another who is not. Ya will do righ' by him. There be you and him. And if fate willna see fit ta have ya see your conclusion, then your life willna be for naught. Fate canna be tha' cruel ta ya both. 'Twill be for Donnchadh."

Gard blinked several times. "Ya be romanticizin' things again, Braelynn. I am not so noble as all tha'. I will have it, and I havena thought any farther than tha'. And if ya think the fates are no' tha' cruel, ya are as naïve as ya be starry-eyed. Fate be a fickle bitch!"

"I dinna care one way or the other. I dinna wish ta figh' wit' ya. As long as Donnchadh be safe for the now, nuthin' else matters."

His lips tightened yet again. "*Donnchadh*," he repeated.

"MontClaire," she whispered, holding his dark gaze.

He inhaled sharply, his nostrils flaring as Brae spoke his name. The hairs at his nape stood.

How much does she know? How long has she known? And does the secrecy even matter any more where Brae is concerned?

She returned his stare, nonplussed. Obviously, she'd been privy to this information for some time, and had treated him no different for it.

When the boy returned, Brae waved farewell. They were both in tears. The lad tried to hide it, she did not. Gard detested her crying.

Brae turned to escape to their tent when a commotion broke out.

"There's been a slaughter!" A fairly rotund English gentleman announced to one and all.

"Go inside," Gard ordered.

"Another poor woman has been attacked. Brutally."

Another? Dread weighted Gard down.

"This time the poor chit's demise was even more heinous than the last. She was not just brutalized. She's been . . . *dismembered.*"

"Dismembered?" Gard repeated, but could not mask the revulsion and disbelief in his voice.

"Aye. The villain chopped her to pieces. With a hatchet, by the look of it. He hacked apart her upper body and strew her pieces about. But he left her legs intact, spreading them wide and smearing them with her blood."

Gard heard mumbles of disgust from some of the men. The English gentleman lowered his voice.

"Even worse, there were bite marks on her legs, mixed in with the blood, making us think that the chew impressions came after the blood soaking. What kind of animal does that?"

"Protect your women, men," the informant warned.

Gard broke out into a cold sweat. The same hapless feeling he had endured when he could not locate Brae returned.

Protect your women!

A shudder racked his body as his mind went automatically to Cowan. Could these attacks be him? *Is he really coming for Brae?* Gard closed his eyes recalling Brae's declaration to his nephew. *"Gard will lay doon his life for me."* The statement had meant nothing to him until this moment, and with great clarity he knew that he would.

"Bain!" Gard roared.

"Aye, sir?"

"You will take up Llachlan's post as your lady's watch."

"Aye, Lord Marschand."

Gard turned toward his quarters only to meet Brae's tear-filled gaze. He should have known she had been listening.

"Bain. We will take half and stay at the inn for possibly one night. The others will remain here to maintain our position."

"Aye, Lord Marschand."

Gard stormed the tent and took up the packs Brae had prepared earlier.

CHAPTER THIRTY-TWO

They rode into the city. Finding lodgings proved more difficult than Gard had anticipated, with London being so overrun with spectators and petitioners. He had not given it enough consideration, his concern for Brae's safety overriding his usual thorough forethought.

They finally secured accommodations in a little hamlet.

Gard ordered Brae a bath and left her to her ablutions.

Sitting with a tankard of brew, he waited for the trencher of food that he planned to take to their room. Gard watched his men. They were much subdued compared to their usual carousing. He was not sure if it was their depleted numbers or his watchful stare that kept them in line this night.

"Wha' be the hold up, MontClaire?" Gard jumped at the sound of the old crone's gritty voice at his side.

"Wha'? How be ye here?" He spoke without thinking, so rattled by her abrupt and unexpected appearance.

"Tha' doesna matter. Wha' matters is ya be draggin' your feet yet again. 'Tis past time ta be gettin' home."

He gathered himself. "So be on your way home, witch. Cease troubling me."

"Why have ye no' claimed her yet?" she persisted.

"She be not mine to claim," he said, taking a long drink from his flagon.

"She bears yor mark. Wha' more proof do ya need? How have ya been able ta resist her? Ya dinna possess *tha'* much character."

Gard gnashed his teeth. What right had she to be so

audacious?

"Bah." She waved a gnarled hand. "Dinna e'en try intimidatin' me, MontClaire. I have been cowed by the best. And ya are clearly no'."

"If you are finished insulting me, you bony old hag, move along. You are wasting my time."

"Ya be wastin' time, MontClaire. And ya be *insultin'* me. I have a reputation ta uphold, and ya be taintin' it by forestallin' me predictions."

"Your predictions? Perhaps you should accept the astuteness of your betters and come to the same conclusion as they. Your sight and your prophecies be rubbish! Nothing more than storytelling for the purpose of entertainment and in my condition, vexation!"

"Ye may figh' it all ya like, MontClaire. But in the end 'twill all turn oot the same. Ya may as weel jus' give in. She already be Lady MontClaire. Ya may no' have claimed her in your stubborn head as yet, but your heart and your body have already done so."

He narrowed his gaze.

She smiled in her toothless way. "Aye," she cackled. "I ken, MontClaire. I ken wha' ya've done."

He leaned over her.

"Here ye be, Lord Marschand." The innkeeper interrupted, distracting him and placing a large tray in front of him.

"Leave me be old wom—" He turned but she was gone. "Where did she go?"

"Who, Lord Marschand?" The innkeeper wiped the surface in front of him, barely paying him any notice.

"The old crone."

He shook his head. "I saw no one."

The cold chill returned to his skin as he searched the room.

"Will that be all, Lord Marschand?"

"Aye," he answered slowly.

"Then I will bid you good night."

Brae heard Gard's footfalls in the corridor.

She had bathed and dressed in a quick and sufficient manner and was combing her wet hair.

Gard opened the door and deftly maneuvered the large platter laden with food into the small chamber.

The moment he set it down, Brae inspected the fare.

Gard stripped off his shirt. Brae was about to close the door when a serving woman appeared with a large flagon of steaming brew. She pressed it into Brae's hands.

"Thank ya," Brae said, bewildered when the woman entered their room.

"She doesna ken, does she, MontClaire?" the woman exclaimed.

Gard inhaled sharply. "Ya will leave us be," he said, using a most menacing tone.

"I dinna ken wha'?" Brae asked.

With lightening speed, Gard attempted to evict the woman.

She ducked under him, moving spryly for her age. She attached herself to Brae's arm before he could reach her.

"Yor name, Mistress?" she asked, taking the pitcher from Brae. She made a good show of pouring the brew into mugs.

"Braelynn," she answered wearily.

"Braelynn. Aye. Tha's righ'."

"Get ye gone, woman. I am tired of your prattle," Gard's voice was low, threatening.

She ignored him. "Have some o' me special brew, Braelynn."

"Wha' is it?"

"'Tis wassail."

"Wassail? Is tha' no' a Yuletide drink?"

"Aye. 'Tis," she answered. "'Tis me own special concoction. Ye'll both enjoy it."

Marschand regarded her sternly.

"'Tis mulled cider and honey mixed with spices and me own unique additive." She smiled toothlessly. "'Tis a notable occasion."

"Oh? Wha's tha'?" Brae asked.

"There be a special couple joinin' this day. A pair near and dear ta me auld heart. I have waited a verra long time ta see them . . ."

"Quit your nattering and be on your way!" Gard warned.

"Keep yor shirt on," the woman retorted, then cackled.

Brae eyed his bare chest, as did the old woman.

"I will go in a moment and let ya two young people begin."

Brae stared at Gard in confusion, hoping he might translate this strange meeting.

But when he did nothing but glare, Brae accepted the cup forced upon her. Tentatively she sniffed the concoction. "Oh, it smells similar ta . . ." She paused, dividing her focus between the pair. "Oh! Smells o' mulled wine," she backtracked as the crafty old lady continued to smile in an odd way.

There was no possible way the woman could know that the aroma reminded her of Gard.

"Aye, smells nice, eh? Reeks o' evrathin' ya ne'er kenned possible, aye?"

"Aye," Brae repeated slowly, mystified by her words and the cider.

"Take a sip. Ye will enjoy it verra much."

Brae took a drink. "Oh, aye, 'tis verra good," Brae said, then sampled it again. "Similar ta red wine, but better. 'Tis sweet yet not overly rich. Tangy but not sour." Brae gazed at

Marschand, then continued, "'Tis like nothin' I could compare it to, yet everythin' all at once." Just like Gard, she mused. The more she drank, the more she craved it.

The woman beamed.

"Wha's your name?" Brae asked.

Gard rocked from foot to foot, impatient to have the crazy hag gone, yet Brae engaged her in conversation.

"They call me Claire." She turned to face Gard.

He assessed her. A strange tingling broke out across his nape.

"You will leave now," he said, having come to the end of his tolerance.

"Ya should try some," the witch coerced. "Ya will enjoy it as weel."

"Aye Gard, ya will like it. It is—"

"Very nice. Aye, you have said that. Many times, in many ways. I would wish to bathe the road from myself, if you would—"

"Claire?" Brae interrupted.

"Aye?"

"Do ya think a lad migh' bring Lord Marschand a fresh bucket o' hot water?"

"Aye, I will see ta it. We mus' keep our lord happy, aye?"

"Aye, thank ya. And for the cider," she said, before taking another sip.

Claire handed Gard a mug of brew. "Ye'll enjoy tha', *MontClaire*," she whispered.

He wrinkled his nose, sniffing at the mug. His eyes widened. "It smells of—"

"Aye, it does. Enjoy them both. Ya have a pleasant evenin', MontClaire," she said quietly before continuing down the darkened hall. "'Tis time," he thought he heard her say as she disappeared, cackling in her wake.

Gard closed the door, shutting her from his mind.

CHAPTER THIRTY-THREE

"She a friend o' yours?" Brae asked, laughing at his expression of distaste. She took another sip of her new favored beverage.

He glared at her and then suspiciously at the mug as if it might bite him.

"Have a sip," Brae encouraged.

He inhaled the steam. The cider's delicate scent reminded him of Brae. Sweet and forbidden. *How can that be?* He took a hesitant sip. And then another. It was just as addictive as Braelynn, too. He tried to call on his anger, to prevent his thoughts and feelings about Brae from coming forth, but he could not seem to gather any to cling to at the moment. He blamed hunger and exhaustion.

They were still enjoying the drink when the boy knocked on the door with the steaming bucket of water. He tipped the pale into the tub, then turned to leave.

"There be a tray o' drink oot here fer ya, yer Lordship."

Gard pulled the board in, finding another full carafe of cider on it. He didn't bother asking Brae if she wanted more. It was obvious by the look of rapture on her face that she did. Handing her the container of liquid, he then began to unlace his breeches.

With a sigh, he sank slowly into the warm tub.

When he looked up, Brae had her eyes closed. Her cheeks were rosy.

It amused him, after all they'd been through, that she was still shy at times.

He didn't know what overcame him, but he decided to make her even more uncomfortable. "I am hungered. What be on the tray?"

She raked her bottom lip with her teeth, but she picked up the tray, then backed toward the tub.

"Ye need no' worry. Ya made the water quite milky looking wit' your soap. Ya canna see anathin'."

She turned fully toward him. After her bath, she had donned one of his shirts. The overlong chemise skimmed her thighs, drawing his hot gaze. Her glorious dark hair, still damp from her bath, flowed freely around her. To see her thus stirred something within his chest. A feeling long past buried and turned to dust, or so he had thought. If he was honest with himself, he had been trying to ignore the foreign and unsettling emotion since the moment he'd met her. A normal life complete with companionship was not for him. Neither wives nor heirs were in his plans.

Brae sat on a low stool close to the side of the tub. She placed the tray on the floor before passing him another mug of the mulled cider. He drank heavily from the tankard.

The shirt that she'd borrowed rode up, exposing her thigh. The scar from their mishap at Ross stared back at him. Reaching out, he stroked the perimeter softly with his finger.

"It truly be my mark," he said, mystified.

Brae cocked her head to the side. "Your mark be a pink moon?" she teased. "'Tis hardly a masculine crest ta embody the devil ya present yourself ta be."

To her absolute amazement, he chortled. The corners of his mouth moved upward more than she'd thought possible. She couldn't help but smile in return. She took his whiskered cheeks into her hands. "Ya are able," she whispered.

"I am able o' wha'?"

"A soldier does smile. Ya jus' laughed. I liked it. I knew ya would be ever more handsome if ya were no' so serious evra moment."

"I have not had reason ta laugh. I guess I forgot how."

"Will ya tell me?" she asked.

His expression shuttered.

She should have known better than to push him. She changed focus, to the food. "Wha' would ya like? There be bread and cheese, which I will admit ta ya I am truly sick of," she said, waving a hunk of flatbread. "No wonder a soldier ne'er smiles. There isna variety or pleasure in his fare. There are these delicious lookin' plum tarts. And if ya be in the mood for meat, there be a tasty lookin' beef and kidney pie."

He was looking rather strange. Dreamlike, almost. He took another long drink of the elixir, draining the cup.

"I dinna care. Surprise me," he answered.

Choosing a meat pie, she tried to pass it to him, but he made no effort to take it. She replaced it on the plate. Using a spoon this time, she raised a piece to his mouth.

As he opened for her, she was fascinated yet again by his amazing mouth.

"Mmm," he hummed. "'Tis good. Try it."

From the same spoon, she sampled the pie. "Mmm, 'tis." Brae knelt at the side of the tub. She was feeling very comfortable with him, almost carefree, like they had done this many times afore. "Try this, though. 'Tis e'en better." She raised a sticky pastry, and he parted his lips and took a man-sized bite. Some of the juice escaped the crust and dripped onto his chin.

She giggled and reached for a linen to wipe it away. "'Tis a good thing ya are in water, yah?"

He studied her in a soft way. For once, he was relaxed and not tense or angry.

"Wha' next?" she asked.

"I am no' really hungry anamore," he said to her surprise. He should be ravenous.

Instead she refilled his cup.

"Will ya tell me?" she asked again. Sobering she searched his gaze.

He took a long drink.

"I will tell ya the tale . . ."

Brae's hopes soared.

" . . . if ya scrub me back."

Reluctant, yet oddly titillated by the request, Brae moved to the end of the tub, where she grabbed a rough cloth and the lye soap. The harsh soap didn't lather well. With circular motions she began washing his broad shoulders.

Gard took his time, probably choosing his words carefully and maybe enjoying her attentions. He was taking so long, Brae believed he had just compelled her to wash him, out of his own selfishness. A trick to have her do his bidding.

Without words he also persuaded her into washing his hair as well. He closed his eyes as she massaged his scalp. For once, he appeared to enjoy her touch.

He took a deep breath. "'Tis all quite simple, really."

Still on her knees, Brae worked her way around the tub. If he was about to impart some truth, she wanted to see his face.

"The same story ya have heard tell all o'er Scotia. My family's lands were confiscated along with their titles. And I have spent the last score o' my life tryin' ta recover wha' is mine by righ'."

The flickering candlelight reflected in his eyes.

"Ya *are* one o' us," Brae exclaimed. "Ya have finally admitted wha' I have waited ta hear. Ye be a Scot. Just as sure and true as me." Overwhelmed with glee, she dove at his lips.

Just as suddenly, she broke away.

"Tell me, tell me evrathin'."

She settled beside the tub, making herself comfortable as she waited to hear his story.

He chuckled. "Ya kenned I be Scot. Righ' from the beginnin'."

"Naw, I wished it so. But ya denied it so often."

"Ye have kenned I was MontClaire for I dinna e'en ken how long. The black-haired Red ratted me oot."

"He didna rat ya oot. He told me the truth aboot himself, not you."

"I am not about to argue with ya, ya will defend Donnchadh until the end."

She was about to speak, but he held up his hand for her silence.

"I was seven. My sister was five. Our father, the Earl of Fife, had his lands and title stripped by the Bishop of St. Andrews. The bishop awarded us time to vacate. But father was more concerned with his people and what might happen to them than anything else. There were some of his folk who he knew would stay and thrive and hold their own against the new regime. But there were others whom he was in the process of relocating. He was too kind-hearted for his own good. And ours. Soldiers stormed the castle, with the Bishop himself. He pulled my father to the parapet, named him a traitor to the king, slit his throat, and threw him from the summit." He spoke so clinically, so unemotionally, as if he recounted someone else's life, someone else's pain.

"Oh, Gard. Did ye witness this?"

"Aye. We all did. We hid in the tunnels until we thought they were gone. Our mother was afraid if they found me they would execute me as well, being the heir. We took wha' we could carry and we fled to her brother's. Our mother didna last the month, so lost wit'oot my da. She couldna live."

Brae's eyes filled with tears and she covered her mouth. "She died o' a broken heart."

"'Twas like she only lived long enough ta make sure Isabella and I reached safety, and then she simply gave up." He blinked very slowly. "She was inconsolable. They loved each other verra much." He said this with derision, just as he had when describing his father as kind-hearted, as though both were a bad trait in Gard's estimation.

"Ya loved them verra much," Brae said. "Is tha' why ye dinna allow yorself"—she swallowed hard—"ta be close ta anaone? Ya dinna want ta feel tha' way again for anaone, afraid tha' they migh' be taken from ya?"

He exhaled. "I am tellin' ya the tale. Wha' I feel or dinna feel isna part o' it. My sire was too soft, and in the end 'twas his downfall. 'Tis much greater to be selfish than selfless. I would do well to remember that." He said it more to himself. Gard took another deep breath before continuing.

"I was ta be fostered afore this happened. My uncle thought 'twould be best for me to go ahead as was planned. I was sent ta Ross . . ."

Brae's mouth dropped open.

"I altered my name and hid my identity from all. Isabella stayed wit' our uncle."

"Ya were fostered at Ross?" Brae said in disbelief.

"Aye. 'Tis where I met Hudson. He trained there as weel. We learned much from Ross. I respected him." Gard would never have admitted this truth at the time, he had been so consumed by hate and grief when he'd first been sent to Ross-shire.

"I ken ya have ne'er been content," Brae said. "But ya

seemed ta have an affinity for your time at Ross. Why did ya then lay siege ta her so many years later?"

"'Twasna supposed ta turn oot the way it did. We were given orders ta take Ross-shire, and we had evra intention of lettin' Ross the man go free, but he was auld and the shock was more than he could take. Hudson and I were sorry for it." Gard trailed his finger over Brae's cheek. "But nuthin' at Ross went as I expected. Ya werena part o' the plan either, Brae. I didna intend ta bring any o' this doon on ya. I didna mean ta bring *me* doon on ya." He grimaced at his choice of words.

Brae filled their mugs again. "So no one kenned who ya were?" she prompted.

"Lord Ross kenned from the beginnin'. When Hudson and I trained together as boys, I grew to trust him and eventually confided in him."

"Ya passed yourself off as an Englishman?"

"When Hudson and I were of age, we went to serve our countries and aye, I portrayed myself as a Frenchman, a Scotsman, a Welshman. Or anathin' I needed ta be."

"Which country did ya serve?" Brae asked.

"I didna serve any, in truth. I served me own agenda under the guise o' bein' a good and dutiful soldier. I did evrathin' I could ta reclaim Mormaer. I was an exemplary soldier. I earned many commendations and the gratitude of the king. I received many commendations from many kings."

"*Kings?*" she echoed.

"I ingratiated myself inta any source o' power which I thought might help regain my due. I was willin' to use any tactic, any leverage, any favor."

"Wha' did ya do for the English King? Ya led more than the siege on Ross, yah?"

"For a time Hudson, Hugh and I were an elite force of hired"—he took a deep breath—"exterminators. We took care of situations and people tha' no one else could. We got inta places tha' couldna be got to." He sighed heavily. "I have done things tha' would send ya runnin' from this room screamin', cursin' me for the devil ya have always accused me o' bein'. I am guilty of the things you ken aboot and others yet that I will ne'er reveal ta anaone until the day the Lord asks me ta account for my sins."

"Ya have killed in the name o' the *English* King?" she said, irreverently.

"Aye."

"Ya have killed your fellow Scotsman for an English King?" she repeated.

Gard knew the admission might destroy any feelings she may have for him. "Aye, ya ken tha' I have. I killed Ross."

"Ya didna kill Ross. Ya said yourself, he was auld. 'Twas his heart. Ya hadna control o'er tha'."

"Braelynn. I told ya, I killed me own brother."

She turned away from him. "Brother-in-law," she corrected, as if that somehow made the sin less. "I ken there must have been a reason for tha'. Ya loved your family. 'Twas an accident. Or ya were defendin' Donnchadh against him."

Gard stood up, water dripping from his body.

With her gaze averted, Brae passed him a towel. He dried off, then wrapped the cloth around his waist.

"Braelynn," he called softly. She turned to face him. "Ya have ta see me as I am. Not as ya wish me ta be. Stop makin' excuses for me. I am not one of the heroes from your poems." For the first time in his life, he wished that he were. "I am the villain in your prose. I have killed wit'oot excuse. All nationalities, including my own countrymen."

She searched his gaze. "Perhaps wha' ya have done doesna matter." Her voice trembled. "But wha' ya do from this moment on should."

He rubbed her cheek. "Why this moment, Brae?" he

whispered, getting lost in her eyes. "Wha' be remarkable aboot this moment?"

"I dinna ken. But do ya no' feel it, too?"

He did feel something, but nothing he cared to examine.

"I dinna care wha' ya have done in the past. I want ta stay wit' ya."

His breath caught—he had not anticipated such a confession.

She raked her lip with her teeth. "I dinna wish for ya ta send me ta Richmond. I dinna want ta live somewhere under pretext o' widowhood, alone, unkennin' o' wha' it was ta be wit' ya. I wish ta stay wit' ya, Gard, in wha'e'er capacity ya will have me." She'd said his name in the harsh Gaelic way. "For as long as ya will allow me ta stay." A teardrop formed on her lashes.

Pain bloomed in his chest. He closed his eyes and swallowed convulsively before he looked at her again. "I have nuthin' ta offer ya, Braelynn. I am a landless knight. A murderer, a thief. An abuser o' women and children." *Your own words.*

"I dinna care if ya are an earl or a soldier. I have naught ta offer ya either. I have done things I am no' proud of."

He tried not to chuckle, she seemed so serious. "Wha' could ya have possibly done, cailin?" He tucked her hair behind her ear and waited for the earth-shattering declaration.

"Ya dinna remember me," she said.

He squinted. "Oh, I remember ya, sweet. Ya be the woman I stole from Ross."

"No. Afore tha'. In the spring, ya chased me inta the crags o' the cliffs."

"Tha' was you?" The corner of his mouth quirked in approval.

"Aye."

"Ya were runnin' communications ta the rebels?" He assumed.

"Aye."

"Weel, dinna try ta convince me tha' ya are ashamed o' tha', Braelynn, because I've been aroond ya enough ta ken ya'd be proud o' tha' truth. Ya would do anathin' for Scotland. Wouldna ya? Jus' as William and John?"

"Aye. I would on not so grand a scale as they, but I played me own little part. But some of the messages I passed ended in the deaths o' people tha' I was tryin' ta save. So I'm as guilty as ya. I have killed me countrymen, too."

He stroked her cheek. "Ya are no' guilty of anathin' but standin' up for wha' ya believe in. There's no fault in tha'."

With sorrow brimming in her eyes she said, "I caught a glimpse of William once. While I was secretin' communications. 'Twas mere days before his capture. I didna speak ta him, only gaped from afar. He was not at all what I expected. From the tales folks tell, he was an impressive ten feet tall and indestructible." Her eyes welled anew. "Yet ta my sadness, he was neither a giant nor was he eternal." She swallowed thickly. "Did ye ken William?"

Gard shook his head. "I didna ken him weel. I was too caught up in me own personal figh' for independence. But his execution did have a profound affect on me, as it did us all. His death solidified my resolve ta fight with any means necessary for what was stolen from my family and me. We need ta preserve wha' we do have, afore they take and destroy evrathin' tha' makes us wha' we are."

"Aye." Brae swiped her wet cheek. "The day ya chased me, wha' were ya doin' there?"

"We were scoutin'. Gettin' the lay o' the land for our siege on Ross. Findin' its strengths and weaknesses."

"Why did ya let me go?" she asked.

He shrugged indifferently. "Ta be honest, I didna consider ya a threat." Yet, now that he knew the truth, he was impressed. On the other hand he was furious for the needless danger she had put herself in when there were able-bodied men who were not as brave.

Brae sat heavily on the end of the bed. She yawned.

Gard grabbed a pair of trews from his pack. Brae averted her gaze while he pulled them on.

It was then, he spied foreign objects in his bag. "Wha's this?" he asked, holding up the book, along with the topaz.

"I thought ya were sendin' me ta Richmond and I wished ta leave ya wit' somethin' ya migh' remember me by. Ya will learn ta read it and enjoy it as I have," she said, her attention on her hands folded in her lap.

Gard tossed the items into his bag, then he sat next to her. "I will never forget ya, Braelynn." Easing his hands into her hair, he coaxed her into bed. Sleepily, she gazed into his eyes, no longer hiding her emotions. What had caused her to all of a sudden reveal her feelings to him?

Her eyelids fluttered. "I canna keep me eyes open," she murmured.

Gard realized he was fatigued also. He gathered Brae into his arms then guided her head to his chest.

In his lethargy, he wondered what had possessed him to reveal his life to her. Surely somehow this too would come back to haunt him.

CHAPTER THIRTY-FOUR

Brae woke in Gard's arms, the sun streaming in the window across from the bed.

By the sound of Gard's deep even breathing, he slept. Brae hazarded a glance up at him, then she seized the opportunity to touch him while she could. He had never allowed her do so for any length of time.

In his relaxed state, he looked so much younger, with no concern or anger marring his sculpted features. She ran her fingers lightly over his beard, then over his mouth.

"Mmm," he mumbled.

Now that she'd been honest with him about her feelings, Brae wished she had the courage to show him. Not vigorously, as he did, yet she was not so naïve as to realize that when he turned to her, it was purely a physical reaction and not a show of the emotion she wished he would convey.

She stared at his lips. How she wished to kiss them.

"Dinna," he warned, his voice sleep-deepened.

Guiltily, her gaze shot to his. He encircled her wrist and removed her hand from his chin. His eyes were once again, a soft brown and not the fathomless black she was so used to.

"I dinna want ta hurt ya, Braelynn. Not you. Not ever."

"But I only wish ta . . ." she said.

Cagily, Gard shook his head, giving her no room for argument.

Sitting up, he moved away from her. "Let us get back to camp."

She did not even try to hide her disappointment. Nevertheless, he had shared more with her last night than the whole time they'd known each other. Surely that meant something.

Only somewhat impatient, Gard held the reins of his horse while Brae fed the animal half her morning meal.

"If you are quite finished spoiling my warhorse, Mistress Galbraith," he said, without heat.

She rubbed the charger's nose. "Wha's the hold up, Marschand?" she teased. "We've been waitin' on ya."

Gard yanked Brae off her feet. She let out a shriek that turned into a musical laugh. Gard tossed her onto the steed, then he leapt up behind.

Brae reclined against his chest and they set off toward camp.

Something had changed drastically for Gard last eve where Brae was concerned. He was feeling differently about her, about many things, and could not explain why. Nor did he want to examine it. However, he blamed the old hag for loosening his tongue. The concoction she had whipped up must have been a truth serum, and with the shared truths came a feeling of intimacy he had never experienced before with any other person.

"Why are we goin' back? I thought ya'd decided ta stay at the inn until Hudson reached us," Brae asked.

"I considered it. But I have since determined to find the offender committing these attacks myself."

Brae stiffened. "Why? The fiend dangerously insane."

"Speaking of my history made me realize I could find and dispatch him faster than the authorities. I will issue my own sentence. There will be no need to wait for a magistrate or a trial." Justice would be swift and final.

A quiver ran through Brae.

"I considered leaving you at the inn, but I believe you were correct. Splitting our numbers at this time could be troublesome. Moreover, you will be safer with me."

"I ken," she said sounding confident.

He was humbled by her trust in him.

After settling Brae at camp and threatening Bain and the rest of the men within an inch of their lives to keep Brae safely in his quarters, Gard spent the remainder of the day speaking to witnesses. Subsequently, after listening to their accounts Gard was reasonably certain he sought Cowan and not some other predator attracted by the crowds. Yet another reason to keep Brae close. Cowan was coming, and Brae was the lure.

By the time he rode into camp, Brae was asleep.

Bain and three others were stationed outside, one sentry at each corner of the pavilion. After Bain's assurance all had been quiet, Gard ducked into his darkened quarters.

Stripping off his shirt, he joined Brae in bed. Without even thinking about it, he pulled her into his arms. She relaxed into his embrace and hugged him in return.

"I'm glad ya are home," she mumbled against his chest.

Home. Was that what they had here? He had not had a home since his parents had died. He pushed all thoughts away and ordered himself to rest.

Just before dawn, Gard's subconscious betrayed him yet again and he turned to Brae. She opened for him, as she always did. And as always Gard denied himself the pleasure of her body.

He sat up, his chest heaving. He rested his hands on his knees for a moment. The second he hesitated, Brae placed her palm against his chest.

"Please dinna leave me."

Seeking strength, he peered heavenward. Gard grabbed his shirt, then headed outside.

"Dinna ya ken wha' it does ta me when ya go elsewhere?"

The agony in her voice disturbed him. "Wha' does it matter?" he rejoined.

"Ya were more open and honest wit' me last eve than I have e'er kenned ya ta be, and I will be the same wit' ya now. It pains me tha' ya go ta someone else, when I would . . . when I . . ." She shook her head and trailed off.

She had said as much before. He kept his back to her when he answered. "I dinna go elsewhere."

"I dinna believe tha'. Ya leave me evra nigh', and most times ya return damp, as if ya have bathed the filth from yourself."

"I dinna have ta explain me actions to ya. I stole ya. We have no obligation ta one another."

Gard tried to ignore the telltale sniffle. He had no patience for her tears. He burst from the shelter and gulped huge breaths of cold air.

"I want there ta be." Her soft voice reached him from inside the canvas and stopped him dead in his tracks. His mind churned with crazy thoughts. With determination, he began to walk away, only to find his feet leading him back toward their quarters.

Brae stood just inside. Her wet eyes widened when he re-entered.

He wound his hand about her nape, yanked her to him, and kissed her with utter abandon. For the first time in his life his body, heart, and mind at odds.

"I dinna want this," he said devouring her lips. "I dinna want a woman. This doesna fit inta my plans."

Just as quickly he thrust her away, then began pacing.

"Ya werena part o' my plans either," she said.

He stopped marching and glared.

Heedless of his silent warning, she continued. "Do ya think this was wha' I imagined of my life? Ta be bullied and brutalized by the likes o' ya?"

"But here ya are practically beggin' for it. Are ya daft?" he retorted.

"Mayhap. But I was ta be an auld married lady by now . . ."

"Dinna remind me!" he exploded. "Ya are forever throwin' MacCrae in my face. Aye, I ruined your plans, but I did ya a favor. And ya have the audacity ta accuse me o' goin' elsewhere! I havena been wit' another woman since Ross."

At first Brae's mouth dropped in surprise, then almost immediately her lips hardened. "Ya mean ya havena been wit' anaone since Ross, so ya admit to, only because Hudson and I saw ya leavin' Islay's tent."

He glowered. "Wha' be ya talkin' aboot. I dinna e'en ken which one she be. I wasna wit' anaone but you at Ross."

She placed her hands on her hips and glared in return.

"There has been no one in my bed but you," Gard explained more precisely. "I return to ya fresh from the nearest, coldest water source ta lessen the immense cravin' ya bring oot in me. Have ya any idea how difficult it is ta lay wit' ya evra nigh' and have *no* relief?"

"Dinna lessen it anamore," she said in a low voice.

He raked his hand through his hair, ready to pull it out. "Ya dinna understand," he ranted. "I will hurt ya."

"Ya may think tha' but evra time I have asked ya ta stop because ya were hurtin' me, ya have. Ya have used your determination ta keep yourself from me all this time. We are learnin' o' each other as we go, Gard. We will learn ta relate ta each other wit'oot ya hurtin' me. I ken ya dinna do it apurpose. We will figure it oot."

He was thinking too much. Brae could not allow him to do that. He had returned when she had called. It had to mean something.

Brae gripped his shirt and yanked him to her, then crushed his lips in a frantic passion-fueled kiss. She fisted her other hand into his chemise and dragged him toward their pallet. Once there, Brae fell backward, using her weight as leverage to bring him down with her. With his lightening-quick reflexes, he braced his arms on either side of her, preventing his mass from crushing her. But Brae kept up the sensual assault on his lips. To her delight he gradually eased on top of her. It was not long before they resumed the dance they had been perfecting for months.

"No, Brae, I dinna want this," he said into her mouth.

Brae took heart. Gard might be lamenting refusal, but he was making no attempt to leave, either. So as not to spook him, Brae cautiously disengaged her grip from his shirt, then ran her hands over his broad shoulders.

"Ya dinna want this, Brae," he reaffirmed, yet he sucked at a spot just below her ear, sending delicious tendrils of sensation all over her body.

"I do want this, Gard," she panted. "And so do you. Quit fightin' it. I can feel how much ya want me. Can ya no' see and feel how much I want ya, too?"

"Ya dinna ken wha' ya are askin', Brae." His chest heaved. "I dinna trust meself. Ya dinna ken wha' I could do to ya. *I* dinna ken wha' I could do to ya."

"It doesna matter. Please, Gard." Incorporating all the tricks she knew, Brae used her mouth and her hips to sway him, undulating in the rhythm he had taught her. She kneaded his toned backside, enticing him to continue. She eased her legs apart, letting him settle between them.

Very slowly she traced around the waistband of his

breeches. She caught the tip of one of the laces and pulled, untying his trews.

"Braelynn," he begged. His voice sounded truly wretched.

On edge, Brae watched his face for any sign he might run. Delicately, she inched his brays over his hips. Gard pushed up on his strong arms taking the majority of his weight off Brae, and he allowed her to slip the material past his buttocks.

Brae's blood rushed. Her hopes soared.

Free now from his trousers, Gard shifted his hips and angled just so. As soon as his hot shaft met her long-suffering flesh, Brae gasped at the unexpected pleasure.

"Ahh, Brae," he implored.

"Oh, Gard," she whispered.

Yet he still seemed to be withholding. He wasn't even as vigorous as he was some mornings with all their clothes on.

At a loss, Brae scrambled for some sensual ploy that might entice him. However, she had not the experience to push him past the point of no return.

"No." He eased away. "I willna let this happen again."

Her heart plummeted. "Nay," she cried. "Please." She wiggled against him shamefully.

"Not until ya are ma wife." He sat up and turned so she could not see his face.

Brae froze, then stared at his bare shoulders, in shock.

He pulled up his trews, not bothering to lace them.

With his head in his hands, he sat on the edge of the pallet. "We will call for a cleric in the morn," he said in a defeatist tone.

"Wha'?" She wheezed. "We dinna need ta do tha'?" she said, confused by his swift turnabout.

Brae sat up behind him. Hesitantly, she reached out and trailed her fingers down his spine. His muscles rippled reflexively. "But, 'tisna wha' ya want, Gard. Ya dinna have ta take me as your wife ta do *this*," she argued. "Ya make your own rules." She shook her head in disbelief. "I was ta be your mistress anyhow, let us simply make it so."

"Ya deserve better than tha'. 'Tis the way 'twill be, or not at all. Unless ya have come ta your senses and ya dinna wish ta stay wit' me?"

"I didna say tha'. I dinna understand your logic. Ya dinna want a wife. Ya dinna e'en desire a woman in your life. Why canna ya merely take what I offer freely and be glad o' it?"

"Because ya are worthy of more!" He punched his open palm. "I stole your chance ta have wha' ya sought. Ya will have a husband. Perhaps not one o' your choice, nor will ya have the life ya thought ya would, but there 'tis. I canna promise not ta hurt ya physically or emotionally, but your choices are dwindlin'. As are mine."

"All this, so tha' ya will give yourself permission ta lay wit' me." Brae blinked. "Ye arna makin' sense. In time, ya will hate me for this decision and regret this rash change o' your plan. Ya will learn ta resent me. I dinna want tha'."

His head was going to explode. Gard needed some time away from her to clear his mind. He was drowning in a rush of emotion he didn't know how to deal with.

In anger, he snatched up his shirt and once again headed for the exit. "You, in time, will also resent me for wha' I have cost ya," he said. "On the morrow, ya will either be ma wife or ya willna. 'Tis your choice."

Again, he was unable to achieve the relative safety of the outside before her voice followed him.

"If ya are sincere, ya dinna have ta call a cleric and we dinna have ta wait until light."

Furious, he turned and raked her with his gaze.

"Have ya forgotten all your customs and traditions so thoroughly then?" she asked.

Confused, he cocked his head.

"Handfastin'," she clarified.

The suggestion left him reeling.

"I thought givin' ya a reprieve and some rest would give ya time ta see reason," he said, carefully.

"I dinna need reprieve. And I am well acquainted by now wit' me reason," she said with confidence. "Perhaps ya be the one tha's in need o' time ta think this through." She took his hand. "In this ya can at least opt ta walk away in the year and a day if ya so choose, as is the custom," she whispered.

There was such sentiment in her eyes he could not look away. "Why, Brae? Why would ya choose ta do this?"

"I think ya ken." Her lovely green orbs filled. "'Tis more than jus' the physical act for me. I have come ta care for ya . . . verra much."

Baffled, he shook his head. Clumsily, he covered her mouth and shushed her. "Dinna." He did not want to hear the words reflected in her eyes.

He shook off her hand, then ransacked his bundle. In his haste, he sent articles of clothing all over the floor, along with her treasured book and the bag of gems.

Gard selected the length of breacanned fabric, the tie that bound him to his lineage. Trembling, he held one end and handed the other to Brae.

He stared into her glistening green eyes, filled with an intensity he had never observed before this moment. Before he lost his nerve, he jumped right in. "I, Donnghardh Marschand MontClaire, take you, Braelynn Galbraith, as my wife for one year add one day." He wound a length of cloth around Brae's wrist.

"I, Braelynn Galbraith," she responded in Gaelic. The language moved him. "Take you, Donnghardh Marschand

MontClaire, as my husband for one year and a day." She draped her end of material over his wrist.

She waited for him to continue. Yet he was uncertain what came next. Only having witnessed one other handfasting, during which he had not cared enough to pay attention.

"May we be made one," Brae continued, winding the fabric once around his hand.

"May we be made one," Gard repeated, looping the tartan about her wrist in turn.

A tear trickled down her cheek. Gard watched its descent, undeserved of such sentiment.

"I give you that which is mine to give," Brae said, wrapping his hand once again.

"I give you that which is mine to give." He followed in word and binding.

"We must drink," she instructed.

He remembered that part and moved toward the tray, able to reach it without having to disturb the cloth. He poured a dram, then lifted the tankard to his lips, but he hesitated. At her nod, he took a sip.

"I pledge to you the first of my cup." He handed her the mug, keeping a hold on it as she raised it to her mouth. She took a taste, keeping her gaze on his all the while.

"I pledge thee the first of my body," she vowed. He inhaled deeply, all his senses flaring momentarily. Gard then drained the flagon, inviting the burn.

"I commit myself to your path in life." She wound the plaid.

"I vow to protect you *with* my life." He in turn encircled the material.

"And I you," she whispered, the sentiment in her gaze when she repeated this pledge was not lost on him. "This to you I avow for one year add one day, if not, we resolve to part without rancor or renew this pledge to one another."

"This to you I so avow," he repeated only the first part of the declaration. There would be no choice given to dissolve this union, for either of them.

"We must give of gifts," she said softly.

Gard spied the topaz he had haphazardly thrown out of his pack and she her favorite book. They bent as one and exchanged the gem and tome.

"'Tis done," she said.

"It has been so, since Ross," he said harshly tugging the length of cloth. With a gasp, she collided with his chest. He swept his hands into her hair — one bare, the other still coiled in the binding tartan.

Tilting her chin, he captured her lips, then backed her to the pallet, where he then frantically worked to free his hand of its wrap.

More calmly, Brae managed to unwind her end, then she embraced him in return.

Greedily, Gard slid his hands under her borrowed shirt, for once reveling in the decadence of her smooth naked skin, instead of denying himself the pleasure.

Brae raised her arms over her head and he swiftly divested her of the last barrier between them.

Shyly, Brae bit her lip as he swept his hot gaze over her voluptuous body.

Gard ground his teeth, his chest rattled, as the animal inside him clawed to get out. She had no idea how fragile his control was.

Once again, she tucked her fingers into his waistband, only to have him swat her away. Instead, Gard gripped her shoulders while sweeping her calves with his leg. He lowered her to the mattress, then eased on top of her as he had numerous times before. But the end result would be different. This time she was all his. From the second he had spied her on the moors at Ross, he had wanted her. Yet what he felt at this moment was much deeper, eclipsing that initial longing tenfold.

Gard could not wait any longer. His heart pounded. Every time his pulse thumped a litany of her name resonated in his mind. *Brae. Brae. Brae.* His body burned to claim her. He had waited an eternity. In selfish haste, he could not even afford her any preparation.

In a frenzy, Gard freed himself from his breeches. He kneed her legs apart.

Brae tensed, her eyes shut tight.

Trembling, Gard guided himself to her glorious heat, then rubbed the head of his aching shaft through her slick cleft.

"Open your eyes, Braelynn," he demanded.

She stared up at him, her expression a mixture of emotions he had no time or inclination to decipher.

"You *are* Lady MontClaire." With a roar, he surged forward, filling her in one fluid thrust.

Brae stiffened at the sudden invasion. For a moment, she experienced some discomfort, accommodating for his size, but it had not hurt exactly. Not like she had anticipated. While he moved, she kept waiting for the pain, surprised to find her body not only adjusting but also eager.

Gard picked up the pace.

Brae closed her eyes and simply listened to Gard's grunts and moans of enthusiasm. She tried to relax sufficiently, in the hopes of experiencing even a modicum of what he seemed to be benefiting from.

Slow familiar heat began to infiltrate her lower body as he glided in and out.

"Come, Brae, love the devil like ya did afore." The sound of his voice and some dreamed memory leapt within her, compelling her move with him.

"Aye, tha's it." He hummed in approval.

Brae matched his rhythm. The pulsing heat inside her built to a welcome ache.

Gard reached between them and swirled his fingers, catching the sweet spot like he had that day upon his horse.

Brae gasped at the delicious burn he stoked. This time she need not be ashamed of what he was making her feel. She moved with him, unable to control the whimper that erupted from her throat.

He rounded faster and added more pressure while circling his hips.

Something deep within burst free. She cried out at the incredible palpitating and overlapping contractions.

Unable to stand his stirring touch, she batted his hand away.

At that moment, he gripped her ankles and forced her knees wide.

"Awww!" he roared, thrusting deep.

His body tensed, his hips juddered erratically. Brae stared up at him. His eyes were closed. His face twisted as if he were in pain. "Uhhh," he grumbled, then collapsed, partially atop her, his breathing harsh in her ear.

For a moment, he remained fully sheathed. Having no control, Brae's insides pulsed and twitched in latent sensation, yet she could feel Gard's body parts reacting in kind.

Before long, Gard removed himself, leaving her bereft of his being. Things between them had escalated so quickly. He had brought her to the ultimate high, but she found herself plummeting twice as fast. Brae withheld tears as sudden emptiness pervaded her.

Gard perched on the side of the pallet.

At a loss, Brae sat up behind him. She longed to touch him, wanting to hold him and needing him to hold her in return. But she was unsure what he would do. If she pushed, would he leave? She didn't want that. Was he already regretting his decision to join with her? Had she not been worth his wait and frustration?

"Ya should wash," he said gruffly.

After pulling his shirt over her head, Brae went to the basin. Embarrassed to be cleansing so intimately with him near, she kept her back to him.

When she had finished, Gard remained sitting in the same place, his head down as if deep in thought. *Or regret.*

"It didna hurt," she said, a little surprised by the fact.

For a split second, Gard met her gaze, then quickly averted his eyes. He cleared his throat but said nothing. Something did not feel right. She had the strangest suspicion she was missing something.

"Bronny told me 'twould hurt the first time," she explained, watching him closely.

He rolled his shoulder while continuing to stare at the floor.

Suddenly, Brae was bombarded by not only vague memories, but also snippets of conversation.

For weeks after she had suffered from the infection at Ross, Brae had been convinced the images of hot kisses and bare entwined limbs were naught but delirious dreams brought on by the high fever and the wine Gard had forced down her throat.

"Ya were dreamin' in your fevered state if ya think there is anythin' kind in me. If ya thought I was gentle or gentlemanly in any way your thoughts are illusory. Wha' else do ya remember? Did I touch ya? Did ya act like ye werena the innocent one touchin' me in return? Ya kissed me in return. Ya opened your legs fer me. Ya invited me in . . . Ya have no idea wha' I could do to ya. Wha' I have already done ta ya."

Brae reached for a chair, steadying herself.

"You do not remember me taking care of you, for if you did, you would not doubt what I tell you. I am not trying to scare you. I am

what I am. All the things you have just described. And the ones that you have not as yet recalled."

"There has been no one but you in my bed."

In addition, as evidenced on her thighs, the morning after Hudson had stitched her leg, she remembered washing away the blood. Then, she'd thought the wound from Gard's dirk had been the culprit of her soreness.

Furthermore, this very night he had refused to love her, without wedding her. *"I willna let this happen again."*

Again? Brae began to tremble.

How many times had he taunted her with, including tonight, *"Are ya lovin' the devil again, Brae?"*

And the moment they'd finished exchanging vows, Brae had said, *"'Tis done"* and he had responded, *"It has been so since Ross."*

How could she not have known? Why had she not felt different? How could he have done this!

Brae stared at her husband. The nonchalant shrug was not one of ignorance or disinterest, but a product of guilt.

"You!" Brae raged.

His gaze snapped to hers, his jaw tightened.

"You . . . We!" She was so angry she could not string two thoughts together let alone words. "Tha' nigh' at Ross!" Enraged, she ran at him. "Ya took my innocence!"

He stood, facing the full-on assault.

Brae slapped his jaw with such force his head snapped sideways. His nostrils flared as he grabbed her wrists. In a stand off, they stared at each other.

She ripped her wrists from his grip. "Are ya no' e'en goin' ta deny it?"

"There be no' denyin' anathin'. Ya may have been ill and feverish, but ya werena against participatin', Braelynn," he justified. "'Twas not as if I forced ya. Ya may not have been in your right mind, but ya were more than willin'. In fact, you turned ta me."

"Ya bastard!" Planting both palms in his chest, she gave him a push, sending him backward onto the pallet. She jumped on him, and pummeled him. "Ya took advantage o' me while I was helpless? Wha' kind o' a man are ya?"

For a few seconds he took her abuse, before wrangling her. "I have ne'er belied wha' kind o' man I am."

"How could ya do tha?" She snatched one hand away and slapped at him.

"Ya kenned wha' I was." He sneered. "Ya kenned I was a bastard, and ya handfasted wit' me anaway."

"Ya said ya would ne'er hurt me. And I believed tha'. Ya took advantage of me, way back then? And we have traipsed all across Scotland, and *this* Godforsaken country, torturin' each other in this verra bed because I thought I was still intact? And for wha'?" She punched him. "We coulda been doin' tha' all along!" She was beyond furious.

To her complete astonishment he began to chuckle. Amusement bubbled from his chest. He threw back his dark head and chortled.

Brae stared at him. She had waited to see him smile and hear his joy, but not at her expense. He was laughing at her. Uproariously so.

"My anger is funny ta ya? Ya laugh at takin' a defenseless woman while she is feverish and then keepin' tha' fact from her for months?"

He grabbed his stomach. "Ya are forever surprisin' me." He continued to snigger. "Ye arena angry tha' I took ya without consent, ya are cross because we coulda been, wha' was it ya said? *Doin' tha' all along.*" He clutched at his ribs. "Does tha' mean ya enjoy it, sweet? Ya did seem ta tha' nigh' as weel."

"Ohhh!" She screamed and continued to beat him until he stopped laughing.

One minute she was thrashing him, the next she was kissing him and longing to have him inside her again. The highs and lows of lovemaking were making her moods extreme.

Gasping, Gard tore his mouth from hers. His dark eyes were not laughing now.

With a bruising hold, he seized her hips.

"Cast your leg over," he demanded.

Uncertain, Brae searched his gaze, then straddled him. He shifted beneath her and for a split second his hardness came into contact with her sex. A thrill shot through her.

He coaxed her to take a seat. With his trews still unlaced his hard shaft lay between them against his stomach. Gard directed her hips, to and fro. The action felt surprisingly good.

A pleasing heavy heat gathered in her lower body.

"Pull my brays down," he insisted.

Brae knelt over him and shoved his trousers out of their way. Yet when she turned around, Gard held his distended flesh upward and watched her expectantly.

Can it be done this way?

Before she could question it, he surged up to meet her. The tip of his manhood seared her flesh.

"Sit," Gard snapped, his jaw tight. The veins in his neck corded.

Slowly, Brae lowered her body. A rush of pleasure ran through her as he filled her.

Air whistled through Gard's clenched teeth.

Gard lifted her bottom, urging her to move up and down. The unfamiliar gesture felt awkward and clumsy, but the delightful pressure she had experienced during their earlier loveplay continued to mount and expand.

Being perched atop him made her incredibly responsive but she did not have the strength or endurance to keep up with his need.

With a growl Gard bucked her off and flipped her onto her back. He nudged open her legs, then plunged inside.

"Ahh, ya feel amazin'. Jus' as I remember." He closed his eyes, as he stroked deep inside her. "I had a taste o' heaven tha' nigh', and ya dinna ken how hard it was ta resist ya. Ya didna jus' lay there like an untried woman." Was he saying that was what she was doing now? She had no idea. It was all so new to her.

"I dinna want ta make a mistake," she whispered.

"There arna mistakes. Do wha' makes ya feel good. Jus' like when ya were strikin' me. Ya were overcome wit' need. Go wit' it. Jus' as we did tha' nigh'. 'Twas why I couldna refuse ya."

As before, he used his fingers to heighten her pleasure.

Gard moaned. "I was afraid ya migh' be wit' child. How would I have explained tha'? Ya dinna ken how relieved I was when I realized ya werena," he panted from exertion.

Her ardor could not have been curtailed any faster than if he'd thrown a bucket of cold loch water on her.

Gard had had every intention of leaving her behind when he departed Ross, well aware of what he had done to her and the consequences of his actions. If not for Robbie Cowan injuring Hudson and setting into motion the events that had occurred since, Brae might have been left alone, expecting a child, and with no memory of how she had gotten that way. And Gard would have never given her another thought.

I am not in need of a wife to produce heirs.

Without Brae's participation, Gard still found his satisfaction. At the last second, he removed himself before he climaxed, coating the crease of her thigh with his seed, before rolling away.

"Ya should wash," he said again. "Better yet, we might return to the inn where ya could bathe properly."

She kept her head down as hot tears scalded her cheeks. "Ya needn't worry. Bronwyn informed me o' what I must do ta prevent a child," Brae said, in a flat tone.

"Gud. Then she had one use," he said, lacing his trews.

"And wha' will happen ta me if I mistakenly become with child?" she asked.

Without warning, he wrenched her arm and spun her to face him. "Ya willna. Do ya understand me? There will be no more mistakes."

"Are ya sayin' handfastin' was a mistake?"

"Aye. Yours. Ya will realize wha' ya have sentenced yourself to soon enough. There will be no child o' this union. By error or apurpose." His fingers bit into her forearm. "Ya willna allow it ta happen merely because a bairn is somethin' *you* desire. Do ya understand? I willna stand for ya conspirin' against me. I heard wha' MacCrae said aboot ya wishin' ta become with child on your weddin' nigh'. It willna be. I dinna desire a child."

It was on the tip of her tongue to remind him that, a few hours ago he did not desire a wife either, but instead she said, "And wha' will happen ta me if it happens no matter how careful we are? Will ya kill me?"

"Nay."

She sighed in relief, only to be doused in his evilness once more.

"I willna eliminate you. But ya willna deliver of a child."

His words chilled her. Would he exterminate the child within her? She would be diligent and never give him the chance.

Absent of humor, he chuckled wickedly. "Ya may be righ'. Perhaps I have no need ta worry. By the look o' horror on your face, 'twould seem ya have no desire to produce my demon spawn."

Brae yanked her arm from his grip. "Let me wash."

Once again, she kept her back to him as she rinsed away his seed. She would have preferred some privacy, not only to bathe but also to gather her frazzled thoughts and nerves.

"I ken when ya were speakin' ta MacCrae ya were only

363

tryin' ta make him hurt as you do, and ya said things tha' ye didna mean, but ya did say somethin' tha' I had never considered. I too wouldna like ye dividin' your time tendin' ta some squallin' brat either. I wouldna stand for it. Ya will attend me above all others. Now come ta bed. Ya need your rest."

In silence, Brae entered the bed. Gard pulled her into his side and easily fell asleep. Brae was not so lucky.

CHAPTER THIRTY-FIVE

Gard woke up next to his wife.
My wife.

When had his life spiraled so out of control to have ended up here? And how could he have let the misfortune that was his life spill over into Brae. And when had he allowed himself to care? Especially for her. He had thought he was incapable of such emotion. He knew firsthand that particular sentiment only left a person vulnerable to hurt. To loss.

Why had he been so overwhelmed by the need to make her his wife before he took her again? At Ross, he had had no misgivings about laying with her, or keeping the fact hidden. Last eve, he had even tried to give her some time to come to her senses by waiting to send for a cleric. However, she hadn't wished to delay. Neither had he. How could that be?

But he did want Braelynn Galbraith. Braelynn *MontClaire*, he amended. Lady MontClaire. His Lady. She made him feel. There was no getting around it. He had tried denying it. Burying it. Killing it. He had attempted to make her hate him. Yet sometimes when she looked at him, it took his breath away. She could not possibly feel for him what he observed in her eyes. For he did not deserve to have anyone have those feelings for him. He couldn't afford to suffer those sentiments for her in return. But he did *feel* . . . something. More than desire, more than need.

Tenderly, he ran his hand over her hair, feeling very possessive at this moment. He imagined Brae wandering the halls of MacDuib Castle. He could picture her there. At his side.

She was his. To do with as he pleased, whenever he wished. His desire welled. He turned to his wife and took his pleasure.

Later, Brae woke, alone. She rolled over and discovered aches and pains in places she had never experienced before.

During the night, Gard had certainly made up for all the times he had denied himself in the last few months. Brae had lost count how many times he had made love to her.

"Ah, ya are awake." Gard entered their quarters with food. "Bain!" he hollered.

"Aye, My Lord." Within seconds Bain and three others entered hauling a large copper tub, followed by boys carrying pails of steaming water.

Brae pulled the blankets high as she watched them at their task.

Once they'd filed out, Gard held his hand out. "Come."

Brae dropped the blanket. Gard inhaled sharply, his hot gaze roaming over her nakedness. Brae took his proffered hand and followed him to the tub.

With his help she stepped into the steaming water. Brae sank down into the restorative heat and closed her eyes briefly as the warmth eased her aches.

"I thought ya would enjoy this."

Brae opened her eyes to find him near.

Gard crouched at the side of the vessel. He laced his fingers into her hair.

Warily, Brae watched him, afraid to give into this softer side of him, knowing how quickly he could turn and snap at her.

"How does tha' feel . . . *wife*?"

"Feels glorious . . . *husband.* Thank ya," she answered, easing some of the tension between them. "I would ask ya ta join me, but ya look as if ya have already taken a dip." The ends of his raven hair were damp.

Interest flared in his eyes, yet he rose to his feet and responded, "I will leave you to your ablutions."

She wanted to ask him to stay but scrambled for words as she stared at his retreating form. He was gone before she could think of anything that might keep him there.

Relaxing into the hot water, Brae submerged right up to her chin, letting her sore muscles work themselves out.

As she soaped herself thoroughly, she reflected on how drastically her life had changed in the preceding hours.

Brae washed her hair. She rinsed off, then stood. She gave her tresses a quick dry, then coiled the thick mass of hair atop her head. Before she could release her hold, calloused hands caressed either side of her neck. She had not heard him re-enter.

"Ya are way too stealthy, husband," Brae said. He moved his hands into her hair, and she released the heavy burden to him. She sagged against him as he massaged her scalp.

"How could ya be so sure 'twas me?" he asked, kissing her jaw.

"Because I ken ya would never allow anyone in here. Ya would be watchin' my *bare* back," she replied, turning to place a small peck on his whiskered cheek.

"And a fine bare back 'tis," he murmured before skimming his lips over her shoulder. "Come my, Lady MontClaire."

The words created chills over her skin.

"We have things we must attend this day." Holding out a rough cloth, he helped her from the tub. Then he dried her before tossing the linen aside. His eyes darkened.

He leaned in and trailed his rough fingers over her skin

before his lips followed in their wake.

Again she closed her eyes as he made her newly invigorated body sing. He worked his way over her highly sensitized breasts, leaving a damp path across her ribs and over her abdomen.

Gripping her hips roughly, he yanked her forward.

Brae gasped when he raked her mound with his teeth, sending a shiver of pleasure up her spine. Then before she knew what he was about, he dragged his tongue through her intimate folds.

Brae jolted, her eyes and mouth opened wide at the unexpected stroke. She stared down at Gard's dark head bowed between her legs. Mortified, she was about to push him away, but he circled his tongue in a sumptuous rhythmic pass, making her a slave to the feeling he induced. Curling her fingers into his hair, she held him to her. At her sudden capitulation, he removed his grasp on her hips and cupped her bottom.

Heavy heat pooled between her legs. "Ah, Donnghardh," she moaned, using the Gaelic pronunciation of his name.

He hummed in response. The vibration sent a zing of pleasure from his lips to her swollen flesh.

Brae fought the pulsating whirlwind of intensity building inside her, reluctant to let the exquisite pleasure-pain be over so soon. But with his hot breath, coupled with the swirl of his talented tongue, he brought her to a fast, devastating climax.

Brae whimpered. Her legs felt weak. For a moment they played a tug of war as he tried to wring every last quiver from her.

He won. Keeping her in his embrace, he pulled her against him. He rested his cheek against her abdomen as her pulse returned to some semblance of a normalcy.

Brae brushed her fingers through his hair as he remained

on his knees before her. Cradling his dark head, she was overwhelmed with love and tenderness to see him this way. *This* was the man she remembered from Ross. She could well see why she would have given in to him so willingly. This man was kind and generous, but needy in his own right. Sadly, she knew this peace would be short lived, and she waited for the word or action that would pull down the mask, the wall of protection he erected to keep himself from hurt.

Slowly, Gard rose to his feet, somewhat shaky himself. He was having a difficult time holding on to his reeling emotions. He wanted to throw his wife down and bury himself in her, but he had vowed early that morning, after taking her for the fifth time in as many hours, that he would leave her alone for a time. Yet when she'd emerged from the tub with her beautiful skin gleaming and sweet-smelling, he could not help himself. He had never done to any woman what he'd just done to her. It was an intimacy he had never afforded himself.

Brae searched his gaze. He was again taken aback by the depth of emotion swimming in her eyes, with an equal amount of healthy apprehension. He deserved that. Undoubtedly, she was waiting for the unpredictable side of his nature to explode, and it inevitably would. Though he dreaded dousing the burning complexity with which she now stared at him.

Instead he cupped her chin and grazed her smooth pale cheek lightly with his thumb.

"Dress." His voice sounded harsh. He kissed her cheek, trying to soften the dictate. "Wear the blue."

Smiling tremulously, she nodded.

Gard took Brae into the city to purchase more dresses. They were of the best quality, elaborately decorated, nothing less for the new Lady MontClaire. However, trying on garments, getting measured, poked, and prodded was the last thing Brae wished to do. She was exhausted and sore and the only one she wanted to be poked and prodded by was Gard, despite her tenderness.

This time Gard remained for the fittings, watching openly with an assessing eye, which only aggravated her further.

As if she were not even there, Gard chose outfits, keeping the seamstress jumping at his every request.

"I dinna need anamore dresses," Brae complained.

"You will be dressed befitting your station," he sniffed.

"Ya mean befittin' *your* station," Brae said in frustration, not thinking before she spoke. She braced for an explosion, surprised when the outburst did not come.

"*That* remains to be seen." He sobered.

Apprehensively, she approached him. Brae wrapped her arms around his waist and was buoyed when he did not push her away. "Ya will regain wha' is yours, Gard. There can be no other ootcome."

"There could be many different conclusions," he responded. "And now that you are my wife, you might be a part of any reward *or* penalty I may suffer." Gard pushed her away.

She had half-expected him to. She finished the alterations without further complaint. Her childish irritation didn't compare to his worries.

Afterward, Gard took her for a noonday meal, then they rode slowly toward camp. Their shelter was the last place she wanted to go and be cooped up again.

"Can we go somewhere?" she blurted.

He cocked his head.

"Somewhere alone other than our quarters and the men,

or the crowds."

Without a word, he wheeled the horse in the opposite direction. They rode for about an hour before he came to a stop in a wide-open field.

"Ya arigh', Braelynn?" he asked in Gaelic, after yanking her from the animal. Her legs were wobbly from sitting on the horse, coupled with the recent physical activity.

"Aye." She was pleased by his concern. It gave her hope for their future that he could feel something for her other than contempt.

He took her hand. "Walk wit' me."

For a time, they wandered in silence. So many questions whirled in Brae's mind, but she was afraid if she opened that particular line, he would revert to the severe, angry Gard. She much preferred the one from early this morning, but he was acting rather uncomfortable in her presence.

"'Tis a lovely day, yah?" she said.

Staring straight ahead, he nodded in agreement.

"I miss my walks," she said conversationally.

"Ya miss your moor," he replied.

"Aye, I guess I do," she admitted.

"Do ya miss your father?"

"I do. But 'twas time for me ta move on as all children mus' do at some point."

Gard cleared his throat. "And do ya miss MacCrae?"

She knew she would have to answer carefully. "Nay, I dinna. Ya were righ', I believe. He was not the man for me."

"I am not the man for ya either, yet here we are," he retorted.

Brae stopped walking and faced him. "I'm not sure ya arena the man for me. 'Twould seem the fates have conspired against ya from the moment ya took hold o' Ross."

A quiver of unease plainly shook him.

"But wha' o' you, Gard? Ya are the one who doesna want

a wife. Wha' o' the loss o' your freedom?"

"'Tis different for a man. I am still free to do as I please."

Brae braced herself. He was about to wound her with words as he did when he felt cornered. Before he could, she continued strolling. She did not wish to hear that in time he would seek out another. She could not take it right now. Her emotions were up and down as it was. She did not need to consider this so soon after their vows. It had been difficult enough thinking he was warming someone else's bed during their travels. But now he was her husband. The dynamics between them were different.

Brae walked to the edge of the water, then sat. Silently, Gard took a seat beside her. The sun warmed her shoulders and fatigue began to weigh her down. Her eyelids grew heavy. Gard leaned against a tree, then held out his hand.

Brae curled in his arms and placed her head on his chest. Comfortable with him, she relaxed and slept.

Gard had never spent such an unproductive, lazy afternoon. Even allowing himself the luxury of an afternoon nap with his wife in his arms.

While she dozed, Gard retrieved the seal from his inside pocket. Since they had crossed the Scottish English border, he had been carrying it on his person.

Brae's words from earlier echoed in his mind, '*Twould seem the fates have conspired against ya from the moment ya took hold o' Ross.*

Absently Gard turned his family's emblem over and over in his hands, as the wind seemed to whisper, *this woman bears your mark.*

Once more, a shiver ran through him. He placed his hand over the back of his neck to stave off the cold tingling there.

Brae shifted in his arms. Her eyes fluttered. She seemed quite worn out from his incessant lovemaking the prior evening. Smiling lazily, she stretched, then kissed his chin.

"Did ya have a good rest?" he asked.

"Aye. The best pillow e'er made." She patted his chest. "Ya look rather relaxed yourself, Gard."

From the moment they had exchanged vows, Brae had taken to using the Gaelic pronunciation of his name. His stomach fluttered every time his true forename passed her sweet lips.

"Aye, had a nap as weel," he confessed.

She giggled. "I bet ya have no' had a catnap since ya were a toddler."

"Ya would be righ'."

She tangled her fingers with his. The moment she noted the seal, she sat up.

"How did ya get it?" she asked. "Ya said tha' it came ta ya as a pair. The gem and your family's seal."

He tensed then placed the MontClaire stamp back into his pocket before he answered. "My sister, Isabella, Donnchadh's mother, brought it to me as a set."

"Isabella?" Brae frowned. "How did she come by it?"

"I didna get the whole of it. We werena able ta speak long. Not tha' we would have even if we'd had the time."

She cocked her head. "Wha' do ya mean?"

"We dinna see eye ta eye on most things. We havena spent much time together since we were children and when we do it ne'er ends weel. We are verra different."

"Is' tha' because ya dinna have much use for women in general, or sibling rivalry?"

"When did I e'er say I had no use for women?" He squinted.

She returned his stare. "Ye didna have ta say it, your actions are verra clear."

The corner of his lip twitched as he grabbed for her. "I have use for you."

"Aye, I ken. And ya have used me many times."

Recalling his vow, he sobered and loosened his grip.

"My sister and I were separated from each other so young. I was overprotective o' her when we were children, but we received verra different upbringin's after our parents died. I made myself strong and trained and plotted and nurtured my need for revenge, while she was coddled and reminded daily o' how important our ancestral position had been. It made her think better o' herself. Gave her lofty thoughts and ambitious schemes o' her own ta marry weel, so tha' she migh' reclaim, if not our inherited role, then one of equal importance."

"And did she marry weel then?"

He snorted. "Naw. She hadna choice but ta marry Donnchadh's father. But e'en in tha', did ya notice, she didna name her child after his sire, as is most common. She named him after our father, so folks would speculate. But to answer your question, much as your former betrothed and your false friend Katie, Isabella and the boy's father were caught in a compromisin' position. Bella refused at first ta marry him, but when she realized she was with child, there wasna choices left for her. She detested the man."

"Then why would she lay wit' him?" Brae asked, naïvely.

Gard raised an eyebrow.

"He forced her then?" she surmised.

"Nay, no' all unions begin as ours did."

"But ours was no' wha' it appeared," she argued.

He raised his hand to her cheek and let it drift down her neck slowly. He traced the swell of her breasts. She wilted under his caress. "Do ya enjoy my touch?"

Her gaze dropped to his lips. "Aye."

"Did ya enjoy last eve?"

"Aye," she whispered. "Parts o' it," she added.

"Then why do ya think people lay together?"

Her eyes rounded. "Oh!"

Following the path of his hand with his gaze, he wanted to bury his face in her flesh, but denying himself, he withdrew now that he'd made his point. "There needs be na force. Men and woman have enjoyed this activity since the beginnin' o' time, and not just ta further the race."

"Women generally dinna have much choice in the men tha' be chosen for them," Brae replied. "But Isabella clearly chose ta be wit' Donnchadh's sire. Why then did she decide she hated him?"

Gard half-smiled. "Again, men and women dinna need ta get along ta participate in tha' particular pastime. Sometimes they jus' get carried away. Ya canna tell me in the beginnin' tha' ya wished ta lay wit' me."

She peered at him through her lashes.

"As ya once said ta me, I couldna stand ya in the ligh' o' day, but I turned ta ya in the nigh'. Ya were the same wit' me. Ya canna abide me during the day, but ya now enjoy my touch. Ya may disagree wit' the way I conduct meself as a person, but you want me as a man. Ya have na objection o' bein' under me."

"Or atop, 'twould seem," she blurted, then blushed furiously.

Unable to help himself, he chuckled. "Ya continue ta surprise me."

"Is tha' true then?" she asked. "Tha' ya still canna abide me durin' the light? Did ya only handfast wit' me ta lay wit' me?"

"Ya ken I didna have ta handfast ta lay wit' ya. I could have done so at any time."

"Then why didna ya? Ya had no misgivin's aboot layin' wit' me when ya thought tha' I would ne'er recall, and ya would have left me at Ross regardless o' whether I be with your child or not, but all of a sudden, now ya feel some kind o' regret is it, tha' made ya wish ta wed me?"

Unable to face the straightforward truth in her statements, he looked away. "I would have been made aware if you were in need, with Hugh holding Ross to keep an eye on you." He shifted and placed his hands on his knees. "As I said, you deserved better than to be labeled as my actions have done to you."

Brae stood, then approached his mount. "Mayhap we should return," she suggested, obviously unhappy with his response.

"I thought you wished to hear of my sister and the seal," he said from close behind her.

"I will hear anathin' ya wish ta tell me."

"Then why now the rush?"

She turned to look at him. "I wish ta hear wha' is in your heart. Not the cold detached Gard Marschand version o' events, the ones ya keep in place so ya willna feel hurt again. And not only wha' pertains ta your family. I wish ta ken how ya really feel aboot the events tha' have occurred between us since ya took Ross. I wish ta speak with Donnghardh MontClaire and ken his heart as weel. For he is the man tha' I believe took care o' me at Ross. He is the man tha' I wish ta be married ta."

He swallowed thickly, anger set his jaw and tensed his body. "Donnghardh MontClaire ceased to exist when his parents did. He will not return. You married me. 'Tis me you will deal with."

"Ya are wrong. Gard is there, I have seen him, and I believe I am in love with him."

Gard felt as if she'd slugged him in the stomach. He grabbed her arms. He knew he was hurting her, but he couldn't stop. "Ya are not!" When she looked away, he bared his teeth like an infuriated animal. "And if ya do, ya are destined to a life o' misery, for ya are in love with a delusion.

Somethin' tha' doesna exist. Some man ya have conjured in your mind o' make-believe." He shook her by the shoulders. "Look at me!" He waited until she did so before he continued. "*This* is me. I am not kind. I am not soft. I willna feel for ya wha' ya think ya feel for me. I willna be weak like my sire. For weakness was his downfall. I am selfish. I want wha' I want. I will do wha'e'er I need ta do ta repossess wha' is mine. I will kill. I will rape. I will plunder. I will lay siege. I will destroy evrathin' in my path ta reclaim it. And I have done all those things, wit' no regret." He glared at her, daring her to question him. Every muscle in his body twitched with tension.

"So how do I fit inta your destructive course, *Lord Marschand*? Will ya destroy me, too? For ya say ya have no regrets, but ya contradict yourself, since ya felt ya needed ta handfast wit' me and give me your name. Which isna e'en your name, because *I deserve better*." She sneered.

He gritted his teeth. "I have no regrets!" he repeated harshly. He was certain she would regret their union before he did. "Ya have no role in my destructive course. Ya will stand aside and watch it happen. One way or the other."

"And wha' am I ta do if it doesna go weel for ya?"

Damn it, she knew better than to prick his temper, yet she refused to stand down. He squeezed her arms, and responded, "Ya will rejoice in your good fortune ta be rid o' me. And ya willna e'en have ta endure the year add a day. Your guise of widowhood willna be a lie."

She wrenched her limbs from his grasp.

Gard tossed her onto his horse, then pulled himself up behind her. "Aye, and all is right with the world," he mocked. "She cannot abide him in the light of day."

"If tha' is wha' ya wish," she retorted. "I will await the nigh'." She crossed her arms.

"As will I." Gard grazed her ear with his lips and was

perversely pleased when a shiver ran through her.

CHAPTER THIRTY-SIX

As they approached their plot in front of the palace, Brae was the first to notice the extra horses.

"Hudson!" she exclaimed, before leaping carelessly from atop Gard's mount and into Lord Richmond's awaiting arms.

"Mistress Galbraith. How good to see you." Hudson hugged her.

Gard swung down to his side. "Lady Marschand," Gard corrected. "You will address her thus."

Every man within earshot seemed to freeze in his tracks. Gard made eye contact with each man, one by one. "You will *all* address her thus." He made sure that each and every one of them acknowledged his order before he met Hudson's surprised gaze.

"Lady Marschand, is it?" Hudson repeated.

Brae stood on her tiptoes as Hudson bowed to accommodate her. "Lady MontClaire," she whispered.

Hudson's features lit up and his grin widened. "Aye. Indeed. 'Tis a grand turn of events. When did this come about?"

Gard yanked Brae into his side and replied, "Last eve."

With a confused yet amused expression, Hudson turned to Brae for further explanation.

"We've handfasted," she said, with a shrug.

"Handfasted?" Hudson repeated. "Is that not some Scots custom where as you may audition a spouse then toss him aside within a time period, when you discover he is lacking?"

"Aye, or he me," Brae replied.

"He will have no reason to cast you aside. There is no deficiency in you, Miss . . . uh, pardon me, Lady Marschand. That may take some getting used to."

"Thank ya, Hudson, for sayin' so."

"Enough," Gard interrupted. "You have made good time, Lord Richmond. We were not expecting you for another two days."

"There was not much reason to delay," he said, intimating that things with his lady wife had not improved.

"We have much to discuss," Gard said. "Wait within," he instructed Brae.

Brae's shoulders sagged as she ducked into their quarters. It would seem Gard was going to keep her from his plans.

Later that evening, Gard and Hudson rejoined Brae. When they entered the shelter speaking companionably, none of Gard's earlier stress showed, to Brae's relief.

"And how is your ladywife, Hudson?" Gard inquired. "Have you smoothed things over and even now enjoy marital bliss?"

"A contradiction in terms, if I've ever heard one," Hudson replied, wryly. "We've come to an understanding, if not achieved forgiveness."

"Ah, let me translate," Gard interrupted. "She has agreed to carry on as the unreasonable wretch that she is, and you will seek your pleasure where you can get it, while still groveling at her feet for absolution."

"Aye, I believe that is correct. You are catching onto the state of marriage quickly, my friend." Hudson clapped him on the shoulder.

Gard rolled his eyes.

Though they joked, Brae was unhappy to learn Hudson's marriage was in discontent. "I'm sorry, ta hear this, Hudson."

Gard scoffed, while Hudson replied, "I appreciate the sentiment, Brae, but I've no one to blame but myself."

"'Tis of no importance," Gard countered. "Her forgiveness or not. You should not have begged for it in the first place. Her feelings are unimportant."

Brae stared over at her husband and said pointedly, "I wonder if the time o' day has anathin' ta do wit' wha' a person can abide."

His black gaze met hers.

"Are my feelin's unimportant?" she asked.

"They are of no consequence. They do not affect me."

Hudson winced and said, "I believe the significance of her feelings will become glaringly obvious to you this night, my friend." Hudson chuckled.

Brae headed for the exit.

"Where do you think you are going?" Gard demanded, chasing her.

"I am in need o' a moment of privacy," she said, never slowing. Her guards fell in place behind her.

Gard let her leave with her security in tow. Bain, two others, and the returning Lachlan from Skye followed. She had not noticed Llach yet, too caught up in her own anger, which suited Gard just fine, much preferring her anger over her imagined *love* for him. Her ire he could handle—'twas the other he had no idea how to manage.

Gard returned to Hudson, who sat smirking at him. "I believe you will pass a chilly, lonely night, my friend. You have no idea how women can wield their bodies as weapons."

"She has done naught but torment me across two nations with her desirous body."

Hudson sobered. "Why did you feel the need to marry her? That was not in the plan."

"I couldn't keep my hands off her. Her nearness made me crazed. I couldn't think of anything else. I must concentrate on the task at hand."

"You did not have to make her your wife to lay with her."

"I couldn't bring myself to use her in that way. I put it off as long as I could. If I had been able to leave her at Richmond I would have been fine, but she is with me *all* the time. And beyond what all of you think, I am human. I couldn't resist her anymore. I tried to keep myself from her for her own sake. I did not want to hurt her. But I couldn't do it any longer."

"You could have had her at any moment. Why the need for permanency?" Hudson pressed.

"'Tisna permanent," Gard snapped, turning from his comrade's penetrating gaze.

"'Tis permanent. I know you, Gard. You have taken this woman for life. You can deny it all you like, but you would not have gone to such lengths simply to bed her."

In frustration Gard threw his hands up. "Perhaps 'twill not be a long union. Depending on the outcome of our meeting with the *new* king."

"But you felt the need to give her your name, perhaps in an attempt to protect her if things do not go well for you?" Hudson narrowed his gaze.

"Having my name might be more of a detriment to her, if things go afoul."

"Is that your reasoning then? You think she will not have a husband for long?"

Brae walked in at that exact moment. Gard saw the flash of hurt that shadowed her expression before she tried to hide it. She'd misunderstood the context of the conversation, missing the first half.

"Be he plottin' how good 'twill be ta be rid o' me in a year's time?" Brae asked Hudson.

"'Tis not what you think you heard, Brae . . ." Hudson stood, and tried to explain, but they were interrupted by a shout from outside.

There was a quick rap on the canvas before Llachlan stuck his head in. "Lord Marschand, there has been another attack."

Gard strode purposefully toward the exit, with Hudson on his heels.

"You will stay here with her." Gard commanded Hudson "Guard her with your life."

"You know I will," Hudson pledged.

Gard glanced at his wife, then ducked outside.

"Of what attacks does he speak?" Hudson inquired.

"There have been some extremely heinous assaults since the population of London has doubled. Gard has made it his mission ta find the guilty party. But so far he has been unsuccessful."

"Gard will get his man. He always does. Do not worry over it, Brae. Or should I say, Lady Marschand." He smiled.

She smiled slightly in response. "Lady MontClaire," she clarified.

"Aye. You are finally aware of his secrets then."

"No' all of them, I'm sure."

"And how do you feel about being the new Lady MontClaire."

"As I told him, I dinna care if I am Lady MontClaire or Lady Marschand or the wife o' a soldier."

Hudson stared at her wide-eyed. "Oh my God," he exclaimed. "You are in love with him, aren't you?"

She bowed her head so he would not see how much this was true.

He sighed. "Oh, Brae. You have made a poor choice of men to love. He will bring you nothing but misery."

She raised teary eyes to his. "I am beginnin' ta realize tha'. But for the now, it doesna change the way I feel for him. But sometimes he isna the man he portrays himself ta be. At times he is kind and there is an understandin' between us tha' I have ne'er afore experienced wit' another person. I want happiness for him more than I wish it for meself. I want him ta possess wha' he has yearned for his whole life afore anathin'. Have ya seen tha' other side o' him, Hudson?" Brae asked, while pulling out a chair for him.

"Aye. But rarely. He protects himself above all things, Brae. He inflicts hurt before he will be hurt. The loss of his parents affected him deeply. He will not allow himself to love like that, not when he knows how fragile life can be. How easily it can be taken away. He will not allow himself to feel for you, Brae. But you must not take it personally."

She laughed at his choice of words. "No 'twould take a much better woman than meself ta make Gard feel anathin'."

"Oh, I would not sell yourself too short there, Lady MontClaire." Hudson held up his hand. "Because I was there the day he swore he'd never take a wife. Gard does not vow lightly. And he broke that declaration to take vows with you. That in itself speaks a great deal."

"Or just goes ta demonstrate how easily he can break his promises," she said dejectedly.

"He does not make them carelessly. He took me to task over my . . . er . . . indiscretion. And as you have seen, he holds *no* esteem for my wife, so it was not her delicate feelings that he stood up for. Even though it is largely accepted men do as they please even after marriage, Gard is not of that belief."

"Why do ya think it affected him so much, Hudson? Why should he care then who ya take ta your bed? He tells me it is different for a man."

"I believe—he has not confided in me, mind you, this is purely supposition on my part alone—that he was deeply affected by his own parents' marriage. They were extremely close to one another, a real love match, which is almost unheard of in nobility. We are matched and traded to further our positions and rank or add to our assets. We do not go into marriage with love as our first compulsion. It is more of a business transaction with the potential of an heir. But his mother and father's love was quite legendary, from what I understand. Gard imagines this love made his father weak, but I believe the union made them strong. They were revered, and I gather feared by others who coveted what they had, and therein came their downfall."

"Their love was their downfall?" Brae frowned.

"That is how Gard sees it. Love is weakness to him."

Brae wanted nothing more in life than love. First her mother's, which she never knew, and then Callum's. She thought that he had loved her, and that their love would never die. Now she wondered if it had ever existed at all. Perhaps Gard was correct. Her expectations were unrealistic because of her books and her own thoughts. Possibly these things were not real.

While pouring Hudson a flask of mead Brae asked, "Hudson? Do ya love your wife?"

He fidgeted. "I care for her. Deeply."

"But if ya had a choice, would ya have married another?" Brae asked taking the seat across from him.

"If I had been given a choice, I might have made a vow similar to Gard's." He tipped his cup to her then took a drink.

"Ya would have wanted to spend yor life alone?"

"Well, I can't say that I would be alone. Men *are* different. We do not need love, per se, but we do enjoy company."

"Aye, men make their own rules, and the women are forced ta abide by them. For we have no choices." Brae did not wish to discuss it any longer. 'Twas a lost cause and hurtful besides. She changed the subject. "Why is it tha' Gard is in custody o' Donnchadh and why is he no' wit' his mother?"

Hudson squirmed again.

When Brae thought he might not answer, she added, "Before ya arrived, Gard and I were discussin' how he recovered the MontClaire seal." She made the statement to make him aware the depth of her knowledge. "Gard mentioned tha' 'twas his sister, Isabella, who returned it ta him."

"Aye," Hudson answered, cautiously.

"How was it she came in contact wit' it? I assumed it was seized by the bishop."

Hudson stroked his chin, as if considering his words carefully. "It was in John Comyn's care."

That made sense. Brae recalled how Llachlan had let slip that Gard had some agreement with Red Comyn. "Again, how did Isabella come to it?"

"She went on the prowl after her *beloved* husband's unfortunate demise. She has her cap set on the younger John Comyn," Hudson explained, then took another sip of ale.

"Ah, she does have lofty dreams doesna she?"

"She will attain him, too. She is lovely and very . . . persuasive." Brae noted something in Hudson's tone, as if he both admired and despised these traits in Gard's sister. Could Hudson have some feeling for Isabella?

"How did the seal come ta be encased in the blue stone?" Brae inquired.

"That was Edward's doing. Just another slap in the face, another insult. One more reminder that if Gard did not do as was directed, his quest would forever go unfulfilled. And now . . ." Hudson sighed. The burden ahead weighed as heavily on him as it did Gard. He shook his head. "It may never come back to him."

"King Edward?" Brae whispered, her thoughts whirling as she recalled the matching stone that she possessed. Remembering Gaveston's words as he'd handed it to her. *Return it to its rightful owner . . .*

"Aye," Hudson broke in. "And now Edward the II may keep Gard from his goal yet again. 'Twill kill him this time or get him killed. I fear for what Gard will do. His behavior is erratic when he is disappointed."

Brae attempted to keep her mind on her fishing expedition and not on the possibilities churning in her head. "And Donnchadh is in Gard's custody, why?"

"He did not tell you?" Hudson frowned.

"Nay, no' all. As ya ken, he doles oot information grudgingly."

"Aye. That he does." Hudson took another deep breath. "Bella is not the motherly type."

For a second time, Brae detected something in the way Hudson spoke her name, this time with familiarity.

"She is too invested in her own ambitions to coddle a child. Gard made him his squire when his mother left him after his father's death. The boy would soon been fostered if not."

"'Twould seem the siblings have quite a lot in common."

Hudson cocked his head.

Brae clarified. "Neither wishes ta further their lineage, too caught up in their own purpose. Isabella in her ambition and Gard in his vengeance."

Hudson sent her an empathetic look. "But you might find hope in the fact that Gard did not abandon the child. He may not have fathering instincts or be gentle in any way, but he did not leave him, as his mother did."

Brae let that sink in. "Wha' happened ta Donnchadh's sire? How was he killed?"

"I almost believe but I cannot prove that the whole ploy was contrived from the beginning by Isabella." Hudson's explanation came to an abrupt halt. "You are very crafty, Lady Marschand. I have become too comfortable in your company and have shared entirely too much."

"Weel then, there is na reason not ta continue." She winked and refilled his cup. "Gard confided in me tha' Isabella had no like for her husband. Is it possible tha' she may have helped herself be rid o' him?" Brae tried to make it seem as if she knew more than she did.

"Gard received information that a group of rebels, led by a notorious thief, were in possession of the seal. We set out after them. It never occurred to us that anything untoward was afoot. When we found them, a fierce battle broke out when the brigands refused to give over what we sought. We killed them all, believing they were the villains." For a moment Hudson looked sick, before he masked it with the cold warrior stare. "We searched every body. There was no seal. Yet when we returned with the bodies, we were revolted to learn that their leader was, in fact, Donnchadh's sire. Gard had no idea who he'd killed until that moment. His brother-in-law and he had never laid eyes on each other."

Brae shook her head in disbelief. "She *set* ya up! How could a woman go ta such lengths ta be rid o' her husband?"

Hudson tilted his head and shrugged.

"'Twas a conspiracy. Wha' kind o' woman does tha'?" Brae railed.

"As you said, an ambitious one," Hudson agreed. "Or on the other hand, perhaps Bella's actions are the result of a child who witnessed her father murdered. Gard turned one direction, she another. They lost everything that day. Their parents, and home, their standing in the realm and each other. They have both erected walls to protect themselves."

Brae was not about to get into that. "So, how is it she explained bein' in possession o' the seal when ya returned?"

"She did not give it over at that time. That is why I have no proof that she is to blame. I'm unsure as to exactly when she came into contact with it."

"I dinna believe ya, Hudson. Ya are convinced she was the orchestrator o' this travesty, ya dinna need proof. And I believe e'en if ya had evidence ya would be hard pressed ta use it against her."

Hudson's mouth twisted.

"Ya lied ta me earlier when ya said ya wouldna have chosen ta marry. Ya are in love wit' her, aren ya, Hudson? Ya make excuses for her as weel as yourself. Ya dinna wish ta believe she be tha' devious."

"You are very perceptive, Mistress Galbraith—" He smiled again at his mistake. "Lady MontClaire. Brae," he said with affection. "You are entirely too intelligent for us soldiers."

"Soldiers dinna need love, Hudson. So how is tha' ya find yourself in love with the deceitful and by your own words lovely Isabella MontClaire?"

"As you say, we do not need it, but sometimes love creeps up and knifes us through the heart, regardless."

"Ya have made a poor choice o' women ta love." She used his own words against him. "I dinna understand how ya can love this woman, Hudson. Ya are a good and kind man. She is no' ana o' those things, from wha' I have learned. I canna see how a man like ya could love a woman like tha'. Your lady wife, the Lady Richmond, is more ta how I see ya, e'en if ya two may be at odds for the now."

"You of all people should understand, Brae. The heart

does not see deeds. How is it you find yourself in love with the thieving, murdering, rapist who is now your husband?"

Brae turned from his inquisitive, all-knowing gaze. "He is no' tha' person all the time," she excused.

"And you will forgive his past deeds so easily because *once in a while* he acts human?"

Brae could not meet his gaze as he continued.

"Bella is not that person all of the time either. I believe she did feel regret, if not over the death of her husband, over how she had involved Gard in it. I believe that is why she retrieved the seal from the Comyn's possession and brought it to Gard in the Tower."

Brae caught her breath. "*He was* in the Tower?" Another piece of the puzzle.

"Aye."

She was afraid to ask. "For what was he in the Tower?"

"The bishop who murdered Donnchadh MontClaire, the first Earl of Fife, Gard's father, was found murdered in his bed. His throat had been cut. Quite a gruesome scene, from what I have been told, his head near separated from his body," Hudson informed her matter-of-factly. "Gard's dirk lay on the pillow next to the bloody scene."

"And he was wrongfully blamed?" she said, aghast.

"He was not wrongfully blamed. An eye for and eye, Braelynn."

Her eyes filled with tears.

"The heart does not know deeds." Hudson reminded.

The heart might not see deeds, but it could not ignore the truth. "How is it tha' he is released from the Tower?" She choked.

Hudson cocked his head. "Some would believe he is still there."

"If 'tis widely kenned tha' Gard committed this act, how is it tha' he expects ta be forgiven and rewarded with an earldom?" She shook her head in confusion.

"The former King Edward's preference, that. So that Gard could lead the missions as Lord Marschand and no one would know him as MontClaire."

"No one does ken him as MontClaire," Brae murmured.

"You would be surprised how many actually do know. Some people in very high places know exactly who he is, and what he has been about for the past many years."

"Then why havena they helped him?" she asked angrily. "As you and Hugh have? They ken who he is and wha' was stolen from him. They could have aided him afore he performed such a heinous act o' revenge."

"Some folks would not like to see Gard rise to any kind of power. He has acquired a reputation among the people who know. And he has also grown legendary among the ones who only know him as Gard Marschand, the devil. But in any persona he is dangerous. He is ruthless. However, people obey him, they follow him. He is highly feared, but vastly respected. And some might think he may have more power and more backing than certain untried . . . king . . . s." He let the word in its plural form resonate, as if the heresy he'd just spoken had reached both realms. "And would-be-kings as well. They all work against him. They would not wish for Gard to see his full potential. He, as any other powerful man, even now is being conspired against from all corners."

"Is it true, tha' the Bruce summoned Isabella ta his crownin' in Gard's stead, as is the tradition of a Mormaer ta crown the kings o' Scotland?"

Hudson nodded gravely.

"Then why would they summon her if the family isna recognized in tha' capacity?"

"Many things go on that do not make sense. Perhaps it was an olive branch on behalf of the Bruce's knowing that

Isabella was in league with the Comyns. Perhaps it was a gesture to Gard from the Bruce. As I said, 'twould be easier for all involved to gain favor with Gard and not become his adversary."

"But ya dinna believe tha' if Gard had been free tha' they would have summoned him ta the crownin' as is his birth righ'?"

"Nay, he would not have been." Hudson shook his head.

"Oh, I bet *she* loved tha', didna she? Feelin' such importance while Gard was locked up." Brae paced. "Then tha' would mean tha' both the Comyns and the Bruces ken exactly who Gard be and still they plot ta keep him doon."

She knew Gard was powerful, just in the way that he carried himself and how people obeyed his every command. She remembered Ferguson's trepidation at the Ross-shire holding, as he had informed the crowd in front of her father and Callum just who was their lord. She recalled as they rode across the country how a mere lift of his arm sent his men rushing to do his bidding, and how vendors and shopkeeps hurried to make him comfortable or fulfill his requirements. And although it was obvious Hudson and Gard were friends, even Hudson, a man that Brae had come to know and respect, with his own commanding air, yielded to Gard's leadership. They were equals as earls, and yet Richmond truly was second to MontClaire.

Knowing more of the story, Brae was even more afraid for Gard now. If he did indeed reacquire his right, he would forever be defending himself, from every corner. His troops, though she could not fathom exact numbers as they were spread all over the two countries, perhaps more, held down the lands as directed by the king. They could not possibly compare with the number of soldiers King Edward or even King Robert possessed.

With her thoughts in turmoil, Brae was quiet for several

minutes, before asking, "Is there actually a man in the Tower in Gard's stead?"

"Aye. That was a stipulation of the former King Edward. He needed for people to believe MontClaire was indeed in the Tower and being punished. When Isabella came to court to uphold Gard's innocence, she spun a tale accusing her deceased husband as the perpetrator who murdered the bishop. She said he had done it out of love and revenge in the name of his wife, unbeknownst to her, of course."

"Of course," Brae repeated.

"I am painting the charming Bella in a very bad light. Your impression of her will be horribly tainted afore you ever meet."

"Any woman who would abandon her child isna a woman tha' I hold in any esteem. Let alone wha' she has done ta Gard." She was feeling quite territorial over all three, Gard, Hudson and Donnchadh. But Hudson's expression of disappointment could not be overlooked. "And perhaps you, too, Lord Richmond. 'Twould almost seem ta me tha' you would have been a glorious catch for the ambitious Isabella MontClaire. The handsome earl of Brittany, with lands, riches, titles and connections o' his own."

He cast his eyes downward. "Aye."

"But perhaps she cast ya aside as she set her sights on the son of the man who migh' be king. Wha' will she do now, Lord Richmond? Now tha' John Comyn the Red has been slain, there isna chance tha' the young one will e'er be more than he is. Will she jump the ship o' Comyn and swim for the shores o' the Bruce? I believe he, too, has male heirs."

He clucked his tongue over his teeth before meeting her gaze. "Do you wish to hear the rest of the story, Lady MontClaire, before your husband returns and puts a stop to his history being discussed? Or will your little fishing expedition go unfulfilled?"

With a roll of her shoulder, Brae acquiesced, knowing she had not fooled him at all.

"Bella came to court and successfully convinced King Edward that her brother was innocent in the murder of the bishop. Although he released him from the Tower, he would not be convinced that Gard was who he proclaimed to be."

Brae stood, intending to replenish the refreshment, but became sidetracked by Hudson's tale.

"As you know, the children, Donnghardh and Isabella, were hidden after their father's murder, and no one was quite sure where they had gone. 'Twas then that Bella produced the seal, and John Comyn stood and confirmed Gard was who he alleged to be. Edward took the seal and proposed to Gard that he might wish to take on a mission or two in the name of the king. He would give him the opportunity to *earn* his place. 'Twas then that the stone was placed over the seal, so that he could not use it until his obligation to the king had been fulfilled. 'Twas soon after that that Gard commissioned the Sons of the Guardians seal for himself and his commanders to use. Then we would know when our correspondence was true."

"Who is in the Tower in his stead?" Brae asked.

"Do not worry over it. He is not an innocent in any way. He deserves to be locked up for one offense or many."

"Llachlan once said that Gard had some kind o' deal with John Comyn ta help him recover his due. Was it more so, tha' John expected Gard's support o'er the Bruce in payment for verifyin' his identity?"

"You are extremely astute, My Lady." Hudson inclined his head.

"There be still one thing tha' concerns me. Well, many things concern me," she explained as she paced. "How was it John Comyn came ta be in possession o' the seal in the first place? If it was confiscated from Donnchadh the First, by the bishop, how did John get it?" She turned concerned eyes to Hudson.

"I can't say it enough, Brae, *many* conspire to keep Gard down. Including his own countrymen, who only have their own agendas and ambitions to see to and not the good of your country. John, to my knowledge, never actually admitted to having the seal. 'Twas Bella who said that is where she retrieved it, and he did not admit or deny this. But there were other rumors spread that led us to believe the Comyns took the seal from the Bruces. 'Twas a lot of finger pointing. And therein lies the intrigue. We may never know the truth of it."

One other thing bothered Brae. How did Isabella know that the Comyns or the Bruces had the seal in the first? Brae did not share this concern with Hudson, but instead voiced another.

"But if either be true, tha' would make one believe tha' either the Comyns or the Bruces wished to quash the powerful Earl of Fife way back when 'twas Gard's father, and the bishop but worked the scheme of men who didna wish for yet another competitor ta be added ta the growing list o' ascendants ta the throne."

"Neither Donnchadh or Gard has claims on the throne," Hudson clarified.

"Naw, but ya said, they wouldna wish for him, neither Donnchadh the First or Gard ta gain the support o' the people, and folks tend to follow powerful men. Nor would they wish ta have Gard throw his sway ta one or the other, either the Bruce or the Comyns' claims, tipping the scales ta one's favor. 'Twas the same wit' William, although he would ne'er be king, he had the support of the people, and both the Bruces and the Comyns *gave* the impression o' workin' wit' him. I myself had seen correspondence tha' led me ta believe they would wish him quieted. Perhaps not dead but they didna need the competition or the division o' the clans."

Hudson nodded his agreement. "Three would-be Kings and how many saviors does one country need to gain and keep its independence?" he asked, wish a raise of his fair eyebrows.

"We dinna need kings or saviors. Our downfall be jus' tha'. Too many leaders and no' enough soldiers. We as Scotsmen need ta band together as one instead o' dividin' and choosin' sides. We could be our own savior as a whole if not for all the misguided ambition o' others."

"Verra weel said, wife." Brae whirled to find Gard standing near the opening of their shelter with his arms crossed. "Ya made the mistake o' discussin' politics wit' her, Hudson?"

"Aye. 'Twould seem your wife is very passionate about many things." Hudson grinned.

"Her passions be none o' your concern," Gard growled, wrapping his arm around his wife's hip possessively.

"How goes the hunt?" Hudson changed the subject.

Gard sent Hudson a stifling look. Brae knew that stare well—Gard did not wish to discuss the specifics of the latest attack in her presence.

"You may join the search party if you wish," Gard suggested.

Hudson nodded and took his leave.

"Ya are bein' passionate again, wife, wit'oot your husband?" Gard asked nuzzling her ear.

Turning in his arms, she wound her own around his neck, kissing him fully. "I much prefer ta display ma passions in your presence," she whispered shyly.

"Ah," he sighed into her mouth. "Then display away."

CHAPTER THIRTY-SEVEN

After several hours of rigorous loving, Brae rested her head on Gard's chest, turning circles lightly over his ribs, her breath warm against his skin.

"Ya seem ta have forgotten your vow o' celibacy this nigh'," Gard said with a chuckle.

"Ya make me forget evrathin'," she admitted.

"I enjoy the way ya punish me, wife."

"No need ta punish meself as weel, as I see it. I did nuthin' wrong."

Gard was pleasantly surprised, not only at her obvious enjoyment of their new intimate relationship, but also that he had not hurt her. Now that she was seeing to his needs regularly, his brutish, animal-like need for immediate gratification had lessened. He took time to explore and enjoy her.

They settled down and slept, only to be awakened early by Hudson.

"Brae. Brae," he called in a harsh whisper.

"Wha' are ya aboot, Hudson, wakin' my wife at such an hour?"

"My apologies, Gard, but I'm in need of assistance."

"From my wife?" he snapped.

"Aye. I have been summoned to a birthing and have no one to help me. I was hoping your new bride might have had some experience with such things, as she also had experience with wounds."

"Aye, a limited knowledge," Brae spoke for herself. "Ya may have ta direct me, but I will aid ya anyway I can. Give me a moment ta dress."

Gard dressed as well, unpleased that his wife's warm body was being dragged from his side.

Unable to tolerate the screeching of the laboring mother, Gard left Braelynn in Hudson's capable care. When she did not return in a timely manner, he went in search of her.

He found his wife and his best friend with their heads together mooning over the new babe.

At first Gard was angry Brae had not returned to him as soon as the child was out. Then he was furious by the way his second and his wife seemed to be so — dare he think it — intimate. They were much better suited to one another than he and she, and 'twas not the first time the rotten thought had crossed his mind.

But when Brae spotted him standing there, the look on her face and in her eyes was soft and sweet, full of such wonder and . . . love. Like a boulder, it slammed him in the chest.

Just as quickly she masked her emotions. She laid the child expertly in its cradle.

"If ya dinna need me anamore, Hudson, I will return wit', Gard."

"Thank you, Brae. You were a great help."

"Gud nigh', Lord Richmond."

"Lady Marschand."

Gard held the flap open for her as he held Hudson's gaze for an overlong moment.

The next morning, Brae awoke alone. She sighed and stretched.

As she got out of bed, she considered checking on the

new mother and the babe.

Last eve, when they had returned to their quarters, Gard had a warm bath waiting along with a tray of food. He had bathed her, fed her, then taken her to bed. The tender nurturer she had known at Ross had returned and she had reveled in his attentions.

Brae selected her clothing for the day, then poured water in the basin and began to wash, but her thoughts kept straying to her husband and all the wonderful things he had done to her with his lips and his tongue. Her body warmed and a delicious heavy heat settled deep within.

She was completely consumed with thoughts of their loveplay and this newfound joy. Yet what could she do to Gard in return that might be equivalent?

Brae pulled on her clothing, finding her skin overly sensitive.

Another wave of sensation fluttered through her as she imagined what it would be like to taste him. Would Gard be receptive of such attentions? She only wished to make him happy, to please him the way he did her. How she wished to make him want her the way she craved him. At least in lovemaking, she did not disappoint him or anger him or disagree with him.

The tent flap stirred, her heart and stomach leapt. She knew it was Gard by his tread. He moved behind her. Seizing her hips, he pulled her against him and nudged her bottom with his hardness.

The simmering warmth in her lower body spread. Even apart, they desired each other. She closed her eyes as he made a line of slow soft kisses across to her ear and jaw.

"Wha' have ya done ta me?" The deep timber of his voice excited her even more. He reached around and covered her breasts, her nipples pearled in his palms. She let her head fall and rest upon his shoulder as he plumped her flesh. "I canna think o' anathin' but you," he said.

A whimper escaped her throat. She turned in his arms. "'Tis as if ya can read me mind," she whispered. "I was jus' thinkin' o' you."

His pupils dilated right before he took her lips in a knee-weakening kiss. He swept her into his arms, then took her to the pallet, where he set her down.

Gard bunched her skirt and ran his hand over her sex, swollen and slick with arousal from her imaginings of him.

"Wha's this?" he sounded almost angry.

"I was hopin' yud return. I couldna stop thinkin' aboot las' nigh'."

Her explanation calmed him yet inflamed him. His fingers danced over her woman's flesh.

"Unh," he groaned, "Brae, ya are wet for me."

Her face heated.

He growled and unlaced his breeches. He nudged her legs apart. Brae pulled up her knees, the way he liked, eager to join with him.

Guiding himself to her, he teased, "Is tha' wha' ya be wantin'?"

"Aye!" she answered, digging her heels in and pushing herself forward, causing him to slide further into her.

Gard filled her completely. Brae closed her eyes on a moan.

He pulled her bodice down, exposing her breasts. "Aye. This is wha' I canna keep from my mind," he murmured. He bowed his head and laved her flesh while maintaining a deep even rhythm with his hips.

His raked her nipple with his teeth. "Your sweet flesh." He circled her with his tongue. She arched against him, lost in the sensual torrent he was creating within her. "Your scorchin' heat surroundin' me." He the licked the hard bud rapidly. "Is this wha' ya hoped I'd come back for?" he panted.

Brae laced her hands into his hair, holding him. "Oh, aye ... your mouth, Gard, your sweet lips do wonderful things ta me."

Brae's inner walls contracted.

Gard shouted and plunged faster, harder.

Brae was bombarded by one wave after another of decadent sensation, as Gard brought them both to the ultimate culmination.

He collapsed at her side.

Gard did not confide that the all-consuming desire Brae had been suffering was exactly the same torment that had lured him back to their quarters. He could not keep his mind to his tasks, imagining her just like this, naked and rumpled from his loving.

Even Hudson had noticed his distraction during training, almost flaying him open with the tip of his sword. Finally, Hudson had cursed at him in frustration, "Just go to her. You are of no use here."

"Is it always this way?" Brae asked, rousing Gard from his reverie.

"I dinna ken." It was not a lie. He had never experienced the like. However, he had never allowed himself to spend this much time in one woman's company. Now he was learning what made this particular woman crave him, even when he wasn't near. Her body ripened, just for him. He smiled at the thought. She wanted him. No other.

Brae sat up and took his cheeks between her palms. Her lips trembled as she returned his grin. Her eyes were heavy-lidded from their loveplay.

"Ya be smilin'," she whispered, tracing his lips.

Gard kissed at her fingertips. "Wha's not ta smile aboot?"

She giggled. "I thought a soldier didna need laughter or lovin'?"

"Perhaps he doesna need them, but a soldier is also intelligent enough ta ken tha' if these gifts are so offered, there isna reason ta turn them doon."

Her smile slipped slightly. "Gifts?"

He cupped her cheek. "Aye, Braelynn, gifts."

Brae leaned in and treated Gard to the most passionate kiss he had ever experienced.

Later, Brae and Gard, lounged, feeding each other bits of pastry.

Brae was surprised Gard had stayed so long, choosing to remain with her instead of returning to his men.

Gard rested on his elbow and said, "I thought ya would be off ta visit the bairn this morn as soon as I turned my back."

"I had evra intention o' seein' them at some point. But I couldna take me mind off other things." She raked his beautiful body with her gaze. " . . . long enough ta e'en finish dressin' meself, let alone leave our quarters decently."

Gard blinked slowly and his lip curled in pure male arrogance.

Brae was surprised to find how comfortable she was becoming in his presence. She was completely nude, yet she had no desire to hide from him.

He reached out and covered her stomach with his large hand. It felt good to have him touch her, and not just because he needed her but because he wanted to.

"'Tisna a curse ta have a child," she whispered. "'Tis also a gift."

He watched her silently. She took hope when he hadn't flown into a rage.

"An addition," she continued, though she did so careful-ly. Perhaps helping Hudson bring the babe into the world had spurred her on. Given the way that she and Gard had been carrying on since the moment they had handfasted, it was possible Brae might already be expecting. If not, it was only a matter of time. Their last few couplings had been so spontaneous that she hadn't taken any precautions, nor had she washed immediately afterward.

"Why would it be so important for ya ta have a child, Braelynn?" He smoothed his hand in a circular pattern over her abdomen.

She looked away and gave her shoulder a delicate shrug. Her feelings for Gard were so strong at the moment, over-whelming and confusing, she didn't know how to put them into words. "I guess, mayhap, I just want ta mother someone."

Her words hung in the air.

"I suppose tha' makes sense, ya have done nothin' but mother Donnchadh, *and* the men, from the moment we crashed inta your life."

Buoyed by the response, Brae lunged ahead. "I've ne'er been close ta the woman who I thought was me mother. I wanted ta be. I guess I wish ta give a child all tha' I believe I've missed oot on. I wouldna overlook those things in our child."

Gard remained very still. She was afraid she had pushed him too hard and he was on the verge of storming out.

"I would try me best ta make him happy. I wouldna do the things she did ta me. I wouldna ignore him. Dinna ya feel like ya missed oot on a childhood too, Gard? Growing up wit'oot your parents. Wit'oot your sister? Would ya not have wished to have kenned wha' your life would have en-tailed had they lived? I'm sure your mother would have dot-ed on ya and your sister. And your da would be verra proud o' the man you've become. A man o' conviction. But I guess tha' is all parents wish for their children. Ta make their lives a little bit better than wha' they had. Would ya no' like the chance ta give a child all tha' ye missed oot on? Can ya imagine a black-haired lad wit' your conviction and my intelligence?" She winked. "He would be a perfect successor for ya." She tried to picture what a child of their joining might produce. She shrugged. "Perhaps I jus' want ta love and ta be loved in return. And children jus' love ya because ye are."

Braelynn wrung her hands together, now embarrassed by her rambling. She tried to smile, but instead her eyes filled. It was just a dream. One her husband did not share. "I guess ya are righ'. My imagination for things is distorted. I guess I jus' always believed tha' a child was a culmination o' a man and a woman. A symbol ta all, wha' two people can feel fer each other."

Gard blinked. "No' evraone feels tha' kind o' sentiment o' couplin', Brae. Sometimes it is jus' the act tha' men crave and no' the result. They dinna need ta love their spouse ta produce offspring. Some men have hordes o' children and ne'er give them a second look. They have them all o'er the country and ne'er lay eyes on 'em again."

Brae looked away. His words hurt, but she would not quit hoping. She could not fathom a life without a child.

"Tha' kind of thinkin' made my father weak, Braelynn. If he hadn't been tryin' ta make me mother happy, none o' this woulda happened."

"Wha' do ya mean?" she asked.

For a moment his expression was bleak. Then all of a sudden he surged forward. Before Brae could take another breath, she was underneath him. He was done talking.

CHAPTER THIRTY-EIGHT

The day of Gard's meeting with the new King of England arrived.

Like a caged animal, Gard paced in front of the pavilions. Brae and Hudson watched on warily. Her husband was more intense than Brae had ever seen him. And she had seen him at his worst. His jaw ticked with tension. The set of his shoulders gave the impression he waited to either receive a blow or charge in fighting.

"'Tis time," Hudson announced.

Gard and Hudson shared a severe expression before Gard swung his attention to Brae. He held her gaze for an interminable moment. The turmoil in his stormy eyes haunted her. Without a word, he turned toward the castle.

Brae released a breath of disappointment. There were many things she wanted to say to him, but his mind was focused on the task at hand — the only thing that had kept him moving forward for the last twenty years — his destiny.

Hudson fell into step beside Gard. They cut an impressive menacingly superior pair, dressed similarly in black. The other men flanked their leader and his second, every one of them with the same single-minded set of determination on their young faces. Brae closed her eyes and sent up a silent prayer for her husband's safe return.

Gard turned to take one last look at his wife. With her eyes closed, and her hands clasped tightly, it appeared she was sending up a silent prayer. *For him.* His heart pounded.

Once again, his feet betrayed him, marching him in the wrong direction.

When Brae opened her eyes, he stood before her.

Her heart was in her eyes. Gard almost regretted coming back. He could not deal with the emotions churning in the emerald depths.

"Ya will stay here," he said gruffly. "Dinna leave your guards."

She placed her palm to his chest. He moved toward her and wound his arms around her.

"Return ta me." She sniffled.

"I will. And I will return an earl," he vowed.

"It doesna matter ta me, if ya are an earl or a soldier." Her voice shook. "I love ya no matter."

He inhaled deeply before pulling away from her. He need not hear those words. Not now. "It matters ta me." He turned to his fate, without another word or backward glance.

Brae waited for what seemed like an eternity. She paced the tent. She mended clothing. She tried to read, but her mind was full of other things.

For the fifth time she stuck her head out of the tent. "Has there been ana word, Bain?"

Bain and others had been left with her while Llachlan had accompanied the earls. Gard might not like Llach, but he respected him and utilized his strengths as a soldier.

Bain shook his head. "I dinna ken if tha' be good or bad, Lady Marschand."

Just then a young lad ran up to them. "Mistress Galbraith?" The boy panted trying to catch his breath.

Bain stepped forward, barring the youngster's progress

from coming any closer.

"Be ye Mistress Galbraith?"

"She be Lady Marschand, gutter rat. Ya would do weel not ta forget tha'! Be on your way, she be na feelin' charitable this day."

"I be lookin' for Brae somethin' Galbraith. Me maw needs her help." The boy's scared gaze darted.

"Your mother?" Brae asked.

"She had a baby. Yester eve, but things arena goin' ta gud, and I canna find the physician tha' aided her. She needs your help."

Brae stepped forward. Bain stopped her. "Ya willna be goin' no where, Lady Marschand."

A no-nonsense expression descended, and it gave Brae pause, but only for a moment. "I must go. Hudson isna here. There is no one else."

"There will be others who can help. Lord Marschand extracted my solemn vow and threatened my life ya would remain here and under my care."

"I will still be under your care," she explained. "Ya will accompany me."

"We are ta remain here." He straightened, staring straight ahead.

"Please, Bain. A child is in need. I mus' go. *We* mus' go."

She could see him wavering. "I will take the brunt of Lord Marschand's anger if he e'en needs become aware o' our absence. Perhaps we will be so quick tha' he will ne'er need ken we were gone. We will return afore he does."

"Please, sir, me maw," the boy begged.

"Arrgghh. Come on men, we will accompany our lady." There were looks exchanged and much grumbling.

The lad led them in the direction of his family's dwelling, darting in and out of the masses. He ran right past the tent that Brae had helped Hudson birth the babe.

"Where be ye goin'?" Brae called.

The boy stopped. "Huh?"

"This be your shelter, yah?" Brae pointed.

"Uh, me maw had ta be moved." He ran on. "Hurry."

Brae and Bain attempted to keep up. The child ran for what seemed like minutes, finally stopping at a wooden hut. He disappeared inside.

Bain pushed the door. Obscurity greeted them, shadows danced from the flicker of a single candle in the corner. Bain placed his arm in front of Brae, barring her progress. His forehead creased deeply. "There be somethin's na righ' here, My Lady."

A strangled noise from within spurred Brae on.

Bain held his hand up to the men behind then he led Brae inside.

"I canna see," Brae said just as someone struck Bain from behind. He pitched forward. Brae made an attempt to grab for him, but his deadweight took them both to the floor.

In a panic Brae looked around squinting in the dim light. A shadow lurked by the door, too large to be the child. A moan from the opposite corner chilled her. Brae tried to cradle Bain's head, yet her hand came away stained with his blood. She whimpered, belatedly realizing her mistake.

"Bain? Bain?" she called, but he was out cold.

The door suddenly swung shut. The deafening thud of the wooden arm latch being dropped into place barring the door, echoed in her mind like a death knell.

"Can I have me coin now?" The boy asked.

"Aye, ya have earned it. Now go oot the back."

Brae heard the boy scurry.

Another moan filled the shed. Just as Brae's eyes were adjusting to the gloom, someone lit a second taper, illuminating the face of the man who had struck Bain.

"What are you saying?" Gard's voice exploded, echoing through the anteroom.

The king's man flinched at Gard's vehemence.

"There must be some mistake, Lord Marschand. The king has not agreed to meet with anyone yet. No petitioners have been seen."

Gard produced the parchment from his pocket. He thrust it into the trembling man's face. "Then what be this? And why were we notified that petitions had begun?"

The man examined the vellum. "'Tis a very good likeness, but 'tis not the king's seal. I'm afraid you have been deceived." Gard looked to Hudson, who stared at him just as baffled.

"How do I know this is not just another elaborate jest on the part of your perverse Liege?" Gard snarled. "He enjoys his games. But I am not one to toy with. I am not one of his amusements. I will not be trifled with."

Hudson wrapped a strong hand around Gard's shoulder. "Watch what you say, my friend," he said quietly. "Do not destroy your chance to be heard."

"He will see me!" Gard demanded. "He will see me now. I have been put off long enough. I have done my duty. I have done *what was* not *my duty*. And I will not leave here this day without what is mine." Gard grabbed the man by the starched ruffled collar. "He will see me . . . now!" Gard fumed.

"What goes on out here?"

Gard let go of the scared little man as he and Hudson both turned toward the voice. Gard could not stifle the growl of frustration when he faced the speaker.

"Speaking of perverse amusements," Hudson said under his breath.

"Piers!" Hudson greeted the man with false jubilation.

"We heard you might be welcomed back. And here you are."

"Richmond," Piers Gaveston responded. "Marschand." He acknowledged Gard dryly. "What seems to be the problem, my Lords? You are bothering our liege with your ranting."

Gard surged forward. Hudson placed his back to Gard's chest, holding him from taking the French knight by the neck. "'Twill not further your cause," Hudson rasped, in exertion. "Your liege would be the one who might clear up this whole mess, Gaveston. We were summoned, this day, this time, to meet with your king."

"There must be some mistake. Edward is seeing no one."

"Save you, you goddamned malefactor!" Gard lunged again. Hudson dug in his heels.

"We do what we must," Piers sniffed. "Am I not correct, Marschand? We are not so different. You have done things you are ashamed of—"

"That is the difference, Gaveston. I may be ashamed. You are not. You will bend over for anyone. Most especially your king."

"Gard!" Hudson warned through gritted teeth.

"You will submit to obtain what you wish. We serve. We kill. We lay siege. We are soldiers. We do what must be done. You simper and bend receiving of the gifts that he thrusts upon you, sacrificing nothing more than your dignity."

"And have you not given of your dignity for your cause, Marschand? You have killed your own countrymen to obtain what you have lost. How is what you do any less degrading than I?"

Hudson again held Gard from strangling the Frenchman.

"At least I am on my feet when I do it, Gaveston, and not on my knees," Gard sneered.

"This is not getting us anywhere," Hudson said. "We wish to speak to the king at his earliest convenience. Might that be possible today? Or might you be able to persuade your liege to start wading through the mounds of petitions? If not for us, for London. The violence that is on the verge of erupting out there needs immediate attention. The sooner people are heard and begin to vacate the city, the better. For everyone."

"I will speak to his Majesty," Piers said with self-importance. "But 'twill not be this day. May I have the missive? I believe his Highness might like to investigate the fraudulent use of his seal. Now the only question remaining, Marschand, is who would want you away from your camp and why? Have you left something very valuable behind?" Gaveston's gaze narrowed.

Gard's heart leapt in his chest and his terror-filled gaze met Hudson's briefly. "Brae!" he shouted and bolted from the vestibule.

Brae gasped as the man crept closer. He smiled. A grotesque sight. "We meet again, Braelynn." His eyes danced with evil insanity.

"Robbie Cowan?" she choked as she began to tremble at the gravity of the situation.

"Oh, aye," he said, in rapture. "I have dreamed o' the day ya would say me name in tha' way. Soon ya will be screamin' it."

Brae squeezed Bain's shoulders and shook him. He was partially on top of her, for the moment protecting her from Cowan. She felt torn, somewhat guilty that she was using him as a shield, but also comforted to have him safeguarding her.

Another groan from the other side of the square cabin

captured Cowan's attention.

"Oh, will ya shut up o'er there." Robbie kicked at the lump on the floor. The unknown victim whimpered pathetically.

"Bain!" She shook him while Robbie's focus was on the moaner. With Bain's weight atop her, she couldn't even reach the dagger strapped to her thigh. "Oh, Bain. Please!" she begged.

"Dinna e'en bother tryin' ta wake him. I have probably addled his peabrain when I hit him. I heard his skull crack." Cowan guffawed. Brae closed her eyes and sent up a prayer for Bain. She smoothed her hands over his hair in comfort.

Robbie took Bain by the boot and pulled him off her. Brae tried to keep his head in her hand so that it would not bounce in the dirt.

"Now," Robbie said. "Come here. I have waited long enough fer ya."

"Donn touch me, Robbie Cowan," Brae threatened. "Lord Marschand's men are still ootside. If we dinna come oot in a timely fashion they will storm this hut. Ya canna stand against them all." She tried to dissuade him as she gained her feet. Cautiously, she backed up.

"There arna men oot there waitin' fer ya. They are loyal ta me. They are now guardin' this place from Marsch."

Could that be true? Or was this ruse simply another trick? Had the men who had accompanied Brae and MacBain betrayed them, or had they suffered the same fate as poor Bain had, and been ambushed by brigands under Cowan's employ?

"As soon as Marsch learns the missive was a fake, he will attempt ta find ya. But 'twill be too late. By then, he will no longer want ya."

Brae's stomach lurched. *The missive is a fake?*

"Ya are wrong aboot tha'. The only way he will leave me

is if I am dead," she said with more confidence than she felt.

"Och, now look who thinks she's special? Ya think because he has kept ya this long tha' ye are dear ta him in some way? Have ya no learned his character as o' yet, ya stupid chit? Ya think ya are loftier than ya were at Ross? Ya are no better than yor friend, Katie, or that whore, Bronwyn."

Did this mean Robbie was unaware that she and Gard had handfasted? She should have known something was wrong when the boy came looking for Braelynn Galbraith and not Lady Marschand.

"'Twas Bronwyn tha' first gave me the idea. She took a bit o' punishment tha' one." Robbie chewed at his fingernail, then spit.

"Idea?" Brae asked, warily.

"Aye. Ta begin my experiments."

"Experiments?" Brae shook her head at his rantings.

"I will admit I was surprised tha' Marsch has kept ya so long. Only makes me more fascinated. And ye, ta be able ta survive a brutal man like Marsch and keep comin' fer more, only makes me wish ta ken wha' possible tortures I could dream up fer ya, tha' ya could survive and continue on. And I have dreamed up the most delicious things fer us, Braelynn."

To her disgust, he palmed himself through his trousers.

"Gard will kill ya," she vowed.

"I ken he will try. But by tha' point, wha' will I care. I will have had ya. 'Tis all I have thought aboot fer months. And when I started killin' 'em while I was still inside 'em . . ." He shuddered, his eyes rolling up in their sockets. "I am done talkin' now, Braelynn. 'Tis time for us." He made a grab for her.

"Tha' was you?" she screeched as she darted away from him. "Ye are the one tha' has been attackin' and killin' these women?"

"Aye. Marsch kens it." He shrugged.

"Marsch kens it? Wha' mean ye?" Brae tried to put the person in the corner between her and Robbie. Brae moved as he did.

"Why do ya think your benefactor has been huntin' the culprit himself and no' lettin' the authorities take care o' it? Marsch only does it himself if no one else can accomplish it. And he kens wha' I be like because we are much the same and he kens how much I wanted ya. I left enough clues fer him tha' he would be sure 'twas me. Perhaps tha' is half o' why he keeps ye aroond, aside from the obvious." His attention lingered on her breasts.

"Wha' are ya talkin' aboot?" Why had Gard not shared this with her? He knew it was Cowan all along but had not warned her?

"Perhaps not only was it a contest ta see which one o' us could have ya."

She didn't know what he was talking about.

"But he doesna want it ta be me. He will be sure ta let ya go once he kens I have been dispatched. But until then he keeps ya aroond so tha' he didna lose ta Robbie Cowan." He thumped his chest.

"Ya are insane. There be na contest!"

He didn't grasp the insult.

"He was always jealous o' the ties tha' bind me ta the Comyns. I have always been more than him."

"Ya will ne'er be more than him!" Brae retorted.

"Tha's wha' his whore sister said, as weel. I'm gonna go after her next. Tha' bitch. Gonna rip her apart wit' me teeth, tha' one. She deserves it, too. The lyin' cat."

"Do ya e'en ken her?" Brae frowned.

"Aye. I ken her. I was gonna ken her good, too. I got her the bauble she but coveted from John. She promised me glorious rewards in return fer it besides. But the lyin' bitch took

414

off wit' the younger John Comyn along with the gem afore I could ram inta her. She will pay. But you first. 'Twill be dually satisfyin' ta have Marschand's whore and then his sister also. Come. I have wanted ta shove meself inta ya since the first I laid eyes on ya runnin' through the moor. But then Marsch had ta have ya first."

Robbie reached across the space and grabbed Brae by the arm so forcefully she cried out. Brae tripped over the poor creature on the floor, causing the individual to cough pitifully. It seemed to incense Robbie further. "Why will ya no shut yor whore mouth? Braelynn willna curse me with talk. She will be perfect in evraway. Yieldin' when I wish her ta. Or a hellcat, nails rippin' at me skin while she bucks beneath me, when I demand it."

He tossed Brae aside in a flurry of heavy skirts. She went down on her hip.

Meanwhile, he fell on the woman on the floor in a crazed flurry of fists. He berated her and screamed obscenities as he beat her. He began to untie his trews.

Brae knew she would regret leaving the poor soul later, if either of them survived, but survival was the only thing she could think of. Her own. And the woman in the cabin would be better off dead from what she had witnessed so far. Brae could not aid Bain while she was trapped, but if she could get away, she would find him some help.

Brae knew that she would not be able to lift the latch on the door without alerting Robbie to her escape. The boy who had lured her there had gone out another way. She had to find it. She scrambled across the floor. A chink of daylight silhouetted the other exit. She had to make it to the outside or she would never leave this hut. She hoped that Robbie was too caught up in the act with the girl to give Brae another thought.

Brae pushed open the door. It creaked noisily. She gritted

her teeth and wrapped her hand around the handle of her dagger just as Robbie grabbed the hem of her skirt, dragging her rearward. Brae screamed as she heard the material rip. She kicked and scratched, but Robbie tackled her. She landed hard, on her back, with Robbie atop her.

Gard's voice echoed inside her head, *Ya need ta be brave enough ta use it.*

Robbie bruised her with his hands. He tore at her flesh with his teeth as he crawled up her body, moving ever closer to her face. Yet she didn't even feel the pain.

Two things happened at once. Bain, who had regained consciousness attacked Robbie—unfortunately, now Brae had the weight of two full-sized men bearing down on her momentarily cutting off her breath—but it didn't stop her from plunging Gard's dagger deep into the side of Robbie's neck.

Robbie stared at her, wide-eyed. He gurgled deep in his throat as hot blood spurted out of his mouth coating Brae's neck and chin. He shook violently, his lips worked but no words formed.

Robbie stilled, his eyes remained wide and staring. Frantic, Brae tried to push him off her, his blood dripping very close to her mouth.

"Bain!" she cried. "Bain, get him off!" She bawled hysterically.

Bain's weight shifted. He rolled the dead man over and then collapsed, unmoving.

"Bain? Bain!" She scrambled to his side. "Bain." She repeated his name and cradled his head, holding her skirt to his wound. "Oh dear God! Please. Bain!" Flickering light from the rear of the cabin caught her eye. Smoke began to billow toward them. Bain must have turned over a candle in his haste.

"Bain. Ya mus' wake up. We need ta get oot o' here." She patted his cheek as the smoke suddenly turned black. She placed her hands under his arms and heaved. In small increments, she dragged his heavy muscled body from the hut.

Brae had to wrench him directly over Robbie's inert body, as she could not move them both in time to get out. The heat rolled ever nearer, smoke choked her as she breathed heavily with exertion. She pulled and tugged the big man until they were well away from the hut which was now fully engulfed in flames. There was no way for Brae to regain entry to save the girl.

"Bain!" She held his head in her lap, while trying to staunch the blood that poured from his head wound. "Please dinna die because o' me!" Her tears fell onto his cheeks and rolled down, leaving clean tracks through the filth he had gathered from being facedown in the dirt.

Brae coughed uncontrollably, frightened that she might attract the attention of the men who had accompanied her and Bain. She had no idea if Robbie had lied to her about their loyalty. Yet no one seemed to be around. No one came to their rescue.

Brae prayed for Bain and for the girl she'd had to abandon in the fiery hut. She didn't know how long they sat there as she contemplated trying to find help for Bain when a shadow emerged from the smoke. Her heart leapt into her already clogged throat.

"Brae?"

"Hudson!" she rasped in relief. Two other men appeared.

"Brae? Oh, thank God! Gard!" Hudson bellowed. "Gard! Here! They're here!"

"Hudson. Bain! Please! Please, he has ta be a'righ'," Brae cried hoarsely. "Fix him!" she pleaded as Hudson knelt next to her. To her shock, Hudson took her face into his hand and drew her into his chest. She accepted his comfort wholeheartedly, just as relieved to see him.

"Are you hurt?" he said into her hair.

"No. Just Bain. Please, Hudson, save him," she sobbed.

"I'll do my best. Here." Hudson handed her a handkerchief from this pocket. "Try to clean yourself up a bit. Gard is going to have apoplexy when he sees you." Hauling her to her feet, Hudson set her away before hunkering down to tend Bain.

Horrified, Brae looked down at herself. How was she supposed to clean up? Robbie's blood had soaked into her gown, darkening it. She was covered in dirt. Her dress was ripped. She knew some of the blood had to be Bain's as well, and she did not know if Cowan's razor-sharp teeth had left any injuries on her person. At the moment, she couldn't feel anything.

The sound of thundering bootfalls hammered in her ears, as if an entire army was closing in. Other shadows emerged from the lingering smoke. The smog swirled, and Gard broke through. Yet he came to an abrupt halt as soon as he laid eyes on her.

Brae suddenly remembered the conversation they'd once had, when she'd asked him to switch places with Callum. Would he be able to forgive her if some unforeseen tragedy, not of her fault, befell her? Robbie had not raped her. But he would have and much worse, given the chance, and Gard did not know one way or the other what had occurred in that hut. Could Gard even now be reliving the same conversation? At the time, he hadn't been able to give her a definitive answer. Could he overlook it in time and still remain with her? Did he now have his answer? Did she? His hesitation seemed to say it all.

His black stare strayed from hers, darting over her blood-stained face and bodice, to the rest of her body, ripped clothing all disheveled and dirty. His gaze returned to hers.

Gard braced his feet apart. Slowly, he raised his arms from his sides, his palms splayed upward in invitation.

Brae choked on a sob and ran at her husband. She collided with his chest. He swung her into his arms as she wept into his neck.

"Brae," he murmured, and coiled his body around her, swallowing her up.

With his wife in his arms, Gard dropped to his knees as the enormity and fear of the situation slammed into him, full bore.

As he and the men had ridden toward the scene, he'd barely been able keep the panic at bay. It clogged his throat and clawed inside his chest. He'd seen what Cowan had done to the other women, and the thought of him ravaging and torturing his wife was beyond what he could bear.

Taking slow inventory, he found her clothing torn, she was covered in dirt and blood. He had no idea if it was hers. Nor could he ascertain the extent of her injuries. He could not think of it. Braelynn was alive, and that was all that mattered. She whimpered against his neck, clinging to him as if he were the only thing holding her together. She whispered his name over and over. He felt that foreign prick behind his eyes again as his heart tried to fly out of his chest.

CHAPTER THIRTY-NINE

At camp, after bathing in warm water which Gard had ordered for her, Brae sat combing her hair when Hudson entered her tent.

"Bain?" Brae asked, rising to her feet.

Hudson gestured for her to remain seated. "The next few hours will tell, Brae, I'm sorry I cannot give you more definitive news. As you once said, head wounds can be tricky."

"Has he gained consciousness again?" Brae asked.

"Not completely. He mumbles, but that has been all." Hudson pressed his fingers to Brae's wrist.

"'Tis a good sign, yah?" she continued at his uncertain expression. "He canna die because o' me."

Hudson did not immediately answer as he counted. "'Tis his duty to protect his lady. 'Tis an honor to die this way."

"'Tis nonsense, Hudson, and ya ken it. 'Tis an honor ta die on the battle field defendin' your country, or ta lose your life for your lord. 'Tis nuthin' more than wasteful for a man like Bain ta lose his life for me at the hands of a madman," she cried.

"Your husband does not happen to agree. He is now standing over the man waiting to express his gratitude. But it was not Bain who saved *your* life, was it, Brae?" Hudson asked.

She ignored his question, not wanting to admit to herself that she had killed a man. "Will ya send Gard ta me? He has not visited me yet."

"I am not sure if he can at the moment, Brae," Hudson admitted.

Gard had not spoken a word since Piers had asked him if he'd left something valuable at camp.

A few short months ago, Gard's first thought would have been his seal and his other jewels, not some woman. Not Braelynn. But his first thought and his last word, had been Brae. She was precious to him. Though Hudson often enjoyed teasing Gard that someday he too would fall in love, Hudson had never actually believed it would happen. Gard was too strong and determined. If he did not want something, by God, it would not be. But it had happened anyway. Gard was in love with his wife.

"Why? He thinks Robbie raped me and he canna live wit' it? He canna forgive me?" Brae cried.

"Nay. That is not it." But how could he explain the complex workings of Gard Marschand when he did not understand the man himself? Yet there were more important issues to deal with at hand. "*Did* he violate you, Braelynn?" Hudson asked, bracing for her response. There would be no telling how Gard would react to that.

"Nay, he did not."

Hudson examined her tearstained features for duplicity. She looked him square in the eye and he believed her.

"But I do have some injuries tha' I believe ya may need ta look after for me." Brae released her hold on her gown, revealing deep and jagged teeth marks and bruising upon her pale skin.

The bastard!

Hudson released a breath he had been unaware he had been holding. "I will need my kit."

Hudson returned with his supplies and patched Brae up. As

he did so, Brae wondered at this new dilemma she found herself in. Should she tell Hudson and Gard what Cowan had revealed about the MontClaire seal and the treachery of Gard's sister? Or could the rantings of a madman even be believed? She watched Hudson's face as he cleaned and stitched her wounds. She decided now was not the time.

After tending the last abrasion, Hudson sat back.

"Thank ya, Hudson," Brae said, squeezing his hand.

"I wish I could stay, but I need to check on Bain."

"I'll be here prayin'," she replied.

Hudson rose and gathered his materials. He cupped Brae's cheek affectionately, then took his leave.

Unable to stop weeping, Brae stretched out on the pallet and waited for her husband to return.

Hudson forced Gard from his vigil at Bain's bedside. He grabbed Gard by the shoulders and directed him towards his quarters.

"Go to your wife, she is asking for you. You are both in need of each other."

Numbly, Gard plodded toward their accommodations.

He ducked inside.

Brae stood near the entrance, looking pale. A billowy white gown hid her shape.

"I thought ya would ne'er come." she greeted quietly. "How is Bain?" The fear in her eyes was evident.

"There isna change," he replied.

"Can I help ye bathe?" she offered hesitantly.

He paused, disregarding the offer. 'Twas the least of his worries. "Are ya hurt?"

"Nay. Hudson fixed me up."

He swallowed with difficulty, approaching her slowly.

They eyed each other openly, uncertain how to proceed.

Gard had no idea what to think, do, feel or say. This was foreign to him, feeling something for another. He did not like it. And the fear was not something he could live with. While searching for Brae, he had kept imagining finding her broken body twisted and mutilated, her dead accusing eyes damning him in eternal sleep for failing her. He had not felt that helpless panic since the day he had watched his father die. Then, he was too small and scared to play the hero. And this time, had he been too late?

"Did he hurt ya?"

Brae met his gaze openly. "Nay. No' seriously. He didna rape me, Gard."

He made no outward reaction, but his blood rushed in his ears.

"He didna rape me," she said, as though repeating it would make him believe her.

"Ya saw firsthand wha' he did ta those other women. Ya ken in your heart tha' if he had done those things ta me, I wouldna be standin' here righ' now. I wouldna live." She yanked the gown from her shoulders, and let it fall, baring herself to him. "Look. I have bruises and marks, but I am whole."

His dark tortured soul held him hostage as she continued her plea.

"I am still yours and yours alone. 'Tis the truth, Gard. I wouldna lie ta ya in this. There would be parts o' me tha' would be too brutalized for me ta lie aboot . . ."

"Caisg, Braelynn." Gard closed his eyes and laid his forehead to hers. "I wasna there. I failed ta protect ya from the bastard."

"'Twasna your fault. He falsified the missive ta lure ya away."

"But I shoulda kenned 'twas too simple. I should have—"

"Caisg, Gard. Ya canna blame yourself. I willna allow it.

Cowan was mad."

"Dinna utter his name again." Gard wound his hands into her soft damp hair.

"Ya gave me the strength and the weapon and the skill. I did wha' ya taught me. I was brave enough ta do it, Gard. Because o' you. I wouldna have been able ta do such a thing back at Ross. Ya have saved my life this day."

Slowly, Brae unlaced his shirt.

"Touch me," she begged. "I need your hands on me."

He had been afraid she would never want a man's touch again. Brae took his hand, placing it at her waist. She then moved his palm over her ribs, forcing him to caress her until his thumb nudged the underside of her breast. She rose on her tiptoes. Her mouth just inches from his, she murmured, "I need ta feel ya, Gard. Please. Erase it for both o' us. I want ta smell ya on me. I want your sweat on my skin. I want ta see only you. Feel . . . hear . . . taste, only you." She kissed his lips and pushed his shirt from his shoulders.

With reverence, Gard lowered her to the pallet.

He made slow gentle love to his wife, branding her with his lips and body in an attempt to make them both forget.

Gard surged into her one last time. "I willna let ya go, one year add a day. Ya are mine, Braelynn," he panted. "For all time."

"For as long as love shall last," she whispered.

The next day, Gard returned to the burnt-out hut, in search of his dagger. He had given his wife a replacement, strapping it to her beautiful white thigh himself. Though he had loathed leaving her, Hudson remained at her side. And knowing Cowan was dead only eased his fear for her in his absence.

Nevertheless Gard required a few minutes alone to sort his scattered emotions. He had not even thought about his quest since the moment he had realized Brae had been abducted. There had not been a day go by, till now, that he had not labored in some way to make some step, however small, to bring his earldom closer to his grasp. Even camped outside the palace had seemed like just another obstacle, another toll he must pay to achieve his goal. But Brae had been more important to him in that moment than anything before her. Now with her safe return, it was essential he turn his attention to what he must do. Yet even now, he wanted nothing more than to return to Brae's side, his dagger bedamned.

Gard bent over Robbie Cowan's scorched body and yanked his blade from what was left of his neck. Tiny particles of crispy ash swirled up into the air and floated on a thin shaft of sunlight.

With one good kick of his boot, Gard sent the remains of Cowan's head into a cloud of dust. "Burn in hell ya bloody bastard."

Gard stepped out into the sunshine. Hooves pounding toward him caught his attention.

Llachlan dropped to his side from atop his galloping mount. "Lord Marschand." He huffed, struggling for of breath. "Your wife has been arrested."

Smartly, Llach took a step in reverse, waiting for the eruption to come. Gard did not disappoint. He wrapped his black-gloved hand about Llach's throat and squeezed.

"What say you, Llachlan o' Skye?" *Not again. She is not taken from me again!*

"Palace guards came ta the camp. They took Lady Marschand. I'm sorry, My Lord." Llachlan attempted to break his hold, only to have it tighten around his neck.

"And Richmond let it happen?" Gard bellowed. "He let them take her?"

"No' exactly, sir. He didna have much choice. There were alotta them. He assaulted one o' the guards and was arrested as weel. He did it apurpose, so the Lady Marschand would-na go alone. He sent me ta fetch ya."

Gard shoved Llach away and mounted his steed.

He looked down at Llachlan and said with determination, "MontClaire." The coarse hairs on his arms stood on end. "Summon them."

"Aye, My Lord MontClaire," Llachlan responded solemnly.

Gard kicked his horse and raced toward the palace.

"Wha' will they do wit' us?" Brae asked Hudson as they were herded into the Tower.

"I expect we will see the inside of the dungeon first." Hudson chuckled.

Brae found it difficult to appreciate his humor, but assumed it was simply his way of trying to keep her calm. Yet she was anything but composed. She had been arrested for the murder of a noble and could be executed before the night was through.

The smell permeating from the damp dark cell clogged Brae's throat. Her feet slid on the wet slimy stones. The guard pushed her into a cell and the iron door closed with the piercing screech of rusted hinges. She heard another clang seal Hudson inside, before their captor's heavy booted footsteps filed away down the hall in a march.

"Hudson?" Her trembling voice echoed.

All of a sudden, his hand appeared between the bars. She latched onto it as if it were her lifeline. "I am here, Brae."

"What's goin' ta happen ta us?"

"Gard will come," Hudson said in a most reassuring tone. "He will take care of everything. Try not to worry."

"Thank ya for assaultin' the guard. I kenned ya did tha' ta accompany me. I dinna want ya punished, but I thank ya for not leavin' me ta this alone."

He squeezed her hand.

"I'm frightened, John," she whispered.

He rubbed her hand with his thumb. "Gard will come."

As time dragged on, Brae tried to stay awake. The thought of sleeping while leaning against the wet green wall did not appeal, but worry and fatigue pulled her under nonetheless.

An enormous uproar startled Brae awake. Clanging metal and shouting followed.

"Hudson?" she called. "Wha's happenin'?"

"I believe your husband has arrived," he said and the smile in his voice buoyed her as much as the prospect that Gard might be near. The ruckus moved closer.

"You will release my wife. Now!" Gard roared, sword in hand, he came into view.

Brae had seen him train, but she had never seen him in battle. He was not delivering killing blows, he was sparing lives while cutting a path to her and Hudson, and it amazed her to watch him in fighting form.

"Gard!" she cried as he backed against her cell, holding the guards at bay. She grabbed onto his shirt seeking his strength and reassurance.

"Are ya a'right?" he snarled out the corner of his mouth, keeping his attention focused on the king's soldiers.

"Aye. Now tha' ye are here."

"What goes on here?" Another voice joined the fray. "Ah, right then," he said as his gaze landed on Gard. "Thought you would gain your own access to the king, Marschand? I dare say 'tis a bold move, but taking the dungeon? Truly. I could think of better ways than to lay siege to the place where you will find yourself once the king realizes your perfidy."

"My wife has been wrongfully jailed. If this is some contrivance of yours, Gaveston, I will gladly join her after dispatching your sorry hide."

"Contrivance? You think I have something to do with this? I was not even aware you had taken a wife. Stand aside Marschand, I would look upon the woman who would saddle herself with the likes of *you* for all eternity."

"Go to hell, Gaveston. Better yet, take a step forward and I will send you there myself." Gard pointed his sword at the man's chest. "I will be a hero among the barons." There were some snickers among the palace guards.

Peeking around Gard's shoulder, Brae tried to get a look at the man in question.

Brae gasped. It was the gentleman from the cliffs who'd rewarded her with the gem! This Gaveston was also the man named in Gard's missive. The one who had been referred to as the Gastonian knight, the young king's companion. *Aye, Piers Gaveston.*

It finally dawned on her. King Edward the First had banished Piers, not to punish him, but to attempt to extinguish the strange relationship between his son, now king, and his cohort. The king was angry that young Edward bestowed lavish gifts and riches on his favorite. Could that have been why he had been fleeing that day they had encountered each other on the cliffs? But who were the men chasing him, and why? His words about the treasure flitted through her mind. *You return it to its true owner, and you will be granted any boon that you ask in reward for saving my life this day . . . I am indebted to you.*

"Perhaps a hero among the barons," Piers retorted, "but you will make an enemy of the most powerful king of the ages," he boasted. "'Twould be a poor choice on your part, ruining the chances of achieving what you seek. *Yet again!*"

The new king was many things, but his unfortunate dead father was more of a ruler than Edward the Second would ever be. And all who knew him, or knew of him, were aware of this fact, spoken or not.

Hudson's snort of derision echoed in the ward.

Yet Gard responded, "Oh, come now, Gaveston, Edward is more interested in his own pursuits than he is England. He will not even by half, compare to his sire."

"You know my influence with him," Gaveston bragged. "You and your cohorts should choose your words more carefully. I may be helpful in your plight, Marschand. I have the ear of the king."

"The ear and various other parts that no other man should have need of," Gard sneered.

The guards snickered again at the notorious and speculated relationship.

Brae was shocked by the way Gard and Hudson questioned and insulted his manhood. He seemed as he should be. Quite handsome. He could have any woman. He appeared a perfect gentleman. But the Lords slurred his relationship with the king, even implying that they might be intimate. Could the rumors be true?

"Easy, Gard," Hudson warned in a low voice.

"Step aside and let me see this wife." Piers daringly backhanded Gard's sword, moving it aside so that he could proceed without being run through.

Brae stood close to Gard, holding his shirt, wishing she could pull him through the bars and throw herself into his arms.

The nobleman's face appeared over Gard's broad shoulder. Brae looked up at him. He was just as she remembered, perhaps a little less disheveled. "Monsieur Gaveston," she whispered.

His eyes narrowed. He was slow to recognize her. One eyebrow rose right before a slight grin spread across his face. "*You* be the Lady Marschand?"

"Aye," she responded with pride.

"Have we met afore, Lady Marschand?" he asked cheekily.

Brae suffered a momentary shiver of fear and uncertainty. She was not sure how to answer so she countered his question with one of her own. "Have ya been ta Scotland?"

"Mmm. Aye, I have. I believe I left something very valuable there at one time." He turned his attention to Richmond in the cell next to hers. "And what do you do here, Richmond, in the prisoners' quarters?"

"'Tis a wrongful arrest," Hudson replied.

Gaveston chuckled. "And why have you been wrongfully detained?"

"Not I. Lady Marschand has been wrongfully accused. *I* have been rightfully obtained."

"You thought to but accompany her then, Richmond?" Gaveston pursed his lips. "Hmm, your steadfast loyalty to Marschand is commendable."

"I protected my lady," Richmond snarled.

Brae was overcome with his constancy. Whether it be through his commitment to Gard or more, it was greatly appreciated.

"Have you ever done so, Gaveston?" Hudson questioned.

Brae again thought to the day she had met the man before. He had promised to protect her if she were found with him.

Gard turned his head and glanced toward Richmond's cell. "Who do you suppose plays the lady, Hudson?" Gard continued the verbal assault on Piers. If Brae did not know better she would think he was having a good time at Gaveston's expense.

"I would regale you my opinion on that, but I may be hanged for heresy afore the sun comes." And in that not so subtle insult, his opinion was sure. The guards around them guffawed again.

Piers ignored the jab. "What have you been accused of, Lady Marschand?"

"I have been accused o' killin' a man," she murmured.

"*You* killed a man? Your crazed husband, I could understand if he killed in cold blood. He was born an assassin. But you? I find that difficult to swallow."

Both Gard and Hudson snorted but deigned for once not to make a jest out of his words.

"Not just a man," one of the guards interjected. "A noble."

"He was the most ignoble man e'er put on this earth," Brae scoffed.

"Careful, Brae," Hudson warned her softly.

"The man attacked me. I but defended meself."

"Whom was the noble?" Gaveston queried.

"He alleged to be a relation of John Comyn," Hudson supplied, trying to cast doubt on that claim. "But 'twas he who perpetrated the attacks plaguing the throngs of people waiting to see the king."

"I had been made aware that you, Marschand, had taken it upon yourself to find the scoundrel. I was unaware that you used your wife as bait—" Piers found the tip of Marschand's sword pointed at his Adam's apple before he could finish his statement.

Hudson rushed on, trying to diffuse the situation. "'Twas also he who fraudulently used the king's seal to lure Lord Marschand to the palace, plotting to have him away from his lady."

"Aww. That may also work in your favor, lady." Gaveston allowed.

Gard lowered his sword.

"I am hopeful, Monsieur Gaveston," Brae said, contrite.

"You may call me Cornwall, if you like," he invited.

"He has named you Duke of Cornwall?" Hudson said incredulously. The guards around them murmured their discontent also.

Piers grinned conspiratorially. "He has not yet made it official. But soon. We are near equals, Richmond."

"Hardly." Hudson sniffed. "The barons will not be happy, Gaveston."

"Mmm. Will they not?" He observed his fingernail as if this fact did not worry him in the least. In truth, he looked like he welcomed their disapproval.

"Gaveston!" the warder chief roared. "Step aside."

"No. This arrangement will not do. I will appeal for them to be moved into more suitable holdings until the Lady Marschand sees trial. She and Richmond should not be housed in this foul accommodation. Come."

"Gaveston," the chief began. "We cannot take your commands as if—"

"I said come. I will take full responsibility. Let them out," he directed, with a wave.

The guards unlocked the two cell doors. Brae dove into Gard's waiting arm.

"And what are we to do with Marschand?" the guard asked.

"You could throw him in Richmond's vacated cell," he suggested with a careless shrug.

Gard brandished his sword menacingly. "You could try," he invited, his mouth curving at the prospect of a good fight. The guards gave him a wide berth.

Hudson, Gard, and Brae followed the king's favorite through the palace halls, the decor becoming more and more resplendent as they went. The guards followed closely.

"Here. Place Lady Marschand in this chamber. The earl may be housed in the room next. Place guards on the door. I will return."

"And what of Marschand?" the exasperated guard inquired.

"Aye, *what of me*, Gaveston? Do you expect me to leave my wife under your care?"

"'Twould seem at the moment, you are out of options, MontClaire," he stated, pointedly using Gard's title for all in the vicinity to hear. "I have put myself out and placed your delicate wife and the earl in more fitting accommodations. I suggest you return to your temporary housing and await the king's summons. Perhaps send your wife and Richmond some more appropriate attire. They will be meeting with the king and representing you, as well as your plight, as they do so." He began to walk away. "Lock them in. Then throw Marschand out," he said over his shoulder.

They locked Richmond in after a small tussle. He did not go in easily. Brae hung onto Gard.

"Come, Marschand, or should I say, *MontClaire*," the guard sneered. "This does not have to be difficult."

Gard turned, giving the leader a black look. "You will give me a moment with my wife." It was as simple as that. The guards withdrew marginally from the power that emanated from Gard MontClaire.

"You will be given but a moment," the chief guard reminded.

Gard backed Brae into the open room. He looked around it as he sheathed his sword. The chamber was lavishly furnished with heavy burgundy brocades trimmed with gold tassels. Hardly accommodations to house a prisoner. What was Gaveston up to? Gard assumed he would not use her in any way inappropriate, believing not only the rumors and the things he himself had witnessed between the king and consort, but relying on his own instinct. Gaveston used people to further his own ambition. Brae could not do that for him.

He hated to leave her alone. Anyone could come in whenever they wished, and she was virtually unprotected.

"Have ya your dagger?" he asked in Gaelic. Gard patted down her thigh checking for himself.

"Aye. Gard, but I do not wish to be here," she answered him in kind, her wide frightened look pulled at his heart. "What if they execute me before you return. What if this is simply a ruse to get you away?"

"He would not have gone to such trouble to move you if he thought you would be executed. He has something planned for you or us, I just don't know what. Try not to answer any questions if you are interrogated. They speak Norman French here. Act as if you cannot speak it or understand it."

"I cannot understand it or speak it fluently. 'Twouldn't be a lie. But there is something that I need you to know before . . . just in case, I don't get a chance to speak to you again."

A knock made Brae jump.

"Gard!"

'Twas Hudson's voice. He hammered on a door that adjoined the two rooms. Gard reluctantly released his wife and approached the entry. In a more hushed tone, Hudson said. "Can you unlock the door? Is there a latch on that side?"

Gard turned the handle and tried the door. It did not budge. He worked the lock from side to side. "It seems to be rusted. I can hear the mechanism working, but it won't release."

"I'll keep trying to find a way in. At least if I can get in, I could get to Brae quickly if need be."

"That would be appreciated," Gard said dryly. "Since you couldn't keep her from being arrested in the first."

"And *you* would have been able to keep her from being arrested if you'd been there? What would you have done differently?"

Gard made a fist and punched the wood. "I should have stopped Cowan afore this happened, and she wouldna be in this situation. Nor would you."

Brae braced her hands on his back trying to calm his anger.

His outburst roused the guards. "Marschand, we are about to use force to remove you from the grounds if you do not first do so willingly," the chief warder yelled from the hall.

Gard took a deep breath, before turning to face his wife. He kissed her soundly. "I will return. And when we leave here, together, I will take ya home."

"Home?" Her lip trembled.

"Aye. Ta Fife. Where we belong." He gave her another quick kiss, then made for the door.

"Gard." She ran after him and threw herself at him, clinging. He turned and held her in his arms tightly.

"Marschand!" the guard roared.

"I mus' go," he whispered.

She looked up at him, and his heart stuttered at the love, sorrow, and fear that he could see in her eyes. "I love you, Gard," she whispered in Gaelic.

Gard blinked slowly, as was his way. He wound his hands into her hair and gently kissed her forehead.

Brae kept her gaze locked on his while he slowly retreated. "Home," he said once more then the guards escorted him away and Brae was locked in.

Hudson continued to work at the door between the rooms. He kept up an endless stretch of conversation, keeping Brae's mind occupied. Brae scoured the room, searching for anything that might be useful to her later. The furniture was heavy ornately carved hardwood. She rifled through drawers finding clean linens and bright white under dresses. A large wardrobe held a riding cloak and other elegant garments. They were of an older fashion but still some of the most beautiful things Brae had ever seen. She wondered what Gard would think of her clothed in one of these, her hair all dressed and bejeweled with pearls or emeralds, befitting the wife of Donnghardh MontClaire. Then she discarded that silly little daydream. She needed to concentrate on keeping her head attached to her body and quit worrying about frivolous things.

"Have you found anything of import, Brae?" Hudson asked.

"There is clothin', linens, a brush and comb, some powder. All lady's things."

"Is there perhaps a letter opener? A feather and ink for writing?"

She opened the last of the drawers. "I found some hairpins. Oh, there be a hat pin."

"Aye, that may work, Brae. Try one in the lock."

Brae rushed over then worked the lock. "God's bones, Hudson, 'tis o' no use." She slapped the door in frustration, and it popped open to her surprise. She laughed out loud and threw herself at him.

"Shhh. We do not want them to know that we can do this." He held her. She felt his chest rumble as he chuckled. "We really need to quit meeting like this. You are a married woman."

"'Twill be Gard tha' ends up bein' a widower if we canna get me oot o' this."

"It will not come to that," he reassured her. "Gard could not handle it."

"Wha'?" Brae frowned.

Hudson cleared his throat. "Let me make sure that this lock will work for us the next time we need it to, shall we?" Brae handed him the hatpin, and he worked the tumblers so they were loose. He flicked the latch again and again. "Now the big test. You go in there, and we will hope I can open the door again once it closes.

It worked.

Hudson walked into her room and looked around. She stuck her head into his room and did the same, a mirror image of hers.

"Do ya have women's things in your room as weel?"

"Aye. I'm thinking of sleeping in one of those long night gowns."

"I would like ta see tha'," she giggled.

"Your husband would not approve."

"Nay, he likes his men in black." She giggled again.

He laughed. "You are a good match for him."

Brae looked at him in surprise.

"Most women would be weeping of their circumstance or bargaining with the guards for their release."

"And how would one go aboot tha'? I have nuthin' ta bargain wit'."

He smiled indulgently "I think I should go to my room and we will close the door just in case the guards check on us. We would not want them to know our little secret. Why don't you try to rest?"

"Oh, a'righ'" she said, disappointed. She did not look forward to being alone with her thoughts.

He closed the door between them. She sat down on the large bed. The silence was deafening.

When she closed her eyes, Gard's handsome face swam before her. She curled up on the bed and cried herself to sleep.

CHAPTER FORTY

Brae heard the lock turn in the door and she bolted upright as an opulently dressed maid shuffled into the room holding a tray.

"Here ye are, Lady MontClaire. Sir Gaveston, er, uh, the Duke of Cornwall has requested I be yor maid. Me name be Morag, I hail from Black Poole."

Brae had to listen carefully. Her accent was very strong and difficult to decipher. Luckily she was not speaking French as Gard had said they might. But Brae was immediately worried when she addressed her as Lady MontClaire. It was out in the open now. Donnghardh Marschand MontClaire was here to make his claim. There was no turning back. And his attention was now divided because of her.

"I have brought ye some sup," Morag finished.

"Has Lord Richmond been served as weel?"

"Wha?" She stared at Brae. "Wha'd'ye say? I cannot understand ye."

Brae would have laughed if she had the energy. Brae pointed to the room beyond. "Lord Richmond," she repeated slowly. "Food?"

"Oh, aye. The earl has been looked after. The Duke has requested ye a bath and I am ta dress yor hair every day until yor trial. Y'are to dress appropriately as well. You may not have time to do so before you are called. You must be ready and waiting every morning."

"My husband has no' yet come wit' me things," Brae explained.

"'Er wha'?"

Brae gritted her teeth and inhaled. "I have no clothing," she spoke slowly, attempting to emulate Gard's English.

"Oh, that does not matter. Lord Gaveston believes the things in this room will be fittin'. I am to take 'em and mend 'em and air 'em out for you. This night you will bathe, and I will help you dress and tend yor hair in the morn."

She went to the closet and started clearing out the heavy dresses. Brae would much prefer to wear the garments Gard had purchased for her. They were more befitting for representing him.

Morag went to the door and a line of maids carried the dresses from the wardrobe then out of the room.

"I will return to help you bathe."

"Oh, ye donn need ta do tha'. I am quite capable o' seein' ta meself."

"Wha'?"

Thankfully one of the other maids understood and translated.

"As you wish."

Once Brae was alone again, she went to the door separating the rooms and listened.

"Hudson?" she called.

"Aye, Braelynn."

"Did they bring ye somethin' ta eat?"

"Aye. You?"

"Aye."

She sighed heavily. The door between them opened. "Why don't I bring one of those chairs closer to the door. I'll stay on my side, you stay on yours, and we can leave the door open and enjoy our meals together."

"I would like tha'," she said gratefully.

He picked up one of the large wooden chairs instead of pulling it, perhaps scraping it across the floor alerting the guards. Setting it down he gestured for her to sit. She did so and he passed her the tray.

Hudson entered his room and collected his meal. He then perched on the seat already located close to the go-between.

They sat facing each other in their respective rooms.

"If we hear a key in the lock, I will push the door closed quickly."

She nodded her understanding. "The maid said she would return wit' a bath."

"We will be vigilant." He smiled reassuringly. "Did you rest? You were quiet for a fair while."

"Aye. I slept some. You?"

He shook his head.

"Soldiers dinna need sleep either?"

"We cannot afford to sleep sometimes. What have you got on your tray there?" he asked.

"Pastries and some kind o' meat. I dinna ken wha' it be."

"'Tis pheasant."

Her mouth curled with distaste. "I am really no' hungry."

"Try to eat. You need to keep up your strength. My guess is by the end of the week we will know our fate. You need to be prepared for whatever may befall us. And Gard. You will need to be strong for him."

"I will be," she whispered. Every time she thought of him, she wanted to cry. She took a bite of the pastry.

It was not long before they heard many footfalls coming. Hudson winked and closed the door between them. Brae hurriedly turned the chair.

The tub was hauled into the room and filled. Brae was left alone. She bathed quickly, pulling on one of the clean linen gowns. She grew tired, even though she had slept earlier. The tub was cleared. Brae called good night to Hudson through the door and then crawled into the big bed, willing herself to sleep.

"Sleepyhead? Are you going to sleep the day away? You are missing everything. You sleep like the dead."

Brae opened her eyes to Gard's tantalizing voice. He spoke Gaelic. She loved to hear the words roll off his tongue.

He grinned. She could not help but do so in return. His smile was devastating. It seemed like such a natural thing for him to do now. She could barely remember when it was a difficult task for him. He was the most beautiful man she had ever seen. She ran her fingers over his mouth, her fingertips over his beard. He caught her hand. "Come. I want to show you everything."

He pulled her out of bed.

"Where are we?" she asked. She looked around. They were in a place she had never seen before.

"Come," he said again, dragging her along. He seemed excited. She had never seen him this way before.

"Where are we?" she asked again as he led her to a window overlooking a beautiful garden at the height of bloom. "Oh, Gard, 'tis amazing." She took a deep breath, filling her nose with the most wonderful fragrances. "Where are we?"

He turned her to face him. He smiled down at her, his brown eyes were full of some emotion she could not name. "We're home."

Brae gasped and sat upright.

They were not home. 'Twas only a dream. She was being held prisoner for murder, awaiting her fate. She might never see Gard's home.

A strange sensation came over her and she could not attribute the feeling completely to the dream. She felt like she was not alone. It took a moment for her eyes to adjust to the darkness. Squinting, she scanned from the right side of the chamber to the left. From the corridor, light from the sconce filtered through the cracks under and around the door casting shadows on the walls. Brae slid soundlessly from the bed and tip-toed to the door. "Hudson?" she whispered, on the verge of hysteria.

"Brae? Are you a'right? What is it?" he answered quickly.

"Are ye righ' here by the door?"

"Aye."

"I feel like there be someone in the room wit' me."

The door opened before she could move. Hudson almost tripped over her. He moved through the room silently and checked about.

"There be no one in the chamber with you." He reassured, patting her forearm.

She leaned against his chest relieved. "Thank ya, John, for puttin' yourself inta this predicament for me." She wound her arms around his waist.

He patted her shoulder. "Get into bed, you need to rest."

"Can ya stay wit' me? Surely the guards willna come in the nigh'?"

"They most like will not. But it is not proper for me to be here with you like this. You are Gard's woman."

She giggled. "Well, o' course I am. And evraone kens it. Ya and I are friends."

He moved her away from him. "Your husband would not see it that way. And frankly, neither do I. Go to bed, Lady MontClaire."

Brae was hurt by his snub. She had thought they were friends. What had she done?

"And if I were you, I would lock the door," he said before he shut it.

Tears scorched her cheeks as she crawled into the big lonely bed.

Her initial impression of Gard and Hudson stood. They were simply the two most confusing men.

CHAPTER FORTY-ONE

Brae ate the morning meal alone, not bothering to see if Hudson had been given his. She was still stinging from his words of last night.

The maid Morag arrived and helped Brae into a green overdress with a cream underskirt. Unfortunately, Gaveston had underestimated the size of the clothing. The garments were at least two sizes too small.

Brae reached for the armoire trying to steady herself and ease the light-headedness that followed the constriction of her rib cage.

"Och, Morag, be this some kind o' English torture then?

"Wha'?"

"The bodice is ta tight."

"'Tis supposed ta be," she reassured. "Look at the difference it has made in yor shape."

Brae looked into the mirror. Her breasts were pushed up indecently, her waist small, the skirt flared out again at her hip.

"Now sit, I will dress yor hair."

Brae eased into the chair. The snug clothing lent her rigid posture. She was forced to take short panting breaths. "Are ya sure tha' I am in need of bein' dressed this way? 'Tis truly uncomfortable," Brae complained.

"I have no idea what ye are sayin'. But I am very good at this. Will take me no time at' all and I will be out of yor hair." Morag laughed at her own joke.

Brae sat quietly, allowing her to brush and pin, coil, and

curl her hair. She thought about Gard and nothing else.

"There ye be, Lady."

"Thank ye," Brae said, not even looking into the glass.

"Have a look see, then. Ye will not recognize yorself."

Brae peered into the glass. If she were ever allowed to see her husband again, he would not recognize her.

"Now pinch your cheeks. Ye have no color at'all."

Brae did not understand, until the woman reached out and twisted Brae's cheeks. "Ouch!" Brae glowered, taking a menacing step toward the other woman. "Wha' was tha' for?"

"Color," the woman stated slowly as if she were daft.

"I will give ya color. Black and blue if ye e'er do tha' ta me again," Brae threatened.

"Oh, you Scotch lasses are nasty."

"You jus' pinched me, ye Black Poolian cow. And we be Scots, na Scotch. Do I look like a pine ta ya?"

"Wha'? I cannot understand ye," Morag retorted.

"Wha'?" Brae repeated. Though she understood, she was just being difficult.

Hudson began to pound on the door upon hearing their raised voices.

"Brae. Brae. What is happening?"

"I be fine, Hudson. This maid o' the Blackened Poole jus' decided ta give me color and I dinna think I need it." Brae placed her hands on her hips as she continued to glower at the maid. "I believe," she said slowly, "ya are done now. Ya may leave."

"Well. I will leave. But only because I am done with ye."

There was a commotion in the hall.

"I will see my wife!"

"Gard!" Brae hollered and ran for the door. It remained unbarred for the maid. Brae threw it open and made a bee-line for her husband. He was surprised to see her free. He dropped the bundles he was holding and embraced her, lifting her off her feet.

"Och, ye are ruinin' yor hair!" the maid yelled.

"Oh, go back ta yor pasture," Brae bellowed, burying her face in Gard's neck. She felt his chest rumble.

He carried her into the room and set her on her feet. She kept a tight hold on him.

Roughly, he pushed her away so that he could look at her. He spanned each of his hands across her cheeks and neck. "Are ye a'righ'?" His dark eyes roved over her face, taking inventory.

"I am all right, physically but I want to come with you. Gard, I am so afraid that I never will be!" she whispered in Gaelic.

"Don't say that. I will get you out of here one way or another," he returned in kind.

It was the *or another* that worried her.

"You must trust me," he said, his voice laden with conviction.

"I do. It's evrathin' and evraone else workin' against us tha' I dinna."

He lowered his gaze. His attention rested on her heaving, pushed-up breasts. He skimmed his hand across her overly rounded flesh. She closed her eyes and enjoyed his touch. He snarled before taking her lips in a bruising kiss. She threw her arms around his neck, her plumped breasts pressed against his chest. He cupped her bottom as he coaxed her toward the bed.

"Marschand, we will not allow you to defile the prisoner," a guard yelled.

Gard, with his exceptional speed, slammed the door, jammed a chair beneath its handle and was back kissing his wife breathless before the guards could react.

Brae kneed her way up onto the bed and began pulling

up her skirts.

Gard followed but stayed her hand. "Not here. The walls have eyes."

"Please," she whimpered, pulling at the laces of his trews. "I miss ya so much. I canna sleep. I dream and I feel like there is someone in the room wit' me."

"Damn it, Braelynn stop afore ya push me beyond my control."

She continued to torment him, rocking her hips.

He gripped her waist. "Quit that. Nor am I blind to your inviting cleavage. I will not love ya for all ta see."

She stopped moving under him and followed his gaze. "Wha' say you?"

"As I said, the walls have eyes. Spies, they are everywhere, watchin', listenin', sometimes for the king, often for their own agenda. 'Tis how they ken wha' goes on. Who migh' be plotting against them. Who's unfaithful. A lot goes on at court."

"Oh!" She covered her bared flesh. "I partook in a bath, wha' if someone . . ."

"I will kill them," he said stonily.

"Hudson also mentioned this last nigh'. Yet I didna understand wha' he meant."

Gard sat up. "He released the lock then?" he said in Gaelic, just in case the eyes in the walls owned ears as well, she assumed.

"Aye."

"And he was in this room with you last eve?"

"Aye, but only to check the chamber for me. I had a dream, and when I woke I felt like I wasn't alone. He was right by the door when I called."

"I can imagine he was." Gard strode to the main door that led to the hallway. Taking the chair out, he threw the barrier open with force. Brae followed, but was blocked by a guard at the entrance. Gard stopped in front of Hudson's door. "You will unlock it," Gard demanded in French.

"I cannot—"

His words were cut off as Gard snatched the keys from the leather at the guard's waist. Gard tried one key, and then the next.

"Give me those." The guard wrested them back then opened the door with the correct key. "At least let it be my decision to unlock it. I am the one in charge here."

As soon as the door was open, Gard went after his second with a vengeance.

Brae could only hear Gard mumbling accusations before flesh met flesh. Furniture overturned, wood splintered. The guards gathered around the opening and jeered however they made no attempt to break it up.

Brae inched toward the unmanned entry. The maid stepped in front of her giving her a glare. "I would not."

Brae slammed the door in her face and ran to the go-between adjoining the two chambers. She listened to the ruckus going on in the next room.

Gard kept his voice low so the guards would not hear the allegations.

"So am I to think that you had yourself arrested to oversee my interests. Am I to learn that you are here to further your own?" Gard slammed his fist into his friend's face.

"Now Gard. You know that my loyalty to you is above all . . . umph." Hudson ran his tongue over his teeth, then fingered the front two as if testing their security.

"I would have believed that at one time. But I have seen the way you look at my wife."

"The same way *you* do?" Hudson remarked, earning himself another jab under the chin.

"She said you were practically sitting on the door. Were you the one in her room?" Gard wound his hands around his former friend's neck.

Hudson attempted to slide his finger up between Gard's hands and his throat. It was of no use as Gard squeezed. Hudson's face reddened and his eyes bulged. Hudson rammed Gard in the ribs. He grunted and loosed his hold. With a push of his legs, Hudson heaved him off. But Gard was good and mad and would not be deterred.

Gard grabbed his collar. "Were you in my wife's room last night," he asked again.

"I was —" Another fist met Hudson's face. "But I only did so at her request. She thought she was not alone. I checked around, reassured her, then I left. I swear."

"Gard!" Brae banged on the door from the other side. "He tells the truth. Caisg!"

"Listen to your wife, Gard. Trust her, if you won't believe me. You know how she feels about you, and if you don't you are blind as well as stupid. She would not betray you with anyone."

"But I know *you*," Gard stormed.

"One lapse. One moment of madness. But it passed. I told her to get to bed and lock the door. I returned —"

There was more pummeling.

"I think you need to quit beating me and ask yourself why you are thrashing me soundly. Perhaps because you have actually developed feelings for her?"

Gard picked Hudson up, only to slam him back down viciously. Hudson coughed, struggling to breathe.

"That's what this is about," Hudson argued. "This is not about me. Or her."

Gard ran out of momentum.

Hudson sat up, pulling a handkerchief from his pocket. He wiped his bloody mouth and nose. "This is about you.

You needed to get your aggression out because you do not know how to deal with your feelings for your wife. Feel better?"

"Not at all. Stand up so I can hit you again."

"Hmm, and no denial."

Gard exhaled as he straightened his clothing.

"I don't understand what the problem is. She is beautiful, intelligent, she owns wit and above all else, she can put up with you."

"I am done. Lock him in," Gard said to the warder. "Open the lady's door."

"You have seen her. Time for you to leave."

Gard glared at the man. "I have brought proper clothing for her." He bent to retrieve the discarded satchel. "She will not be trussed up like a plump Christmas goose with all her wares on display for the multitude to enjoy." He rounded on the maid, who cowered. "She will wear her own things that are decent for my wife to be seen in."

"She is no' bein' seen." The maid dared.

Gard glowered. "Why are you still here?"

She gasped and flew off down the hall.

Gard gestured for them to open the door.

Brae sat in the chair in front of the glass, her head down. He barred the entry, affording them some privacy.

Gard dropped her case. "You will change," he demanded.

"But you will not," she said quietly.

He frowned. "Ya kenned I wouldna. So, dinna question me now."

"Why did ya do tha'? Hudson is your friend, and e'en though he doesna wish ta be here, he put himself in jeopardy outta loyalty ta you."

"His actions arna so noble."

She shook her head.

He moved behind her and began to loosen her clothing.

449

She relaxed and took several deep breaths. "How is it English ladies breathe in such garments? I am truly light-headed."

"You will not set foot out of here looking like that again," he said in his most stern English, so there would be no misunderstanding in his meaning.

"'Twasna by me choice."

He turned her in the chair. He leaned down inches from her face. "But when we get home . . ." he said in Gaelic, as his eyes followed his hands to her freed breasts. His body tightened.

Her eyes glazed and her lips parted. Her reaction did not help his situation.

"Change. I mus' go," he ordered, using all his willpower not to ravage his wife.

While she changed, Gard searched the walls for peep-holes. Carefully rearranging furniture and tapestries, he was fairly confident he had covered them all. He had to get her out of here.

"Has anyone been to question you?"

"Nay."

"Gaveston?"

"Nay. I havena seen him."

Gard walked toward the exit. She followed. Her eyes were glassy with unshed tears. Gard swallowed. A hard knot had formed in his throat.

"'Twillna be long now," he reassured her.

She laid her head on his chest, then placed her arms around him.

"Wha' was your dream?" he asked holding her.

"My dream?"

"Ya said ya had a dream afore ya felt like there be someone in your room. Was it a good dream, or a nightmare?"

"'Twas a good dream."

"Wha' did ya dream tha' was good, Braelynn?"

"I dreamt we were home."

When he closed his eyes, he could already see her there. He cleared his throat and set her away from him.

"I will attempt to return if I am so permitted," he said almost too formally, before opening the door. Tears rolled down her cheeks as the guards locked her in. That image was now branded in his memory.

Gard wanted nothing more than to stay and hold her, and when the time came, he would take the punishment in her stead.

CHAPTER FORTY-TWO

A full sennight passed. Brae and Hudson were fed regularly. Brae dressed everyday in the garments Gard left, hoping each day would be the one she had some say in what fate might befall her. In the beginning she had been so afraid that she only had a few hours left on this earth, but now she just wanted desperately for something to happen. A trial, a punishment. Something. The waiting was unbearable. She had not seen Gard again. Was it because they would not permit him, or did he not wish to see her? Was he even now exalting in the fact that he did not have to endure a year plus a day?

Locked up, she had too much time to think. The extra hours played with her thoughts and made her imagine things that may not even be. Was she going mad?

She and Hudson had a routine. With the door open, they ate their meals together. Hudson had found a chess set on his side and had taught her to play. They had several close calls keeping their secret hidden from the guards or the maids. And they took turns reading to each other from the tomes Gard had brought in her bag.

By the end of the week, she had convinced him to teach her French. He laughed often at her pronunciation. "Your brogue keeps you from perfection, Brae. But the rolling r's are wonderful due to that guttural Gaelic you and Gard so covet."

She bit her lip at the mention of his name. "Where do ya think he has been?"

"I believe they will not permit him visitation. We are prisoners, after all."

Brae bowed her head.

"He would not leave you alone this long by choice," Hudson reassured.

"I dinna ken aboot tha'. Wha' will happen ta you, John?"

"Don't worry yourself over me."

"But I do. I dinna want ya ta be hurt because o' me. Wha' is the worst possible punishment ya migh' receive for assaultin' one o' the guards."

"The worst?" He shrugged. "Most like a flogging."

She closed her eyes and tried to stave off the tears that trickled down her cheeks. "I'm sorry."

He reached across the space between them and squeezed her hand. "I'm not. I would do it again. In fact, I would trade places with you if I were permitted."

She blinked. "Gard is verra lucky ta have such loyalty in his men. In you."

"'Tis not about Gard, Brae. 'Tis you. I am just as loyal to you. You are his lady. I would do anything for Gard. But I would for you as well. Not because it is expected of me as his man. I have come to care for you, Brae. I feel rather protective of you."

She felt much the same for him. She was about to tell him so when they heard marching in the hall, bearing down on them. Hudson gave her a reassuring wink and closed the door between them quickly.

Brae heard the lock being opened next door and then the low murmur of voices. Hudson's voice rose. There was what sounded like a scuffle. The door slammed, more heavy footfalls followed leading away from her location. Then complete silence.

She listened for many minutes. There was nothing.

"Oh, dear God." Had they beat him?

"Hudson," she cried quietly at the door. "John?" She tried again. There was no sound, not even a moan. Was he unconscious? She worried her lip before pushing the door. Hesitant, she peered into the chamber before she stepped in. It was empty. She fell to her knees and prayed that he was only switched and not executed.

She went back to her room, then closed the door. Perhaps they would bring him back after his punishment. He would need her attention for his wounds. She could always use the linens as bandages if need be.

The day dragged on and the shadows grew long. Hudson did not return.

Her evening meal was delivered. When the guard unlocked the door, she pleaded with him. "Where was Lord Richmond taken?"

He shrugged carelessly as he placed the tray on the side table.

"Was he taken to the dungeon?"

"I do not know," he answered impatiently.

"Please, I must ken if he be a'righ'?"

"I do not know," he repeated, before locking her in.

She tried to eat but instead ended up pacing until darkness fell. She changed into a linen gown, then tried to rest. It was too quiet. She heard nothing but the occasional cough or murmur from the guards in the hall. When she finally did sleep, she dreamed that Hudson had been beheaded. She woke up crying.

In the morning, the maid Morag arrived. Brae sat before the mirror.

"Err, what have ye been doing, Lady. Ye look like death. Oh, er, sorry tha'. 'Tis quite possible, id'nit. But 'tis good to know that you will have resolution soon, eh?"

"I will?"

"Och. Did they not tell you? Your trial has been set. You

will see the king this day."

Brae shuddered. Morag held up a gown for her to put on. They had argued everyday about what she would wear.

"Na." Brae went to the wardrobe and pulled out her blue gown. "I will wear this, this day. I will represent my husband."

"Och, aye, sure I am tha' he be proud o' all this."

Brae tried to ignore the taunt. She had her own doubts, she did not appreciate the miserable maid adding to her fears.

After donning the blue dress, Brae went to her bag and pulled out the long piece of green and blue check on red MacDuib cloth. With reverence she fashioned it around her hips as close to the same as she could remember to how Gard had tied it. She sat down in front of the glass and brushed her own hair. When the woman tried to style it, Brae all but slapped her hands away. "I will do it meself. If I'm to meet my fate this day, I will do it lookin' as me."

Brae began to plait her hair in the thin fishbone style. As simple as it was, it made a dramatic intricate look. And she knew that Gard liked her hair plaited.

The maid watched her. "Let me. I've watched enough, I see how it goes. Do you wish it pulled up and pinned against your nape?"

"No, let it drape and tie it."

The maid finished the plait, securing it. She then took tiny drop pearls and placed them throughout.

"Aye, that's quite nice that," Morag praised.

"Thank ya."

"I will leave you now. Good luck to you, Lady MontClaire."

"Thank ya."

"Don forget to pinch yor cheeks, Lady," she added cheekily, letting herself out.

Brae did not think her color or lack thereof would matter if her head were soon severed from her body.

Alone again, Brae prowled the room. Wandering to the window she tried to look down on the courtyard below. There were a lot of people teeming about. *Where is Gard?*

One last thing. She took one of the hatpins and tore the stitching out of her carpetbag, retrieving the stone Piers had given her so many months ago. Perhaps if she returned it to its rightful owner, whom she now assumed was Edward, she could walk away with her head *and* her husband. She covertly placed it deep into her pocket just in case someone were still able to watch her. She made sure Gard's dagger was secure on her thigh. And she waited.

CHAPTER FORTY-THREE

Just after the noonday meal had been cleared away, Brae was summoned and escorted to a large room, crowded with people. They murmured and pointed at her when she was led in. Brae kept her head down while surreptitiously scanning for Gard.

The crowd parted as she passed with her guards. She was led to the front of the room, where a man sat in an elaborately decorated chair she assumed was the throne, and in turn supposed the man sitting in it, looking bored and unpleased, must be the new King Edward. She was surprised he sported a crown when, to her knowledge, a coronation had not yet taken place.

Piers Gaveston sat at his side. He smiled, stood, and extended his hand to her.

Brae placed hers in his.

He bent over it, keeping his sparkling gaze on her. He kissed the back of her hand drawing the king's attention. "You look lovely, Lady Marschand," Gaveston said. He seemed overly excited by the coming festivities.

"Thank ya, Monsieur Gaveston," she whispered, forgetting his directive to address him as the earl. "Where is my husband?" she asked worriedly.

Edward broke in, speaking French. Brae did not catch all of what he said, but he made some comment that she might have forgotten something.

"You must curtsey to your king, lady," Gaveston said indulgently.

Brae stood straight and met Gaveston's gaze directly. If she were to die this day for killing that horrible man Cowan, then she would die standing tall as a proud Scotsman when she did so. "I will not."

Piers' expression dropped. "But you must."

The king said something Brae did not understand, as one of the guards kicked Brae's knees out from under her, sending her down to the floor.

The king smirked.

As Brae tried to recover without losing her complete dignity, there was a commotion to her right. The sentry who'd tripped her was cut down in one fell swoop. Then Gard was by her side. She wanted to throw her arms around him. Instead, she reached for his hand.

"Stay down," Gard commanded as he knelt beside her.

"Ah, Marschand. 'Tis you. I should have known by the commotion that always seems to accompany you," Piers said.

"Gaveston, I should have known by the simpering," Gard sneered.

"Who be on his knees now?" Piers grinned nastily.

Gard growled, baring his teeth.

The king leaned toward Piers, speaking French.

Brae whispered, "Where be Hudson?"

"Here Brae," came his deep voice from behind. For a moment, he gripped her shoulder.

"Oh, thank God." She squeezed his hand and took an enormous breath of relief before he released his hold.

The king finally nodded, and Gard helped Brae to her feet. Piers spoke French. Brae caught only snippets, which included Gard's name. Hudson's lessons in French did not help her understand much of their language due to the speed with which they spoke. Hudson leaned in and interpreted for her.

"Gaveston asks the king if he recalls Gard Marschand."

"Oui, Monsieur Marschand. Welcome. But I have just received your petition, I was not yet expecting you."

"I am not here on behalf of Gard Marschand, Your Majesty." Hudson translated as Gard responded. "I come before you as Donnghardh Marschand MontClaire, the next Earl of Fife. As you know."

The king's eyes widened. He inhaled and waved a handkerchief delicately under his chin. There was a murmur among the people present.

"This is my wife. Lady Braelynn Marschand MontClaire. She has been accused of a crime. I seek your clemency. I believe the court owes me this, for all that I, and my men have done to further its cause, and in the name of the king."

"And why would I grant you anything, Marschand?"

"The former King Edward, God rest his soul, guaranteed that my earldom would be reinstated when certain tasks had been met. Those duties have been carried out, and I would now collect on what was promised."

"My sire promised many things to many people. Those bargains were struck between him and them. I do not see that I should be held accountable for things I have no way of knowing. *I* have pledged you nothing."

"Your father's legacy is vast. You have much to live up to. These first decisions that you make under your new reign will define what kind of king you will be. And what your people will come to expect. Choose carefully." Gard's deep voice gave one and all in attendance the impression of power.

The king pursed his thin lips, while looking sideways at his favorite. Piers leaned in and spoke only for the king to hear.

"Of what has your wife been accused?" The king asked.

"Murder, sire," Piers provided quickly before Gard could

King Edward frowned. "Mmm. Whom did she murder?"

"Robbie Cowan, a relative of John the Comyn," Piers replied.

"Mmm. One less. She did us a favor." Edward shrugged.

"He was a nobleman, sire. It cannot be overlooked."

"Robbie Cowan was not a nobleman," Hudson spoke over her shoulder also in French.

"Richmond?" The king perked up and sat forward.

"Aye, Your Highness," Hudson responded.

"Mmm mmm. Come," Edward said excitedly. "Where I can see you."

Hudson exhaled heavily but did as requested. Brae effectively lost her translator.

It was Piers Gaveston's turn to react uncomfortably at the king's interest in Hudson. Edward reached out and let his fingertips run over Hudson's sleeve. Hudson visibly cringed, fisting his hands at his side.

Brae finally took a good look at Hudson, turning her attention then to her husband. They were both dressed in red and blue tunics crested with black and gold crescent moons. They were dressed in his family colors, to make a statement. Gard was in essence signifying to the king and his court that he would not accept any other outcome from this meeting than reclaiming his earldom.

"I see that you back your man. As you always have," King Edward spoke. Brae was unsure that she had translated his words properly, struggling to keep up. "I respect that. But you must also recognize that particular loyalty will not lead you onward in your own ambitions, Lord Richmond."

Piers shuffled.

"I have achieved all that was ever expected of me, Your Majesty. And more than I'd ever anticipated. I have, in my loyalty to Lord MontClaire through your sire, done as I should."

"You should be rewarded for your loyalty and bravery to this court through my father."

Edward raised his hand, summoning one of his courtiers to his side.

"Sire," Hudson waved off whatever the king was about to offer.

Gard interrupted, "Through your own admission, King Edward, and promise of reward, you acknowledge we have labored to further your cause and that of your father. We would have you hold to his word."

King Edward turned an expressionless gaze toward Gard. Brae surmised, though Hudson and Piers titillated Edward, Gard intimidated him. But who would not be unnerved by the aura of power, authority, and determination that rolled off him?

The king's attention strayed to Brae. "What say you, Lady Marschand? Have you naught to add in your own defense? Will you have your husband try to sway me with his influence?"

Gard repeated the king's words to her in English.

Brae leaned toward Gard. "Am I ta speak in English or Gaelic?"

"English," he responded.

"I be Lady MontClaire," she began by correcting his inaccuracy. Brae believed he could understand her, but Piers relayed her words.

The king bristled at the amendment.

"I am perhaps guilty of takin' a man's life. But it was in defense of mine own. I was attacked wit'oot provocation. I had na choice but ta defend meself. And I believe my husband's influence be more on this court than it be for me. Might I also remind one and all o' a man whom committed murder on a nobleman in a kirk, no less, then na so long after declared himself a king. I dinna see how we be so different. At least, in my circumstance, I was in defense o' me life."

Gard twisted Brae's arm in warning.

Gard was aware of Gaveston's editing of Brae's speech, omitting the last part altogether when she had referred to the murder of John Comyn before the high altar of Greyfriars Church in Dumfries, at the Bruce's hand. Nevertheless, Gard was not confident of how much the king truly understood.

Piers met Gard's gaze briefly. If he was looking for gratitude, he would not receive it. Instead Gard granted him a menacing sneer. *What is he up to?*

"You do not seem to be worse for wear, *Lady Marschand*," the king responded.

Gard squeezed Brae's hand, warning her not to comment again, that the king but addressed her thus with purpose — in an attempt to get a rise, by denying Gard's claim as MontClaire.

"It has been a sennight since the attack and ma wounds have all but healed," Brae responded.

"I tended them myself, Your Majesty," Hudson added.

"Oh, and what a fine physician you are, Lord Richmond. I remember when you attended me. You have the hands of a healer," he simpered, turning his attention to Brae. "You are very lucky, Lady Marschand, to have such remarkable men stand in your defense."

"I am truly blessed," she agreed.

He sighed heavily. "We will see." He looked away as if he were finished with her before asking, "From where is it that you hale, Lady Marschand?"

"From Ross-shire."

"Aye, Ross-shire. There seems to be some question as to your activities before leaving said shire." The king's words hung heavy in the air.

Her grip tightened on Gard's.

"Are you in fact acquainted with a Vicar Dufferin?" Edward asked.

"Aye," she replied.

"'Twould seem the lady you chose to align yourself with, Lord Marschand, is not so loyal to England. It causes me great concern that two of my most promising men may be in danger of harboring and perhaps unknowingly passing state secrets. It seems rather questionable to me. *And* your devotion has always been in question, Marschand, even to my father." Edward gestured. "Bring in the witness."

Gard straightened.

"Wha' did he say?" Brae whispered.

"Witness," Gard snapped.

Gard turned as two royal guards escorted Callum MacCrae into the proceedings. MacCrae was a little worse for wear, dirty, his hair messed but not half as bad as it would after Gard got his hands on him. They had a score to settle, and this latest escapade pushed the limit.

"What is this, Edward?" Piers inquired, obviously unaware.

"Please tell the court who you are and what you know of the Lady Marschand's activities in Ross-shire."

"Huh?" Callum responded.

"Yes, MacCrae, tell us who you are and what you know of the lady's activities," Hudson translated the French, adding in English, "And then prepare to meet your maker."

"I am Callum MacCrae. Braelynn Galbraith, *the new Lady Marschand*," he sneered, "and I were once betrothed. During our betrothal it came ta my attention tha' she be passin' messages ta and from the rebels loyal ta Scotland."

A collective gasp resonated through the crowd.

"Be this true, Lady Marschand? I may be able to overlook the death of some deviate that prayed on women and committed such atrocities in my realm and who may or may not be loosely related to the Comyns, but I cannot in all that is good, overlook treason."

"'Tisna treason," Brae retorted. "Ya are no —"

"Brae!" Gard warned her gravely, twisting her arm painfully this time.

She yanked away from his grip and pushed him in the chest as hard as she could, causing him to take a step. "If I am ta die, I will do it as I have lived, Gard, the true and proud Scot tha' I be."

Gard wondered if that was an affront to the way he lived his own life, all but hiding his heritage while he sought his revenge, but he ignored it for now. "Ya willna die, I willna let it happen!" he growled. "But ya arna helpin' me. Ya canna provoke him."

The king began to laugh. "I was skeptical at first, Marschand, when I heard that you had taken a wife. I wondered what kind of woman would be able to stand up to you. Then I was advised that you had stolen her and forced her to bed you, then wed you. I would see that you have found one that can hold her own."

"Aye, I am also truly blessed," Gard responded dryly.

"You are much suited, 'twould seem." The smile slipped from the king's thin lips. "Murderers both," he added.

Brae gasped. Gard refused to be distracted from the question at hand. "I would ask MacCrae if he has any evidence, besides his own supposition, as to my wife's alleged treachery."

"I have na written proof, but I ken wha' she was aboot. Ye can ask anaone at Ross, e'en me own wife as ta Mistress Galbraith's whereaboots ana given day. She was fore'er on the moors. A gud and decent woman doesna wander the moors alone. Wha' other business would she be aboot?"

"Perhaps she simply enjoyed a nice stroll," Hudson intervened.

"I believe I can clear this up, Your Majesty," Gard said turning. "Would that be the man in question?" Gard pointed at the Vicar Dufferin. He too was dressed in the MontClaire tunic.

"Aye. Tha' be him," Callum verified.

"Dufferin is one of my men," Gard said. "If Braelynn indeed passed missives, 'twas communication sent between my men and myself. She was not running messages to the rebels. In essence, unbeknownst to anyone, she toiled for me. And in turn then, Your Majesty, for your father. For you."

The king appeared unconvinced as Gard continued his argument. "As you can see, Your Majesty, MacCrae holds bitter resentment that I took his betrothed from under his nose and but seeks vengeance against us."

"Ya raped her and stole her from her family, ya bastard!" Callum bellowed.

The king's eyes widened, as did Gaveston's.

"Be that precise?" Edward turned to Brae.

"Nay," Gard denied.

"I will hear it from the lady."

"Nay, he did no'," Brae denied.

"Tha's a lie. I saw her, after he defiled her, I saw it." Callum bounced in rage.

"'Tis true I was besieged and frightened and I put up a fight afore I kenned wha' they were aboot. I was wounded in the figh' o' me own mistake. Tha' be wha' Callum witnessed. I tried ta explain tha' ta him on several occasions, but he didna wish ta accept as true. Believin' I had nuthin', I left Ross o' ma own free will wit' Lord MontClaire and his men," Brae explained.

"And were you forced into wedlock with this man?"

"Nay, 'twas ma choice."

"Did the infamous Vicar Dufferin perform the blessing?" Edward mocked.

"Nay, we are handfasted," Brae clarified.

"Ahh, so it is not a union recognized by the church," the king commented.

"But a union no less recognized by God," Brae said.

The king directed his next statement to Gard alone. "Would you permit the vicar to wed you this very moment? Making the union something more permanent. A unification that you will not be permitted to leave at the end of one year?" The king's eyes narrowed, watching for Gard's reaction.

Brae inhaled sharply at Gard's side.

He wondered at that but replied, "Aye, I would marry my wife again this moment."

Brae exhaled.

"But the vicar is not truly a cleric."

"Wha'!" MacCrae exclaimed.

Gard continued. "As I said, he is one of my men. He is a soldier. Braelynn Galbraith Marschand MontClaire be my wife in every way that is important. God acknowledges it, as do I, as does she, and not one witness in this room will dispute that fact." He spread his menacing black gaze to all around them. Gard took Brae's hand. "She be my wife."

"Mmm." The king pondered a moment. "I will acknowledge that I am aware of your service to my father and in turn myself and this court and this country, therefore, I will give you a choice, Gard Marschand." He still refused to address him as MontClaire. Edward paused and stood, moving behind the huge ornate chair as if shielding himself from Gard before he made his declaration. "You may either leave here this day fully restored with lands and title as promised by my sire, King Edward the First. Donnghardh Marschand MontClaire, the Earl of Fife." All awaited with bated breath. "Or," he offered. "You may depart with your wife." He waved his hand indicating Brae's form. "But you will not have both."

Brae's shoulders slumped and she hung her head. She would understand his choice. He had lived, breathed, killed, fought and bled to regain his birthright, and avenge his father's death.

Hudson glared at Gard before flanking Brae's side. He braced his hand on her shoulder, attempting to comfort her.

"'Tis a verra simple choice, tha'." Gard heard Brae's surprised gasp as he used his brogue in front of these people, no longer hiding his true identity.

Gard pulled Brae's hand up to his chest. She looked at him, her heart and the pain in her eyes of the choice that she believed he would make. He deserved that, he realized. She had no idea the depth of what he felt for her. "Let us go home," he said to her in Gaelic.

Her eyes widened and searched his, her mouth opened and closed. "Home?" she asked tremulously.

Gard helped her from the dais.

Dozens of shocked faces greeted them, they too assuming his choice would not have been Brae.

"Be sure, Marschand. There will be no going back," Edward taunted. "I will eliminate the Earldom of Fife permanently. It will cease to exist. You will never have this chance again. Nor will your heirs. The Mormaerdom will be stricken. It will be no more."

Gard did not pause. He kept moving as the crowd parted for them. "I be more than certain."

"You will refrain from using the MontClaire name. You will be known forever more as Marschand and nothing more," the king jeered.

Shocked, Brae followed, unable to believe what was happening.

Gard nodded, while staring straight ahead, digesting what must have been a hurtful blow.

Brae turned to her right and exchanged a look with Hudson. His eyes were shuttered. She remembered the conversation they'd had. *"Some people would not like to see Gard rise to any kind of power. He acquired a reputation among the people who know. And he has also grown legendary among the ones who do not and only know him as Gard Marschand. But in any persona he is dangerous. He is ruthless. But people obey him, they follow him. And some might think he may have more power and more backing than certain untried . . . king . . . s. And would-be-kings as well. They work against him. They would not wish for Gard to see his full potential. He, as any other powerful man, even now being conspired against from all corners."* The king would enjoy this outcome.

A bout of nausea washed over Brae. "Gard." She pulled him to a stop. She looked up at him and for a moment was speechless. He'd transformed as if he was a different person, one without the weight of the world on his shoulders. Even his eyes were a soft brown and not black bottomless pits she was used to. For the first time he looked at ease. Just a man. She believed she was seeing the real Donnghardh. He was no longer hiding.

Her heart broke. "Dinna do this. Ya will regret it. Ya have sacrificed too much ta leave it like this. This isna the way it was supposed ta end, Gard. Ya need ta take wha' is yors."

"I be takin' wha' be mine. I have na regrets, Brae." He shook his dark head.

"But ya will in time. Ya will hate me, ya will blame me, perhaps resent me, for losin' it for ya. 'Tis ma fault." She dissolved into tears.

"Brae." He tucked his finger under her chin forcing her to face him. "Do ya remember wha' ya said ta me? It doesna matter to ya if I be an Earl or a soldier." The corners of his mouth lifted slightly in wonder. "I have come ta realize it doesna matter ta me either." His lips curved a little more and his eyes warmed. Brae's knees trembled. "Ya will ne'er ken the fear I felt when Cowan had ya. And these past days wit'oot ya by my side and in ma bed have been the longest most torturous I've ever endured. I have dreamed, breathed, and bled for the day tha' I would return ta MacDuib castle as its earl. But I can no longer see meself there wit'oot ya by my side. The earldom means nuthin' wit'oot ya, Brae."

His eyes pricked. He swallowed with difficulty. He had come to care for her. She stood up to him and understood him, like no one else. Gard enjoyed not only her body but also her mind and her quick wit. He confided things in her, things he had never shared with anyone, save Hudson. He had come to rely on her counsel as he also did Hudson. She made him see things and feel things he would never have known. She even made him realize the error of his ways with Donnchadh. She tolerated his moods and fits of anger. At one time, he had believed that there was only one thing he was willing to give his life for. He had been wrong. He would give up his earldom. He would give his life. He would die for her.

The old crone was right, he thought briefly, remembering her words. *"Ye will ne'er get back wha' ye seek withoot her. Ye mus' let go o' yor auld ways. Ye mus' open yor heart. For if ye dinna ye will lose evrathin'."* He recalled how he had responded. *"I have already lost everything. They cannot take more. There is nothing left."*

"Ye be wrong," she had countered. *"Ye will soon come ta realize tha' fact. Soon ye will ken that wha' ye have made yor life's*

purpose ta win back will mean nuthin' wit'oot the one tha' bares yor mark. For she be the key ta evrathin' ye seek."

"Brae, I . . . have . . . come . . . ta . . ." He paused. "Ya don ken how hard this is fer me." He hesitated, taking a deep breath before rushing on. "I . . . love ya, too, Braelynn."

Tears rolled freely down her cheeks.

Gard realized in that moment that her happiness meant more to him than his own vendetta, for her happiness would produce his own. He reached out and softly skimmed his knuckles over her abdomen. "We will create"—he swallowed thickly before he could continue—"our own . . . MontClaire." He stared straight into her eyes. "Let us go home, sweet."

She smiled almost wearily, taking his proffered hand. "Where would tha' be?" she asked as she walked by his side.

"For now, 'twill be Ross, I suppose. We still hold it. It is mine. Edward willna bother ta repossess it. I believe he may have some other more pressing matters ahead. I have many holdings still in my possession. I am sure he will discover this in time. We will stop and collect Donnchadh from Richmond first."

Brae laced her arm around her husband's, holding onto him tightly.

CHAPTER FORTY-FOUR

Brae and Gard had barely made it half way through the crowd when Piers Gaveston's voice stopped them. "Lady Marschand. Lady Marschand. Wait."

Brae's heart plummeted.

They paused and turned as one to face him. "'Twould be an excellent time to ask for that boon."

"Boon?" Gard barked. "Wha' be ye talkin' aboot, Gaveston?"

"Ah, Marschand, that brogue does become you. Perhaps if you'd been using it all along, you would be one of *his* favorites as well. Come," he said to Brae.

Brae closed her eyes. If she asked for this, Gard would forever need to defend himself. If the earldom ceased to exist, they could perhaps lead a semblance of a normal life. But how could she be so selfish when he had just been so selfless? Brae followed Piers.

Gard and Hudson trailed Brae and Gaveston to the dais.

"You have the audacity to come before me again, Lady Marsch—"

"Please, Your Highness, I would ask your patience," Piers simpered. "Show him," Piers directed Brae.

Apprehensively Brae dug into her pocket and produced the large gem in the palm of her hand.

"How did you get that?" The king demanded in French.

Gard asked in Gaelic.

And Hudson cursed in English.

"You told me you lost it," Edward accused Piers.

471

"No, I wanted your father to believe that I had lost it," he explained. "'Twas in my possession when he banished me."

"And how did *she* get it?"

"When I was—" Piers began.

"Non!" Edward exclaimed, angry, for the moment, with his favorite. "I will hear it from her."

All eyes turned to Brae. She kept hers downcast. "Last April, I was on the moors. Walkin', as I enjoy, takin' pleasure in the early spring when all of a sudden, horsemen appeared. Fearin' for ma safety, I fled. I ran for the cliffs seeking sanctuary. But I wasna alone. Monsieur Gaveston was in the caves. 'Twas he who was bein' pursued."

"Do either of you know who might have been chasing me that day, my Lords?" Piers asked, his attention swaying between Gard and Hudson.

Both men shrugged non-committally.

"Continue on," the king said in stilted English to Brae.

"Monsieur Gaveston asked me to guide him from the caves. And perhaps by usin' some distraction, lead the men seekin' him away from his location."

"Ya asked my wife ta redirect a pack o' men from ya?" Gard accused.

"She was not your wife then," Piers pointed out.

"'Twould be two months afore ya laid siege ta Ross, afore I met ya," Brae said quietly, afraid Gard might believe she kept this from him for some other reason. Would he and Hudson think she was like his sister, Isabella, holding onto the hopes of bettering her options?

"E'en so, ye sent a woman ta deviate your pursuers on another course? Do ya ken wha' woulda happened ta her if they'd caught her?" Gard asked angrily.

"The same thing that befell her at your hand, Marschand. No one here believes you did not defile this woman when you laid siege," Piers argued.

Hudson stepped between the two men in anticipation of Gard's next move.

"Keep on, Lady Marschand," the king gestured impatiently.

"I agreed ta divert them, and Monsieur Gaveston rewarded me wit' the gem. He said I could either sell it, that it was verra valuable. Or tha' if I were ta return it to its rightful owner, I would most certainly be given ana boon o' my askin'."

"Why did you not use it to gain your freedom from the Tower?"

"I didna think o' it," she replied honestly.

"Or is it more like you have played this court and your husband to your own advantage." The king spoke in French. Brae did not understand until Hudson translated.

"You were about to walk away with something very valuable to me, only to claim your boon at some other more opportune situation that will further you or your husband's agenda."

Hudson relayed the king's words. Gard would not even look at her.

"I didna think o' it," she repeated to Hudson.

"If I may, your Highness." Hudson stepped forward on her behalf. "I believe she speaks the truth. There is no artifice in Braelynn, Lady Marschand," he amended. "No pretence, no deception. I have known her these past months and through not only word and deed, I would assure you, she is genuine. She did not think to use the gem to further any such ambition of her own accord or that of her husband, because the idea frankly would never occur to her to use it, or call in some favor to gain any title, freedom or riches. She is unlike any woman you will ever meet at court. Or perhaps anywhere."

"That is a glowing recommendation, Lord Richmond. But

473

I find that difficult to believe. I have never met a woman or man for that matter that would not lie, cheat, steal, kill or lay with the enemy to further all those things which you have stated."

"You have never before met Lady Marschand."

"She has no allegiance to myself, or the Bruce, 'twould seem by her own deprecating commentary. I would ask of your opinion, Marschand but by the look of your miserable visage, I gather you did not know of her reward and are even now questioning her loyalty to you, as well."

"You would be wrong. I have no such doubts. Richmond speaks the truth. 'Tis Gaveston's intent that I question."

The king addressed Gaveston. "Why is it you did not inform me of the topaz's whereabouts as soon as you realized who she was?"

"You know me, sire, I enjoyed watching it play out. Have you not yourself enjoyed Marschand's twisting in the wind? But now I believe the lady knows exactly what boon she must collect."

The king's lips hardened, his eyes narrowed as he realized what Piers had just proposed.

"She saved my life, sire. What might that mean to you? To the court?"

Edward turned to Brae.

She hesitated, imagining a more simple life, if she did not collect. She felt light-headed, sick to her stomach again. She dared not look at Gard. "I would," she began, her voice shaking with uncertainty, "request Donnghardh Marschand MontClaire be declared Earl of Fife, as be his birthrigh' and through his bravery and selflessness in service ta the king." Her vision tunneled.

"Your request is granted." Edward held out his hand. Brae dropped the gem into it. Turning, she weaved her way through the crowd seeking the outdoors, Hudson close on her heels.

"Brae." Hudson stopped her. "You did the right thing."

She moved out into the sunshine and was greeted by a sea of red and blue tunics as far as she could see. Gard appeared at her side.

"The Earl of Fife!" Hudson roared jubilantly to the crowd, throwing his fist in the air. They erupted in one uproarious cheer.

Gard's followers were vast.

Gard took Brae's hand. She turned to look at him in surprise. His mouth quirked. "Did I no' say this day migh' have many different ootcomes?"

"Why are they all here? Why did they not storm the castle when he threatened ta strike your title from the realm? Ya were willin' ta walk away wit'oot it?"

"I *was* willin' ta walk away wit'oot it. But I wasna willin' ta walk away wit'oot you. Their orders were ta release their Lady from the executioner if need be."

The queasiness doubled.

"Does King Edward ken tha' this show o' force be here?" she asked shakily. She did not want her husband at war with the English.

Gard shrugged. "We can assume by now tha' he does."

All of a sudden, his wife looked rather pale and unsteady. She swayed against him and her eyes fluttered shut.

"Hudson!" Gard yelled as he gathered his wife into his arms. Hudson was by their sides in an instant. He placed his hand against her chest.

"Wha's wrong?" Gard asked worriedly.

"I believe she's developed a fit of the vapors."

"Brae? A fit o' the vapors? Naw. She isna like tha'. There mus' be somethin' wrong. She's sick. Fix her."

"Gard. She has just escaped the executioner's axe. Faced down a king. Discovered that you were willing to give up your life's labor for her. And more difficult to believe than any other thing that has befallen her this day, she learned that her husband loves her. The man with no feelings, no emotion, the devil himself, who vowed to me that he would never allow himself to be caught in such useless human emotion. Let alone walking out, of a palace no less, the Lady MontClaire, and into an army that now sees her as its Lady, ready to defend her as it would its master. I wonder how that might overwhelm her?"

"Ya sure. Tha' is all then?"

Hudson chuckled. "Aye, that is all."

Gard picked her up and began the short trek to their pavilion. He would be happy to see the last of England, the last of tent living, and regain a permanent place to lay their heads.

With an expression of deep concern, Hudson fell into step beside him.

"What!" Gard snapped.

Hudson looked at him sheepishly as he moved the tent flap aside. "Unless —"

Gard growled. He laid his wife on their pallet before turning. "Unless wha'?" he bellowed.

Hudson appeared to brace himself for whatever reaction might come. "She may be with child."

Gard's balance wavered.

Hudson lowered Gard to the nearest stool but hovered as if at any moment he expected anger, the throwing of objects, bellowing, perhaps even having to throw himself in front of Brae to protect her and the child from his murderous rage. But even to his own astonishment, anger was not the emotion he suffered.

When no outburst came, Hudson relaxed his stance. "Not

The Devil Take You

the reaction I was expecting, my friend. 'Tis truly a strange day."

Gard dragged a shaky hand through his beard. "She could be?" he asked his friend.

"Well, 'tis a distinct possibility. Is it not?"

"O' course."

Hudson turned his palms up. "Then time will tell."

Gard looked over at his wife. "Llachlan!" he bellowed over Hudson's shoulder.

"Aye, Lord MontClaire?"

"Begin disassembling. Ready the troops."

"Aye." Llach left to carry out his orders.

"What's the hurry?" Hudson asked.

"I need ta get her home if she carries a child."

"You have plenty of time, Gard, it will not arrive tomorrow."

"She needs a home." He began throwing their belongings into a corner. "We still have ta reach Richmond and collect Donnchadh. Then travel ta Ross afore we can make Mac-Duib. I dinna want her doin' all tha' travelin' while she's na feelin' weel or when she can no longer sit a horse."

"Then send her directly on to MacDuib." Hudson reasoned.

"But I need ta see ta Ross and discharge Hugh and —"

"What has that to do with her? Send her on."

"Nay. She stays wit' me."

Hudson chuckled.

Brae sighed and Gard was by her side before she opened her eyes.

"Wha' happened?" she asked.

"Hudson believes ya may have fainted o'er all tha' has befallen ya this day."

Her eyes fluttered. "Aye, it has been a day quite like na other," she admitted.

"How do ya feel now?"

Exhaling heavily, she tried to sit up, her face paling. "Ohhh." She eased down once more.

Hudson handed Gard a cool cloth. He laid it on her forehead.

"Ahh, tha' feels lovely," she said, keeping her eyes closed.

Gard spanned his hand across her stomach, and she covered it with her own. "Hudson believes ya may be more than simply overwhelmed." His voice was deep and full of meaning.

Brae stilled, then removed the cloth from her head. Her startled gaze met his. He was disappointed to see the latent fear and apprehension there. His long-ago threat to exterminate any issue was still lingering, his more recent avowal to create MontClaire evidently not to be trusted by his dubious wife.

His mouth twitched. "'Twould seem we have already begun ta rebuild MontClaire."

"And would tha' be a'righ' if tha' be true?" she asked slowly.

"Is ma word not trustworthy to ya?"

"Ye once told me never ta trust ya. Tha' ya will do wha'e'er ya wanted whene'er ya wished."

He cleared his throat. "Tha' was different."

"Aye, 'twould seem many things are different. But a child isna somethin' ya could e'en abide, let alone imagine not so long ago."

"We are learnin' o' each other as we go, we will figure it oot," he said. "And we will adjust as need be. I canna say tha' I willna be put oot by the time ya willna be able ta tend me, as we talked aboot afore, but I still have ya all ta meself for . . . how long migh' it be, Hudson?"

"I believe you have until next spring. April, perhaps."

"So we be needin' ta get home. Do ya think ya can ride?"

"Oh, aye." She smiled before looping her arms around his neck. Gard sought her lips.

"I'll take my leave," Hudson said, ducking out.

"Migh' ya be able ta do somethin' more afore we ride?" Gard asked. He had been without her for a sennight.

"Oh, aye!"

He needed to remind himself to be gentle, not wanting to hurt her or the child, but it was difficult, while she was so enthusiastic, and he had been so deprived.

"I have missed ya," she said, reaching for his laces.

"I have missed ya as weel."

"I love ya, Gard." She said this so easily and with such feeling.

Warmth bloomed in his chest. "An' I you, Brae." 'Twould seem the sentiment would become easier for him to declare with every utterance.

CHAPTER FORTY-FIVE

Brae rode along in Gard's lap atop his horse as she willed her stomach to settle. She closed her eyes, but it only made the nausea worse.

They had already been to Richmond, where Hudson was informed his wife had moved out of the manner, with a handful of household staff, the family jewels, and silver. She left him a note which he did not share with Brae or Gard, but the impression given was one of finality.

They gathered Donnchadh and endured a tearful farewell with Hudson, who promised to make the trip to Fife next year as soon as the snows cleared, long before the babe was due so that he could be there for the delivery.

Today they would make Ross. Brae was grateful Gard seemed to be taking her condition in his stride. Hudson had kept up a steady lecture of what to expect all the way from London to Richmond. She tried not to complain or hold up their progress with frequent stops for either her bladder or her stomach. But it was not easy. She attempted to keep her misery from Gard, knowing he could not deal with it. His fits of anger were sporadic, either with her, or the men, or poor Donnchadh. Brae was so happy to see Donnchadh. If 'twas possible he had grown in the few weeks since they had been apart. She watched him ride ahead of them.

"He has grown," Gard said apparently reading her mind.

"Aye. He looks more like ya evraday. The young lasses at MacDuib will compete for his attentions." Brae smiled up at her husband.

"He willna be accompanyin' us ana further."

Brae sat up quickly, almost clipping his chin in her haste, but before she could protest her stomach rebelled. "Let me doon. Let me doon!" Gard lowered her to the ground and rode on quickly as was his habit. He pointed to Llachlan of Skye, but Bain and Donnchadh were both standing by waiting for her.

Donnchadh handed her a rag. She wiped her mouth. "Thank ya," she said tiredly.

"When will this cease?" he asked, with concern.

"Soon. I promise. Hudson said the sickness will be o'er soon." Hudson had said some women felt better after a few months, but then others were sick their whole time. Brae prayed she would be the former.

Bain reached down. Brae took his proffered hand and he helped her stand. She weaved against his solid chest, grateful he was alive and well. "Must ye men always be savin' me from somethin'?"

"Mus' ya always be in need o' savin'?" Bain teased, winking wickedly.

How lucky she was to be surrounded by such handsome men.

"As I recall I was the one needin' savin'."

"Och, ye recall nuthin' o' tha' day." Playfully she swatted at his broad chest. "And we saved each other, I do believe."

Bain sobered. "Jus' take a moment, Lady MontClaire." He smiled before she could remind him again to call her by her name. But only when Gard was out of earshot. "Brae," he amended affectionately. "We can stand here how e'er long it takes."

"Then we may be standin' here 'til next May."

He chuckled. Brae held onto him as she closed her eyes and concentrated on breathing in then out. She smiled as the dizziness passed.

"Better now?"

"Aye. Have I mentioned tha' I am verra thankful tha' ya didna die, Bain."

"Tha's the first time this day, My Lady." He smiled.

"Ye will unhand me wife, MacBain." Gard's deep voice cut in.

He nodded and withdrew as usual. Gard took her hand and they walked for a time. Donnchadh followed closely, mounted and leading Gard's horse.

"Better?" Gard asked.

"Aye, 'tis gettin' better," she lied. "Why will ya no' permit Donnchadh ta accompany us?"

"'Tis long past time for him ta be fostered," he explained.

"Then he should be fostered under you. Wit' us." Her emotions were so raw she began to cry at the thought of him being so far away. She stopped walking.

"He will stay here at Ross." Gard brooked no argument.

"And who will he be fostered under if ya be dischargin' Hugh? Donnchadh should be wit' his family."

"He will be fostered under Llachlan and Bain."

"Ya be leavin' Llachlan and Bain in charge here?" On one hand she felt better that they would be here to watch over Donnchadh and teach him. Other than Gard and Hudson there were no better men, in her opinion, but she felt as if she were losing them, too. They had been her guards, but more over they had been kind to her. They were like the big brothers she never had. Her new large family was dwindling rapidly. Even Bronwyn had chosen to stay at Richmond, not accompanying Llachlan to his new designation. She wondered if Gard had something to do with that particular decision between them.

"Aye."

"But why canna Donnchadh come home wit' us until he is older and then return ta Ross when he be ready?" She wiped at her eyes.

"He be ready. 'Tis long past time for him ta be trained. And ye coddlin' him willna make him a man."

She trembled at his criticism. "Bodes well for wha' ya will think o' me parentin' this child." She pouted, placing her hand protectively over her stomach.

"Tha' be different. And tha' be another problem. 'Twould no' be good ta have two heirs under the same roof." Forcibly he removed her hand and replaced it with his own. She was finally showing some sign beyond the sickness. He rubbed her barely notable protrusion. His chest expanded a little. "This child be the next Earl o' Fife. Donnchadh is no'."

"Oh!" The thought had never occurred to her.

"'Tis best for Donnchadh ta be here at Ross and learn ta ken his people and they him."

"His people?"

"Aye, Ross will be Donnchadh's."

"Ross will be Donnchadh's?" she echoed, as the importance of what he'd said dawned on her.

"Aye. He will be the Earl o' Ross, as my heir."

She threw her arms around his neck and hugged her husband. He lifted her off her feet and embraced her in return. "Does he ken?" she asked.

"I believe he does now," Gard answered putting her down. They looked up to find Donnchadh dismounting. Brae could see the emotion in his eyes.

"Truly?" Donnchadh asked Gard.

"Aye. You will learn, ya will train, ya will have ta work hard, but, aye, Donnchadh, you are Ross."

Donnchadh reached out to shake Gard's hand. They shook like gentleman, but as the boy pulled his hand away, he was overwhelmed. He flung his arms around his uncle and embraced him. Brae had to laugh at the look on Gard's face. He did not know what to do. Donnchadh released him, then swallowed Brae in a big hug that she accepted with as much shared excitement for him.

"Here now. Be careful. She be delicate." Gard pushed at his nephew's shoulder.

"Come. I canna wait ta get there." The excited new laird of Ross mounted his horse in one giant man-sized leap, then headed off leaving in a cloud of dust.

"Aye, come, let us get ya where ya may rest. And one step closer ta home."

"The poor child will ne'er ken who he be," Brae said, attracting a strange frown from her husband. "Let me see if I can get it a'righ'. Donnchadh Ruadh Dubhán MontClaire Ross. When will he be kenned as jus' one?"

"He *will* be kenned as simply one. Ross."

Gard helped her onto the horse as the Vicar Dufferin, who was not a vicar at all, rode by. He gave them a nod.

"Gard, somethin' be still botherin' me. If the Vicar Dufferin isna a vicar, does tha' mean tha' Callum and Katie are no' really married?" Brae had not yet had a chance to speak to the feigned cleric, but she would guess that he did not even have a stutter. How silly he must think her to have spent so much time pouring over his would-be sermons.

"Wha' does it matter to ya?" Brae settled against Gard's chest as he clicked the reins urging the steed forward.

"Weel, it doesna where Callum is concerned, but Katie was ma friend. And there be the child."

"Duff officiates a handfastin' similar ta wha' we did. He is merely a witness directin' their vows. They are as married as we are."

She looked at him suspiciously. "Ya do consider us married do ya no'?" She watched him carefully.

"Aye!" he exclaimed, his ire rose at her implication. "Do ya no'?"

"Aye," she said softly.

"But ya would like a blessin' from a cleric." Gard breathed. "Would tha' make it righ' for ya? I will summon one when we reach Ross."

"Na. I wish ta be united again at Fife. In our home. On yer land. And it doesna have ta be in front o' a cleric. We could jus' repeat our vows ta each other. I feel as ya do when ya stated our case ta Edward. We are married, and God acknowledges it as weel, or he wouldna have gifted me wit' this child."

"Gifted *us*," Gard corrected, placing his hand over the slight bump.

"Do ya mean it?" Her eyes searched his.

"Aye, I believe evrathin' aboot ya has been a gift." He pulled her close and nuzzled her neck.

She giggled. "Ya have not always thought tha'."

"Naw, but neither have you aboot me. I dinna why? I am a verra amiable man," he joked.

"Soldiers dinna need jests," she reminded him.

"I am an earl." He winked.

"Aye, but ya still be a soldier. Ya ken ya will be called at some point by either Edward or the Bruce."

"Mmm, and ya may have put me in a bad place wit' both," he pointed out.

"Do ya care?"

"Naw," he answered unconcerned. "But ya do owe me an explanation as ta why ya kept the gem a secret from me," he said idly.

"I didna do it apurpose. I kept it a secret from ya in the beginnin' for obvious reasons. We kept things from one another, na trustin' each other. But I did realize tha' the gem I had and the blue tha' covered yor seal were one in the same. 'Twas then tha' I realized King Edward mus' be the owner o' the stone. But I didna ken who Piers was until we made the palace. I had no idea how one related ta the other until then.

Then there wasna time ta tell ya anathin'. Please believe me. I didna keep it from ya for any underhanded purpose."

"While ya are tellin' me truths, ya can tell me aboot the slight hesitation righ' afore ya asked the king ta see me restored."

Ashamed, she bowed her head. "I did hesitate for a moment," she confessed. "Wonderin' wha' 'twould be like ta jus' lead a simple life as Gard and Brae Marschand. I'm afraid ya are goin' ta have ta defend yourself time and again ta keep wha' ya have, your life long struggle isna o'er and I guess I thought, for an instant, 'twould be nice na ta have ta worry aboot ya."

His mouth lifted at the corner. "I have a feelin' ya would worry aboot me whether I be a soldier, an earl, or a farmer, aye?" A slight breeze caused Brae a shiver. Gard pulled his cloak more closely around them.

"Aye, ye, Donnchadh, and Hudson, all. And then there is Bain and Llachlan and —"

"Cease! Have some faith in me, wife. In all o' us."

They rode for a moment in silence, lost in thought.

"Gard? Who do ya think brought Callum ta court as a witness against me?"

"I think Edward went lookin' for someone ta bear witness against ya. Against us. Or mayhap 'twas much more simple than tha'. Mayhap MacCrae caught wind o' wha' went on at court through Hudson's wife and he took it upon himself ta attempt ta stuff the lining o' his own pockets. I dinna ken, but when I catch up ta him, we will have our answers."

She didn't comment. In the past she would have asked for Gard's leniency in this for Katie's sake, but not this time. Callum had sealed his own fate.

"Gard? I have thought o' one other thing tha' migh' be a problem."

"Och. Wha's tha'?" Gard's knees tensed around the horse.

"Wha' if your heir be a girl?"

He smoothed his hand over her stomach, his fingers rested indecently low. "Then we will jus' keep tryin' until ya give me a male heir."

"I canna imagine ya arrangin' betrothals for your daughters." She giggled. "Ya will be a verra protective Da, I believe."

"Da . . ." he whispered. "I am goin' ta be someone's Da," he said as if that had just dawned on him. "Daughters?" He stressed the *s* on the end making it plural.

"Aye. Ya ken your luck, Gard. There will surely be a passel o' girls afore ya achieve a boy."

"Surely," he agreed dryly.

He took her hand and she turned to face him.

Gard could still see the uncertainty in her eyes. He slowed his mount. Even though at times they had achieved this easy banter, she was still unsure of him. He wanted to ease her fears. He was learning. He felt differently, and not just because he had claimed his due. He had been given something he did not even know that he wanted or missed. The misery that had pushed down on him for years was lifted. He had hope. He had love. He had Brae. "Ya are findin' it hard ta accept, aye, Brae?"

He all but cradled her head as her beautiful green eyes searched his.

"Tha' I could so easily turn aboot?" he explained.

"Ya were so sure tha' ya didna want these things. Me. A bairn. Ya threatened ta rid me o' any child? And now . . ." She bit her lip and shrugged as her eyes glazed.

He closed his eyes in regret. On opening them, he said, "I did. And I be sorry tha', Braelynn. I was still tryin' ta come ta terms wit' me own feelin's aboot evrathin'." He took another deep breath, finding it difficult to describe all the changes and things that he felt. He was not good at explaining himself or his feelings. He never even admitted them to himself, let alone another person. "Brae, I have spent me life doin' things tha' I am na sure tha' I will e'er be forgiven."

She started to shake her head, but he stopped her by continuing, "I have spent me life bein' selfish and livin' for only me. I was of a single-minded purpose. Nuthin' else entered inta me thinkin'. Until you. I guess I didna believe tha' I o' all people deserved ta have these things . . . a wife . . . and love. I didna e'er imagine those things would be relevant ta me. And certainly no' the responsibility o' a child. Look wha' I have done ta Donnchadh. Look at the things tha' I have done ta you. Ya have na idea wha' it felt like for me when ya told me tha' ya loved me. Still when ya say it . . . I canna believe it."

"Ya seemed so angry the first few times I said it."

"Aye, because I guess I'm still waitin' for ya ta come ta your senses." She shook her head in denial, but he rushed on, "Or for God ta say, here Donnghardh, ya had a taste of heaven, now I be takin' it all away from ya for all the evil ya have done."

His eyes pricked. "Jus' like afore, Brae, when he took me family from me." His throat tightened. He swallowed convulsively. "I dinna think I could survive it again. Naw wit'oot ya."

"Ya werena bein' punished then. 'Twasna somethin' tha' you did. Ya were too young ta have done anathin'. 'Twasna God's punishment. 'Twas an evil man tha' took your family. Ya will ne'er have ta endure tha', again, Gard. I would ne'er leave ya. Naw o' me own choice. I have seen your worst, and I began ta love ya anyway."

"But wha' if it na be o' your choice? Wha' if God punishes me by takin' ya?"

"We canna worry o'er things tha' we cannot control, Gard. We mus' live for the now and na think or worry o'er things tha' may ne'er be. And e'en if somethin' God forbid were ta happen ta me, I will love ya e'en in death."

"Tha' isna good enough, Brae." He wanted confirmation, he needed a guarantee that nothing would befall his new family.

"Ya will have this child, Gard, tha' is part o' you and part o' me. And God willin' there will be many more. They will need ya. And I will depend on ya ta be there for them. 'Tisna so different for me, my love, I worry o'er wha' is ta come. I am jus' as afraid tha' ya will be pulled inta quarrels na o' your makin' by ones tha' seek ta harm ya. And then 'twill be me tha' be alone wit'oot ya."

"I guess I jus' wanted ta protect meself from . . . feelin'. This is wha' I have always believed made me father weak. He felt too strongly, he loved too much. Especially me mother, and look wha' happened ta them. I feel these things . . ." He pounded his chest.

Brae smiled and nuzzled into his neck for a moment, then sat back and looked at him with brilliant emerald eyes.

He continued, "And I am overwhelmed sometimes wit' all tha' I feel for ya. And aboot the child. I have protected meself all this time from feelin' anathin'. Anathin' but anger. I lived off it. I fed off o' it. I thrived on it. But ya broke righ' through all tha' and ya made me feel. I hated ya for it. And now tha' be all I seem ta do. At times I still want ta protect meself. I dinna want ta be like me father. 'Twill make me weak."

"Lovin' each other doesna make us weak, Gard, it makes us strong." Brae interlaced her fingers with his as they neared Ross.

Gard reined the horse to follow the others.

"Who be worryin' now, My Lord MontClaire? Ya ken

wha' Hudson would say, yah?" She tried to imitate Hudson's deep voice and accent. "Sometimes, I believe you are a woman, Gard."

A rush of air left his mouth as he tried to keep her from knowing he found her amusing. "I am na sure anaone save you and he would dare accuse me o' such," he said, lifting a dark brow.

"Na, I would ne'er . . ." She feigned denial and smiled at him as he allowed her to lift him from his despair. "I love ya, Donnghardh," she said.

"An' I you, Braelynn."

CHAPTER FORTY-SIX

They made Ross, where Gard obtained a suite for Brae to rest. She was grateful to sleep in a real bed. She slept the rest of the day and was marginally aware of her husband's presence during the night, but he was gone when she awoke. Gard made sure there was a bath waiting, along with several dishes that might entice her flagging appetite, since she and food had not agreed with each other of late.

To Brae's relief, Gard had also decided to wait a few more days before setting out for Fife. The man was truly considerate of her needs.

Brae looked out of her window, spying the grass below, and thought of the day afore, when after training, Gard had approached Donnchadh. Brae had been surprised at first, thinking her husband must have truly turned away from his dark side.

Gard had set up barriers at either end of the space they were in. "'Tis an amusement tha' I used ta play wit' my da," he had explained. "Ya need ta try ta get the ball from me, but ya canna use your hands." Brae had smiled, realizing he had been about to show the boy a game. There was truly hope for them all.

"And how am I ta do tha'?" the boy had asked, carefully. Brae often found Donnchadh approached Gard with a healthy dose of wariness, as she used to in the beginning, waiting for his unpredictable temper to flare.

Gard threw the ball down to the ground. "Use your feet, your brain, your head, and some strategy. And use the speed

I ken ya have. I have seen ya try ta ootrun me."

"Aye, and I have ne'er been able ta elude ya."

Gard had ignored him. "Ya mus' try ta kick the ball wit' your feet inta tha' goal o'er there, but ya mus' also keep me from doin' the same in your goal here." Gard had pointed in to the opposite barricade.

Gard started off slowly at first until Donnchadh understood the game. Then Gard used his size, skill, and speed to get by the boy and score many times.

Donnchadh became dispirited until Gard gave him a bit of encouragement.

"My da used ta do the same thing ta me, Donnchadh. Usin' his grown-up size ta dominate me. Use your head, lad. Look past your frustration. Think. Ya ken I mus' have some weakness. Find it. Use it ta your advantage."

Brae realized what he was doing. Just as Gard's father must have been doing with him when he taught him the game. Aye, 'twas fun and it gave them time to spend together, but he was showing him all the skills he would need to be a good soldier and a good leader. He would have to conceal and work through his frustration and find his opponent's weakness to gain the upper hand.

Brae fell a little more in love with the man as she watched him with his nephew. She tried to see him with his sons. Dark-haired boys just like Donnchadh.

At one point, some of the other younger men came around wanting to join, but Gard waved them off, wanting this one-on-one time with his heir.

Gard was not easy on the lad. He had not let him score a goal, making him earn it instead. It took a good long time. And when he had finally scored against his teacher, Gard seemed just as pleased as the boy.

"I got it in!" Donnchadh had yelled, then pumped his fist in the air. Gard clapped him around the shoulder, and they laughed together. *Gard laughing!* Brae shook her head at the sight. He could not be more handsome.

The play resumed, and Donnchadh was able to record a point against his mentor, quickly.

"Ya see, Donnchadh, try no' ta let your emotions cloud your thinkin'. Evra'one has a weakness. Step back and find it, then ya can use it ta your advantage and be the one tha' comes oot on top."

The young one had added another to his tally, and then the real game was on. They went at each other like true competitors. Brae had been exhausted just watching them.

The game had wound down, and the two sweaty dark-headed combatants strode toward the loch to wash. It turned into a foot race to see who could get there first, and then a swimming contest of laps ensued.

It had been an amazing sight to see them both so carefree. It did Brae's heart good.

She moved away from the window still smiling over the memory. She bathed, dressed and attempted to choke down some gruel. She plaited her hair before going in search of her husband.

As she descended the stairs slowly, a bout of dizziness overtook her. She found Donnchadh at her side before she made it halfway. "Ya are a fine master already," she complimented him, trying to smile but failing abysmally as they looked down over the great hall of the lad's new holding.

"I hope ta be. Was it your idea?" he asked.

"Nay. No' at'all. I was jus' as stunned as ya were. But ya ken, I am inclined ta believe he intended ta give ya Ross all along. Wha' other reason would he have made ya his squire and dragged ya all o'er the countryside wit' him if not for this verra ootcome. 'Tis no' as if ya enjoyed each other's company. And I ken, also, tha' he was fostered here at Ross, and although 'twas a torturous time for him because o' the loss of his parents, he confided in me tha' he was grateful for the time he spent here. Ross has a special place in his heart, 'twould seem. And so do ya."

"Aye, and not so long ago, I believed he didna e'en own one." The boy chuckled as they made the bottom of the stairs.

She turned to him affectionately and rubbed his black head. "Thank ya, my Red Black Duncan Ross. I am goin' ta miss ya."

The side of his lip pulled tight. "'Twasna so long ago tha' ya didna think *I* had a heart either, aye?" He tried to joke.

"Naw, 'tis jus' you MontClaire men, ya like people ta think tha'."

Brae surveyed the room in search of Gard, but she was brought up short when she found him with a raven-haired woman hanging on his arm.

"Dubhán." Flustered, she lapsed in her old name for him. "Who be tha' woman wit' Gard?"

"*Tha'* would be my mother," he said, his voice flat.

"Oh!" Brae was immediately angry. "How be she here?"

"I dinna ken. She has not sought me oot as o' yet. Perhaps she has forgotten me altogether now. She is most like here ta get whate'er she can oot o' Uncle."

Brae highly doubted Isabella would forget her son now that Gard had made Donnchadh the new Ross. His over-ambitious mother would surely use her son's influence when he finally attained the leadership role.

Brae tightened her grip on the boy protectively. "Donnchadh, ya will be careful. She—"

He patted her hand in comfort. "I ken all aboot me mother. Ya dinna need ta worry aboot me. Llach and Bain will look after things until I am able. She canna get anathin' until then. And I have a long memory."

Brae smiled again, some of the anxiousness left her. "Ya

are goin' ta be a great overlord, my Dubhán. I am so verra proud o' ya already."

"I havena done anathin' yet."

"Oh, aye, ya have. Ya have come a long way since ya spit in me food."

His cheeks reddened, and he avoided her stare.

"Ya did *worse* than spit in me food, didna ya?" Brae wrinkled her nose. "Donn tell me, I dinna wish ta ken. Food isna me favorite thing jus' now and merely thinkin' o' wha' ya migh' have done turns me already roilin' stomach."

"Can we forget aboot tha'?" he asked. "'Twasna one of me finer days."

"Forget wha'? I canna recall wha' we were talkin' aboot." He laughed, and Brae did too, attracting the attention of her husband as well as the woman at his side.

Brae scrutinized the woman, but realized she was also being assessed.

Gard and Isabella began to walk in their direction. Donnchadh stood straighter as Brae squeezed his arm, which she was still using as her anchor. Gard's expression was rigid with irritation.

Surprisingly, Gard dropped his sister's arm and raised his palms to Brae's cheeks and observed her, as Donnchadh and his mother embraced awkwardly in greeting.

"How be ye feelin'?" Concern darkened his gaze. He stroked his thumb over her cheekbone. "Ya are pale and ya still look like ya could sleep for the next sennight."

She smiled. "I slept verra weel. 'Tis this beautiful Scottish air, 'twill make me whole and hale in no time. I'm glad ta be home. Weel, almost home. No need ta concern yourself. I'm fine." She reassured.

"Did ya find the stuffs I left for ya this morn?"

"Aye, thank ya. 'Twas verra kind." She squeezed his hand.

"Did ya find anathin' ta your likin'?"

"I had some gruel."

He placed his hand over her stomach. "She is goin' ta be a fussy sort, aye?"

Brae giggled. "I believe ya are gettin' used ta this idea o' pendin' fatherhood. Mayhap ya may e'en be lookin' forward ta meetin' your heir. Him or her?"

"I am lookin' forward ta all the work it migh' take ta get me a male heir. I have thought long and hard on the matter."

The dark promise in his eyes warmed her and helped her forget the nausea for a moment.

"And if she looks anathin' like her mother, I am lockin' her up—lockin' all o' them up—until I get me male heir. I will begin work on a tower o' me own as soon as we make home."

"And mayhap I will lock *him* up if he looks anathin' like his father. Wit' all those other MacDuib lasses aroond, we dinna need tha' many more runnin' wild tryin' ta distract our future earl, eh?"

He grinned. It was becoming easier for him. Brae forgot about all the others milling around, she rose on tiptoe and kissed him.

"Be ya feelin' weel enough ta return ta our room?" he whispered against her mouth.

"Oh, aye," she agreed wholeheartedly.

Not even waiting for her to walk up under her own power, Gard scooped her up and took the steps two at a time, foregoing proper introductions between Brae and Isabella.

Later, Brae held onto Gard's arm tightly, as they descended the stairs. Dizziness plagued her unmercifully.

Brae observed the people around, recognizing most of them.

Donnchadh and his mother were deep in conversation, their dark heads tilted together. Isabella was draped in a low cut deep blue dress, her raven tresses arranged beautifully about her pale face. Her dark-eyed gaze drifted over to Gard. The resemblance was obvious, but on Isabella the dark hair and eyes gave such an exotic look. Brae could well see why Hudson might be drawn to her. She was stunning.

"She is lovely," Brae commented.

"Aye. On the outside, at least," Gard commented. "Come. Let us get this o'er wit'."

"Gard. Wait. There be somethin' I need ta tell ya." She caught his arm.

His dark eyebrow lifted. "More secrets, wife?" Although, he had forgiven her for keeping the topaz a secret from him, she knew it still bothered him that she had felt the need to.

"Weel, nay. 'Tis jus' somethin' tha' I havena wished ta think aboot, but now tha' she be here, I remembered tha' I didna tell ya."

"Wha'?" he asked, dread clouded his handsome face.

"When Robbie Cowan lured me." She swallowed. "He said tha' he was the one tha' stole your seal."

"He wha'?" he blustered.

"He said tha' he took it at Isabella's urgings. Tha' she promised him . . . she promised him . . ."

"I can well imagine wha' she vowed!"

"Aye, she would do *tha'* for him if he but took the seal for her."

Gard's features twisted in revulsion. "And did he say? Did she fulfill her pledge?"

"Nay, she didna. Cowan said he was goin' ta come for her when he was finished wit' me — if ya didna kill him first — tha' she still owed him, and he would be sure ta collect."

Air streamed from his nostrils like an angry dragon. "And did he say from whom he stole the seal?"

"He said she used all her wiles as distraction so tha' he could take the seal from the Comyns."

Gard's lips tightened even more in fury. As Hudson had said, it would seem everyone plotted against him—the Comyns and perhaps his own sister.

"But Robbie Cowan wasna a reliable sort. Mayhap he just said tha' ta scare me more than I already was."

"Tha' doesna e'en make sense, Brae, for he hadna intention o' lettin' ya leave tha' hut, wha' significance would tha' have served. 'Tis an easy enough circumstance ta believe. I ken how she works." His black eyes surveyed Isabella from across the room. "She has no' bothered wit' me since she returned the seal. But I have had time ta think. She didna e'en return it ta *me*, but ta King Edward. She is only here now ta reap the rewards now tha' I have attained my title. She will think she is also entitled ta reclaim our past. But why should I, Brae? I have given evrathin' o' myself. I have done things tha' I am ashamed o'. I avenged our father's death at me own hand, and e'en spent time imprisoned for it. I killed her husband. And, I would most like do all those deeds again. And wha' has she done? Gone from parlor ta parlor, livin' off the generosity o' other people from castle ta palace, hopped from one Earl's bed ta next a Duke, ta the Comyns. Where would she have gone next? Ta the Bruce's? Wha' am I ta do?"

Brae thought he was just trying to work it out, not that he wanted her opinion, until he stared at her expectantly.

"I am na sure tha' anathin' she did was ana different than ya, Gard." Brae recalled the conversation she'd had with Hudson. He had said Gard had gone one way, and Isabella the other, after the murder of their father.

Gard's black eyes simmered with rage.

Brae also recollected the exchange with Donnchadh. He could not wait until he was big and strong so that he would not be pushed around. Brae had explained to him that women were not so lucky.

"Gard, do ya remember tellin' me tha' 'tis different for a man. Then ya mus' understand things be different for a woman. We do not possess the same weapons as ya men. Just like when ya showed me how ta use your dirk ta defend meself. Ya said I had ta be more wily since I dinna possess the strength ta stand against an opponent."

Frowning, Gard nodded.

"Isabella witnessed the same thing tha' ya did, the day your sire was killed, and she was e'en younger. Ya both lost your mother so soon after, then ya yourself were fostered. There was no one there ta explain things ta her, ta comfort her. Can ya imagine how scared she mus' have been? Ya used wha' ya had. Your strength, your anger, and your strategy, jus' as ya demonstrated ta Donnchadh on the field jus' the other day. And Isabella has used wha' she has, the things tha' she possessed ta attempt the verra same as you. 'Tisna wha' I woulda done, but Hudson tells me women can be as different as weel. Perhaps she jus' did wha' she thought she needed ta do, simply ta survive. Jus' as ya did. All the wrong actions, for all the righ' reasons. She did bring the seal and John Comyn ta vouch for ya? He didna have ta do tha'. But neither did she."

He pursed his lips. "But she be the female. She needed me ta regain my title so tha' she may take her proper place as weel."

Brae went on. "Mayhap she be jus' as ashamed by some of her actions as ya be, Gard. Ya didna ken wha' be in her mind. And she may be the same as you and would do all the same again. Ya will ne'er ken until ya ask her. Mind ya, I donn ken how she can forgive herself for abandonin' Donnchadh. Or wha' she contrived tha' ended in her husband's death. Or wha' she did ta you and Hudson tha' led ya after the man. I dinna ken the answer, love. But perhaps as I said ta ya once afore . . . mayhap it doesna matter what deeds were done in the past. Wha' matters now is wha' she so chooses ta do from this moment on?"

"And wha' be of such import at this moment?" he asked quietly, his obsidian eyes glittered with emotion. He had asked her that question once afore.

"Perhaps evraone deserves a second chance. We all are in need o' some forgiveness. Hudson explained ta me tha' none of the things tha' she may have done can be confirmed. Except where Donnchadh is concerned, o' course."

The corner of his mouth twitched. "Ya can forgive evrathin' but tha', canna ya, Brae. Evrathin' but leavin' her son. Ya are the boy's greatest defender."

"He deserves one. But ya ken, perhaps e'en her leavin' was a blessin' in disguise for Donnchadh at least, for he had ya."

Gard's face twisted, most like for the way he had treated the lad at times.

"Lads need a father, as much as a daughter needs a mother. Aye, ya may have been hard on him in some things, but I am told soldiers need ta be tough. As I said, things can be turned aroond, deeds measured for the present and not the past. I am verra happy tha' I have gotten ta ken him. Almost as grateful as I am for meetin' you." She rubbed her tummy. "'Tis time for new beginnin's, Gard, for all o' us."

To her surprise, he again enveloped her in a large embrace, for all to see. "How is it ya got so wise, wife?"

She smiled up at him. "'Tis a gift."

He chuckled. "Aye. 'Tis *all* a gift." His hand drifted over her abdomen. "Come meet your new sister." He took Brae's arm.

"Ya ken, husband, I happen ta ken Hudson migh' have some latent feelin's for your sister. And now tha' she doesna need ta chase the Comyns or anaone else ta further her quest ta marry well, mayhap there be a chance if ya can wrangle an annulment for Hudson, tha' is, since his wife did in fact abandon him—"

"Are ya now a matchmaker, wife?" Gard interrupted her scheming.

"Weel?" She shrugged, batting her eyelashes.

"One obstacle at a time, wife, one at a time!"

EPILOGUE

Fife, Scotland, 1308

"Braelynn, come, if we dinna leave taday we will miss the weddin'. Is tha' wha' ya want? Ya have delayed our trip many days as it is," Gard asked for the fourth time, becoming exasperated. He was about to grab her and bodily remove her from the chamber. "Ya willna have ana time wit' Donnchadh either if ya hinder our travel ana further."

"Nay. I wish ta see Hudson and your sister wed, and ya ken I look forward ta seein' Donnchadh e'en more than the festivities. I bet he looks like a full-grown man by now but . . . I dinna wish ta leave *him*." Her tearful gaze met his before falling to the barely six-month-old child in the cradle. "He is ta young ta be wit'oot me for an o'erlong time."

"'Twill be but a sennight, Brae. He will survive tha' long wit'oot ya. The staff will look after him. The women dote on him jus' as much as you do. He willna e'en realize ya be gone." He knew the minute the words left his mouth that he had said the wrong thing.

Her features crumpled, and she looked up at him, lip trembling.

It tore at his heart to see her so distraught over leaving the babe. Things were much easier when he had no feelings.

Brae turned away and headed for the door as she pulled on her traveling gloves. She knew he had not meant it as it sounded, but in her fragile state it still upset her. Gard had changed much in the year they had been together, but he was still quick to erupt into temper or say hurtful things before he thought. Brae tried to keep it in mind but sometimes she had to watch her own temper. They had had some rip-roaring rows that usually ended in some rough but very satisfying love play.

Brae waited by the door, turning when she did not hear her husband's footsteps behind her. He had his own dark head bent over the cradle. Brae tiptoed closer.

Donnghardh the Second looked up at his papa and smiled, kicking his arms and his legs in excitement over his father's attention. Fatherhood had changed Gard more than any other event in his life, not his marriage or even regaining his due. Being young Donnghardh's father had softened him, though he would never admit it, but Brae had seen the man melt when his child grinned at him.

"Gard. Be ya comin'?"

After an overlong moment, Gard scooped up his son into his massive arms. "Pack his things, he will be accompanyin' us."

"Wha'?" She giggled at his pronouncement. "Do ya mean it?" She ran for the bureau, not giving him a chance to change his mind. "Claire!" Brae yelled for her stiff English maid. The extreme and efficient woman with the sinewy but able body who'd assisted Hudson in bringing young Donnghardh into the world barreled into the room. "Ya mus' help me pack young Donnghardh's things, please," Brae rushed.

The maid placed her hands on her hips. "You cannot take that child traveling. I will not allow it."

Brae's eyes widened, and she paused packing the bairn's belongings. "Ya willna permit it?" Brae sputtered at her nerve.

"Nay. He is much too young to be seen. You will bring him home with all sorts of ailments. Is that what you want? To expose him to disease?"

Brae considered her words, but Gard would have none of it.

"Mayhap ya would prefer packin' your own belongin's, Claire," he roared loud enough to shake the rafters. Luckily young Donnghardh was used to his outbursts by now and did not even flinch. "We will be takin' our child on our travels. Ya either assist your lady, or ya will forfeit your position in my household."

The maid opened her mouth to argue. Gard's eyes turned black and he held up his hand, saying naught. Brae had not seen him use that particular gesture for a very long time, and it was all that was needed. Claire was a nervy sort, and in some instances Brae appreciated it, but Claire could not stand up to Gard.

"Aye, My Lord MontClaire," she said, humbly assisting Brae and taking over completely the overseeing of the young master's things.

Brae approached her handsome husband and amazingly beautiful son. She crooked her finger at Gard, and he bent, accommodating. She took his bearded cheeks into her hands and planted a warm kiss to his generous lips.

He handled the child in one arm while pulling Brae against him with the other. "Wha' was tha' aboot?" he asked.

"It has been a long time since I saw ya wield your power. I found it quite appealin'."

"Ya kiss me like tha' again and I'll be wieldin' power all o'er this room."

She could not pass up that challenge. She kissed him with more heat.

"Claire!" Gard bellowed. "Take this child and quit this

room."

"My Lord," she protested. "I have many things to—"

Deliberately, Gard advanced on the maid who, from time to time, eerily reminded him of the old crone—and yet more recently reminiscent of his own nanny. He shook his head, but that simply could not be.

Gard thrust the baby into Claire's arms, then escorted her out of the room. He slammed the door, then turned on Brae, stalking her. She weaved toward their enormous bed as she had many times afore. He dove at her, taking them both down onto the bedding. He kissed her ravenously, pulling at her clothes.

"Ya are goin' ta ruin my travelin' ensemble and delay our progress yet again," she gasped with the sound of pleasure he had grown to love.

He continued to kiss a trail down her neck heading for her ample breasts, still nicely rounded from the child. "Do ya care?" he growled, right before he pulled forcefully on the scoop of her neckline. He closed his lips over her ripe flesh.

She moaned, while holding and directing his head. "Na, I dinna."

Gard was not gentle with her, but sometimes, which he enjoyed about her, she did not need tenderness. He took what she offered quickly, and then held her in his arms in a blanket of her heavy traveling skirts. She snuggled into his chest, sighing, her arm coming to rest over his stomach. 'Twas her habit right afore she fell asleep. He was about to nudge her into wakefulness, but he stopped himself in spite of their time restriction. Gard knew she required sleep. The child was draining, and she needed to rest when she could. Travel would be delayed yet another day. Hudson and Isabella would have to wait for them. Gard pulled Brae closer.

Her hand found his beard and she stroked him softly before her hand eventually went limp.

He caressed her soft dark hair, and he summoned the memory of the day he had hauled her up onto his horse by it. Little had he known that one hasty decision would so drastically change his life. And hers. It was a strange beginning, to say the least. Not that he was complaining. She really was the greatest gift he had ever received. Aye, it was satisfying to have his title and his home after all the torment and toil it took, but Braelynn, and now his son, were the things he treasured most.

Gard closed his eyes and drifted, his eyes growing heavy, opening and closing as he fought sleep. He allowed himself the luxury of thinking of his parents. He did not do so often, having learned long ago to keep them from his mind. But he was surprised to find the pain was not nearly as excruciating as it once had been. He imagined if they could look down on him, wherever they might be, and see how much his life had changed, whether they would be astonished to find their son had finally found peace with the past and love for his future. Perhaps even legendary love reminiscent of their own.

Who could ever have predicted the Devil of Fife would take a wife. He chuckled sleepily at his own whimsy. He had been in Braelynn's soft company for too long.

"Wha' be ya laughin' o'er?" she asked sleepily.

"I believe your penchant for verse has finally rubbed off on me."

"And ya learned how ta laugh as weel. My work here be done," she mumbled, smiling into his chest.

"Naw, my sweet, I predict your stay in purgatory has only jus' begun."

"Weel, if lovin' the devil be wrong, I dinna wish ta be righ'."

"Don fret, love, there be nuthin' wrong aboot it." Gard

grinned widely, relaxing into heavenly sleep.

YOU MAY ALSO ENJOY THE FOLLOWING FROM EXTASY BOOKS INC:

Running
H.K. Carlton

Excerpt

"If we are going to do this, Miss Cambridge, we have to do it all the way. You cannot pick and choose who you are going to give to us. You can't protect them any longer. You need to tell me everything you know and you must be completely honest. We take them all or we take no one. It's up to you."

Her gaze darted as she tried to read me. She didn't trust me, either. Her full lips stretched into a thin hard line of indecision.

"We are not on opposite sides here, Miss Cambridge." She stiffened at my words and her head cocked slightly to the side. I must be getting through to her. "This is a two way street. We need to trust each other."

"I've heard that before, Agent," she said quietly. "They are just words. You want what you can get from me."

"And you need what I can give you," I answered.

She raked her lip with her teeth and then inhaled deeply before pulling another photo out. "Gunner. I'm sorry, I don't know his real name. I never did, that's all we used to call him. But give me a few minutes with your database and I could come up with that for you." She nodded towards my computer." She flipped over the picture. "But I see you've already done that—Herb Gunderson," she read. "No wonder he preferred Gunner." She smiled slightly and looked at me sideways.

She really was attractive. I couldn't deny that.

Her eyes narrowed. "Why do I feel like I'm not telling you anything you don't already know?"

"You are filling in plenty of the finer points that we were uninformed of. And maybe there are a few details that I can pass on to you. We can fill in the gaps for each other, be as prepared as we can be."

Sceptically, she looked up at me through her bangs.

"Are there photos in that pile of the three men that were killed that day?" I asked gently, knowing it must have been a difficult day for her.

Pursing her lips, she sighed. I knew then that she was fully aware that I knew those three photos were in the file. But she didn't call me on it. Shuffling through, she pulled them out.

"That's Jeffy. Dale." She lined them up on my desk. "And this is Trenton." Her voice softened. The mildness indicated she'd cared for this man. Absently she stroked the photo with her left thumb. I examined the kind-faced man as he smiled back at her.

"He was your driver.

"Yes, he was my driver. He was my friend."

I wasn't good at comforting. I cleared my throat. "Let's make categories as we go. Men who are still in your father's employ. Those who are in hiding. And those who are . . . uh . . . no longer with us," I suggested, not so delicately. I began to throw the photos into their respective piles. "All right. Tom, Buddy, in the current employ pile."

She put the four men in hiding into the middle stack. "Gunner, Teddy, Phil and Jason in the . . . hidden file." She smiled and gave me a slight wink as if she hadn't just made reference to a computer operating system like some kind of computer geek. I was almost unsure I'd seen it. Was she joking? I was quickly reassessing my preconceived impression of Holly Cambridge. Perhaps she wasn't just a bubble headed blonde.

"Do you know where these men are?"

"No. I don't." She looked into my eyes as if challenging me to either see the truth or detect the lie. I'd interrogated hundreds of informants and or criminals in my time. Liars, award winning actors most of them. And even after my earlier attempt to intimidate her, and our awareness of each other's mistrust, for some reason she wanted me to believe she was telling me the truth before she continued. "I have done some research of my own. I vaguely remembered a conversation I'd inadvertently overheard about the Caymans." I didn't consider the inadvertent part, but I did believe she didn't know where the men were hiding. "Apparently, William Cambridge owns an island. But, I guess, that isn't a surprise to you, like it was to me."

I confirmed with a nod.

"I travelled there." She dragged her lip with her teeth. It was a nervous habit, and sensual as all get out.

"You took a trip there? I thought you just said . . ."

"No. After I left. By myself. I tried to find them, thinking that might be where they would go."

She'd gone alone? I had no record of her ever leaving the country. Not even under one of her aliases. Why were we not aware of this? Although, I reasoned, from the ages of eighteen to the present, her whereabouts had been sketchy at best. She'd taken to hiding like a fish to water.

"And what did you find?"

"I couldn't locate them. I have no proof, but from the clues I did find and the people I spoke to, I think my father had them killed. I believe he is more cold and sinister than even I believed. Even after all these men had done and sacrificed for him and our family, they were no longer useful to him. He doesn't leave loose ends, Agent Orton."

She had detached herself from William Cambridge. I noted it earlier how she referenced him as either the formal my father or William Cambridge, trying to depersonalize or distance herself from him. She didn't refer to him as my dad, which might be considered an appellation.

Holly looked at me then and I knew that she was fully aware of her own predicament. She was a loose end that William Cambridge either needed to tie up or cut away completely. Perhaps it had been that precise realization that convinced her to come to us. She was scared, and she knew we could protect her. It must have been absolute shell shock for her to leave the safe and sheltered Cambridge life to live completely on her own. So young and unprepared, unprotected. Always on the move, on the lookout for family and enemy alike. Looking over her shoulder, just waiting to be captured or killed. It was only a matter of time. She must have realized she couldn't stay out there on her own anymore. She'd given it a valiant effort. I'd give her that. But she'd finally come to her senses and come to the Bureau.

"Until we have proof, will we leave them in the hidden file?" She asked holding up the pictures.

"All right." I nodded. "Unknown, for the time being." She returned them to the middle stack. I pointed at the kind-faced man that had been her chauffer and friend. I was departmentalizing and sorting in my own mind and didn't think before I spoke. "Deceased. They are no longer important."

Her expressive eyes widened, turning cold. "If we are going to do this," she spat my own words back at me. "You need to respect my people. Those people are important to me. Dead or alive. They may be nothing but gangsters and criminals to a straight-laced lawman like yourself, but they were my family. My team. The people who had my back and ultimately gave their lives for mine. You will not dismiss them as collateral damage. If you expect me to respect you and yours, then you need to acknowledge and respect mine, Agent." Although her voice was angry, I saw that she was struggling to hold back tears that threatened to break the tough exterior she was attempting to maintain.

"The ones that remain, are no longer yours, Miss Cambridge, and you need to accept and acknowledge that, and separate yourself from your tender feelings. These are the people we are going after at your request."

"I don't think we can work together," she said, at length, as if she had a choice.

She was halfway to the door when I heard myself say, "I apologize for my insensitive comments, Miss Cambridge." What was I doing? She was halfway to no longer being my problem. I should have just let her walk out. But I needed this case. I wanted it. And I could admit to myself now, looking back—it was much more that made me stop her that day. There was just something about her. I wanted to know more. My fierce curiosity and quest to know all gnawed at me. And I knew I had just scratched the surface of Miss Holly Cambridge. My preconceived idea of the mafia princess was rapidly evaporating as she challenged me at every turn. No one tested me. She was not fitting into the box I had placed her in before she'd even walked through my door.

She stopped at the sound of my voice but she didn't turn in my direction.

"Are you finished psychoanalyzing me, Agent Orton?" she said, as if she could read my thoughts. She did turn then. "Go ahead. Profile me. Is it really that great a feat, Agent, when you think you have all the answers right there in that file? As I said before, you don't know me."

Again. A Challenge. I could not resist.

"The mob boss' daughter. Mafia princess. Protected. Sheltered. Spoiled. Poor little rich girl. No friends. No social life. Lonely." I looked down at the file one last time, leaving behind what I thought I knew about her and turned to what I had gleaned since she walked in the door. "You turned to books and school to fill the void." I recognized her need for knowledge and detail only because I, too, possessed those qualities. "You are quiet. Shy. You pay attention, absorb, observe, research. You listen and learn. You have known from an early age what's right and what's wrong. Your character is so strong that the life style that you were forced to live warred with your own morals and ethics, which you did not learn from your father or the people around you. A father who was cold to you most of your life, ignoring you and your sister. Perhaps he is even unbalanced, bi-polar, paranoid. You threw your energies and your money into charitable organizations, in an attempt to ease your own conscience. You gravitated towards the men around you to replace the family and friends you didn't have."

I thought of her caressing the edge of the photograph of her driver and the way she'd staunchly defended her employees, her team, as she'd referred to them. "The criminals around you became your own dysfunctional family."

She sneered at me when I referred to them as criminals. "You could no longer endure that amoral life, so you sacrificed your own. You want nothing more than to belong. To be loved. To live a quiet normal life." I took a shot in the dark with this one. "With a husband. Perhaps even a child." I could have smiled at how easy it was getting. I walked towards her with every intention of continuing, as we kept our focus on each other. I was just getting warmed up.

"My turn, Agent Best?" she remarked, sarcastically.

"Oh, be my guest," I invited, smugly. If nothing else, we knew how to antagonize one another. This should be good.

"FBI. Special Agent." She began slowly, as I had. "Single-minded. Career man. Cold. Stiff. Curious. Almost obsessively so. Your quest for knowledge is your driving force." I was no longer smiling.

"You have to know everything about each person and everything around you. You have known from your earliest memory that this would ultimately be your career. You followed in your father's footsteps. Also a career man. You are an only child. Also no friends, no social life. You moved around a lot as a child because of your father's career, but that isn't the reason you didn't make friends. Your intelligence and your intellect was way too complex for children your own age. You found them boring, tedious, unintelligent compared to your advanced IQ. Knowledge came easy to you. You didn't have time or make time for baseball or football. You also turned to books not to fill an emotional void, as you intimated that I did, but to fill your insatiable appetite for knowledge, and that drove you to learn as much and as fast as you possibly could, to fill that massive brain. You are the classic over-achiever. You graduated high school early and entered an accelerated program to fast track you into an Ivy League school. I'm going to guess, Harvard. Only because it is the best law school and would impress the Bureau. You would settle for nothing less than the best. You are a strict disciplinarian. You are ruled by rules. A perfectionist. You cannot commit to a long-term relationship because your passion is your work. How am I doing, best?"

"You have obviously accessed my personnel file. Which is a federal offence, Miss Cambridge," I accused, stiffly, crossing my arms.

"I have done no such thing, Agent Orton. Go ahead," she invited gesturing towards my computer. "Check. If your file has been accessed recently it will be flagged."

"Then Sid or Trey gave it to you."

"That would also not have been procedure. I can assure you, they did not. You know neither of them would ever give an agent's file to an informant, and again, you can check."

I stared at her. Obviously she was a better liar than I'd realized.

"It was interesting meeting you, Agent Orton. Have a good day."

She walked out the door. I couldn't believe it. She didn't want to work with me.

I followed out into the hallway. But she was gone. The elevator must have been ready and waiting for her departure.

"Maeve. Have security stop Miss Cambridge before she leaves the building."

"Miss Cambridge, sir?"

"Yes. She just exited my office."

"I didn't see her leave."

"She just left. Thirty seconds ago, at most."

"I'm sorry. I didn't see her, sir."

"Call down, and notify the desk, anyway. I want her stopped before she exits the building."

Another thing she had been able to convince Trey and Sid, which I also disagreed with, was no protection. She needed to be in protective custody. It was imperative for the kind of mission she'd convinced them to undertake. She needed to be corralled.

That was the first of many occasions in which she disappeared without a trace. According to the security guards, she'd not taken the elevator down. She was not picked up on the cameras in the stairwells either.

I was so angry. There had to be an explanation. I called Sid's office, thinking she'd gone to him to complain about me. He guaranteed me he hadn't seen her since he'd left her in my capable hands.

I contacted Trey and he gave me the same song and dance. Trey assured me I didn't need to worry. She was quite capable of taking care of herself and she would make contact with us when she was ready.

That wasn't good enough. We were the FBI, for Christ's sake. We made the rules. We were in charge.

I sent out half my team after her. As they searched I accessed my file. I don't know how she'd done it, but according to the log, my file hadn't been accessed since I myself had done so eight months ago to update my new address when I moved into my penthouse apartment. There was no way she could have come so close to the details of my life without having seen my file.

My street agents called in one by one. There was no sign of her.

ABOUT THE AUTHOR

H K Carlton is a multi-published Canadian author of romance and its varied sub-genres. From naughty to nice, historical to contemporary, time travel to space travel, and everything in between.

Variety is creativity's playground—It's where you'll find me.

www.ingramcontent.com/pod-product-compliance
Lightning Source LLC
Chambersburg PA
CBHW071628260626
47170CB00001B/7